THE AMBER PANELS OF KÖNIGSBERG

David Eilers

TABLE OF CONTENTS

BALTIC SEA AREA 1930s
Polish Corridor to Baltic Sea splits Germany into two parts

Norway

Finland

Sweden

★ ST. PETERSBURG

Estonia

Russia

Latvia

Baltic Sea

Denmark

Lithuania

DANZIG ★   ★KONIGSBERG
         Germany

Polish Corridor added after WWII

★
BERLIN

Poland

Germany

Czechoslovakia

BALTIC SEA AREA 2013

Norway

Finland

Sweden

★ ST. PETERSBURG

Estonia

Russia

Baltic Sea

Latvia

Denmark

Lithuania

★ GDANSK
(Danzig)

★ KALININGRAD
(Konigsberg)

★ BERLIN

Poland

Belarus

Germany

Czech
Republic

Ukraine

Slovakia

January 20th, 1945

The Amber Panels were real . . . and really did vanish

CHAPTER 1: KATYA HAIDER

Fifteen-year-old Katya Haider awoke wrapped in her father's long wool overcoat, its familiar musky odor a reminder of her former life. She reluctantly sat up and folded her legs into a crossed position. The teenager brushed her long gray-blue plaid skirt with her hands as if doing so would remove the creases. Then she planted her elbows on her knees and cradled her head in her hands to wait for the fog of sleep to lift. Her greasy brown hair hung like a curtain around her face creating a sense of privacy in the one-room cellar where she and fifteen other refugees had spent the night.

Katya's bones ached from another night of sleep on the hard wooden floor. She reached behind her and unrolled the dirty brown sweater that had been her pillow. She no longer cared that it didn't match her skirt or her light blue

1

blouse. She slid the sweater over her head and it fell easily around her thin physique, one that hungered for food.

Resigned to living another day, Katya stood and inhaled a deep breath, the stale air thick with the stench of unwashed bodies. She felt for the rope tied around her middle and pressed its fist-sized knot into the empty cavity below her breastbone — a technique she'd learned to counter the gnaw of hunger. This morning it wasn't working; it was imperative she find food today.

She slid her arms through her father's long-sleeved coat and buttoned the front. The hem reached almost to her ankles. She patted the coat's pockets to make sure the notebook, pencil and knife were still there. Katya had promised her father she'd keep a diary while he was away at the Eastern Front, a diary they could share when they were reunited, whenever that might be. He'd left in 1942 and been gone for three years, but it felt like a lifetime.

Katya squinted at the early morning light penetrating the single mud-spattered window located high on the cellar's east wall that illuminated the stairway against the far wall. She started tentatively toward the stairs. To her right a mother slept soundly alongside her three young children. Next to the woman slept Hans, a kind one-legged veteran of the Great War; he carried a gun and kept an eye out for her. To her left were three more women, an infant girl, two boys aged about ten and twelve, and a sick old man who coughed. They were new to the cellar.

A crude handrail worn smooth from use guided Katya as she slowly climbed the dark staircase, each step squeaking underfoot. When she reached the door, she groped for the doorknob. The teenager pushed the door open and emerged from the cellar into the destroyed barbershop. She blinked as her eyes adjusted to the bright light. Her boots clunked quietly as she crossed the ceramic tile floor of the former business and approached the entry door with the broken glass. She'd been lucky to find the boots two months ago before it got cold, because after the bombing she'd been left with only thin summer shoes.

"The nasty Brits," she muttered for the thousandth time, as it was they who had transformed her life.

She opened the door and stepped into the bitter January cold. The salty wind from the Baltic Sea threw her coat to one side nearly blowing her over.

"Brrr", she grumbled, reaching into the coat's upper pocket for her wool hat, the one her grandmother had knit for her the previous Christmas. She'd found the treasured keepsake amongst the rubble that had once been her family's home. Its pale green yarn had become stained and gray from use. She pulled it over her head; its simple shape framed Katya's pretty face.

She turned left to walk along the old sidewalk. She passed two horse carcasses half-stripped of meat. They'd appeared last month and smelled at first, but the cold dampened the stench. Rats had dined on them, until they'd frozen solid.

Neither the rats nor the dead horses bothered her anymore. It had become a common sight in Königsberg. Food was only available to the lucky few with ration coupons. She'd been lucky herself the prior week when she'd found a brown coupon, good for bread. She'd redeemed it at Kahl's Bakery for a warm loaf and rationed it over several days, savoring every bite. Today she had no coupons; today she sought a *Stammessen*, a coupon-less meal she'd have to find, or beg for, or steal.

Hunger, death, and loneliness were constant reminders of how her beloved city of Königsberg, formerly the capital of the country of Prussia and now the capital of the German state of East Prussia, had been transformed by two nights of allied bombings in July 1944. Prior to the bombing, the seven-hundred-year-old city's rich history was evident from the beautiful architecture and its cosmopolitan population. After the bombing Katya became one of two hundred thousand homeless people living among a city in ruins. Tens of thousands had been killed, including her mother, grandparents and neighbors. The bombs had destroyed downtown Königsberg and leveled her family's apartment building.

Despite the destruction, Katya felt lucky, because a series of miracles had saved her. Katya's mother had needed her father's coat repaired so it could be donated to the German Army as required by the Führer. On the day of the first bombing Katya went across town to her mother's friend Ulrike's apartment to get the coat sewn. It was late in the evening when Ulrike finished, so Katya agreed to wait until morning to return home.

That night the city exploded with bombs, fires, and sirens. Nearby buildings collapsed, smoke filled the streets, and yelling for loved ones continued throughout the night. Incredibly, Ulrike's apartment wasn't destroyed. For Katya's safety, Ulrike insisted Katya remain with her. Two nights after the bombing, worried sick about her family, Katya snuck out of Ulrike's with her father's coat. She slowly navigated the dark city streets toward home. Halfway there, warning sirens sounded. Suddenly the streets erupted with activity as people dressed in sleeping gowns bolted from their apartments to a nearby bomb shelter. Katya followed them.

Deep in the shelter amongst strangers she curled inside her father's jacket listening to the sounds of explosions. The next day she re-emerged with everyone else to see that the second bombing was worse than the first. Beautiful Königsberg was a relic, a burning shell.

Downtown suffered the greatest damage and was still burning intensely, so there was no going home. Katya walked back to Ulrike's, only to discover her building had been destroyed as well. Out of options, Katya followed other people to an outlying city park, where they waited for the fires to subside. While there she heard many rumors. Some people argued the Russians would come and kill them all. Others said they would be spared. Some still believed the German Army would keep the Russian Army out of East Prussia. Katya didn't know what to believe.

She remained at the park for a week until she felt safe enough to return to her family's downtown home. Katya's trek into the city lasted several hours until she finally reached her former home. She discovered that all three stories of her family's former apartment building had been destroyed. After sifting through the rubble, she found nothing she could identify. She gave up the search and sat on a box across the street so she could view her former home. That's when she glanced down and found her bonnet. She never understood how her bonnet escaped the apartment and landed on the street. Later that day she wrote in her diary:

Father, I am sitting in the street outside our home. It is now a pile of blackened bricks. I do not know if mother, grandmother, and grandfather are alive or dead. I don't understand why this is happening? I hope they escaped, but I fear they haven't. So many have died. What do I do until you return? I haven't read a letter from you since October of 1943, but Mom explained you've been too busy to write. I hope you return home — wait, there is no home. Just return soon to me. Please be safe! Love -K

***

A brisk gust of wind shook Katya as she stepped off a sidewalk to avoid debris from a demolished shoe store that extended into the middle of the street. She was heading to the old Cathedral on Kneiphof Island near old town to check if any food had arrived. It was her daily ritual. The priests always said to come the following day, but only rarely could they provide any food. She wondered why God wouldn't bless them.

The thought of food made her reach for the knot. It reminded her of Herr Besk's most important rule: *Outsmart the enemy.* Herr Besk was the second teacher she'd had last year. The first, Herr Kleinter, had vanished midway through the school year. More and more often, adults just disappeared, present one day and gone the next.

Herr Besk was a plump man with a long gray beard that fell to a point. He'd never explained to Katya's high school classmates what had happened to Herr Kleinter. It was as if Herr Kleinter had never existed. Herr Besk even stopped teaching normal lessons, replacing math and literature with lectures about the German struggle for victory and the history of Prussia. He also provided instruction on survival techniques.

She could still hear Herr Besk's deep booming voice telling them, *I grew up on a rural farm and we often had to go without food. So, you are a little hungry? Imagine how the soldiers on the front feel. They need food more than you so they can defend our beautiful city, our beautiful country. But, if you feel a little hungry, I have a rope trick to teach you. You can always outsmart the enemy, even if the enemy is hunger.*

With her father fighting for their lives, Katya wore the knot to symbolize her solidarity with him. By eating less she hoped her father would have more food. So, she reduced what she ate and wore the rope and knot with pride. But after the bombs destroyed the city in July, the rope changed from a symbol of solidarity into a necessity.

An overachiever and the daughter of a German literature professor, Katya always pursued her school studies with zeal. She applied the survival lessons she learned from Herr Besk. Besides shelter, water and food, she was always on alert for dissidents, keeping her pocket knife with her in case of trouble, and walking purposefully like she knew where she was headed, even if she didn't. She felt her father would be proud of her efforts, which she recorded as entries in her diary.

Katya's footsteps echoed through the abandoned buildings on Drumm Strasse. She strode by the Biophon Theater's sign that clung to the broken facade of a theater that no longer existed, its roof now collapsed onto its velvet seats. She turned the corner at the next intersection, checking for streetcars as she continued across Steindamm Allee. The tram tracks had been heavily damaged by the bombs, but within two weeks the resilient Prussians had put them back into service. When Katya reached Kahl's Bakery she saw children milling about begging for bread coupons. Adults had more sympathy for the very young than they did for a fifteen-year-old. Katya had little chance of receiving charity.

Katya turned down Entschierse Platz, a short alley. Overhead a large banner declared the *Wunderwaffen,* or *Wonder Weapons,* were nearly finished and would stop the Russians from overtaking East Prussia. She scrambled over a ten-foot high pile of charred bricks from a collapsed wall, blackening her hands, then scurried east across Gesekus Platz toward Kant Strasse. Across Kant Strasse loomed Königsberg Castle.

Unlike Bavaria's famous Neuschwanstein Castle with its graceful spires and cream-colored walls, the castle in downtown Königsberg had muscular, long brick walls anchored at its corners by stout gray-plastered turrets. On the castle's far side from where Katya stood, a newer Gothic tower jutted high into the air topped with a steep conical roof. This was the bell tower where musicians assembled to play concerts on pleasant summer days.

Massive stone retaining walls encircled the castle's landscaped grounds, which raised the complex above the surrounding streets. The retaining wall grew taller as Kant Strasse dropped downhill toward Kaiser Wilhelm Platz, making the castle high and imposing when approached from the south. Last month Katya had discovered the retaining wall had been damaged during the bombings and that she could squeeze through a narrow crevice. When she reached the other side of the wall, Katya realized she'd entered an underground tunnel. Feeling frightened, she'd slipped back out. Today, flapping in the January wind, large red and white banners hung from the retaining walls promoting the German fight.

Katya turned to her right to look south on Kant Strasse. Passed the shopkeepers' awnings she spied the Krämer Bridge. Beyond the bridge she could see the rubble left from the bombing of the enormous Königsberg Cathedral. The old cathedral had been built on Kneiphof Island in the middle of the Pregel River. Katya remembered how sunshine once lit up the cathedral through stained-glass windows that depicted the history of Prussia. She remembered the soothing mellow tones of music that flowed throughout the church whenever the powerful Baroque organ was played. Now, no music could be heard and no windows remained for the sun to brighten.

Seeing Kneiphof Island reminded Katya of the time she and her parents had attempted the Eulerian Walk to try and solve the famous Seven Bridges Problem of Königsberg. She was only ten years old when her father explained that seven bridges linked Kneiphof Island and another smaller island in the Pregel River to the surrounding city of Königsberg. He told her it was impossible to find a path that crossed all seven bridges once and only once. Certain she could figure out a way, she led them around for nearly three kilometers over one bridge and then others until they'd crossed the sixth bridge. At that point she couldn't figure out a way to cross the seventh bridge without crossing back over the sixth. Her father explained that sometimes a problem is just that way: an unsolvable seven bridges problem.

Like most everything else, the July bombings had destroyed two of the seven original bridges. She wondered, if the bridges were never rebuilt, would an impossible problem be referred to as a five bridges problem?

Continuing on, Katya walked south until she entered the center of old town at Kaiser Wilhelm Platz, just outside the southwest corner of the castle. Katya gazed back at the castle's damaged south side and saw a ragtag group of trucks parked along side it. Amazingly, none were *gazogenes*, trucks that ran on burning wood, coal or coke. Instead, these were gasoline-powered trucks, vehicles she rarely saw anymore. She paused to watch.

An unusual number of men were mingling around the trucks. Three of them wore the völkisch sig runes, or the SS symbols. Her father said the sig, the swastika, and other rune symbols invoked a simple-minded notion of a bygone Prussian era that had never existed. Until the day he was drafted, her father had resisted the Nazi Party's interpretation of the German past, because the Party trampled on the free pursuit of knowledge.

The other men near the trucks were *Volkssturm,* or *Volunteers,* sixteen-year-old boys ordered to defend Königsberg from Russian soldiers. Dressed in green wool knee-length jackets, matching pants, and black boots, the Volkssturm shuffled around trying to keep warm. Katya recognized a teenager named Oskar Ballheim, a boy she'd met last fall when she went to a *Kirche Jesu Christi der Heiligen der Letzten Tage,* or *Church of Jesus Christ of Latter Day Saints.* Katya learned she could get food most every day there, so she'd returned often for several months.

She made some friends at the church, but it took her a while to earn Oskar's confidence, because he was quiet. In time, she won him over and, in return, he treated her with a kindness she relished. One day they snuck into an abandoned house to talk. After sharing her memory of the bombings, he described how his family huddled with others in a bomb shelter protected by an iron door. The heat from the fires outside the shelter caused the shelter doors to seize shut. They waited an entire day after the bombings for the doors to cool enough to open.

During their last meeting in late November Oskar confided to her that serving in the Volkssturm scared him. He was told he'd have to defend the city to his death, but he wasn't ready to die. He wanted to escape, yet didn't want to disappoint his parents. Katya comforted him with a hug that turned into a brief, exhilarating kiss.

In December, the National Socialist Party took possession of the church building. When she'd appeared at the church she was told the church has been disbanded. Feeling lost and alone, she didn't know where to turn.

She'd returned several more times, but never saw anyone she recognized. So, Katya had resorted to begging or stealing food.

Now, upon seeing Oskar once again, a feeling of joy welled up inside her, however she resisted the urge to run over to him. She didn't dare approach him with the Volkssturm and SS around him.

Katya thought this gathering of men meant there must be food nearby. If so, the logical place for it would be inside the castle. Her eyes shifted back to the fissure she'd explored last month. If she wanted food, she knew she'd have to sneak back through the crack to find it, but this time she'd have to be brave. She'd have to explore the castle's spooky tunnels.

Katya started across the plaza towards the castle wall. She knew there used to be a restaurant in the dungeon area of the castle called the Blutgericht. The bombings had closed the restaurant, but she thought it still might have leftover cans of food and was the most likely place the soldiers would be fed. All she needed was a distraction so she could slip through the narrow crevice.

Her thoughts were interrupted by the noise of motorcars coming from the direction of Krämer Bridge. She saw three Mercedes four-door Cabriolets bearing Nazi Party flags on their front fenders. They rounded the corner onto Kant Strasse and drove in her direction. The three cars turned right near her and slowed to a stop alongside the trucks. The Volkssturm, seeing the approach of important dignitaries, quickly formed a line and dutifully saluted, their right arms raised in Nazi precision.

Katya saw her opportunity and darted across Kant Strasse to the retaining wall. She moved north along the wall until she found the familiar break. A quick glance confirmed the few people on the sidewalk were watching the cars and soldiers. She took two deep breaths inward and slipped through the crevice. She emerged from the wall into the passageway as she'd done before.

Katya's heart beat swiftly as she pressed against the tunnel's rough wall and listened for any sound. A dim bulb lit the passageway with yellow light, revealing a long north and south corridor parallel to Kant Strasse. The tunnel's walls consisted of roughly mortared stone bricks of random sizes that still reeked of smoke from the bombing's fires. The walls reached up and formed a pointed arch. The somewhat warmer temperature inside the tunnel gave Katya some relief from the cold Baltic winds outside.

Satisfied she was alone, she quietly made her way north over the crude cobblestone floor. Soon, she arrived at an intersecting passageway. Another bulb hung from the ceiling and provided additional light. Katya turned to her right and walked twenty feet or so, where the tunnel steered her to a solid wood door.

Katya listened carefully a moment, gently grasped the door's metal knob, twisted it, and pushed on the door. It gave way. She peered inside, but it was difficult to see through the room's darkness. The dim yellow glow from the tunnel's bulb revealed stacked chairs and wood crates near the door.

She reached inside the door and slid her hand down the wall hoping to find a light switch. Her hand bumped a protrusion with a push-button toggle. She pushed the button inward and four lights came on. Katya was in an immense storage area stacked with boxes, couches, tables, desks and chairs. Some of the furniture surprised her with its plain construction. Other chairs and tables were ornately carved and ostentatious. The couches were all padded with varying colors of fabrics. Many pieces were stacked on top of one another to conserve space. Unlike the tunnel, the walls of this room were smooth. The floor consisted of large red tiles, precisely laid. Katya was certain she was now inside the castle.

Closing the tunnel's door behind her, she realized it didn't look like a door at all, but a smooth plaster panel similar to the surrounding walls. When she examined it more closely, she discovered the opening mechanism was hidden in a small niche in the wall. Once she was satisfied she could safely exit, she made her way through the furniture to the far wall, where she came to a pair of heavy wooden doors.

The first door wouldn't budge, but the other one was unlocked. She cracked it opened and peeked into a plain tiled hallway. Her confidence growing, she slipped out of the storage room and tiptoed along an empty corridor until she came to a set of wide stone stairs. She climbed to a landing, paused to listen, and continued up to what she assumed was the first floor of the castle.

The top step transitioned into a floor of alternating brown and cream tiles. The ceiling of the stairway rose to meet the much higher ceiling of the first floor creating a spacious volume. The hallway ended to her immediate left where a small window framed by richly detailed wood indicated how beautiful the castle had been before the bombings. She looked right into a fifty feet hallway that terminated at a carved panel door.

Her heart pounded as Katya continued her exploration toward the door at the end of the hallway. The ceiling was bordered with ornate mouldings, darkly stained. She liked the beauty of the trim with its disciplined and precise designs. Katya passed two doors on her left as she walked. The right wall had no doors, but was divided into sections by wood trim where she imagined large paintings once hung. She assumed all the castle's valuables and furniture had been removed and stored elsewhere either before or after the bombings.

Katya imagined life as a princess, of long elegant dresses and satin slippers. She approached the hallway door pretending a handsome king and beautiful queen awaited her presence on the other side. There was a ball being held in her honor and, somewhere inside the castle, there was a prince ready to sweep her off her feet and carry her away.

Katya, with thoughts of royalty in her head, put her ear to the door hoping to hear dancing and music, but expecting to hear nothing; instead, she heard footsteps. Her dreams were instantly replaced by the reality of her situation. She cursed herself for dropping her guard, for allowing her teenage self to distract her from her mission. She considered fleeing, but then the noise ceased. *Strange*, she thought. She listened a little longer. Suddenly, the steps resumed, only louder this time. She realized several people were close to the other side of the door.

Oh no!

She immediately retraced her steps to the last side door she'd passed, turned the knob and pressed down on the door as she opened it, a skill she'd learned to quiet the squeaky doors at home.

Slipping inside, Katya carefully closed the door behind her and found herself inside a small study. Wooden shelves inset into the western wall were bare. Four tall thin mirrors hung opposite the north facing windows. Sunlight filtered through sheer covered windows with tall drapes at each side. The room had been stripped of furniture, art and books. No trace of carpet remained on the ornate inlaid wood floor. As she sought a hiding spot, she heard the hall door close and several sets of boots traversing the tile floor. Seeing a small door on the east wall, she hurried to it.

Katya opened up the door, revealing an empty closet. She stepped inside and closed the door. The closet was dark, except for a gap at the bottom of the door. She heard the hall door open and close. She lowered herself to the closet floor and turned on her side. The floor felt cold against her cheek, so she pulled her father's lapel between the floor and her face. It provided a little comfort.

From under the door Katya saw the room's door open and watched three sets of black leather boots enter the room. After shutting the door the three people gathered to face each other.

One man broke the silence, a youthful voice asking in German, "Doctor Rhode, what can I do for you?" The man's accent was not East Prussian. It sounded more like Katya's neighbor Herr Gebler's Austrian accent.

Dr. Rhode's commanding voice responded sternly, "Herr Weiner, Gautleiter Koch has changed his mind. He has created a simple plan to ensure you deliver the right boxes to the right destinations. He has painted a train symbol on the boxes destined for the Harz Mountains via the train; the boxes to be shipped from Pillau have ship symbols; and the boxes to the Sternwart brewery in Königsberg have keg symbols. Your orders are to guard the Harz Mountain shipment with most of your men. They must deliver the Amber Panels no matter the obstacles. They must understand the critical importance of their missions. Any questions?" Dr. Rhode sounded familiarly East Prussian.

"No Doctor!" replied Herr Weiner's youthful voice.

Katya heard the rattle of paper. Dr. Rhode's resumed his instructions, "Use this map to reach the salt mine. DO NOT let this map out of your hands. Do you understand? The code word is *bernstein*. Repeat it back to me."

"BERNSTEIN, Dr. Rhode!"

"Herr Weiner, you are dismissed. Heil Hitler!"

With a click of his boots, the young man pivoted and exited the room.

Dr. Rhode spoke again, but his tone was friendlier and more intimate, "Fritz, I have a private matter to discuss."

"Alfred, what can I do for you?" Katya felt Fritz and Dr. Alfred Rhode must be friends. She thought Fritz's accent was similar to several college students her father had taught, but she couldn't remember where they were from.

Katya had occasionally attended his classes and felt pride whenever she watched him lecture.

"I expect to die in Königsberg, Fritz. Gautleiter Koch's SS troops will insure that. He badly wants the Amber Panels for himself. As soon as the panels leave this castle the SS will kill anyone who knows their true location."

Dr. Rhode paused as if to underscore the weight of his statement, and then continued, "As you know, Gautleiter Koch controls all of East Prussia, but he is crazy. He wants the panels for himself, just like Hitler did. I refuse to let either man steal the panels from the German people. Therefore, I need you, Fritz. I need you to hide the Amber Panels. You must see that the boxes marked with a ship reach your boat in Pillau, then depart as soon as you can. Shoot anyone who gets in your way."

"But Alfred," pleaded Fritz with familiarity, "aren't the Russian troops more than a month away? Gautleiter Koch says that . . . "

"No," interrupted Dr. Rhode, "the Russians will be here in two weeks, maybe less, and they are furious with us, Fritz. Yesterday, I spoke with a woman refugee from a small town near the Russian border that dressed as a man to escape the Russians. She told me her town was sacked by them. As she made her escape she saw three elderly farmers nailed to barn doors. Old men! That scared her even more, so she ran five kilometers until she arrived at a train station, but it was mobbed by people. She said the train was stuffed with people like a sausage. As it pulled out of the station she saw thousands of people along a riverbank slowly crossing a bridge to stay ahead of retreating German tanks and infantry. A moment late the Russian tanks appeared. She said both German and Russian tanks rolled over refugees as if they were blades of grass. The refugees who didn't move fast disappeared under the tanks."

"My God!" cried Fritz.

Katya put her hand to her mouth, gasping silently from behind the door.

"Unfortunately, this woman's story is not unique. The situation is desperate! I'm ashamed to say it, but we are responsible for our own fate. I told you that I traveled to the Eastern Front and Leningrad to bring the panels back to Königsberg, but I never told you what I witnessed. Some of our soldiers committed terrible crimes in Russia. It seems we will all be responsible for their actions. Other contacts of mine confirmed Russia's plan to wipe the Germans from East Prussia. I predict the Russians will reach and destroy Königsberg, and then do the same to Berlin. We can brand the Russians as dogs all we want, but they are really bears, mad fighting bears," Alfred told him, audibly frustrated.

Katya's mind was spinning. *The war was lost? What does that mean for my father?* Tears welled, then dripped silently off her eyes onto the coat's collar.

Dr. Rhode continued, "Unfortunately for us, the Russian soldiers will judge our fate. The Bolsheviks won't find their graves in East Prussia; Instead, I am confident they will dig ours."

Fritz asked, "Are you saying we don't have the defenses to protect Königsberg either? Last week I heard Gautleiter

Koch promise that the tank traps being created by the Volkssturm would stop the tanks and save the city. He said that *our walls may be broken, but our hearts are not.*"

"Fritz, I heard the same thing. But the Volkssturm consists of young teenage boys and old men. They cannot fight the Russians. Have you heard about the weapons they were issued to defend against the Russian tanks? The men over at Quittainen were issued Italian muskets and fifteen cartridges each. It is so bad that General Guderian, the man in charge of the Eastern Front, warned the Führer in October that he could not stop the Russians. The General shared the information with me, pleading with me to move the museum's art collection as soon as possible. Even worse, I spoke confidentially with Admiral Dönitz during my trip to Berlin at Christmas. He told me that Stalin and Churchill have already agreed Königsberg will become part of the Soviet Union at the end of the war."

"What!" exclaimed Fritz, shocked at the news that Stalin and communism would rule over East Prussia, "Gauleiter Koch has lied even more than I thought. If General Guderian can't stop them, who can? It seems hopeless!"

"Precisely Fritz. General Guderian told the Führer the Russians have eleven soldiers for each one of ours, seven tanks for every German tank, and twenty times more artillery than we do. Germany is lost."

"Why is Gauleiter Koch so insistent on defending Königsberg if the High Command knows all is lost? Shouldn't we be evacuating?" implored Fritz.

"Leaders from East Prussia are urging people to evacuate. They have told them to head west, because we will be safer with the Western Armies. But, Gautleiter Koch will hear none of it. He wants Königsberg defended until every last man is killed. Did you hear that he even wants the Hitler Youth to be organized to defend the city? Can you imagine twelve-year-old boys in the Volkssturm fighting seasoned Russian soldiers to save Königsberg? That's a death sentence for them," insisted Dr. Rhode, "you want to know the worst part? The brave Gautleiter has moved his base of operations out of Königsberg. He has abandoned his huge estate for a hotel in Pillau. There he has a small plane, a ship, and two ice-breakers ready to save himself, not if, but when the Russians break through."

Fritz growled, "Gautleiter Koch is a traitor!"

"Agreed. And you know where the precious Amber Panels are supposed to go? To his *other* estate in Western Germany," said Dr. Rhode with disgust. "Looking back, I feel immense shame for capitulating to his demands for the other artifacts. I should have fought him harder."

"Alfred," said Fritz, consoling him, "had you resisted, he would have killed you as easily as he butters his bread. On my way here today, I saw a dozen German soldiers hanging in the trees. One wore a sign proclaiming they were German traitors and warning other German soldiers to stand and fight or die. The SS killed them. They trample anyone who defies them. Many brave German citizens sick of the Nazi Party have died fighting against the SS. Had you tried, you would be dead. Do not be hard on yourself."

"Perhaps you are right. But, I've had enough. I couldn't fulfill his request for the panels. They symbolize what Königsberg was. They represent the height of German amber artisans. I must save them!" asserted Dr. Rhode. Then, he dropped his voice to nearly a whisper, "So, despite what you just heard me tell Herr Weiner, the panels are in the boxes marked with a ship, not a train. Only you and I are aware of that. I ask you, my friend, to take charge of evacuating the panels."

"Even Koch doesn't know?" replied Fritz with a whisper just loud enough for Katya to hear him.

"Most importantly, Fritz, he should never know. With Koch in Pillau, I have a brief time to challenge him. I convinced him that if the panels went by ship, they would be hard to track and would likely be sunk by Russian submarines. I figured he would listen to me. After all, I am the one that suggested storing them after the first British bombing last summer."

"And it is good you did that, Alfred, or they would have been destroyed during the second bombing. Who would have thought that the castle's former torture chamber would become a safe place for storing priceless treasure," remarked Fritz.

"Yes, but I realized something after storing the panels in the dungeon. Hiding the panels isn't enough; we must hide their trail, too. Therefore, a few months ago I launched a new strategy. Are you familiar with the Second Boer War?"

"Generally," responded Fritz with interest, "it was fought between the British and the Dutch settlers in South Africa around 1900. Why do you ask?"

"During the Boer War a British Officer named Robert Baden-Powell commanded a force of 1,500 soldiers that faced a Boer force of 8,000 soldiers. His mission was to defend the town of Mafeking. Knowing he couldn't defeat them outright, Baden-Powell turned to subterfuge. He built fake forts. He made the town's citizens carry around boxes of mines, which were actually filled with sand, to convince the enemy and local spies that the British had lots of mines, then marked fake minefields with signs. The man drafted fake letters to convince the Boers that more British troops were on their way. Guns, searchlights and other equipment were moved around town to make it appear the town was better fortified than it actually was. By confounding the enemy, Baden-Powell was able to keep the Boers at bay for over two hundred days. Eventually, the British arrived with reinforcements that secured a victory over the Boers. My point is that we must create deceptions to cover the trail of the Amber Panels in order to confuse both our friends and our foes."

"Alfred, your plan makes sense, but I didn't know you were such a student of military history," marveled Fritz.

"I am not. But, I was a Boy Scout in 1910. The founder of the Boy Scouts was the same Robert Baden-Powell. His victory against the Boers was common knowledge between the other boys and myself."

"So, have you got a plan?"

Katya listened as Dr. Alfred Rhode sketched out the entirety of his plan.

Dr. Rhode's voice softened, "I have another favor to ask. I ask that you take my son Weinhold along with you and the panels. He is five; he has no future here. No children have a future here. If my wife Gertrude and I escape this hell, then the three of us will reunite. I promise that. If not, at least I will have saved my child."

Fritz countered, "We have known each other a long time. I'm sure all three of you can escape tonight. Let us at least try!"

"No. Koch still has the resources to hunt me down. The SS informed me they have orders to kill Gertrude if I disappear. She is a virtual prisoner. It's a seven bridges problem. I'm doubtful any path will provide a solution for me. You know I am right."

"I hope you are wrong," said Fritz sadly.

"I am at peace with my decision. Besides, my work is here. I can save the panels by maintaining the ruse. As for Weinhold, you've been like an uncle to my son. I'm confident you will raise him well. I know I ask a lot of you, but these are difficult times. Tonight I will send Weinhold with his nanny Karina to the ship. They will be there by nightfall. I expect you will have the panels loaded onto your ship by then."

"Karina? I have never been introduced to her. What happened to Elizabeth?"

"We have no idea. She left home last month with some ration stamps to buy meat and never returned. It took us a week to find another nanny we could trust. My wife found Karina in a cafe of all places.

"I will look for Karina and the boy at the ship tonight. We have quite a journey before us."

"Thank you," responded Dr. Rhode, his deep voice breaking with emotion.

Katya saw the boots move closer and heard the sounds of back slaps.

"God speed to you Fritz," said Dr. Rhode gathering his composure, "now, let us show a brave face for the men."

Katya sat up after the two men left the room and the sounds of their boots faded down the hall. A far door opened and closed. Silence embraced her.

For the first time, she had doubts that her father was alive. Even worse, she had doubts that Germany could win the war. She knew she could stay in Königsberg no longer. The thought of Russian soldiers terrified her; yet, where could she go? She'd heard rumors of people walking westward to Danzig over the frozen Frisches Lagoon, but this had to be done at night to hide from Russian planes. She wondered why God had made this winter of all winters the coldest in memory.

Katya had heard people say they would take a train to escape the city, but she had no money for a ticket. She'd heard local ships were charging even higher fares to transport people from the city.

However, when she reconsidered Dr. Rhode's plan, she thought maybe she could create a ruse of her own. Ten minutes later, fifteen-year-old Katya emerged from the castle with a plan for escaping Königsberg.

June 15th, 2013

Puget Sound 2013
Puget Sound, Peninsulas & Islands

PORT TOWNSEND
★
● FORT FLAGLER

Marrowstone Island

Mutiny Bay

Whidbey Island

EVERETT
★

★
MUKILTEO

Olympic Peninsula

Puget Sound

Bainbridge Island

Discovery Park
●
★
SEATTLE

Kitsap Peninsula
★
BREMERTON

CHAPTER 2: PEEN ROGERS

A black terrier hurled himself down the concrete front porch of a Magnolia Bluff home in Seattle. The dog's legs blurred as it accelerated toward Peen Rogers' bicycle. Peen anticipated the terrier's chase by downshifting his bike and increasing his spin-rate. He gripped the handlebars tightly and sped faster, powering the bike with legs accustomed to sprinting. He fully expected to outrun the Rodent, Peen's nickname for the dog.

From the corner of his eye he watched the Rodent dart across the sidewalk and into the road, oblivious to any vehicles. Peen admired the dog's ability to singularly focus on its target with no regard for its own safety. One day while chasing Peen, the Rodent caused a Honda Civic to veer into a Ford Bronco. No one was hurt, but there was plenty of damage. Today there was no traffic, so Peen swung into the middle of the road to maintain distance from the dog's snapping jaws. How the Rodent was free to chase bicycles every day was a mystery to Peen.

The Rodent swung behind Peen trailing him by a short car-length. His bark reached a pitched frenzy and his wiry tail swirled like a propeller. Peen reacted by pedaling faster, his black basketball shorts and green t-shirt flapping in the wind. Sweat dripped off his wavy black hair and down his forehead onto his Gargoyle sunglasses. His legs alternated between pushing down and pulling up on the pedals to drive more power to the bike and maintain his lead over the terrier.

The Rodent continued his frenetic barking, unable to close ground. Then suddenly, bored by the chase, the terrier slowed, and the distance between them quickly widened. Satisfied his nemesis was leaving, the dog delivered one last bark, daring Peen to return. Their ritual complete, Peen continued on his training ride, while the Rodent trotted back home.

Peen could avoid the Rodent by riding a different route, but outracing the terrier gave him a certain satisfaction and enlivened the normally uneventful ride. While he enjoyed riding, preparing for August's annual two-hundred mile Seattle-to-Portland bicycle ride, or the STP as it was called locally, meant training four times a week, forty to sixty miles at a time. With three months of hard rides behind him, Peen felt confident he could beat his long time friend Chase Jennings.

The idea to race one another surfaced last month on Valentine's Day. Since neither had a girlfriend, they'd decided to go have a few beers and shoot some pool. Both men were "pushing forty" and kidded each other about their respective ages that evolved into an argument about who was faster on a bike. To settle the matter, they decided to enter the STP. To up the stakes, the winner would have to buy the loser a new bike. It was a dumb bet, and they were old enough to know better, but now pride was on the line, accompanied by exchanges of friendly jabs such as one was too fat to ride a two-wheeled bike or the other was too ugly to get a date.

Peen had plenty of time to train. The web development company he'd founded in early 2001 had collapsed during the 2007 recession, leaving him jobless and nearly homeless. With more time than money, he was motivated to win because couldn't afford to buy Chase a new bike. Peen knew Chase had the money to buy a new bike and was too busy at his hospital job to train for the ride, so Peen was confident he could win the bet. Still, being a competitor, Peen was not one to leave a bet to chance.

He rounded a corner when his phone's digital bell sounded, a signal that a text message had arrived. Rather than checking his phone right away, he'd wait until his coffee shop stopping-point halfway through the ride. While Peen took his training seriously, he wasn't above mixing business with pleasure. He liked to stop at the Starbucks in Magnolia to see if any cute women were sipping lattes outside. If there were, he'd strike up a conversation. He'd even created a one-line opening line. He'd ask, *if there are no Magnolia trees on Magnolia Bluff, then how did Magnolia Bluff get its name?* If a woman didn't know, but reached for her phone to google the answer, his interest in her increased. If she didn't feel like looking or didn't care, his interest waned. He preferred his women curious and smart.

Peen slowed for an intersection on westbound McLaren Street just south of Discovery Park. The pace and scenery of the Seattle neighborhood contrasted sharply with the busier streets he'd left behind. Trees thick with early summer leaves shaded the road on one side, while the manicured lawns of nearby houses lined the other. McLaren dropped sharply downhill into the heart of the neighborhood's quiet center.

Peen enjoyed the peaceful street, coasting along without hurry. The microclimate created by the trees offered a cool respite on this unusually warm June day.

Near the bottom of the hill he approached a three-way stop at McLaren and Perkins Lane. This marked the end of the seventeenth mile of his forty-mile workout. Unlike most of Magnolia Bluff, which was packed with homes on small lots, this intersection was bordered by dense vegetation, screening the street from neighboring houses. Evergreens, mostly Douglas Fir, towered over the south side of the intersection. Madrona trees and ivy covered the northern side.

Peen slowed at the intersection and reached down for his water bottle. Just then a car approached from behind, startling him. His focus broken, he fumbled the plastic bottle, dropping it onto the road. He braked to a complete stop in frustration.

"Shit," swore Peen. He pulled his sneakers from the old-school pedal straps, dropped his feet to the ground and straddled the bike. Peen's six-foot, leggy body ran with sweat. He removed his helmet, resigned to let the car pass before retrieving his bottle.

But, instead of passing by, the car slowed to a stop next to Peen, an *Escalade* according to the logo on the passenger door. Breathing heavily, Peen checked out the black Cadillac SUV, a four-door with a body that looked like it had just rolled off a car lot. The Escalade remained motionless until the passenger door's tinted front window lowered. Then the rear passenger door opened.

Still thinking about his water bottle, Peen's mind shifted to the scene next him. He thought, *Do they want directions?*

A man in the front passenger seat leaned forward and looked up at Peen. The man wore a long sleeved blue shirt with no tie. His light brown beard was trimmed short, stubble like, and his hair was cut in a similar manner. Dark sunglasses made his age difficult to determine. He showed no emotion.

The man spoke, "We can see you are tired, Mr. Rogers. Please join us for a short ride." His tone was demanding and his accent sounded European, perhaps Slavic.

Before Peen could answer, a man built like a diesel train, dressed in a black dress shirt, dark gray jacket and matching slacks, emerged from the passenger-side rear door. The Diesel was a real cue ball, a Russian version of a Japanese sumo wrestler, with no hair and no beard and round features.

Still straddling his bike, Peen turned back to the man who had spoken to him. Before considering his options or an escape route, Peen responded by declining the demand,

"I don't know how you know my name, but my mother told me never to ride with strangers. I also don't like to be told what to do."

"Your cooperation isn't necessary, Mr. Rogers. Besides, your mother is dead," said the man, as if to confirm that he knew all about Peen, "she won't care. Let my associate show you his identification."

The Diesel lifted up the right hem of his jacket, revealing a handgun. Peen didn't know a derringer from a police issue pistol, but one thing seemed certain, these kooks were serious.

"What the hell? Who are you? Are you robbing me? I have a five-dollar bill and you can have it, but I don't have my wallet or any ID cards with me."

"No, I am not here to rob you. I am here to talk with you."

"Well let's get this over with because I need to get on with my ride."

Ignoring Peen, the man in the car calmly gave the Diesel an order, "Please help Mr. Rogers into the car."

The Diesel stepped forward, grabbed Peen, and pulled him from his bike with one arm. Peen's helmet dropped to the ground along with his glasses, while the bike fell against the two of them. Still holding Peen, the Diesel grabbed Peen's bike, picked it up and tossed it into the bushes. Peen's phone fell from his bike's front pannier to the ground. Seeing the phone, the Diesel stepped on it and twisted his foot. The plastic gave way with a loud crack.

"HEY!! My bike, my phone!" yelled Peen, surprised by the Diesel's strength. Peen was strong and weighed one hundred and ninety pounds, yet was being manhandled with ease.

The Diesel shoved Peen into the car, ignoring his protests. Instead of physically resisting, Peen moved inside resolutely, causing the Diesel to lose his balance and hit his head on the top of the SUV. The man didn't make a sound, but clearly grimaced as he followed Peen into the car.

"Fine. I'm here. Who the hell are you and what do you want?" demanded Peen, as he looked around the car. Next to him sat the Diesel. In the front passenger seat was the man who'd asked him questions. In the driver's seat was a third man, whose bald head was visible from behind.

Peen's question was met by silence as the driver U-turned the Cadillac and drove east back up McLaren. Peen heard the auto lock of the doors engage.

Peen tried a second question, "Where are we going?"

"You aren't asking the questions. I am. My name is Damon," he announced as he turned in the passenger seat to look at Peen. Damon removed his sunglasses revealing someone older than Peen had expected, perhaps in his late forties. His gaze was intense, dark and unblinking. Peen returned the man's stare with equal intensity. He hated to lose, even if it was a staring contest, something he'd practiced after reading a book about Steve Jobs' use of staring to unnerve others. Peen wondered if Damon had read the same book.

"Well then, ask me something so I can get out of here," insisted Peen.

"Why the hurry Mr. Rogers? Aren't you curious at all?"

"Nope," lied Peen.

"Tell me what you know about your uncle and the Amber Panels," demanded Damon menacingly.

Peen squinted at Damon, "What are you talking about? What are those?"

"Nice try," replied Damon, "we know your uncle is Professor Edmund Rogers and don't bother denying it, because we have already confirmed you are Peen Rogers."

Peen was confused. He'd never heard of any panels, "As I said, Mr. Damon, I know nothing about them. Why don't you just ask my uncle?"

Damon responded with a wicked, short snort, "We would like to, but we can't speak face to face at the moment. Seems your uncle is buried in his work right now. So, you have two options. Either tell us what you know or we will hurt you until you do."

Peen hated ultimatums even more than being told what to do. His mouth began to out-race prudence, "Perhaps it hasn't registered on your transistor-sized brain, but I know even less than you do. I don't know where my uncle is and I don't know what an amber *tunnel* is. I dropped by my uncle's office this morning, but he wasn't there. Shit, I don't follow his research about *timber* panels any more than he follows the details of my love life, which I hope he doesn't follow at all, not that there is a whole lot to follow."

"You mean *Amber Panels*," responded Damon sternly.

"I actually meant my love life," sneered Peen.

Damon glowered, "Clearly you do not take me seriously. Perhaps this will help."

Damon looked at the Diesel, nodded, and said, "Fiat justitia, pereat mundus."

"What does that mean?" asked Peen.

Before Damon could answer Peen felt an elbow slam his rib cage, forcing him into the door to his left. The elbow knocked the wind out of him. As Peen fought for a breath of air Damon told him, "It is Latin. It means, *let there be justice, though the world perish.* I think of the phrase as an ethic that guides my actions."

Peen raised himself back to vertical.

"What are you thinking now Mr. Rogers?"

"I think," Peen wheezed, "you took a very perverse ethics class."

"Mr. Rogers, since we have some time together, let me tell you what will happen if you do not cooperate. A few years ago a man . . . "

Peen didn't care about the story. He just wanted out of the car. Peen studied the driver for a moment. His shaved head revealed dark brown skin. Except for a difference in skin color, the Diesel and the Driver could be relatives. In the rear view mirror he noticed a red birthmark covering half of the Driver's right cheek, but aviator sunglasses covered his eyes. On his hands were black leather gloves that matched the black leather jacket he wore. Perhaps that explained why the air conditioning was blasting in the car.

While Damon continued to talk, Peen noted how far they'd traveled up McLaren Street. They were about to overtake a bicycler who was also traveling eastward on their side of the road. Ignoring an oncoming car, the Driver of the Escalade began to swerve around the biker.

Realizing an opportunity, Peen coolly shifted his weight, positioning himself for the inevitable event, anticipating it by only a moment. The oncoming car suddenly braked and turned directly into the path of the Cadillac to avoid that dumbest, but most predictable animal, the Rodent, who darted across the street to attack the cycler. Faced by the oncoming car, the Cadillac veered to the right and chirped to a stop, almost hitting the cycler. Damon, who had been sitting awkwardly, was thrown into the dashboard.

While the others were caught off-guard, Peen popped the door lock, pushed the door open, and leapt from the car. He stumbled on the pavement, crashed to the ground, rolled, and then jumped to his feet. Peen heard Damon yell at his men, "Get him! He's escaped!"

Peen ran around the front of the car to the bicyclist, who had stopped after watching the near collision. The Rodent yapped madly from a few feet away. Peen, seeing another opportunity, knocked the distracted rider off his bike and onto the sidewalk.

"Sorry!" yelled Peen as he picked up the bike. The stunned biker watched Peen mount the bike and take off. The Rodent, seeing Peen ride away, gave chase. Above the Rodent's yapping, Peen heard the angry biker yelling for someone to call the police. The noise subsided as he raced toward an intersection. Behind him, the Rodent slowed, gave one last bark, then trotted back home triumphantly.

Peen rode fast. He rounded a sharp corner and raced south on Magnolia Boulevard, his legs pumping as fast as he could push them. The bike was a bit too short for his long legs, leaving him feeling cramped. *Beggars can't be choosers,* he thought as he frantically searched for his next move. Then he heard the screeching of tires behind him.

Though Peen's surprise tactic had given him a short lead, the Escalade was gaining fast. The lack of traffic in the slow-paced neighborhood played to the car's advantage. The Cadillac roared up behind Peen. Fearing they'd run into him, Peen swerved across the road into a driveway. He leapt off the bike and hoisted it over his shoulder. As he ran to the side of the house, Peen heard the SUV stop, its door slam, and the roar of its engine as it raced away.

Peen didn't look back as he entered the house's backyard, but assumed someone was chasing him. He sprinted across a grassy yard surrounded by a six-foot cedar-slatted fence. With no other exit, Peen approached the rear of the yard and threw the bike over the fence. In one motion he pulled himself up and over the fence, landing in a garden bed on the other side. So focused on fleeing, Peen didn't notice there were rose bushes until their thorns swiped painfully across his face. He brushed the stems aside, scratching his arms and cheeks painfully as he untangled himself from the bush. He grabbed the bike, hoisted it to his shoulder, and, after navigating a backyard full of lawn furniture and kids' toys, he dashed around the side of the brick house.

Peen emerged into the front yard, his heart pounding as he dropped the bike to the ground and jumped onto it. He steered across the front lawn, negotiated a short driveway, and entered the street. Peen feared the car was rounding the block. Reacting more than thinking, he angrily scolded himself, *Jesus Peen, you need a better plan than this.*

Desperately pedaling north on a quiet neighborhood street, he heard the screech of tires behind him. He looked back to see the Cadillac no more than a hundred yards away. Looking ahead he saw Discovery Park was only a short distance away and realized the park could provide a good escape.

Peen sprinted the remainder of the street until it ended at a busy four lane arterial, where he turned right. He glanced forward at the oncoming traffic. Then he spotted the entrance to the park just ahead of him on his left. Unlike all the other entrances, this one had concrete posts that prohibited cars from entering it.

Peen gripped the handlebars firmly, lifted his butt off the seat, and sprinted to reach the park's entry gate. Over his panting he heard a car screeching from behind; Peen didn't need to look back to know it was the Cadillac.

The only gap in the oncoming traffic forced Peen to careen across the street earlier than he planned. With no shoulder, he rode the last twenty yards with cars honking at him for going the wrong direction. He slowed just enough to make an abrupt left turn and threaded his way through the pillars into the park.

He looked back to see the Cadillac brake to a stop. The Driver and Peen exchanged looks. The Driver waited for two cars to pass and then flipped a loud U-turn to travel west. Peen wondered if the strangers knew about the car entrance to Discovery Park farther west. Were they headed there? As Peen resumed pedaling, he quickly devised a plan to cut through a nearby lot, race through the eastern portion of the park, and exit at the northeast entrance.

To execute his plan, he steered onto a short trail and then onto Discovery Park's paved southern parking lot. He spotted only one car in the lot. Beyond the lot, Peen rode past a clearing and onto a paved narrow two-lane road. He threaded through a set of concrete posts that blocked vehicle traffic. Past the posts, the road turned to gravel and dirt, not ideal for the bike, but the quickest way across the heavily forested park. Just then he heard the familiar sound of screeching tires.

"Shit," he grumbled. Glancing over his shoulder Peen realized that if they wanted him badly enough, they could circumvent the concrete barriers by driving on the grass and striking a pile of stacked wood. If Damon made it past that obstacle, there would be little to stop him from catching Peen.

The uneven gravel road shook the bike, forcing him to tightly grip the handlebars. As he fought for control, he tried to think of a trail that a car couldn't navigate, but nothing came to him. He mentally mapped Discovery Park: a mile long and a mile wide it had multiple entrances on the south side, where Peen and the SUV had both entered, and two on the east side. There were no entrances on the west, which terminated at Puget Sound, or on the north side, due to the way the ship canal divided the city of Seattle. So, if the concrete posts blocked Damon, Peen knew he could escape. Otherwise the chase would continue. Until then, Peen had to ride hard.

His legs burned as he churned over the gravel. He badly needed a rest to catch his breath. Looking up he estimated he was halfway down California Way, a road that bisected much of the park. He shifted his butt on the seat attempting to provide some relief to his tired body, but it didn't help. As he tried shifting to his other cheek he heard an explosion of metal and wood.

He didn't dare turn around, for fear of losing control, but he was sure the Cadillac had just run into the woodpile. He focused his senses to the unfolding events behind him, listening for clues. Other noises erupted. He couldn't make sense of them. Finally, with the gravel road leveling temporarily, Peen snatched a look backward. The Cadillac was swerving onto the road spraying gravel to one side. It was coming fast.

Ahead, Peen spotted two small parallel ditches across the road too deep to ride through. Rather than steer around them, Peen stopped pedaling, compressed his legs against the top bar, and pulled up on the bike. He sailed over the first ditch, made a smooth landing, and then repeated the move over the second ditch. This time the front wheel skidded slightly. He regained control and resumed pedaling.

Peen knew the vehicle would have to slow for the ditches, which would buy him time. The Escalade was only thirty yards behind when the sound of it braking for the ditch gave Peen hope. He had gained more distance by the time the SUV had navigated the second ditch. The sound of flying gravel resumed, but Peen barely noticed due to the exhilaration he felt at reaching the end of California Way where it terminated at Washington Avenue.

Peen rounded the corner onto Washington. A moment later, he rounded another corner onto Discovery Park

Boulevard. He glanced to his right and saw the Cadillac turning onto Washington.

Fortunately for Peen, Discovery Park Boulevard angled downhill, allowing him to accelerate. Near the end of the boulevard was an entrance onto the park's loop trail, a single-track trail too narrow for the SUV. If he could stay ahead of Damon long enough, he could reach the trail. However, the Cadillac, now back on the pavement, was closing the gap between them quickly.

Peen estimated the loop trail was a quarter mile ahead of him, while the SUV was only fifty yards behind. His heart dropped when he realized they would catch him before he could reach the loop trail. He needed another option, but the steep slopes and dense vegetation of the boulevard hillsides provided no escape. As he frantically considered his next move he heard consecutive popping noises and yelling from behind.

Holy Shit, those assholes are shooting at me!

Desperate, Peen spied the park's Veterans Cemetery entrance just ahead. He'd never considered the cemetery an option because the entrance and the exit were the same road; he'd be trapped if he entered. His only chance would be to scale the tall chain-link fence that surrounds the cemetery. But then, with a flash, he realized he'd only be a short distance from the northernmost entrance to the park. But, the tall fence was topped with security wire; it would definitely be a gamble.

With only seconds to decide, Peen slowed dramatically and veered in front of two oncoming cars. Surprised by Peen's move, the oncoming car braked to avoid hitting

Peen. A second car collided into the back of the first car with a loud crunch. Damon's driver, surprised by Peen's move, sped by the two cars as their drivers stopped to check for damage. The Driver past the accident, spun the car around, then raced back until he reached the turn for the cemetery.

The entrance to the cemetery angled up, launching Peen and the bike into the air. As he flew he fought to maintain control. He landed hard onto the driveway. Ahead, Peen could see the cemetery's paved drive was turning to gravel and diverging as if he was approaching the home plate of a baseball diamond. One road angled right and the other left. The two roads reached outward until they turned toward each other and met at an imaginary second base far across the cemetery. Inside the diamond drive were rows of headstones.

When Peen arrived at 'home plate', instead of turning right or left, he rode straight onto the grass between rows of graves on a direct line for 'second base'. They provided a perfect path for him to reach the other side of the cemetery, yet were too narrow for the Cadillac.

My apologies everyone, thought Peen as he careened between the graves. He quickly emerged at the far side just as the Cadillac roared into the cemetery. He glanced back to see it turn left.

He turned his attention to the fence before him, a standard eight-foot tall chain-link fence with three strands of barbed wire on top installed at an outward angle to deter unwanted visitors. Just beyond the fence were numerous large fir trees and beyond them was a remote park building with no cars around it.

Peen hopped off the bike, grabbed it with two hands, wheeled in a circle, then let it go like an Olympic hammer throw. He hoped the bike would rotate horizontally through the air and land on its side to minimize damage. At least that was the plan. But as the bike flew over the fence it rotated straight into a fir tree, then tumbled down several limbs to the ground. Despite the plan's poor execution, the bike survived.

Peen turned to see the Cadillac rounding the last turn; now it was headed straight at him. He had one chance to traverse the fence or be trapped. Backing up, he held his breath, and ran at it. Peen leapt up extending his right foot. Just as his foot made contact with the fence, he forced his left leg upward. As his shoes dug into the links, he drove his right leg up and reached for the top of the chain-link fence, pulling and pushing his body up until he could crouch on top of the fence and use the barbed wire portion to steady himself.

Peen raised up and put a foot on the angled rail that supported the barbed wire. As the sounds of the SUV grew louder, he took two quick steps along the rail, then leapt toward a large fir tree branch.

This move wasn't completely novel for him. As a kid, he and his buddies often leapt from a friend's garage roof, grabbed a branch, and rode it to the ground. But, being eighty pounds heavier than his thirteen-year-old self, the branch partially slowed his descent, then snapped. He fell hard onto the ground, his left arm pinned under his side. He felt a flash of pain, but there was no time for pain.

Peen stood, grabbed the bike, and lugged it around to the side of the park building as the Cadillac skidded to a stop. The SUV sat motionless. Then, the tires spun and gravel flew once again as the Driver raced for the cemetery's exit.

Clearly, they aren't done with me, thought Peen.

Peen ticked through his options. He knew of one place he could go and not be chased by Damon's car: the Ballard Locks, the western terminus of Seattle's Lake Washington Ship Canal where boats were raised and lowered to and from the salt water of Puget Sound and the fresh water of Lake Union. Luckily, the locks were a short ride from here.

CHAPTER 3: GRISTO

Peen's arm hurt. Sweat stung his scratched face. His legs felt like anchors. His body ached for rest, but his mind urged him forward: *Just get to the locks*. He had to repeat it several times before his body responded. Peen forced himself back on the bike, placed his feet on the pedals, and rode north across Texas Way. He looked east toward a parking lot, then glanced west and saw no sign of the Cadillac.

Peen gripped the handlebars and headed down 40th Avenue. A view of the ship canal in the distance renewed his hope of escape. He rounded the junction at Commodore Way and sprinted eastward. The downward slope allowed Peen to shift to eighteenth gear and gain plenty of speed on the arrow-straight road. A half-mile ahead a train trestle crossed over Commodore Way. Just past the trestle was the entrance to the Hiram Chittenden Locks, known locally as the Ballard Locks.

Peen reached the flat portion of Commodore Way, pedaled vigorously for the trestle. Hearing a noise from behind, he glanced back and spotted a red minivan approaching him, followed by a white truck. Tailing the truck was the *Cadillac.*

Shit! What is it going to take to ditch these guys?

He steered to the center of his lane to force the van and truck to stay behind him, blocking Damon. The minivan driver honked the horn as Peen approached the trestle.

Peen looked back again. To his surprise, the Cadillac was in the oncoming lane ready to pass the truck and minivan. Before it could get close, Peen sped under the trestle and veered left into a small parking lot, then maneuvered the bike onto a paved trail. He rounded the trail onto a promenade atop the locks' southern embankment. A quarter-mile east was the entrance to the locks.

Rather than follow Peen into the parking lot, the Cadillac continued east along Commodore Way and climbed a short hill. Peen lost sight of the Cadillac as it disappeared behind a stand of trees.

Peen rode fast, ignoring signs on the promenade that ordered him to dismount. He didn't stop until he reached the entrance to the walkway along the locks' wide spillway, where fresh lake water dropped into the saltwater of Puget Sound. The walkway was clogged with tourists, so Peen dismounted and tossed the bike aside, then began running across the spillway's one hundred yard long path.

Part way across, a group of tourists posing for a picture blocked his path. Peen nervously looked behind and spotted the Diesel's large body rumbling down the concrete path toward the spillway.

I can outrun this guy, Peen thought, *but only if the lock gates stay shut and these tourists move.* That was the one hitch in Peen's plan. There were two sets of locks Peen had to cross to reach the Ballard side of the canal. The only way to cross them was over the watertight doors, or gates, which doubled as pedestrian walkways, but only when they were in the closed position.

With a brusque, "Excuse me," Peen pushed his way past the tourists. They complained noisily, while Peen moved forward, threading his way around additional tourists. He cleared the spillway and stood atop the south concrete pier of the small lock.

Peen saw that both sets of gates were shut because a lift was in progress. He sprinted to the nearest set of gates and crossed over them between the handrails.

With the small lock behind him, Peen now faced the large lock. He looked to his right toward the closest gate and saw it blocked by a large group of tourists taking pictures of the boats inside the lock. He could see no way around them.

Peen looked left. He could see the western gates were open and the last two boats were leaving the lock's chamber. Aware the gates would close as soon as the last vessel cleared the chamber, he thought he could escape across those gates. He looked back and saw the Diesel had nearly crossed the spillway. Peen's lead had diminished to five seconds.

Peen began running west, his path narrowing temporarily as he rounded a small building. Suddenly, a foot-high bollard with a wet paint sign was in front of him. He hurdled over the bollard, stumbling as he landed. After regaining his balance he picked up speed.

The concrete pier stretched two hundred feet before him. Steel railings lined both sides of the pier. Down the middle were more bollards with wet paint signs. To his left Peen noticed the roiling currents below the pier: the water looked dangerous.

Peen looked ahead and saw the western gates were still open. A wooden three-masted schooner was just clearing the gates. Behind it, the last sailboat, a single-masted thirty-footer, was slowly motoring toward the gates. Peen had hoped the western gates would be closed before he reached them, but now he realized they wouldn't shut in time. He knew the Diesel would catch him.

As Peen approached the end of the pier, he considered his options. He could turn and fight, but the Diesel had a gun. Also, the man was twice Peen's weight.

He could jump from the concrete platform into the frigid water, a leap of about twenty feet. However, he rejected that option, because he knew there were powerful pumps nearby that could pull him under the water. Between that, the strong current, and the cold water, he didn't think he could last long swimming in it.

Just then, Peen realized he was running at the same pace as the small sailboat, which was very close to the lock's sidewall nearest Peen.

Relying on instinct rather than common sense, Peen angled to his right, then swung himself over the railing. He landed on top of the huge lock's gate, which was still in the open position, and continued running atop it. Nothing blocked his path beyond the end of the gate. Keeping pace with the sailboat, he sprinted, knowing he was about to make an insane leap of faith.

On his final step, Peen launched off the end of the gate. He grabbed the handrail, swung clockwise, then let go, hoping to catch hold of the boat's mast. Twenty feet above the water, he extended his arms before him as his legs churned the air, giving tourists a sight they'd never forget.

Unfortunately for Peen, his timing was off. Gravity pulled him down sooner than he'd planned. As he began to fall, his right foot snagged a mast stay, knocking him off balance. To compensate, he reached for the mast with both arms. His right arm caught the mast, but a sharp pain seared through his injured left arm forcing him to release his grip. Unable to catch the mast firmly, his body pivoted around the mast. Unable to withstand the rotational force, he lost hold of the mast.

Freefalling, he caught another stay with his left leg, careened off of it, and tumbled through the air. Peen relaxed his body, resigned to his fate. He landed in the cold, murky water head first, barely missing the boat's starboard gunnel.

The sailboat's skipper witnessed the entire mishap. He'd watched helplessly as a crazy tourist attacked his boat, then tumbled over the side into the water, while tourists snapped pictures and videos, then uploaded them to their favorite sites.

The Diesel was running fast as he watched Peen's unexpected move. He was distracted just long enough to miss seeing a bollard. He tripped over it, full-speed, and landed hard, sliding into a solid metal post.

Peen, fully submerged, found the salt water disorienting at first. The shock of his situation was replaced by the need to reach the surface. He opened his eyes and looked around until he saw sunlight, then noticed the hull of a boat. Peen kicked himself upward as fast as he could, his hunger for air overcoming any fear.

He surfaced, gasping, when a life preserver bounced off his head. He grabbed it and held on tight, while the boat dragged him away from the lock's chamber. The skipper steered the boat over to a northern concrete wall near a barnacle-encrusted metal ladder. The boat's fenders cushioned it against the wall as the skipper put the boat into neutral, more or less bringing the vessel to a stop.

The boat's small wake gently lapped against the concrete wall as Peen kicked to the ladder. He grabbed onto the bottom rung with his good arm, the barnacles imprinting themselves onto it. Releasing the preserver, he waved with his sore arm and shouted thanks to the skipper. The captain gave Peen a silent nod, then motored quietly away.

Peen began his slow ascent. In addition to being physically and mentally spent, he was now cold and wet. His arm hurt, so he could only use it sparingly. It was only eleven in the morning and he wondered what else could possibly happen to him today.

Cresting the concrete wall, Peen was relieved to see two police officers waiting for him. They helped him off the ladder and directed him to a grassy knoll where he collapsed. From there, he had a view back across the locks. A youthful looking officer with freckles asked him a question, but Peen was looking for the Diesel. While he didn't see him, Peen did see a crowd gathered at the spot where the Diesel had been. Relieved the chase appeared to be finished, he laid his head on the grass.

The freckled officer repeated his questions, "Sir, can you hear me? Are you okay?"

Peen tried to shake off the fog of exhaustion. Instead, he rambled, "My arm, left arm, is killing me. My face stings. Did you get them?"

The officer, somewhat impatient, asked Peen calmly, but sternly, "Get who, sir? What happened to your face? Does anything else hurt?"

Peen struggled to gather his wits, "Yes, that is all that hurts. Did you get the guy who was chasing me?"

A tall lanky officer with a moustache spoke, "There is someone down on the lock platform, but we don't know anything more. So, what the hell was that stunt about?"

Peen answered, "As soon as I find out, you'll be the first to know. Some guys chased me and shot at me. Then that big guy ran after me. I had no choice. I had to jump."

"You say you were chased and that was why you jumped off the lock?"

"I had to get away," said Peen, closing his eyes. His body shivered from the cold. What he wanted to do was climb into a warm bed and go to sleep. However, that wasn't happening any time soon.

✻✻✻

Damon looked through the binoculars again. Strangely, Gristo didn't move. Even worse, a crowd had gathered around the fallen man. Watching Peen escape had made Damon Kant angry, but seeing his bodyguard Gristo collapse onto the ground had him worried. Damon had known Gristo a long time. He'd hired Gristo when he first took control of his father's estate in the 1990s. Since then, he'd proven to be a smart and capable ally. Damon knew the man didn't give up easily. If he was on the ground it meant Gristo was seriously hurt.

Whatever the injury, Damon couldn't risk getting involved. Gristo would have to handle the problem himself for now. He turned and ran back up the park's walkway to the Cadillac. Opening the door, he barked at the Driver, "Get out of here now!"

As the Driver pulled away, Damon thought to himself, *For a guy who didn't know anything, Peen worked very hard to escape. Peen's got to return home sometime. We'll be waiting.*

CHAPTER 4: OFFICER LARRY JACOBS

"The FBI will be here any moment to speak with you," advised Officer Jacobs.

Peen released an impatient sigh and shifted his weight on the uncomfortable metal chair. He'd been at the station since just before noon. The Seattle Police had already recorded his statement, but the FBI still wanted to speak with him in person before he left. He didn't know why they wanted to speak with him. He was tired of waiting and his stomach was rumbling.

Jacobs sat across the desk from Peen completing his report. The officer was in his mid thirties, stocky, and fit. His demeanor was friendly, yet business-like. With light blond hair, blue eyes, and square features, Peen imagined Jacobs descended directly from a clan of Norwegian Vikings, a safe assumption given the Ballard neighborhood's Scandinavian roots.

Other than the sound of Jacobs tapping on the keyboard, only the buzz of the fluorescent ceiling lights interrupted the silence. With nothing to do, Peen's mind drifted back to the locks.

The officers who'd helped Peen from the ladder had seen him jump. They'd escorted him to the grass, and wrapped him in an emergency blanket. When Medic One arrived, the EMT examined Peen's arm and thought his ulna bone might be fractured. He recommended an x-ray. Peen said that he couldn't afford any medical treatment and would rather let the arm heal than be billed some ridiculous amount for treatment he probably didn't need.

Following Medic One's departure, the officers brought him to the Police Department's North Precinct to file a report and possibly file a reckless endangerment charge against him. Peen reminded them he'd been chased. He was still awaiting final word on the charges.

As he waited, Peen looked around the office. He'd never been to a police station and realized his only experience with law enforcement came from television shows such as Barney Miller, Hill Street Blues, and Law and Order.

Peen looked at the gray janitorial overalls he'd been given to replace his wet shorts and shirt. They were too big, but he was warm and dry. In fact, except for being bored, he had no complaints.

Jacobs glanced up from his paperwork and smiled, but he wasn't looking at Peen. The officer was looking past him. Peen turned to see a fit, tall man in a dark blue suit, white shirt, and a British style tie with blue and gray diagonal stripes. He showed little emotion as he approached. He directed his gaze squarely at Peen, measuring him. Peen returned his gaze, thinking this must be the FBI guy. He looked like he'd just read lines for a remake of the X-files. Only the brown gauze wrap on his left hand was out of place.

"Hi Larry! How are you?" yelled the approaching man to Jacobs in an surprisingly jovial manner. Jacobs stood and greeted the man with a hearty handshake.

"Great! I'm really good," responded Jacobs. Looking at his friend's injured hand he asked, "How are you Michael? How's your pinky?"

"Better," he said, lifting his gauze-wrapped hand, "the doc says I fractured it. But, give me a few weeks and I'll be dunking again."

"Michael, the only dunks you've ever made were on your son's Little Tikes hoop," teased Jacobs as he tapped Jorden on the chest with the back of his hand. Turning to Peen he said, "You should have seen this guy's finger. We were playing some three-on-three when the basketball hit Michael's hand. All of a sudden, blood was spurting out of his pinky all over the floor. Bone was sticking out. Man, it was gross."

"Larry's overselling. It was barely a flesh wound. Well, maybe a broken bone, too. Just know I could have kept playing. I could have beaten you all with just my right hand, but then, I didn't want to make you look bad."

"Maybe next time," said Jacobs, shifting his gaze toward Peen, "anyway, this is the guy I wanted you to meet. Peen Rogers, Michael Jorden. Michael Jorden, Peen Rogers."

"Peen did a double take. *Michael Jordan*?" he asked.

"Yeah, I get that look a lot. It's Jorden with an *e*," corrected Jorden.

"Gotcha," said Peen, "that fracture must have hurt!"

"Yeah it did. Your face must hurt, too. No offense, it's a mess. Listen, for the record, the names might sound the same, but I know my limitations. The only things *the* Mike and I have in common are our smarts, good looks, and black skin. I'd like to have paychecks in common, too, however I doubt the FBI will find my service quite so valuable. Maybe, if I can just milk the free agent thing, I still might have a chance."

"Don't give up your day job, Michael," laughed Jacobs.

Jacobs offered Jorden a chair, but Jorden sat on the edge of the desk, while Jacobs retook his seat. Jorden's smile slipped from his face and he asumed a sterner FBI character. Taking a deep breath, he said, "So, I understand you are Peen Rogers?"

"Generally. At least on normal days I am, but after today, I'm not sure I want to be," replied Peen.

"Understandable given what you've been through. I know this NBA wanna-be has drowned you with questions, but I want to re-address some of them," said Jorden as he pulled out a small note pad. "Your name is Peen Rogers. You are thirty-nine years old and live in an apartment at 375 West De Haro Lane in Seattle?"

"Yup," affirmed Peen.

"Where are you employed?"

"The economy crushed my company, so I'm unemployed or underemployed at the moment. I make a little side money, but don't have a steady job."

"So, what do you do for income?" inquired Jorden.

Peen felt he had nothing to hide and relaxed more with each answer, "I do a little consulting and web development, however that doesn't generate much money. After my web company went under, I had some money saved, so I took some time to travel, thinking the economy would turn around. Obviously, it hasn't. So, I've been earning enough to survive while I figure out what I'm going to do next."

"Where have you traveled in the last couple of years, Mr. Rogers? Did you make any enemies along the way?"

Peen thought about his recent cross country road trip from Seattle to the East Coast and back, "I'm not aware of any. I spent six months driving to and from New York, staying with friends or camping. Mostly, I tried to avoid people. I returned this spring and, apart from my consulting, have been looking for a new opportunity, but haven't found anything yet."

"Where do your parents live?"

"Dad passed away five years ago. Mom died when I was only twenty."

"I'm sorry to hear that Mr. Rogers," uttered Jorden with genuine sympathy.

"It's life. Nothing to be done about it," shrugged Peen without emotion. He didn't like discussing their deaths.

"Any siblings, grandparents, or any other relatives?" Jorden already knew the answer since he'd spoken with Jacobs on his way to the station.

"Just my uncle, Edmund."

"Do you two have a good relationship?"

"Yes. My uncle and I get along, but our busy lives kept us distant in the past, despite the fact we've both lived in Seattle all our lives. That changed last December when he nearly died from a heart attack. Since then, we've been trying to spend more time together. In fact, I dropped by his office earlier today to wish him a happy birthday, but he wasn't there. He told me he'd be around there today, which was odd, because normally he avoids being there."

"And you told Officer Jacobs that this Damon fellow specifically mentioned your uncle?"

"Yes. Damon demanded to know where my uncle was."

"And how did you respond, Mr. Rogers?"

"I told them I had no idea where he was."

"Do you have any idea where these guys are from?" probed Jorden. So far he wasn't totally buying Peen's story and wondered if he'd concocted it to cover his leap onto the sailboat mast. He and Jacobs initially suspected the jump was some kind of social media stunt. However, after identifying the man who'd been injured at the locks, Jorden decided to visit the station and give Peen the opportunity to explain what happened.

Tired and hungry, Peen appealed with more emotion, "As I told Officer Jacobs, I have no clue. The leader's name was Damon and he spoke with an accent. It was Slavic or Eastern European or Russian; I couldn't tell for sure. He wanted information on something called amber panels, but I've never heard of them."

"What does your uncle do for a living?" asked Jorden.

"He's a professor of art history at the University of Washington. If the panels are old and European, he probably knows about them," said Peen. His uncle had been passionate about art and history since the age of twenty, when he spent a summer traveling Europe by train.

"It makes sense that if your uncle knows something about these amber panels, Damon might be hunting him to get that information. You mentioned they wanted to ask you some questions. What questions did they ask you?"

"None other than the ones I've mentioned. They didn't really have a chance. I was only in the car a minute or two, before the dog ran in front of the car, nearly causing an accident. That's when I made my getaway, at least I hope I've gotten away. Based on their relentlessness, I have this feeling I'll see them again."

"Have you ever traveled internationally?" asked Jorden.

Peen wondered where Jorden was heading with his questions. "Yeah," said Peen, "I spent three months biking and working around New Zealand a couple decades ago. I visited Eastern Europe a few years ago. And, of course, I've been to Canada and Mexico. Outside of that, I've been too busy to travel overseas."

"Do you have any strong relationships with any Europeans, particularly Eastern Europeans? Or do you or any of your friends have any strong relationships with any Europeans?" asked Jorden directly, watching all of Peen's reactions closely.

"None that stands out," answered Peen slowly, "I don't understand what you want from me."

"I just want the truth. This could be a very serious problem for your uncle and, as you've already experienced, for you too," asserted Jorden as he crossed his arms, "remember the guy at the locks?"

"Let's just say I have a Kodak moment of the guy permanently imprinted on my synapses. But, I am curious about him. I never saw him after I leapt to the sailboat. What happened to him?"

Agent Jorden looked at Jacobs, "You didn't tell him?"

"No, because I haven't received any more information," responded Jacobs.

Jorden turned back to Peen, "The guy's name is Dimitri Galprom. According to Interpol, he goes by the name Gristo. Witnesses at the scene reported to police that while he was chasing you at the locks, Gristo tripped over a bollard. As he fell he smacked his head against the railing, causing a spinal cord injury that has left him paralyzed from the neck down. After he fell, he started speaking in a language nobody understood. Then two tourists from Ukraine who'd witnessed the chase recognized the language. They said he was mentioning a man named Damon and complaining about fools and amber. Then he fell silent. He's refused to say anything else since. Currently, the doctors at Puget Sound Medical Center are evaluating him."

Jacobs piped up, "So, he won't be chasing anyone any time soon?"

"Nope," said Jorden, "even if he was healthy, he wouldn't be chasing anyone, because it turns out Gristo is wanted in Germany, Britain, and Poland for art thefts. Europol is particularly interested in him."

"Europol? I've heard of Interpol, but not Europol," remarked Peen.

"Europol focuses on internal EU communication, while Interpol is much larger and more internationally focused. Europol has developed an expertise in information and intelligence analysis. They also specialize in art theft. Did you know that behind drugs and arms, art theft is the third most profitable crime in the world? There are major players involved who are as ruthless as drug and arms gangs. That's the type of people who were chasing you."

"Ooooh. Not good," groaned Peen. As he listened to this news, he felt even luckier he'd escaped. He wondered if his uncle had been as fortunate. Based on Jorden's information, it sounded as if Damon had the resources to find him again. Peen knew he'd have to watch his back.

"Europol has linked Gristo with several mysterious deaths. Also, Gristo is a known accomplice of Damon Severloh, who goes by several aliases. His name for the last few years has been Damon Kant."

Peen nodded his head in understanding, "Ahhh, most likely the very same Damon I met today."

"Exactly," concurred Jorden. He paused for a moment and took a breath, "This is important Mr. Rogers. Europol wants Damon even worse than Gristo. My question for you is, what does Damon want with you? If he was chasing you, I imagine he relayed the reason to you clearly. Do you know what that reason might be? Because, my gut tells me you're not telling me everything you know."

"No, I don't know why he's chasing me. I rarely go to museums. I'm too broke to own art. I'm just a tech guy who has built and run tech companies. Today, I was riding my bike, minding my own business, when these guys kidnapped me, or at least tried. I can't imagine why they were chasing me," explained Peen. "If my uncle knows something, he's never told me."

"Have you made contact with your uncle yet?"

"As I said, I visited his office. I wanted to wish him a happy birthday. He's sixty today and that was extra special for him since his heart attack last December. When I couldn't find him at the office, I called and then emailed him, but I still haven't heard back. Of course, it's possible he called after I was chased, but Gristo destroyed my phone. So, I haven't checked my messages for a while."

At that moment Peen remembered the text he'd received while riding his bike. It could have been his uncle, but his uncle rarely texted him. But, with his phone destroyed, how could he get to it? Maybe his buddy Chase knew how.

"I guess that is it for now," said Agent Jorden, looking less than satisfied. He stood, reached into his pocket, and handed Peen his card, "If Damon contacts you again or you hear from your uncle, please call me, okay? Your life may depend on it, Mr. Rogers."

"Thanks Agent Jorden with an *e*," said Peen smiling as he stood and shook Jorden's hand.

Jorden rolled his eyes, turned and walked away. Peen sat back down and thought, *Now, how will I find my uncle?*

Just then Jacobs announced he was finished. He told Peen that, because of the circumstances, there wouldn't be any charges. But, if he tried it again, whatever the reason, he'd be in big trouble.

Wanting to leave as soon as possible, Peen asked, "Can you give me a ride?"

"I'd like to help you, but we aren't a shuttle service," replied Jacobs matter-of-factly.

"Can I at least make a call? My friend can pick me up."

"Yep, there's a phone along the hallway wall you can use. Just dial nine first. And please don't forget to return the overalls."

"Sure thing," responded Peen, as he stood and flapped the wide pant legs, "they aren't my style anyway."

Peen exited the office and looked for the phone to call his friend Chase Jennings. Chase would help him out.

✳✳✳

Moments after Peen left the precinct, Agent Jorden returned to Jacobs' office. As he sat down, his cell phone buzzed. He recognized the number and answered right away, Jacob's listened to Jorden as he spoke, "Yes, a black Cadillac Escalade at the south side of the locks before noon. What? No video cameras yet? That's frustrating. Okay, thanks for the update."

"Who was that, Michael?"

"A friend from Homeland Security," Jorden informed him, "DHS was supposed to install cameras in all the Ballard Locks' parking lots last year, but my friend just informed me they haven't done it yet. You know, the locks are now considered a potential terrorist target. Can you imagine the damage if the locks were blown?"

"Oh, that would be a bad, bad day. Water from Lake Union and Lake Washington would pour into Puget Sound. Everyone connected with the ship canal — marinas, houseboats, restaurants, not to mention fish runs — would be affected. The damage would be immense. I'd never thought about that," exclaimed Jacobs.

"Fortunately, DHS *has* thought of it. They just haven't moved fast enough on it yet," said Jorden in frustration.

Jacobs nodded his head, "That's too bad about the cameras. Having those plates would have been helpful. However, I do think Rogers is on the level with us."

"Yep, I agree, though I wouldn't say he is telling us everything he knows. I do believe Rogers felt like he was running for his life. Why else would someone be crazy enough to jump off the locks?" Jorden noted. "If Gristo was chasing Rogers, then Damon thinks he knows something very important."

"Do you know anything about the panels he mentioned?" asked Jacobs.

Jorden responded, "Nope. But, what Damon is hunting doesn't really concern me; what concerns me is that the Europeans want Damon. Because of that, I've recommended that the FBI tag Damon a terrorist. That way when we get a plate on the Cadillac we can locate it more quickly."

"Is that legal, Michael? Don't they have to represent a threat to national security? I thought it took more than art theft to land on our watch lists."

Jorden looked at his friend and raised an eyebrow, "Don't forget, Damon is wanted for murder, too."

"Oh, yeah. I forgot that little detail."

"Besides," added Jorden, "nabbing Damon would be a great cross-agency win. The FBI has been encouraging us to aide foreign intelligence agencies, because we are relying on each other more and more as criminals have globalized. For example, I'm waiting on a scan of Damon's face from Europol as we speak. With the Trapwire, and soon the Intellistreet programs, I think we'll have enough cameras around the city that we ought to be able to spot him using facial recognition software."

"I've heard of Trapwire," Jacobs said to Jorden. Then he asked, "Doesn't that system combine cameras and software to spot suspicious activity?"

"Yes," affirmed Jorden, "the system predicts potential terrorist attacks by monitoring the behavior of people throughout the United States. Numerous cameras in major cities capture footage on a continuous basis. That footage is analyzed in real-time by software capable of identifying suspicious behavior."

"So Michael, how does the Intellistreet program you mentioned earlier differ from Trapwire?"

"The Intellistreet program has cameras, microphones and speakers in street lights. It's a way to expand into the suburbs where many terrorists live. The system records pedestrian and road traffic, listens to conversations, and can be used to broadcast civic announcements. Farmington Hills in Michigan was chosen as a pilot program city. Now Homeland plans to expand to more areas. Seattle and Los Angeles are already retrofitting their streetlights for new technologies like Intellistreet."

"Jesus," voiced Jacobs with concern, "can it get more Orwellian than that? Not that I don't find the tools useful, but, to be blunt, it kind of gives me the creeps."

Jorden countered, "Well, it could be worse. The Europeans are experimenting with a variety of technologies. For example, the Dutch police have announced they are developing a mobile scanner that will see through people's clothing, similar to what DHS uses in airports. Some British cities use the loudspeaker capabilities of the streetlights to chastise citizens for littering or other minor offenses. Personally, I don't see us going that far. As long as people behave, they'll be fine."

Jacobs shook his head, "Yeah, I've heard that argument a lot these last few years."

Jorden continued, "Well frankly, I can't imagine *not* having this technology. Without it, we can't track people like Damon. With our license plate camera collection points, we can corral him in no time once we confirm the Cadillac's license plates."

"Well, just don't abuse it or the government will take it away," warned Jacobs, "I do hope some of it trickles down for our use, but it still makes me uneasy."

Jorden responded, "Hopefully these systems will be around for a long time. We just need to get it right."

CHAPTER 5: CHASE JENNINGS

"And here I thought spilling maple syrup on my living room carpet would top any story you had today. But nooooo, you've got international terrorists chasing you, a death-defying leap from the Ballard Locks, and an interview with an FBI agent. Have you no shame?" complained Chase Jennings after hearing Peen's story.

"Don't forget I scratched my face and arms," goaded Peen as he pointed to his cheek.

Chase and Peen were at PHO 21, a Vietnamese soup restaurant on Capitol Hill, named partly in honor of the 1962 *Century 21 Exposition*, the world's fair Seattle hosted, a fair dedicated to the space race and all things futuristic.

Just now the 1960s instrumental hit *Telstar* was playing in the background.

"Peen, I'm staring right at you and I can say, unequivocally, you've never looked more handsome. Those scratches add dignity to your face and compliment your dark hair. They give you character!"

As Peen grabbed his glass and took a sip of water, his gaze drifted across an interior at odds with its menu. The only visual nods to Vietnam, apart from the food, were three bamboo plants anchoring one corner. Colorful posters from 1962 hung around the room at eye level: an orange and gold Space Needle, these days painted white; a sparkling nighttime photo of the amusement ride area known as the Gayway; the clear plastic elevator called the Bubbleator, due to its spherical shape; the Spacearium theater; the Home of Living Light; and several Skyride overviews of swoop-roofed pavilions decorated with futuristic blobs and curves. Even the fair's "Girls of the Galaxy" peepshow had a space-age theme. The poster closest to Peen was of the Washington State Pavilion, a cluster of six rectangular buildings wrapped around three sides of a large reflecting pool. Hovering over the pool like stepping-stones was a multi-level plaza that guided visitors to the main entrance. Above the plaza soared five elegant, arched structures, like towering lacey white gazebos. This complex later became the Pacific Science Center, a place Peen knew very well because he'd spent a summer working there as a Science Camp counselor. For Seattleites, the lacey gazebos are nearly as iconic as the Space Needle. Peen knew that most people were unfamiliar with the name of their architect, Minoru Yamasaki, but everyone would recognize a pair of other buildings he had designed: The World Trade Towers in New York City.

"Fortunately, I'm more than just a pretty face," Peen finally responded.

"Whatever," Chase chided, hoping to deflate the stress Peen felt. Just then, the background music shifted from *Telstar* to the *Peppermint Twist*. Peen started rocking his shoulders to the beat, which made them both laugh.

Chase added, "I love the campiness of this place."

"Only on Capitol Hill could this work," replied Peen.

"Yup, guaranteed counterculture all the way."

As if on cue, a petite female server with bright red hair and a nose ring delivered large bowls of soup. She wore tight-fitting jeans and a brown t-shirt with the *PHO 21* logo over her left breast. Normally, Peen would have flirted with her, but he was too hungry. After she set down the soup, he added squirts of sriracha and hoisin sauce to the soup, then juiced in a lime chunk and tossed in Thai basil leaves. Next he scooped up a pair of chopsticks, swirled the ingredients together, and sucked some hot rice noodles from his bowl. The soup was spicy and satisfying.

"Damn, Peen," said Chase, "do you know what this means? It means there was absolutely no value in spilling all that syrup on my carpet. Did I mention the carpet was only six weeks old? Have you got any idea how hard it is to clean syrup out of a carpet? Probably not, I certainly had *no* idea."

Peen didn't reply. Instead, Chase watched him wolf down the first few slurps of the noodle soup. Then Peen slowed to enjoy the remainder of it. As he watched his friend with concern, Chase absentmindedly wound the long thin rice noodles onto chopsticks. He always ate the noodles first, before sifting through the beef stock in search of tripe, brisket fat, and slices of round steak.

Chase set down his chopsticks, took a drink of water, and, hoping to humor Peen some more, acknowledged he'd lost, "Alright, so you did have the worst morning. On the bright side, you'd better be thankful I keep some clothes at the office. Lucky we're the same size."

"Thanks man. I really appreciate the clothes," said Peen as he looked from his soup to his friend. Chase's face was a blend of his Korean mother and African father, both of them immigrants who met at an English language class soon after they'd arrived. Unable to agree on a traditional Korean or African name, they'd sifted through famous American names before choosing the obscure last name of former Supreme Court Chief Justice, Salmon P. Chase.

Unlike his namesake, Chase had a full head of hair, wild and black. By using various hair products, his hair started smooth and compact in the morning. By midday it was several inches off his scalp. By evening, if he didn't have it ponytailed, his hair grew untamed, like Albert Einstein's.

"Hey, if I were chased by terrorists, you'd let me borrow your clothes, wouldn't you?" asked Chase as he settled against the back of the booth. He absentmindedly stroked his fingers through his hair. Without waiting for an answer he continued, "Now, back to your problem, Peen. You want Dimitri's room number so you can question him about your uncle? Right?"

Peen's decision to contact Chase was not just because they were best friends, but also because he'd worked at Puget Sound Medical Center for six years as a financial analyst and aspired to CFO of the company some day. If anyone could get him information on Gristo, it was Chase.

"Yeah, I need a room number."

Chased grilled his friend, "Do you see any problems at all with that plan?"

"What could go wrong?" smirked Peen sarcastically.

"Oh, I don't know. Maybe I could get fired?"

"You won't get fired," argued Peen, "just deny, deny, deny. You'll be fine."

"Easy for you to say, but denials won't keep me from being fired," countered Chase.

"You won't get fired. You can talk yourself out of anything," said Peen trying to think of an example, "Remember that time we were caught by your mom with Miller Lite in your car?"

Chase chuckled, "Yeah. She stormed into the living room wagging her finger at me." He stopped talking, laughing too hard to continue.

Peen was laughing too, "I was stunned. I'd never seen your polite, quiet mother yell like that."

"Neither had I, Peen!"

"But, you kept your wits about you and explained how the beer wasn't yours, because you'd never drink it. You even described how it included chemically modified hop extracts and other bizarre ingredients I can't remember any more," added Peen.

"Oh yeah, I lucked out. Earlier in the week we were studying food ingredients that went into popular foods like Twinkies. I threw in anything I could come up with, sulfates, diglycerides, and a couple others," laughed Chase.

"Then you told your mom that you and I would never drink that shit. You said the word *shit* to your mom! She was speechless! Finally, you explained how we'd stolen the beer from some friends who were already drunk and planned to drive to another party. You argued that we were just trying to protect them."

"Of course, Peen. She'd just accused her seventeen year-old son of drinking alcohol, only to find out he was doing a good deed."

Peen's hard laughter subsided to a chuckle, "And then she left the room without saying anything."

Chase quieted down as well. Then he said thoughtfully, "You know, she apologized later that night. Of course, I accepted it."

"I didn't know that. Did you ever tell her the truth?"

"No," replied Chase nonchalantly, "I didn't want to crush her image of me. She didn't really want to know that you and I had gotten drunk with two older girls. The next day my head hurt so much from our drinking that I wanted to find out what they'd put into the beer. My research scared me off of most beers."

"See, that's exactly why I'm not worried about getting you into trouble," argued Peen. He knew his friend could get into trouble for releasing the information, but Chase could worm his way out of anything. He'd always been great at managing disagreements.

Peen and Chase first met when they were thrust together as debate partners during their junior year in high school. Peen signed up for the class because his girlfriend, Michelle, had signed up for it. But, one week into the school year they split. By then it was too late to find another class, so Peen was stuck in a debate.

Peen's first partner was Jeremy Bingle, a cocky rich kid who thought he was a better debater than he actually was. One month later, Jeremy's parents moved to San Diego. Peen was relieved to be rid of him.

A few days later, Chase appeared in debate class after his family moved to Seattle from Salt Lake City. Since neither Peen nor Chase had a partner, the teacher paired them together.

Their relationship began poorly. Chase had been through two years of debate and didn't think Peen took the *game* of debate seriously enough. He considered Peen a jock that thought he was smart just by showing up for a debate class.

In fact, Chase had read Peen correctly. During their first competition, Peen and Chase encountered a pair of seniors from Lindbergh High. The national topic for that year was: *Resolved: the United States Government should adopt a health care system providing free basic care for anyone at the poverty level or below.*

Chase and Peen had taken the affirmative stance, arguing for universal care and for a specific plan. Chase went first and outlined the problem and the plan. One of the Lindbergh debaters countered with evidence that suggested their plan couldn't work. When it was Peen's turn to speak Chase gave him a USNWR article that blunted the attack. Peen spoke forcefully enough, but subsequently faced a cross-examination. During it, one of the Lindbergh debaters asked Peen, "You claimed your evidence came from USNWR?"

Introducing evidence into a debate required citing its origin to insure it came from a credible source. Peen responded, "Yes, it was the July 9th issue of USNWR."

Then the Lindbergh debater asked, "What does USNWR stand for?"

Chase was familiar with that line of questioning. Students often borrowed or bought evidence from others, but some didn't know what the acronyms of the published sources represented. For example, USNWR stood for U. S. News and World Report. Chase wondered if Peen knew the answer. If Peen couldn't answer this simple question, the Lindbergh guys would win the debate. Chase remembered watching Peen's face redden as he struggled for the answer.

Peen interlocked his fingers and twisted his hands looking upward as if the answer was on the ceiling.

"USNWR is an acronym for United States National World Report," Peen guessed. When Peen sat down, Chase's menacing stare told him all he needed to know; he'd guessed wrong.

Peen and Chase lost that debate. If Chase was mad at Peen, Peen was even madder at himself. Peen hated losing and he especially hated looking like a fool. He resolved to take debate more seriously. Seeing Peen taking debate more seriously made Chase take Peen more seriously. In their next debate tournament, they won their division. As their partnership flourished, a friendship bloomed. Chase began to play basketball with Peen, while Peen's grades improved. Over the next two years, Peen and Chase terrorized the high school debate scene with a total of 72 wins and 4 losses.

Peen finished his Pho soup and looked across the table at Chase. His friend was no longer the awkward geek he'd been in high school. His skinny frame had filled out, partly due to his love for cooking and partly from his love of lacrosse, a sport he'd embraced during college.

A ping from Chase's cell phone announced a text message. After checking the phone, he handed it to Peen, "My assistant found the room number. Remember, you never got it from me. My question is, should you be doing this at all?"

"Never heard a word from you," agreed Peen as he read the number E-325 on the screen, "and, yes, if I don't try and talk with Gristo, I will regret it. I need to know why they are chasing me so aggressively and why they want my uncle so badly. After my visit with Gristo, I plan to drop by my uncle's office one more time. I know visiting both places is risky, but I need to learn more."

"How was your uncle feeling when you last saw him? Could he have had another heart attack?"

"I guess that's possible. Last week he told me he's been feeling better. He's on pace with what the cardiac surgeon projected. Two weeks ago he started to walk regularly, though he told me last week he still feels winded after only a half-mile."

"You said his aorta was partially blocked, right?"

"Yep."

"Well, if he's in trouble, it can't be helping his heart."

Peen took a deep breath, "That's one reason I'm so worried about him. You know, we've made some good strides in repairing our relationship. Well, repairing isn't the right term. Restoring it is better. We just got too busy with our own lives to concern ourselves with the other. At least, now I know what has kept him busy. I bet he's been chasing those Amber Panels for years."

"Did you google them yet?" asked Chase, "because I did a quick search."

"No, I came straight here. I haven't been near a computer. By the way Chase, thanks again for covering the cab ride from the precinct."

Chase shrugged it off as no big deal. He was more interested in telling Peen what he'd learned. "Well, I took a quick look and I can better understand why those guys were chasing you. In 1701 the King of Prussia ordered the construction of wall panels made from amber, a material widely available in Prussia. They used tons of the fossilized resin, you know like the amber stones in the movie Jurassic Park. The amber was sliced and fitted into interlocking pieces like a mosaic. A decade later, Russia's Peter the Great acquired the unfinished panels. In the mid-eighteenth century the Russians completed them and installed them onto the walls of a palace room, calling it the Amber Room. Sometime later it was labeled a world wonder." Chase stopped talking and sipped his water.

Peen responded, "I've never heard of the Amber Room."

"Neither had I," said Chase. "Now, fast forward to World War II. The Germans plundered the Amber Room and shipped the Amber Panels back to Königsberg, where they were installed in a castle. When the Russians overtook Königsberg in 1945, they searched the castle, but never found the panels."

"So, that explains why Damon is searching for them," concluded Peen, "a missing wonder of the world would be a great treasure to find. It amazes me no one has found them yet."

Chase added, "Most believe the panels were destroyed in Königsberg after it was bombed. Ironically, a team of Germans and Russians re-created the panels in 2003."

"Well, aren't those two countries getting along famously now?" said Peen with heavy sarcasm, "they even did an art project together!"

"That's funny," chuckled Chase.

"Whether Uncle Edmund really knows something about the panels or not, Damon thinks he does. And that's a problem."

"Yep," agreed Chase. Then he gulped down the remainder of his water.

"Hey," said Peen, "that reminds me, do you know how to access a text online? I received one this morning, but never got a chance to look at it. Is there any way to look that up through my carrier?"

"Normally you can't. Remember how I set you up with Google Voice?"

"Yeah, however I never use it," admitted Peen, "I meant to learn more about it, but never quite got to it."

"Why am I not surprised? As I explained when we created your account, Google Voice will record the text messages for you, as long as your text message is routed through them to your phone. That's what I like about it, and why I urged you to set it up that way."

"Chase, am I about to hear *I told you so*?"

"Who me? C'mon Peen, I'd never kick you when you are down."

"Yes you would," argued Peen.

"True, I would. Yes, I TOLD YOU someday you'd thank me."

"Can you look up the text for me? I have no clue how to do it."

"Sure. Just a sec," said Chase. He jumped to Google Voice using his web browser and opened Peen's account. Chase tapped away on his iPhone as Peen watched.

"I see one text from earlier today," explained Chase," but it's kind of cryptic. I wonder if there's a problem with the software. All I see are the numbers seventeen, zero, nineteen, and forty-five, and then the name *Ft Flagler*. Does that mean anything to you?"

Puzzled, Peen took the phone to look at the text. The pattern was too cryptic for him to make sense of it, "Nope, it means nothing, but that's my uncle's phone number. He never texts me, so I can't imagine why he would now. I hope Gristo has some answers, because I'm getting more and more concerned."

Still thinking about the panels, Chase asked, "I wonder what the panels are worth given there are new ones?"

Peen rumpled his brows and shook his head back and forth, "No idea. I'd imagine someone could make some big bucks locating the originals."

Chase nodded his head in agreement then remembered something, "By the way, how are you going to get past the security guard at Dimitri's door?"

"Didn't know there was one."

"Actually, I don't know either," admitted Chase, "I'm just trying to think ahead. But, if this dude is as bad as your FBI agent says, it wouldn't be unusual to keep a security guard posted."

Peen thought a moment and then responded, "Maybe, but the guy is supposed to have a serious spinal cord injury. He's not going to be walking out of that room anytime soon."

"True, but the guard might be there to protect him from people like you," said Chase pointing at Peen.

"I guess I'll hop that puddle when I get to it," answered Peen as he slid to the end of the bench and stood up, "Chase, I'm off. Mind taking care of the bill?"

"Not a problem," responded Chase, "I need to roll as well. I have a busy afternoon. By the way, keep my cell. I suspect you'll need it until you get another one. I can live with my work cell for a few days." Chase stood and pulled out his wallet. He shoved some money in Peen's direction and said, "Also, here's some cash for you. I figure you'd need that, too. Be careful my friend."

Peen gave Chase a hearty hug, "Chase you're a good friend. I'll let you know how all this ends."

"Hell yeah Peen, I expect a full report!"

✳✳✳

Ten minutes later Peen arrived at the Puget Sound Medical Center on Broadway. The massive complex loomed above Peen as he approached the entrance. Peen had visited patients in the hospital a variety of times over the past two decades, most recently when his uncle was recovering from his heart operation. So, when he entered the lobby, he didn't need any directions.

Peen rounded a third floor nursing station in the east wing of the hospital and spotted the room. He was relieved to see no security guards posted at the door. Peen surveyed the long bright corridor for hospital staff. A woman at the nurse's station was engrossed in a call and two men dressed in green orderlies moved swiftly, turned, and disappeared down another corridor. Otherwise, it was unexpectedly quiet.

Peen stood by Gristo's door and listened. Hearing nothing, he took a breath, placed his right hand on the door's lever handle, and shoved down until he felt a soft click. He pushed the door inward a few inches and peered into the room. Except for the patient, it was empty. Peen slipped inside, shut the door, and crossed to the bed. Even before he saw the face, Peen recognized the huge body.

Gristo laid face up, his body strapped to a backboard covered by a white sheet. Various cords tethered him to electronic monitors like a marionette. Occasional beeping from the machines provided the only signs of life.

The patient seemed oblivious to Peen's presence. Peen touched Gristo's temple to see if he'd get a reaction.

Gristo's eyes blinked open, then grew wider when he recognized his visitor.

"I didn't hear you enter, Mr. Rogers," said Gristo, his English thick with a Slavic accent. He spoke with a rasp, "It didn't take you long to find me."

"Do you understand why I'm here?" asked Peen.

"Yes," the man wheezed as he spoke, "but why should I tell you anything?"

"Because, if you think about it, I'm your last opportunity to help Damon. I might make mistakes and give Damon an opportunity to grab me again." Peen paused to let Gristo absorb what he'd said and then added, "Besides, given your situation, your people may kill you soon. So you really have nothing to lose."

The big man said nothing. He showed no emotion. Then, in a deliberate voice he said, "Yes, I am a liability." He halted, coughed and then continued, "It is not you; it is about the panels."

Frustrated, Peen clenched his jaw and spoke forcefully, "I don't care about any panels. Where is my UNCLE?"

Gristo took a moment and then said, slowly, "Your uncle is trapped. All we want is to trade you for the . . . "

Gristo tried to finish his thought, but his throat was phlegmy and coughing was difficult. Gristo moved his lips, but no sound came out. Peen made out the word water and ran over to the sink.

"Where are the cups?" he asked. Then he remembered the water fountain he'd passed earlier in the corridor had cups, "I'll be right back with some water."

Peen stepped into the hall. In his haste, he nearly bumped into an elderly patient limping slowly down the corridor. A female nurse aiding the old man gave Peen a dirty look. He veered around the pair and passed the nursing station, trying to look calm. He could have asked for a cup there, but he didn't want to involve anyone else. Peen passed two other nurses and dodged a worker on a ladder repairing a ceiling light. He turned a corner and stopped at a water fountain. He pulled out a cup from the dispenser and filled it.

As Peen walked back toward Gristo's room, the nursing station buzzers erupted. A female nurse jumped from behind the counter and sprinted to the room, quickly followed by a male nurse. Peen followed them into Gristo's room. When he moved closer to see what the nurses were doing, he saw a trickle of blood oozing out of Gristo's left temple and onto the sheet.

"He's been shot!" shouted the female nurse.

The next few moments were a blur of activity as the nurses tried to revive Gristo. Peen's mind raced, wondering how anyone could have entered and exited the room so quickly. As he watched the scene unfold his heart leapt when the realization suddenly hit him: he might be the number one suspect.

While the mayhem intensified, Peen's instincts told him to flee. He backed out of the room into the corridor and searched for the nearest exit sign. He was fifteen feet away from it when he heard a loud voice demand, "Hey! You! Get back here!" The voice sounded familiar, but he couldn't place it.

If the person who yelled thought Peen would stop, they were in for a surprise. Peen's adrenaline spiked as he bolted through the exit door into a stairway. He moved to the top of the steps, grabbed hold of the hand railings on both sides, and executed a jump-slide move he'd mastered in high school. Pain seared through his sore left arm. By opening and closing his hands on the railing, he controlled the speed of his descent as he jumped a flight of stairs with each leap. At the bottom of each flight he landed with a thud, absorbing the impact with his strong legs. He repeated the process four more times, his arm throbbing and his hands on fire until he reached the ground floor.

Fortunately for Peen, the stairs had an emergency exit door. Peen ignored the warning and set off the alarm as he passed through the door. He did not look back to see if he was being chased; his focus was on finding a place to hide.

Peen sprinted across the four lanes of Broadway Avenue. He disappeared into Seattle University's campus. He emerged from a garden between two buildings and ran along East Marion Street until he reached Twelfth Avenue. Spying a sandwich shop, he darted across the street, then glanced behind to see if anyone was following him. He was about to enter the shop when he spotted a Seattle Metro bus approaching from his right.

Peen turned and saw a bus stop just up the sidewalk from him. Without knowing its destination, he ran to it and waited. As the bus approached, Peen's next destination streamed across the electronic sign: University District.

"Perfect," huffed Peen as he hopped aboard and fed the fare box a ten-dollar bill, understanding he'd receive no change. The cost was worth it, because he could easily disappear within the huge University of Washington campus. More importantly, there were several places his uncle might be on campus. If he couldn't find him, he'd break into his office at the history department's building. Maybe that would yield some clues.

CHAPTER 6: DAMON KANT

Damon Kant leaned back against a cinder block wall in the lower Queen Anne neighborhood where First Avenue West intersects West John Street, a few blocks from the Seattle Center. He awaited an update on Peen and also the operation at the silo, which was proving more difficult than he'd anticipated. In one hand he held a chocolate shake from *Dick's*, a local fast-food chain. The other hand held a burger, half-eaten. As he chewed a bite, he took a sip of the shake.

Damon pondered the loss of his longtime friend. Gristo had helped Damon recover countless artifacts from all over the world, among them two Van Gogh paintings stolen from France during World War II, a set of Ming Dynasty rice bowls that had disappeared during the Japanese occupation of China, matching thirteenth century Durer tapestries smuggled into Bolivia by former German SS troops, and more. Gristo had been a trusted confidant and colleague for over a decade.

But, given Gristo's injury, there no chance for a recovery. *It had to be done*, Damon thought, *he'd become a liability.* Gristo knew most of Damon's secrets. Any chance Gristo might talk warranted his elimination. Damon had shared these concerns with Gristo, who'd agreed to a grisly plan: Damon would use Gristo as bait. Dressed as a doctor, Damon would wait for Peen to appear. Once he did, Gristo would speak with Peen. At some point, Gristo would fake a cough and ask for water. While he searched for some water, Damon would slip into the room, shoot Gristo, and wait in the bathroom. When Peen reappeared in the room, Damon planned to stick him with a muscle relaxant, drop him in a wheel chair, and roll him out of the hospital.

But, what Damon hadn't counted on was Peen leaving so quickly. Damon exited the bathroom door just after Peen left Gristo's room. Damon tried to give chase, but a team of people rushed through the doorway to help with Gristo. By the time Damon got around them, Peen made it to the stairwell. He yelled at Peen, but Peen never responded. Damon sprinted down the hall. By the time Damon arrived at the stairs, Peen was gone. Even worse, there weren't enough of Damon's people to watch all the exits. Damon's only hope now was that Gristo gave Peen enough information to keep him searching for his uncle.

A noisy bus approached, disrupting Damon's train of thought. As the bus rumbled by, a swirl of warm air blew across him. He took another bite of the burger, still leaning against the wall. He'd grown tired of sitting in the 2011 Cadillac Escalade his assistant Arista Kharkov had purchased from a classified ad. She'd paid cash for it. Buying the vehicle was more expensive than renting one, but the title was still in the previous owner's name. If the police traced the license plate, they would be led to the previous owner rather than to Damon.

Just to be safe, they also stole a couple sets of plates off of parked cars. That way, if they ran into trouble, they could swap different plates onto the vehicle. The tactic might not fool real cops, but it would fool any cameras. When they were done with the car, Arista would get it licensed and insured through a shell company and then resell it or have it stolen.

He looked east over the Seattle Center buildings to the iconic Space Needle, the only landmark Damon recognized. He'd been to Seattle twice, this being his second time. The first time he'd come to retrieve *Still Life: Vase with Five Sunflowers*, the famous painting by Vincent Van Gogh. The painting had been lost during World War II following the American air raids in Japan. How it reached Seattle from Japan was unclear, but information about the painting landed on a black market web forum used by Damon and others to hunt unique treasures. Submitters of leads were well paid. Damon learned through the site that the owner had the painting appraised. Using information the appraiser posted to the forum, Damon located the owner's house. When he and Gristo entered the residence early on a Sunday morning they found the fifty-three year-old owner eating breakfast. Gristo held the man as Damon explained that the painting was a lost treasure, so the man had no right to it. He said the man should claim it was stolen and submit the loss to his insurance company. The man refused Damon's offer and paid for it with his life.

Lost treasure, Damon chuckled. If only the world knew how many *lost* treasures passed through collectors hands every year as fortunes ebbed and flowed. The public was mostly ignorant; Damon, however, knew how the world really worked. Wealthy, powerful people skirted laws so they could buy or sell whatever they desired.

He knew some of his acts were crimes, but Damon took pride in his work. He'd rescued and restored about a thousand works. The price to civilized society for his efforts was his temporary enjoyment of the art. He liked to display restored pieces in special rooms of his estate for a few months, sometimes years. Eventually, he'd trade the objects for other pieces or donate them to museums.

He'd been pursuing lost art for years, yet the world barely knew the good work he'd accomplished. If certain countries did find out, they would immediately demand he return the art to them. Damon was convinced they cared little or nothing for the art itself or its cultural importance, they simply wanted to satisfy their political needs with the return of the treasure, where it would likely sit in a storage room where no one could enjoy it.

When anyone challenged Damon's stance on lost art, he'd cite America's Smithsonian Museum, the world's largest museum complex, with nineteen museums. He'd explain that while it does amazing work and has massive amounts of floor space, the Smithsonian could only show two percent of its collection at any given time. Because of its size, many important artifacts aren't restored, maintained or exhibited as they should be. So, Damon argued, to anyone who would listen, that he played a critical role in the art world, since most of the art and artifacts in his collection would still be lost and continuing to deteriorate had he not recovered them. The higher moral value was not museum ownership; the higher moral value was saving them, and that's what he did.

Damon believed the end justified his means, but he'd had to break laws at times. Because of this, at least eight countries from China to Australia plus several in the European Union were after him. Fortunately, he had no problem evading authorities. With his vast fortune he could buy himself out of any situation, purchase a new identity, or escape on private transportation. And, if he did get caught, particularly in Europe, he could pull a few strings with Prime Ministers and Cabinet leaders, to whom he'd calculatedly given rare artifacts. In America, however, he'd not yet cultivated a strong network, since he'd had more success finding valuable pieces elsewhere. Therefore, he had to be more careful in the U.S.

Damon kept the scope of his collection private. He might be bold with his wealth, but not ostentatious. Anything else would have shamed his mother. She'd inspired his love for art. Only the people he employed had an inkling of his collection's size. He needed these people to direct and perform the restoration process, and to insure the art was placed in its proper environment.

Damon was born in Gdansk, a place his parents and grandparents had emigrated to during World War II. His mother was an art professor, one of the first women in Poland to attain that honor. His father was a well-liked and successful politician who thrived as a businessman during the collapse of communism in Poland. He'd been integral in helping transform Gdansk from a drab Soviet city into a modern European one. Along the way, his father laid the foundation for building a fortune in real estate.

When Damon turned eighteen, his parents sent him to Princeton University in America. There, he became fluent in English, adding to his fluency in German, and Polish, along with a passing understanding of Russian. During his freshman year in college he gravitated toward art and humanities classes. Though the classes could be engaging at times, he was restless. He didn't know what he wanted to do or who he wanted to be; yet during that year, in 1990, many changes were reshaping Gdansk.

That partly explained why, by the end of his first year, he was homesick. Damon followed the news from Poland closely and couldn't wait to go back. He returned to Gdansk for the summer of 1990, but when the summer ended, he didn't want to return for his sophomore year, but his parents demanded it.

That year he qualified for the Humanities Honors Program, which the students called the Great White Whales club, after the men credited with shaping Western intellectual thinking. Following an intense semester reading Virgil, Herodotus, Thucydides, Faust, Don Quixote, and others, the spring semester brought enlightenment in the form of the Philosophical Revolution and the Age of Reason. Unlike the fall semester's readings from antiquity, Damon found the spring semester's philosophical ideas of Descartes, Hobbes, Locke and Hume more approachable. Their struggles for freedom and reason resonated with him due to his father's struggle in Poland for political autonomy. However, no thinker resonated more clearly to Damon than Immanuel Kant. For him, Kant's ideas of moral authority and his use of reason echoed his own perspectives: In a world of competing morals, it was critical to make the best choices by following the highest moral path, or greatest good no matter the consequences, if a person was to truly pursue life properly.

Equally important to Damon, Kant argued that using reason, without applying real world experiences, only leads to thoughtful illusions. Nearing the end of his sophomore year, and convinced that he needed more real world experiences of his own, Damon was ready to leave college. But in April 1991, before he had a chance to convince his parents that leaving college was the proper path, they were mysteriously murdered.

Their deaths were a consequence of the rapid change unfolding in his home country. Neither the country of Poland nor the city of Gdansk were prepared for the changes necessary to transform the country from communism to capitalism. While Damon's father was well situated for the change and had substantial control over properties and policies in Gdansk, others had different ideas about who should control the politics and real estate.

Upon learning of his parents' death, and having no siblings, Damon returned to Poland to take control of his parents' estate and his parents' problems. He didn't know it at the time, but he was in for far more reality than he'd ever imagined.

As he hunted for his parents' killers, he continued his father's project: the re-development of Gdansk. Over time, he built a network capable of handling sometimes dubious activities. Using these people, Damon hunted the killers, eventually learning that a gang called Little Eye, one of the strongest criminal rings in Poland, had been behind the murders. In 1992, he captured the two men from Little Eye responsible for his parents' deaths. As demonstration of his resolve and the strength of his network, Damon delivered a message to Little Eye by personally presenting the killers' middle fingers to the leader of the gang.

Damon played a successful role in the rebuilding of Gdansk, realizing his father's vision. Despite the large fortune Damon amassed during the 1990s, he'd never relished his role in Gdansk; it was more his father's dream than his. While he was grateful to honor his father's memory, Damon wanted his own dream, a goal to pursue that was his own.

In 1995, he relinquished control of the construction business and removed himself from its day-to-day operations, choosing instead to dedicate himself to his passion for art full time. It gave him far more satisfaction than constructing buildings and was an endeavor that allowed him to honor his mother's memory.

Hunting important artifacts was his primary focus until the year 2001, the tenth anniversary of his parents' death. That year he was invited to visit Kaliningrad, a city in Kaliningrad Oblast, a satellite state of Russia, as part of a conference on Immanuel Kant, who'd lived and died in the city during the eighteenth century when the city was called

Königsberg and governed by the Kingdom of Prussia. Like Gdansk had done a decade earlier, Kaliningrad was re-opening itself to western ideas and thoughts.

Damon embraced the opportunity to visit the home city of his hero, Kant. But, rather than being enchanted by the experience, he was saddened by Kaliningrad. It was saddled with a myriad of economic and health issues. Gone was the historic castle, church and old town that had defined the beautiful city he'd seen in pictures. Damon was troubled that no one in Kaliningrad had created a vision for rebuilding the city as his father had done with Gdansk.

That visit to Kaliningrad changed his life. For the first time he understood his father's desire to rebuild Gdansk and the challenges he must have faced to launch that project. Walking the promenade along the river in Kaliningrad, Damon realized he had the connections, the experience, and the money to lead the rebirth of Kant's home city. This was now his own dream, a way to secure his name in history: the reconstruction of Königsberg.

So determined was he to execute his mission, he legally changed his name to Damon Kant. To bolster his moral authority, he even had a fake document created that suggested a distant familial connection to Immanuel Kant.

That had happened twelve years ago. Since that time, he'd helped to rebuild the great cathedral in the center of Königsberg. He'd also organized the group that developed plans for rebuilding Königsberg Castle. He'd even tried convincing authorities to change the University of Kaliningrad's name back to the University of Königsberg.

However, they'd balked at that notion, choosing instead to name it Immanuel Kant Baltic Federal University.

Despite all of his accomplishments, Damon's most important goal eluded him. He wanted to put his signature on the city, to give it something unique. After much thought, he'd decided to find the Amber Panels, restore them, and use them as the carrot for getting the castle rebuilt. He felt strongly that the castle project, combined with others he had in mind, would attract tourists from all over the world, which would mean more money for the economically crippled region. The economic ripples meant more of the old city could be restored into a jewel that rivaled, albeit on a smaller scale, the great cities of Europe. Eventually, he believed, just as the city of Leningrad had been renamed St. Petersburg in 1991, Kaliningrad could be renamed Königsberg.

But the search for the Amber Panels proved far more difficult than he'd imagined. Despite the high value of other artifacts he'd hunted, none were as rife with rumors and dead-ends than the panels. Credible witnesses, still alive from World War II, would swear they'd seen the panels being moved, yet their stories proved unreliable. Competing maps surfaced, one indicating the panels had been buried in a salt mine, while another reported them under a brewery. None proved correct. Damon hired divers to investigate three sunken ships in the Baltic Sea. All they found were rusted steel and bones.

His European and Russian contacts, normally dependable, created more confusion. One claim contradicted others. In one case a Wehrmacht soldier stated he'd been at the castle and had been part of a group assigned to load the boxes on the trucks, escort them to a waiting train, then transfer them to the train. He accompanied the boxes to Allenstein, before being forced off the train after fighting with another soldier. He'd taken a later train so he could track down the offending soldier. A day later he discovered the man he'd fought with was dead. His body was surrounded by the bodies of other men from Königsberg alongside the tracks outside of Frankfurt. He'd never known who'd killed them.

Eventually, Damon's patience and payments paid off. One month ago he acquired copies of a German diary. Copies of the diary had been located by one of Damon's informants. They were stolen from a translator who was deciphering them for a professor named Edmund Rogers.

Damon was growing impatient as he paced in front of the cinder block wall. *Where would Peen Rogers go first, his home in Magnolia or his uncle's home in lower Queen Anne?* He wondered.

Damon called Arista, She was stationed at a nearby hotel, acting as communication central and monitoring the hidden microphones in both the Professor and Peen's apartments. She monitored their progress at the Tamanachee Reservation, as well, which they'd code-named the *Ant Farm*.

"Any updates?" asked Damon without a greeting when Arista answered the phone.

"No," said Arista, "*Nephew* reports no activity."

Nephew was the code name for Peen's apartment, "Have you heard anything from *Uncle*?"

Arista was also monitoring Professor Edmund Rogers' apartment, codenamed *Uncle*. Damon arranged to have the apartment bugged as part of a housekeeping ruse used on Edmund. Arista told him it wouldn't work, but Damon assured her it would, because he'd hired an appealing woman to make the offer. To Arista's surprise, the maid was successful.

"No. I have heard nothing."

"What about the *Ant Farm*?" probed Damon.

"The men have not breached the front door, but report it will only take one or two hours. Is there anything you would like me to do?"

"No. Just keep me informed."

"Of course," responded Arista. "When are you heading back to the *Ant Farm*?"

"I can make the morning meeting. Until then, I plan to pursue the nephew. I am unhappy he has escaped twice."

"Do you really think he will be of use?"

"Yes. The nephew will act as leverage over the professor, to keep him from doing anything foolish."

"You should not do anything foolish either."

"I will do what I must. Securing the nephew is the right move. Call me when you have news," ordered Damon before he hung up the phone. The last thing he needed was Arista questioning his motives. He was confident it would all work out, because it always did for Damon.

CHAPTER 7: LESLIE PORTER

Peen knocked on his uncle's office door. The sounds of his raps echoed down the empty corridor. Whether to save power or because university maintenance hadn't replaced the bulbs, only half the ceiling lights worked. Beige walls interrupted by doors for visiting and tenured professors lined both sides of the dim corridor. Most professors and students had gone home for the day. The building felt lifeless, but given the day's events, Peen liked it that way.

Peen knocked for a second time, but it too went unanswered. There were no windows, so Peen couldn't verify whether his uncle was inside or not, but he didn't really expect to find his uncle here anyway. His uncle often avoided the office, preferring to work at home where there were fewer distractions. When he was at the office, there were too many students seeking help on papers, asking for grade changes, or wanting to know what they'd missed when they should have been attending class. He complained that most students were too distracted by jobs, relationships, apathy, or other extracurricular activities to be full-time, serious students who wanted to learn.

Peen checked the time on Chase's iPhone: 3:30pm, late in the day by history department standards. He glanced down the hall and then looked to the door. He was uncertain about his next step. Should he try to break into the room? As he puzzled over his situation, the sounds of a xylophone startled him. Then he heard the theme song for Grey's Anatomy. As he dug into his pocked for his phone he thought, *Only Chase would use that.*

An *unknown* notice flashed across the screen where there should have been a phone number. Guessing it could be Chase, Peen answered, "Hello?"

"Jesus, Peen. What the hell did you do? Did you shoot the guy?" implored Chase.

"Well Chase, that answers a question I had. So you know about the shooting?"

Chase replied sarcastically, "Well, the hospital generally likes to inform its senior staff when there's been a shooting at the hospital. For Christ's sake Peen, where are you? Did you turn yourself in?"

"Uhhh, no."

"I'll take that as a *no I didn't turn myself in because I had no idea the police were looking for me* response."

"Something like that. Look, I didn't shoot the guy . . . "

Chase interrupted him, "Duh, I figured that, Peen. But the police want to talk to you, mainly because they think you *did* shoot the guy. Or at least you know who did."

"Did you talk to the police?"

"Not exactly. More like they talked to me. The police figured out pretty quickly you were involved. That dope Jimmy down in marketing identified you. He's the guy you pissed off at Moe's bar last month."

"Oh yeah, I remember him. He made me so mad! He's the guy that shoved Amy causing her to spill her beer, right? He won't forget that black eye."

"Trust me, Peen, he hasn't forgotten," Chase told him.

"What happened?"

"The police interviewed witnesses by sharing your picture from the security camera footage. According to a friend of mine named Betty, as soon as Jimmy saw your picture, he told them your name was Peen Rogers and claimed you were an asshole. Then he told them I'm your best friend. Minutes later they were interviewing me."

Peen groaned, "If anyone's a jerk, it's Jimmy. Maybe I shouldn't have hit him, but he was drunk and had no reason to push Amy that way. He had it coming, because he just wouldn't back down."

"I know. I was there genius," Chase reminded Peen. "Anyhow, the next thing I know, the police are in my office asking me if I know where you are. They argued that I knew you were in the hospital, then tried to pry out a confession from me claiming I would be charged as an accomplice if I didn't cooperate."

"What did you say?"

"Deny, deny, deny was streaming through my brain. I denied knowing anything about your visit, but did admit knowing you. I offered them your cell phone number, your normal training routes, and your favorite hangouts. I told them that even if you were in the hospital, you're incapable of killing someone. Furthermore, I informed them you didn't own any guns, abhorred violence, were part of the anti-war effort at school, and anything else I could think of to make it appear you are a complete pacifist."

Peen chuckled, "In other words you were lying like hell for me. Weren't you laying it on a little too thick though?"

"Like molasses. But I figured they knew we were best friends, so they'd expect nothing less. I agreed to help locate you, because I know you're innocent," explained Chase. Then he added, "You are innocent, aren't you?"

"Of course. The guy was alive the moment I left the room to get him some water. When I returned with the cup of water, he was dead. Realizing I was suspect numero uno, I bolted."

"So, what are you going to do now?"

"Three things. First, I'm going to break into my uncle's office. Second, I'm going learn more about the Amber Panels. Third, if I don't learn anything here, I'll go to my uncle's apartment. If I'm going to be chased, shot at, and accused of murder, I'm sure as hell going to figure out why it is happening!"

"What can I do to help?" volunteered Chase.

For all their bantering, Peen knew Chase would do anything for him, but he really didn't want to drag Chase into this any deeper, "Just sit tight buddy. I have to do some things on my own. The less you know, the better."

"Good luck, Peen. I think you're gonna to need it."

"Thanks Chase."

Peen hung up the phone. While talking with Chase, Peen had meandered down the hall. He always walked when he talked. It helped him think. He turned back toward his uncle's office to knock one more time. As he approached the door, someone turned the corner at the other end of the hall and began walking toward him.

Startled at first, Peen relaxed when he saw the person was a female wearing purple shorts, a white t-shirt, and a purple baseball cap with a gold Husky silhouette on it. The book bag slung over her left shoulder and her youthful looks suggested she was a student. He stopped at his uncle's door and knocked on it. There was still no answer.

Peen pretended to be reading a tiny paper schedule hanging on the door as the woman approached. He glanced at her. She returned his gaze, looked at the door, and then back at Peen. She looked annoyed.

"Still not there?" she asked. She was shorter than Peen first thought. On a tall day she was probably five-foot two. She had the build of a soccer player, somewhat stocky yet lean and fit.

She added, "That means I wasted another trip over here to check on him. Do you have any idea where Professor Rogers is right now?"

"I don't know, but I'd like to find him," replied Peen.

"So does my roommate Tora."

"Why's that?"

The woman grasped the strap of her book bag and shifted her weight to keep the strap from slipping off her shoulder, "Because, Professor Rogers is on Tora's dissertation committee. She just finished her prospectus

103

and needs him to meet with the other members of her committee so they can sign off on it. Until then, she can't start work on her dissertation."

"How long has she, I mean Tora," he stopped, wondering if he was pronouncing the name correctly, "is that Tora Tora Tora, like the old movie?"

"It's actually short for Victoria, but Tora is spelled the same as the movie name."

"Gotcha. When did Tora last see him?"

"She spoke with him on the phone a few days ago to schedule today's committee meeting, but he never showed. She was *sooo* pissed," explained the young woman. "Since the committee couldn't get ahold of him either, they decided to forgo a decision on her dissertation topic."

Peen knew his uncle would never miss a meeting like that. It just corroborated what Gristo had told him. His uncle needed help. Peen rubbed his face with his hand and asked, "And she's had no contact with him?"

"Nope, she's tried texting, emailing, and calling him all day. Nothing. None of the office staff have seen him today either. She asked me to stop by one more time before coming home. Why are you looking for him?"

He raised his hand to shake hers, "He's my uncle. My name's Peen Rogers. I haven't seen him since last week, but then I wasn't looking for him until this morning. So, what's your name?"

She reached to shake his outstretched hand, "I'm Leslie. Leslie Porter. You said Peen, right?"

"Yes, Peen."

"Peen, did you happen to search for your uncle in some raspberry bushes?" she said pointing to his face.

"Not raspberries, but rose bushes," corrected Peen. He quickly changed the subject, "Leslie, could I talk you into introducing me to your roommate? I'm very concerned about Uncle Edmund. Any information would be helpful."

She looked up at him. Peen thought she was evaluating him, probably wondering if she could trust him.

"Do you have a car?" she asked.

"Nope, I took the bus here."

"That makes it easier. Our condo is just a couple blocks from campus, so it's a short walk. We can go right after I slide my paper under Professor Willoughby's door." Leslie motioned for him to follow her and added gleefully, "I'm so psyched! It's my last paper of the quarter."

Since it was mid-June, Peen thought that odd, "Isn't it a little late to be handing in a paper?"

"About a month late. I got very sick at the beginning of May. It was horrible!" she complained. "My instructors took pity on me and gave me extra time to complete my final projects."

"That was nice of them. What's your paper on?"

"Technology as a historical driver of changes in management structures. It's for 639, Business History," she responded as they walked.

"Interesting," said Peen. Assuming she was in her senior year, he asked, "What's your major?"

Leslie winced with a bit of a sigh, "Actually, I'm a graduate student getting my MBA. My undergrad degree was in finance."

"Cool. I got my degree in finance, too, from the University of Puget Sound in Tacoma."

"Really?" Leslie said, showing more interest, "what do you do now?"

"Not to dash your hopes, but I'm thoroughly unemployed," admitted Peen. He held the door for her as they exited the building. He scouted their surroundings for anyone suspicious, "In fact, I have never been employed in the field of finance."

"So you got a finance degree and never used it?"

"Sad, but true," acknowledged Peen. "Right before I graduated a few of us were walking with a finance professor to class. Someone asked her about the value of a company and its relation to its Beta. Of course, you understand that the magnitude of a company's risk versus the market is implied by the size of its beta coefficient, which is simply a number used to represent the volatility of its past revenue."

"Yep, we've had to calculate those coefficients."

"Well, my professor said something I'll never forget. She explained that most investors buy stocks for reasons other than their true value, partly because most investors have no idea how to accurately value a company. Instead, a herd mentality drives value, with most people following others in and out of the market. That knowledge disillusioned me. I felt my analytical skills were my strongest attribute. I'd hoped it was about sound judgment, but realized for many it was just a game. So, rather than gamble on someone else's company, I decided to start my own company in 1995."

"How old are you Peen?" Leslie asked, "I thought you were around thirty."

"I'm thirty-nine. My fortieth birthday is in three months. A friend of mine says he's got a big party planned, but won't tell me what's happening. I'm just supposed to show up and expect the unexpected. I have this feeling it's gonna involve alcohol," chuckled Peen.

It felt good to laugh and talk.

CHAPTER 8: AGENT MICHAEL JORDEN

A jarring metallic buzz interrupted Agent Michael Jorden's dream. He'd been chasing pigeons along Alki Beach, while six judges on a barge scored his effort by raising white cards. He was trying to read his scores when his eyes blinked open.

As his surroundings came into focus, Jorden heard the buzzing sound again. *I am in my office*, he thought. *My phone. That sound is my phone. Where is it?*

The FBI agent pulled his feet down from his desk and tilted upright in his chair. He traced the sound of the buzzing to his phone. It was vibrating against his aluminum water bottle.

He lunged for the phone, but, still foggy, knocked over his water bottle. Fortunately, the lid remained tight and no water spilled onto his keyboard like it had last year. Since then, he always put the cap on his bottle.

With one hand Jorden righted the bottle. With the other hand he grabbed the cell phone. He looked at the screen and saw it was Officer Larry Jacobs calling him.

"Hello Larry," Jorden answered as he cleared his voice, "you woke me from the strangest dream."

"Power napping again?" asked Jacobs, "how do you get away with that?"

"Larry, I keep telling you that power naps are better for your body than drinking caffeine. Just fifteen minutes a day. You should try it."

"Your office must have far more privacy than mine. I'll stick to my caffeine."

"Your loss. So, you're calling again? Twice in one day? Should my wife be worried?" joked Jorden.

"Tell your wife that she's way more beautiful than me, so she's got nothing to worry about. However, you and I have something to worry about. I just got word Gristo is dead. He was shot right in his hospital bed. The main suspect running from the scene matched the description of one Peen Rogers, the guy from earlier today. I thought you might want to know."

"Aww shiiitttt, Larry! Did Peen do it? I don't see Peen as a shooter. He didn't own any registered weapons, so I doubt he had a gun to use and didn't seem like the type that could find a black market one quickly."

"I agree. But, they did discover a gun with a silencer in the bathroom of Gristo's hospital room. Whether it was Peen's or not, someone had to leave it there. Just the same, he was running from the scene. Perhaps he's more deeply involved than we suspected?" suggested Jacobs.

"Perhaps," Jorden said to himself as much as Jacobs, "have you apprehended him yet?"

"Nope, he got away. Hospital security cameras showed him running across Broadway Street and disappearing into Seattle University's campus. He hasn't been seen since."

"Can you tell me which detective has been assigned to the case?"

"Nope," responded Jacobs, "but I should know soon and will connect you two when I hear."

"Thanks for the update Larry. If I learn any more about Damon or the Cadillac I'll let you know," said Jorden. They exchanged goodbyes as Jorden pondered who was more dangerous, Peen or Damon. Maybe he'd misread Peen.

CHAPTER 9: TORA ARMSTRONG

It was 4:00pm when Peen and Leslie approached the entrance to Tora's building. As they walked up the front steps, Leslie explained that three years ago Tora's brother, Bryan, had taken a job as a river guide and was moving his stuff to Boise, Idaho. He was descending Interstate 80 on the eastern slope of the Oregon's Blue Mountains when the brakes on Bryan's rental truck failed. About that time he encountered a line of cars halted due to construction. Unable to brake, Bryan swerved the truck onto the right shoulder above a shallow canyon. The van leapt over the shoulder's edge and nose-dived to the bottom. The first people to reach Bryan learned he hadn't died on impact. He apologized over and over, repeating the phrase, "I'm sorry, the brakes, they didn't work." He died five minutes after they pulled him from the wreckage.

The family sued the rental company, using the company's own maintenance logs and depositions from previous renters of the same truck. All had reported problems with it. The rental company agreed to settle out of court, but Tora had to contractually agree never to go public with the details. Leslie admitted she didn't know the settlement size, but guessed it was in the multi-millions.

With both her parents overseas, Tora was put in charge of Bryan's estate. The settlement allowed Tora to purchase a condo and pursue her academic interests without having to work or apply for a loan, a luxury most graduate students don't have. Tora offered Leslie a free place to stay, because Tora had the room and enjoyed her company.

Peen held the door open, then followed Leslie into the foyer. This wasn't typical student housing; instead, it had the decor of an upscale hotel. The waiting area had upholstered couches and a flat screen television on one side of the lobby and a security desk on the other.

"Hiiii Ralph," said Leslie sweetly to the young security guard as they walked past the counter to the elevator. The guard was large enough to be a starting tackle on the UW football team.

"Hi Leslie," he responded, "your day been good?"

"Oh yeah," she replied, "and, my last paper is handed in for the year! Woo Hoo! By the way, this is Peen Rogers. He's here to see Tora." She hesitated and then added, "Did Tora mention we're having a party this evening? There'll be around twenty people coming through. Tora was supposed to send down a list."

"Yep, got the list. And, congrats to you Leslie! Nice to meet you, Mr. Rogers."

"Thanks, you too," replied Peen over his shoulder as they stepped into the waiting elevator.

Leslie pressed the top button marked fifteen.

"Wow, the penthouse!" Peen remarked. "If I'd known grad students had it this nice, I would have gone back for a graduate degree!"

"I know, right? I lived in a basement apartment my first year of grad school. I could hear the owners of the house upstairs having sex," she blurted out to Peen's surprise, "I kind of think they did that on purpose. After the first few times, I kept my iPod turned on and my ear-buds in whenever I was there."

"I'm sure that was weird," said Peen, looking down at Leslie. Leslie looked up at him, wrinkled her face, and nodded her head in agreement.

The elevator opened onto a small lobby, all taupe and cream-colored with the usual potted plants. A long skylight guided them down a corridor. Leslie led him past two other doors, before halting at the end of the corridor at a pair of tall double doors.

"These are cool!" Peen said as he put his hands on them to feel the carvings. They were old weathered wood divided into panels. The top section had lion faces carved onto them. Below that two scepters separated carved leaves, all of which was framed by a raised border of leaves. The lower section was larger, filled with carved architectural elements — plinth, Doric columns, and an arch — surrounding a pastoral scene.

"Tora rescued them from a building in downtown Seattle," explained Leslie as she opened the right hand door, "when Tora remodeled this space, she hunted Craigslist for vintage doors and found these. The story is they originally swung in a Swiss castle, before being imported from Europe during the Depression. Their size was a problem for most people, but not for Tora!"

"They are beautiful. Tora has some great taste," said Peen as he examined the thickness of the door, estimating it was three inches.

"Yes she does," agreed Tora.

They stepped into a small foyer with a Tuscan feel accentuated by dark wood floors and textured walls. On the left wall hung a wrought iron coat rack holding jackets and hats. Below that was a dark, richly carved sitting bench. The dark floor extended into an open large room.

As they entered a short hallway the rich smell of Thai food danced past him: cilantro, garlic, and lemongrass. *These people are serious about food*, thought Peen. The hall gave way to a spacious kitchen with an island in the center topped by a brownish-white marble slab.

"Hi Tora. I stopped by the co-op and picked up some coconut milk," announced Leslie, "but couldn't find any tamarind. Also, I did pick up something, or someone, you didn't ask for, but you two have something in common."

"What do you mean?" said Tora, too focused on her cooking to turn around, "you picked up some guy? Congrats. You must be in quite a mood after handing in your paper."

"Even better," responded Leslie, "I brought him home for you. Turn around and meet Peen Rogers, Professor Rogers' nephew. Peen, this is Tora Armstrong."

"What?" exclaimed Tora. She turned to look at him. Her face brightened, then she moved forward to shake Peen's hand.

Peen estimated she was in her late twenties. Her medium build made the blue jeans and white t-shirt she wore look great. *Artists do it Colorfully* was playfully written across her shirt in rainbow colors. Tora's blond hair was pulled back into a short ponytail.

"Any relative of Professor Rogers is a friend of mine," said Tora. Noting the scrapes on his face she asked, "Did you run into a blackberry bush or a nasty cat?"

"Neither. A band of international terrorists chased me on my bike. I leaped over a fence and landed on a rose bush. Pretty ordinary day really."

"Oh, I know what you mean," laughed Tora, dismissing his explanation, "just the other day I had to fend off a group of three burglars using only a pair of salmon bone tweezers. I killed two and chased off the third, but developed a nasty hangnail in the process."

Peen wasn't surprised she hadn't taken his story seriously, so playing along he said, "Well, if you can do that with salmon tweezers, I'd hate to face you in a dark alley with a rolling pin."

"Au contraire. I think you'd find me fun in a dark alley, especially if I had my rolling pin."

Tora turned back to watch the food on the stove, "So Les, did you bring the playful Mr. Rogers home just for me or do you have ulterior motives?"

"Well, you said you wanted a new man servant. He appears physically fit. I haven't checked his teeth closely yet, but they appear to be in working order. Doesn't smell to bad, for a guy that is. He seemed pathetic enough, like that old dog we brought home last week. Peen promised he could do windows, wash clothes, or perform any other demeaning tasks you needed."

"Yeah," added Peen, "Leslie also mentioned there might be some more demanding jobs as well, such as some plumbing maintenance?"

"Oh, my plumbing is quite fine, thank you," countered Tora with a smirk. "What was your name again?"

"Peen Rogers."

"What kind of name is Peen? It's not very suitable for a man servant."

"When I was younger my parents let me play football," began Peen. He'd polished his explanation over the years, "One day while messing around with my father he asked me to tackle him. I ran up to him as fast as I could and hit him hard in the leg, but it was too hard. Dad crumpled to the ground. He said it was like getting hit by a ballpeen hammer. He limped for two weeks and if anyone asked him why, he said he got hit by a ballpeen hammer, which eventually got shortened to Peen. I legally changed my name to it. I've been told I can be hard-headed at times, so Peen fits me."

"What's your real name?"

"Peen."

"I mean, before you changed it."

"Forgettable. My original name was forgettable."

"I can see that Peen-as-in-hard-headed is the perfect name for you. You're probably too stubborn to be a viable manservant, aren't you?"

Peen nodded his head in agreement.

"What use do we have for you then?"

"Since my value as a manservant has become suspect, perhaps I can be of another use. I understand from Leslie that you need my uncle."

"I sure do!" responded Tora in a much more serious tone, "he won't answer his cell phone, his home phone, or his office phone! He hasn't returned any of my messages. It's driving me crazy! Where is the bastard . . . I mean your uncle . . . no offense."

"None taken, Tora. And, I don't know. I'm having no luck finding him either. But I need to find him, uh that bastard, as well. Do you have any clues where he might have gone?"

Tora, returning to the stove, responded, "Believe me, Peen, if I knew where he was, I wouldn't be cooking Thai food right now." She paused a moment and said, more to herself than to Leslie and Peen, "Okay, that's not very helpful." Then, more loudly, "When I saw him last week, he looked pretty ragged. He clearly needed a haircut and more sleep. I spoke to him a few days ago, too. The call was short, but he assured me he'd attend my dissertation committee meeting."

"Did he say what he was working on?" asked Peen.

"Nope. I was to self-absorbed in my own stuff to ask."

"Well, Tora, I think I know what's been keeping him busy, but the question is, where is he now? Have you checked his apartment in lower Queen Anne?"

"I've never been there," she said as she squirted a little more fish sauce into her soup.

"The problem is I have no car," said Peen. Then he asked, turning on the charm, "Want to go with me and check it out?"

Tora reduced the burner's heat. She turned back to look at Peen, "You and me? We? You barely know me. I could be a mass murderer or something."

Peen was surprised at her response, "I'm willing to take my chances with you. And, I'm willing to leave my personal info with Leslie, just in case you have any worries about me."

"Works for me. Besides, I recognize you from a picture in Professor Rogers' office," smiled Tora. "Frankly, I've been cooking all day and could use a change of pace. How about we eat a quick bite and go?"

"I'm all for that, Tora, but what about your dinner party? I didn't mean to interrupt it."

"Oh, I can handle that," volunteered Leslie.

"Thanks Leslie," replied Tora, "it's only 4:30pm. Dinner's all ready anyway. People will be trickling over here for the next couple of hours. They're mostly grad student friends wanting free drinks and food. They'll probably hang around all night. I'm sure we won't be gone long. So let's eat, you do like Thai, don't you?"

"Well, let me put it this way," said Peen, pausing and moving to the stove to examine the entrees. Spread over the burners and on the stainless griddle were pots of different sizes, "Your peanut sauce is smooth, yet has some texture of crushed peanuts suggesting you used both freshly ground peanuts and smooth peanut butter. The yellow suggests you used some curry powder or turmeric.

Your Pad Thai looks exceptional; the noodles are firm and not greasy. I hate greasy noodles."

He picked up a spoon, dipped it into a pot on the stove, and took a taste, "Mmmmm. Nice balance of lime, garlic, Thai peppers, and lemongrass. I see some Kaffir lime leaves and a chunk of galangal, too. It must be Tom Ka Gai or something similar? And, your Salmon curry appears cooked just the way I like it, with red basil and red and green peppers. Finally, the beef curry looks tasty."

"Actually Beef Panang."

"Oops, my mistake. The lime leaves and ground peanuts are a dead giveaway."

Leslie, who'd been watching the two flirt, couldn't help herself, "Oh no, please don't tell me you are a foodie, too. One of you is bad enough!"

"No," countered Peen, "I'm not a foodie. I eat plenty of crap. But, I do like to cook."

"Well Mr. Rogers, since you know your way around a kitchen, maybe you'd make a fine man-servant after all!"

"Not likely. I'm hard to train."

"Fair enough Peen," she said. Reaching for a plate, she suggested to him, "Sit yourself at the table and I'll play servant this time."

Chapter 10: Stella Campinelli

After Peen & Tora finished eating, Tora led Peen downstairs to her condominium's garage where her blue 1969 Volkswagen Beetle was parked.

"This is your car?" asked Peen, surprised by her choice in vehicles, "I mean, you live in this beautiful condo and you drive an old bug? I have nothing against VWs, but somehow I pictured you driving something more modern."

Climbing into the car, Tora replied, "You aren't the first person to wonder that. I'm just attached to VWs. But don't be fooled by its serene exterior. This antique is not your grandpa's Volkswagen."

Peen slid into the passenger seat as she started the car. One revolution of the car's engine and he could tell her car had extra power under its rear hood, "I see what you mean. This bug has juice."

"It's more than juiced — it's nimble too. This is an awesome, perfect city car. I just love it!" she said with glee. "Where do we need to go?"

"His apartment is located in lower Queen Anne just west of the Seattle Center."

Tora exited her driveway and headed south, "Okay Double-O-Seven, how did you really get those scratches?"

"You think I was kidding don't you?" said Peen flatly. He understood how unbelievable it all sounded. Had he not lived through it, he wouldn't have believed it either. He looked over at her as she drove. Tora gazed ahead, patiently waiting for his explanation. He began, "This morning started out like any other. I woke up, answered emails, authored a post for my tech website and made scrambled eggs and bacon for breakfast. Then, because Uncle Edmund told me that he planned to spend time in his office this week, I drove there to surprise him for his 60th birthday. But, he never showed up, so I returned home. I've been training for the STP, so I went out for a ride. The next thing I know some guys I'd never seen before kidnapped me. They asked me questions I couldn't answer and made threats. Luckily, I broke free of the car and stole a bicycle in order to get away. Later on I jumped a fence and landed in a rose bush. I barely remember the thorns, because my focus was on running and riding as fast as I could. At one point they even shot at me!"

Tora interrupted him, "Hold on Peen. Is this really the truth? You understand this sounds pretty wild? And, you are a bicycle thief to boot?"

"I swear, Tora, everything I'm telling you happened. I am not sure I believe it and I lived through it!" added Peen. He'd become animated and was moving his hands as his story unfolded, "Honestly, I forgot all about the bike until just now. Yes, I stole a bike, jumped a fence, and landed in rose bushes. I also climbed over a second fence, a cemetery fence to be exact, and rode the stolen bike to the locks. The chase didn't end until I, and you really won't believe this one, I jumped off the side of the locks and tried to grab a sailboat mast, but that . . . "

"Wait, you mean *the Ballard Locks*? You jumped from the side of the *Ballard Locks*?"

"Yep. I had to jump. I was trapped. If you'd seen the guy chasing me you would have jumped too," argued Peen.

"Oh shit. Are they still after you? Should I be with you right now?" responded Tora.

"No need to worry. I haven't been chased in over an hour. And, the other good news is that one of the guys chasing me is dead."

"Okay," she said cautiously, "I suppose that's a plus. Did they say why they wanted the professor?"

"They said it had to do with something called amber panels. Do you know anything about them?"

The words burst from Tora, "Ohhh Myyyy Godddd . . . *the Amber Panels*? The ones lost during World War II. One of the most important artifacts to disappear during the war?"

"I can't be one hundred percent sure. I don't know enough. So, you know about them?"

"Wow, do I," exclaimed Tora, "I've been an art history grad student studying under Professor Rogers, I mean your uncle, for three years. His specialty is the cultural implications of wartime art theft, which has become of great interest to me as well. I haven't studied the panels specifically, but I'm generally familiar with their loss in Königsberg at the end of World War II. However, I didn't know he was actively searching for the panels."

Excited to find someone who knew about the panels, Peen considered multiple questions before blurting out, "So tell me Tora, how much would they be worth? Enough to kill someone?"

"The value of the amber would depend on the condition, which could well be poor after all these years. But as a three-hundred-year-old work of art they would be invaluable. Their greatest value might be political. If a country, rather than an individual, gained control of the panels, they could be a powerful negotiating tool."

"What do you mean? Negotiate for what?" asked Peen, feeling stupid for not realizing there might be a bigger picture than just greed.

"At the end of World War II, Europe was a disaster, a stew of destruction, desperation, crime, power, and hunger. Soldiers from all sides were grabbing what they could. Art and artifacts were shipped back home. Items of value were buried in caverns, tunnels, salt mines or any other place a plunderer thought they could locate in the future. To give you perspective, the Russians alone have documented more than a million items that are still missing from World War II. One million! The Nazis confiscated over half-a-million documented items from Poland alone. In fact, Germany still has items stolen during World War II that have yet to be returned to their respective owners due to breakdowns in negotiations."

"Really?" said Peen shaking his head. "I had no idea."

"Even worse, more and more of these items are being pushed underground, due to the efforts of many museums and auction houses, and rightly so, to research the provenance, or the history, of all significant artifacts before selling them. If sellers have any concerns about the provenance, they are choosing not to come forward, because the sellers run the risk of losing the items if the artifacts are identified as stolen. And, for the artifacts held by governments, the more time that passes, the more awkward it becomes for a country, say Germany, to admit they still possess stolen items," explained Tora. The Volkswagen's tires hummed on the grated surface as Tora crossed over University Bridge toward the south side of the ship canal.

Peen responded, "That makes sense. Are there many private collectors who trade in art?"

"It's hard to say," she responded. Tora wrinkled her brow to think, "For example, I recently read about a collector from Las Vegas who died a few years ago. He made a fortune as the founder of a large casino, but I don't remember his name. Anyway, he built a collection claimed to be worth $1.5 million that included Nazi Party cars and some of Hitler's possessions."

"Maybe he's some type of Neo-Nazi?" speculated Peen.

Tora shook her head no, "Based on what I've read the collector wasn't. He was just a private collector who was fascinated with history. At one time he had the largest car collection in the world, so his Nazi paraphernalia was only a small part of his overall collection. He kept the Nazi Party items in a private room. The world wouldn't have known about his collection if he hadn't held two event parties inside the room for some of his workers during the late 1980s. Unless a collector makes a mistake like that guy did, people outside the private collector world will never know about it. After the public learned of that guy's collection, for obvious reasons, Jewish groups condemned the collection, the FBI investigated him as a possible Neo-Nazi, and the Nevada Gaming Commission fined him a million dollars. They claimed he damaged their image, but I think it was really to remind the wealthy casinos owners not to be so publicly stupid."

"Where'd the collection go?" asked Peen.

"I never learned," she answered, "the guy issued a public apology and said people misunderstood his reason for collecting it. He sold it during the early 1990s, but to whom and for how much I couldn't say."

"Tora, it amazes me that items like that can appear and disappear with such ease. I can see why Uncle Edmund was so interested in lost art."

"Which is why I chose him as the head of my dissertation committee. Peen, he really is one of the best."

"Do the Amber Panels legally belong to anyone?"

"They belong to the Russians without a doubt. After all, they owned the panels for over 300 years before the Nazis swept into Russia and took them. Given the panels were stolen rather than lost, it seems to me that the Russians clearly have a rightful claim to them, if they still exist," answered Tora as she looked over her shoulder while changing lanes.

"You don't think they exist?"

"Treasure hunters have been searching for them since the war ended. That's almost seventy years. Unlike smaller pieces of art, hiding the panels would be difficult. If professionally packaged, they might fill twenty-five crates or more."

Peen asked her, "Why did the Nazis want so much art?"

"The answer is complicated. The Nazi Party created a detailed art collection system, funneling most of the stolen artifacts through Paris. Hermann Göring, the morphine addict who launched the Gestapo, created a system to divide the most valuable pieces of art between himself and Hitler, but plenty of others profited, too. Beyond that, World War II wasn't just a battle over political boundaries and land. As with most wars, it was about cultural subjugation, domination and punishment."

Tora grew quiet as she slowed to a stop at a red light along Eastlake Avenue and collected her thoughts. She looked to her right through a space between two buildings and saw the television towers on top of Queen Anne Hill.

"Let me ask you two questions, Peen. The first requires you to be a Seahawk football fan."

"It's fair to say I'm a fair-weather fan and we know how often the weather is fair in Seattle," chuckled Peen.

"True. But did you watch the 2006 Super Bowl that the Seahawks lost? Many fans claimed that poor refereeing cost them the game."

"I remember it well. I couldn't stop yelling at the television. Seattle fans fumed after the game."

"Good. Now, keep that in mind as I ask my second question. Did Germany win or lose World War I?"

"Uhhh . . . is this some kind of trick question?" wondered Peen as he parsed her words.

"No, Mr. Paranoid," giggled Tora, "just tell me what you were taught."

"Well, Germany lost. The Allies won."

"Exactly. That's what we were taught. However, at the end of World War I, many Germans felt that the war had been a tie. In fact, many towns treated their returning veterans as heroes. After four years of war, they'd barely lost any land at the time the armistice was signed in November of 1918. But, all the armistice did was halt fighting. It wasn't until eight months later that the Treaty of Versailles was drafted. When the German people learned about the terms of the treaty, many were shocked and confused by it."

Reaching the south side of Lake Union, Tora turned right onto Broad Street and came to a stop at Westlake Avenue. She continued, "To put it into perspective, imagine that you had a big bet on the Seahawks winning the Superbowl and you lost all your money. You'd be quick to blame the refs and the system, because you believed the system stole the game from the Seahawks. That experience might confirm that the NFL system was stacked against the Seahawks. Now, imagine if the entire city had bet financially on the outcome. How mad would they be?"

"Pretty ticked," said Peen nodding his head. He understood where Tora was going with her argument.

"Well, the entire country of Germany bet on the war and thought they had tied. Then the other team's refs arrived to announce, through the Versailles Treaty, that the game wasn't a tie, but rather a crushing defeat for Germany. The cultural, economic and political realities of the Versailles Treaty helped push Germany further into an inflationary abyss that wreaked havoc on their livelihoods and on their own sense of what it meant to be German. In the northern part of Germany, for example, the treaty created a *Polish Corridor*, a narrow area of land that gave Poland access to the Baltic Sea, but also divided East Prussia from the rest of Germany. It's like giving Canada access to the Caribbean by carving a fifty-mile-wide Canadian pathway through the United States."

Peen uttered, "Ouch! I imagine that couldn't have been too popular."

"You're right, the Germans weren't happy. At the time, the city of Königsberg was considered the eastern capital of Germany, with Berlin the western capital. Now, I don't want to sound apologetic, because pre World War I Germany was eager to start a fight. However, from the German perspective, right or wrong, few were prepared for the consequences of the Versailles treaty. So the treaty, coupled with the economic difficulties in Europe, laid the groundwork for a radical group to seize control of Germany. Compounding Germany's troubles was the legitimate fear that communism might roll into Russia. The German Communist Party in the 1920s and early 1930s was strong. During the 1932 election the right wing Nazi Party, embracing Christianity and militarism, battled for votes and support against the secular Communist Party. In the middle of this political saga was the powerful, popular, and comparatively moderate leader Paul Hindenburg, the aging President of Germany who was tired of politics. By 1932 he was an old man. Before he retired, he wanted to meet his most likely successor. At the time Hitler was the front-runner for winning the 1932 Presidential race. The meeting between the two went poorly. Hindenburg was so disturbed by Hitler, he prophesized Germany would become a dictatorship under him. His fear of Hitler was so strong that rather than retire he ran for re-election so Hitler couldn't win." Tora came to a stop to allow a bushy-faced man in tattered clothes to finish crossing the street.

Peen watched the man slowly amble without regard to anyone else. He asked, "Is that when Hitler gained power? I thought he'd been elected?"

"Nope," said Tora. She sped up a little until clogged traffic halted her progress, "Actually, Hindenburg triumphed in the 1932 election and Hitler came in second. But, that didn't stop Hitler. He led a behind-the-scenes campaign to overtake the government. They pressured an increasingly senile Hindenburg to relinquish power. The political machinations were complex, but Hindenburg's decline allowed the Nazi Party and Hitler to gain control of Germany. Of course, I'm oversimplifying what happened, but before long Germany climbed out of its economic and cultural malaise."

"That's all good Tora, but you didn't answer my original question. Why did they want the art?"

"Patience Peen, I'm just about there," she responded. "As Germany improved, the Nazi Party wanted to reclaim the land lost due to the Versailles Treaty and regain the best of High German Culture. Hitler, a long time art lover, established a special military arm specifically for collecting, organizing, cataloging, and distributing any art his troops could locate. And, while Hitler, Göring and others were stealing art for themselves, much of what they considered *High German Art* was scheduled to go to the German city of Linz, where Hitler was building his Führermuseum. Hitler intended to replace Vienna with Linz as the cultural center of Europe and the Führermuseum was to be a centerpiece of Linz . . . "

Peen interrupted Tora, "Drive to Third Avenue West and we'll park there. I want to be a little ways from Uncle Edmund's apartment building just to be on the safe side. We can enter from the back on Second Avenue West. Whether or not my uncle found the panels, those cretins who chased me seemed to be convinced he did, which means they won't stop looking for me. If they're watching his place, it's likely from the front and not the back."

"Good point," agreed Tora. Then she had an idea, "Peen, why don't you grab my gray hoodie from the back seat? The more we can disguise you the better. Also, how do we get into the apartment? Do you have a key?"

"Normally I do," he said with a slight groan as he twisted around to reach into the back. Peen grabbed the hoodie and slipped it over his head, "But my key is at my apartment and I don't dare go there. Instead, I'll have my uncle's building manager let us inside. She knows me."

"Works for me," she answered, "does the hoodie feel ok? It's an extra large."

"Fits fine," he replied.

Tora steered her Volkswagen down Third Avenue West until Peen motioned for her to park. She backed into a vacant parking place.

Tora climbed out of the car and put her hand to her forehead to block the sun. She looked west across Puget Sound. The sun still hung high above the Olympic Mountains on the far side of the sound. A light breeze added to a perfect late afternoon.

Tora contemplated the quiet neighborhood that surrounded her. Unlike nearby Belltown, a hip area for twenty-something partiers, this area of Seattle had lost some of its identity following the NBA Seattle Sonics' move to Oklahoma.

She looked at Peen, who stood near the front of the Volkswagen, his clean-shaven face and short, light brown hair protruding slightly from her hoodie. It fit Peen, because it had been Kent's, her ex-boyfriend, but she didn't think Peen needed to know that. In fact, it was kind of strange seeing Peen wearing something so familiar. Despite their breakup, her ex-boyfriend had asked Tora to keep it, to remember that there had been good times. But, those times ended five months ago when he took a finance job at Goldman Sachs in London. Kent had asked her to go with him, but, as she'd explained to her friends, she *had* to complete her PhD. She'd also known, deep down, that Kent wasn't the guy for her. He was too self-conscious about what other people thought of him, while she was more carefree and adventurous.

Kent wouldn't have sanctioned this adventure with Peen. He would be texting or calling her, warning her not to go for all the obvious reasons: It could be dangerous, she didn't know Peen, and she was supposed to be hosting a party. So, this opportunity to take a chance, to jump into the unknown was a perfect example of why she couldn't envision herself with Kent.

Tora had been absorbed in her classwork for the past year in preparation for her dissertation. She'd spent days and nights tied to her computer researching and writing, which combined her life-long love of art with a newer passion for history. Having settled on a topic, and just needing approval from her committee to get started, her dissertation would argue that the use of landscape and imagery in paintings and illustrations by Western artists during the nineteenth century constructed an identity of the American West that was more fantasy than fact.

The toll of Tora's graduate work had been the complete destruction of her social life. In fact, the party she was holding tonight, and was now missing, was the first one she'd held in ten months. But that was Tora, she followed her passions. She could forget to eat, pay bills, or call her boyfriend. If she was focused on something, she was relentless . . . a word her friends said defined her.

So why am I here? she asked herself again. She knew it was more than just hunting for the Professor. Of course, she had to locate Dr. Rogers so he could approve her dissertation. That was the whole point of yesterday's meeting. But also, after immersing herself in the last century for months, this was a chance to escape academia and live in the present, to feel her heart pound at danger and spend time with an attractive man. Given this chance, she was going to take it.

Besides, she wanted to get to know Peen Rogers better. He exuded a self-confidence that she found appealing, mixed with a dose of humbleness. She thought his modesty was a sign that he'd seen and lived life and had bumps and bruises to show for it. He certainly had the facial scars to prove it! Strangely, she'd trusted him instantly and felt safe still, despite the circumstances and the story he told.

Physically, she thought he was well-built and had nice facial features, but was not classically gorgeous. Peen had a purposefulness that was contagious, at least for Tora, and it felt good to be captivated by someone else's world for a little while.

***

Observing no suspicious activity near Edmund Rogers' apartment, Peen and Tora approached the building's back entrance. The six-story mocha colored brick apartment building had stood for decades.

Peen explained there were three entrances. The main entrance to the lobby door was on First Avenue West. A second entrance was in the apartment's underground parking lot. A third door was near the delivery entrance at the building's rear, the one they now approached from Second Avenue West.

Though Peen called it a back entrance, it was still well maintained. Garden beds splashed with bleeding hearts, purple irises, and white daisies flanked the door.

He'd been calm on the drive, but now Peen felt anxious, not unwarranted given his day so far. His senses were sharp. He examined every car, watching for the Cadillac. He searched for anyone not dressed in shorts, which would be a crime on this beautiful day. His adrenaline was pumping and he was sweating, but fought to stay calm. He didn't want to make Tora nervous. To her credit she handled the situation without a trace of concern.

Peen opened the door and held it for Tora as she walked through. He followed her into a narrow hallway. It had a modern feel, suggesting a recent remodel. That hallway intersected another. Beyond the intersection was a set of stairs.

Peen said in a low voice, "Around this corner to the right is the hallway to the front door. I want you to check out the lobby to see if anything seems suspicious. If it is all clear, then we'll head to the manager's apartment."

Following his directions, Tora walked down the hallway toward the door. This corridor was larger, a place designed more for mingling. To her left a series of mailboxes was inset into the wall. On her right was an alcove with west-facing windows. Inside the alcove were several tall palm plants, a loveseat, and denim covered chairs. A flat-screen television hung in one corner. Tora saw no one in the hallway or alcove, so she continued.

Just past the mailboxes a large entry way opened to the east. Tora walked to the front doors and peered out of them for a moment. She only saw empty parked cars and, across the street, several office buildings.

She turned back and continued down the main hall. At the far end was an elevator. On her right she spotted a room with tables and a computer. She thought it was a meeting room of some kind. She gazed inside, but saw no one. She looked to see if there was anywhere else people might be, but saw nothing.

Her mission complete, she started back toward Peen. She was just to the alcove when a bell rang behind her, signaling the arrival of an elevator. The noise startled Tora, but she ignored it and kept walking. Suddenly, Tora heard an older female voice yell, "Becky! Becky, is that you?"

Tora's heart pounded as she turned to see an elderly woman exit the elevator and approach her. To Tora's amazement the woman was dressed in a rose-pink Faberge bikini. Tiny strings held what little fabric there was in place. However, it wasn't the size of the bikini that surprised her; she'd seen similar ones. It was the fact the woman wearing it was north of sixty years old.

Out of embarrassment, Tora's eyes shifted away from the approaching woman, yet sheer curiosity forced her to take another look. As the initial shock receded, Tora had to admit that despite her silver hair, age spots, and wrinkles, the woman had the body to wear a bikini. She seemed to have the confidence, too.

Tora was still adjusting to the situation when the woman spoke again, "Oh okay, I'm sorry dear, you look like my granddaughter Becky from the back. I guess it was just wishful thinking." The woman continued, "You know, I haven't seen her in three months. Since she had her baby, I have barely heard from her but once a week or so."

"That's a shame," said Tora, wondering why the woman kept talking with her after recognizing she wasn't Becky.

"Well, okay, you know," responded the woman, "yes it is, but not unexpected. You see, I had three kids of my own and I know how demanding it can be. I bet you couldn't guess I had any kids at all by looking as this body," she added clearly proud of the way she looked. She shifted her hips and held her arms wide.

"No, I would have never guessed that," agreed Tora, feeling trapped.

"Neither would I," announced Peen as he approached Tora from behind, "how are you feeling today Stella?"

"Oh, okay. Hi Peen! I feel great, thank you for asking, Peen. I haven't seen you in a couple weeks. What have you been doing with yourself?" As he neared she noticed the cuts and scrapes on his face, "Okay, WOW! What happened to your face, dear boy?"

"A bike accident. It will heal in no time, Stella."

"Okay, great! I'm glad to hear that. I've told you to be careful riding that thing," she scolded.

"I know, but there were some extenuating circumstances."

"So, introduce me to your cute friend, Peen," said Stella.

"Stella, this is Tora . . . uhm . . . what's your last name again, Tora?"

"Armstrong," Tora offered, appearing unoffended by Peen's forgetfulness.

"That's right," responded Peen feeling a little guilty. "Tora Armstrong, this is Stella Campinelli. She's the apartment manager here."

"Nice to meet you Stella," said Tora.

"Wonderful to meet you, Tora. I was going to ask if you two were dating, but it seems unlikely since Peen can't remember your last name," teased Stella.

"I can forgive him. We just met a couple hours ago," chuckled Tora.

"Okay, you know in my day, I did more than just date in a couple hour time frame!" Stella admitted, shaking her head with a wrinkled smile that suggested a litany of sins. "Oh, the sixties were so much fun!"

Quickly changing the subject, Peen asked Stella, "Say, have you seen Uncle Edmund around here lately?"

"Well," she paused, shifting her eyes and searching her brain, "yes, I saw him a couple of days ago, but not since then. I'm guessing he went to his cabin near Port Townsend."

"He has a cabin?" responded Peen, jolted by the news, "near Port Townsend?"

"Of course! It's the place where he goes to write. You know how he would disappear sometimes for a couple days? Well, he finally admitted to me where he went. I guess he's been going up there for a year now. I don't know why he'd keep that a secret from you, but he must have had his reasons."

"Strange that he never mentioned it to me."

"Well, okay, that is strange Peen. He was never specific about it with me either until a few days ago. We bumped into each other . . . upstairs," she said with a smile, shifting her eyes upward, "he told me he planned to drive to his cabin along the beach and asked me if I wanted to meet him there. He said it wasn't far from Port Townsend."

Peen and Tora looked at each other. Their eyes lit up in agreement. "Did he give you an address?" asked Peen.

Stella continued, "He mentioned the address, hoping I'd want to go. But you know, I'm a people person, a city person. I'm not much for spending time in the sticks."

"Could I get the address Stella?"

"Well, I didn't think I'd need it, so I never wrote it down." Stella put her hands onto her hips, shifted her weight, and crinkled her face in thought. Then she said, "I'm trying to remember the house numbers, but my memory is so bad. God, I'm becoming useless."

"That's fine Stella, just take your time," said Peen.

"You know who would know? Edmund's friend Ian Cadmeyer. Edmund told me Ian lived in Port Townsend, which is how he got to know the area. Ian runs a little store up there called Bernstein Antiques, or something like that. Edmund gave me some beautiful earrings he got there."

"Professor Cadmeyer?" asked Tora, surprised.

"Well, yes, I believe he worked at the University of Washington. I met him once, three months ago. He

141

dropped off a package for Edmund. He was a handsome man, tall, lanky, with lots of gray hair."

As Stella talked, Tora pulled her phone from her pocket and googled Cadmeyer's name. Moments later she found an address.

"Yep, here it is. Bernstein Fine Arts is at 1008 Water St, Port Townsend," said Tora as she tapped the phone a few more times. "Peen, check this out."

Tora held the phone so Peen could see it.

"Hmm, that's not a coincidence," he said quietly.

"What's not?" asked Stella.

"Nothing important," answered Peen, "thanks for the information, Stella. Can you do me a favor? I forgot my key at my place. Will you please let us into Uncle Edmund's apartment?"

"Oh, I can do you one better. Two days ago Edmund asked me to change the locks on his door. He said he'd lost his key and was concerned about his safety. He had me make an extra key for you. Let me run and get it. I'll be back in a flash."

Stella turned and walked to her nearby first-floor apartment. She returned a minute later.

"Here you go, Peen."

"Thanks Stella! I appreciate that. Can I ask you one more favor?"

"Okay, yeah, of course! You just name it."

"Great. Please don't tell anybody else about Professor Cadmeyer or my uncle's place. Actually, don't say anything until you've spoken to me or my uncle," requested Peen.

"My lips are sealed," responded Stella, dragging her finger along her lips.

"Thanks, see you soon I hope," said Peen as he turned and walked away. Tora followed with a small wave, "Nice to meet you Stella."

"You as well, Tora! Bye Peen."

Peen guided Tora back to the stairs and, out of earshot, whispered, "Now *that* is something you don't hear everyday. She's *sealing* her lips. If you hadn't figured it out, Stella is the local busybody – both figuratively and literally. If it's happening in or around this building, she usually knows about it, partly because she's the manager here. If you get her going, she'll chatter on and on and on. That's why I walked up to you two. I thought I'd better save you from her."

"I appreciate the thought, but I'm a big girl. So what's with her and the bikini? I mean it's warm, but not exactly bikini weather."

"Stella always wears skimpy clothes. My uncle says she grew up on the beaches of Southern California. Apparently, she never left them. She's always been proud of her figure. In fact, one day she showed up at my uncle's door wearing just a towel asking if she could borrow a cube of butter. I was in the apartment by myself. I invited her in and stepped into the kitchen to get the butter. When I returned with the butter, she reached for it with the hand holding her towel and *accidently* dropped the towel."

"What'd she say?" asked Tora suspiciously as they approached the stairs.

"*Ooops, you know, I'm just so clumsy sometimes,*" replied Peen, badly imitating her voice, "then she took her time bending over to retrieve the towel. I will say she has a great body for someone her age; I complimented her accordingly. You want to bet she pulled the same stunt on my uncle? Obviously, those two hit the sack, but then according to my uncle she keeps several of the men in the building busy."

"I seeee," said Tora raising her right eyebrow in a Spock-like manner, "don't tell me you are one of the men she has kept busy?"

"Well, I'd love to answer that question, but I'd rather just torture you with the unknown. Perhaps I can invent something amusing later," teased Peen as they climbed the stairs, "so bernstein is the same thing as amber?"

"According to that website I showed you, bernstein is the German word for amber. Could there be a connection between Professor Cadmeyer and the panels?"

"Anything is possible at this point. So you know this Cadmeyer guy?"

"I met him at a couple Humanities Department faculty parties. Professor Rogers said Cadmeyer was as much a mentor as he ever had. He is a sharp old man who studied European history and then moved into art history as more of a hobby than as an academic, or so it seemed to me," noted Tora.

"I suggest once we examine Uncle Edmund's apartment, assuming he's not there, which I'm sure he isn't, that Port Townsend would be the next logical place to look. Since you already know Cadmeyer, you'd be a big help," hinted Peen. He paused and then asked outright, "Would you consider going up there with me?"

Tora hadn't considered that possibility at all. Taking a quick jaunt to downtown Seattle was one thing, but making a several hour trip north to Port Townsend was something else, "How about we discuss it after we check out the apartment," she said to deflect the question.

"Works for me," he responded with a smile, borrowing the phrase she'd used several times.

They exited the stairs onto the third floor. Peen pointed in front of them, "Uncle Edmund's apartment is the last one on the left."

So far, except for Stella, Peen and Tora had encountered no one, which suited Peen just fine. His nervousness had subsided while talking with Stella. Plus, he was in familiar surroundings. But now, approaching the door, his heart sped up.

Peen knocked on the door. Receiving no answer to his first knock, Peen rapped on the door more loudly a second time. The apartment remained silent, so Peen opened the door with the key. He stepped into the apartment and shouted, "Uncle Edmund, are you here?"

No one answered. As he looked around the living area, he gasped, "Oh my God!"

Chapter 11: Running For Shelter

From Peen's reaction, Tora expected to see everything topsy-turvy, papers scattered, clothes strewn, and lamps on the floor. She gently shoved Peen aside to get a good look.

The room was divided into three sections. To the left was a study, with neatly ordered bookshelves and a clean desk. Papers atop the file cabinet were neatly piled. To her right, two couches were arranged in a tidy "L" before a television screen.

Tora was confused, "I don't understand, Peen. What is so *Oh my Godish* about this place?"

"It's too clean!" he said emphatically. "Usually when I come here, cleaning is the first priority. I find cups stained with dried milk or coffee all over. There are always papers and books scattered across his desk and on the floor. To be honest, he's a slob."

Tora half-listened to his response, because she'd spotted an unusual painting across the room, one the size of a shoebox lid. She moved get a closer look.

The painting lacked the proper perspective giving it a primitive appearance. It depicted two men, one standing in waist-deep water holding a big net. The other stood on the shore grasping a shovel in his left hand. Behind the two men were several mounds, haystacks or hills, or both, and sky, or maybe clouds. Whatever the background, it was clear the men in the foreground were the focal point.

"Peen, come here. You have to see this."

Peen, still in shock at the cleanliness of the apartment, approached her. He stood slightly behind Tora, his right leg and arm gently leaned against the back of her left leg and arm. She didn't move away.

"Do you know what this is?"

"Two men dressed for Halloween?" he kidded.

"No, this appears to be an early painting depicting men collecting amber, probably from the Baltic Sea."

"Funny. I've never thought much about it," he responded, studying it more closely, "I'm guessing the baskets across their chests aren't for carrying babies?"

"Right. Those woven baskets are designed to carry amber. See the huge net that hangs off the pole over the man's shoulder and the way it extends forward? That's called a scoopstone net."

"I didn't know amber floated," said Peen. He could have admitted that he didn't know anything about amber, but he was pretty sure Tora had already figured that out, "So all they had to do was scoop the amber from the water and drop it into their baskets?"

"Yes," Tora replied, "but it wasn't always that easy. It took cold weather storms to loosen large amounts of amber from the sea floor. I suspect these men were freezing their cojones off as they struggled in frigid water to gather the amber. It was unpleasant work."

"Amazing. So, this is what it took to gather amber for the Amber Panels?"

"Amber can be excavated using traditional mining methods or scooped from the water like this painting demonstrates. It can even be collected off the beach. The people that collected amber for the Amber Panels were likely paid in salt. Do you want to apply for the job?" joked Tora, turning to look at Peen.

"Actually, salt as a payment method doesn't surprise me," replied Peen, happy to share a bit of history that he knew, "before coin and paper currency became standard, value was represented in other ways. Salt had an intrinsic value, because people could use it or trade with it. But, sometimes people accepted value for things they never used, like huge rocks."

"Huh?" responded Tora with fascination, "I've heard of beads, shells, salt and other items, being traded, but never large rocks."

Peen explained, "In the Yap Islands of Micronesia, they used huge rocks as a means of exchange. Some were impossible to move. There is a story about a rock that fell off a boat and settled to the floor of a lagoon. It was too heavy to remove from the lagoon's bottom, so the islanders left it there. Despite its location, it was still assigned value and traded."

Peen continued, "It sounds strange at first, but if you think about it there is no more value in the rock than with our paper currency. The value is somewhat arbitrary and assigned. At least with a large rock you could sit on it if you wanted; the dollar bill is less useful. "

"Well, if you were cold you could burn it," countered Tora. "Not that it would warm you much."

"Very true. I like your resourcefulness," said Peen nodding.

Looking back at the painting, Tora added, "This painting confirms the Professor had a bigger passion for amber than I knew."

"How old is this painting?"

"Judging by the poor depth perspective and the age of the surrounding frame, I'd guess it might be several hundred years old. I can tell more by looking at the canvas and the stretcher on the back," said Tora. "Should I remove it from the wall?"

"Yeah, go ahead, I'll start looking through his bedroom for the address."

Peen walked away as Tora carefully lifted the small painting off its hook and spun it around. She yelled, "Judging by the back of this artwork, I'd say it was painted around 1703."

"That's pretty precise, why do you believe that?" he responded from the bedroom.

Tora hollered back, "Because a label on the back reads 1703. It has a title as well: *The Amber Hunters*. Oh, and guess what else it says on the label?"

"What?"

"Peen, the framing was done by Bernstein Fine Arts."

He appeared from the bedroom, "Oh, I didn't see that coming. Do you suppose Cadmeyer framed it?"

"I don't know. I guess we'll find out if we go there," noted Tora, rehanging the painting.

Peen caught the *we* in her comment. It sounded to him like she was ready for a trip to Port Townsend.

Tora broke his train of thought, "You mentioned this room was a surprise?"

"Uncle Edmund spends most of his time researching and writing, so the fact that his place is so clean, is . . . well it's puzzling."

"Maybe he got himself a cleaning service?"

"It's possible," agreed Peen, "after all, he never told me about the place in Port Townsend."

"Perhaps he never told you about the cleaning service, either," remarked Tora.

"I can't imagine he'd ever let a maid near his desk, because he sure never wanted me to touch his papers."

"Perhaps," was all Peen said. "Hey, since you're done with that painting, would you do me a favor and watch the hall for Damon's men. It would make me feel better."

"Good idea. It would make me feel better, too," admitted Tora, revealing for the first time that she might be a little nervous.

Tora moved to the apartment's entrance. She peered out the door. Relieved she saw nothing, she pulled out her phone and began to text Leslie, but before she could send the text she heard a noise. Looking back down the hall, she saw two professional-looking men dressed in sport coats and jeans cresting the stairs. They turned in her direction.

As soon as they saw Tora, they began running toward her. She reeled backward in surprise. Tora slammed the door and locked it, hearing them shout something in a language she didn't recognize. "We need to get out of here. There are two men running toward the front door."

"Time to go," shouted Peen as he herded Tora into the bedroom with him. He shut the door and pushed a button on the doorknob to lock it, despite knowing the lock would be useless. He bolted to the bedroom window next to the fire escape, unlocked it, and slid it to the left. In the other room they heard the sound of splintering wood.

"They sure knock loud," muttered Peen as he kicked the window screen loose. Peen scrambled out the window. Tora followed. As he slid the window shut, they heard the sounds of the bedroom door being forced open.

Tora glanced at the grated metal landing they were standing on. Below them, a sturdy fire escape wound down the side of the building.

"Quick, follow me," yelled Peen urgently. He led the way down, his sore arm aching as he used his hands to slide-jump down the stairs as he'd done at the hospital. Tora only did half a flight at a time, but it was still faster than running down each step. They were down three flights before they heard the men above them jump onto the fire escape.

Peen shouted, "Go, go, go." He was talking to himself as much as to her.

At the bottom of the stairs, Tora noticed that security bars formed a covered enclosure that kept people from entering the fire escape from the sidewalk.

Peen pushed the exit door's emergency latch. The door swung open with a loud clang. Tora followed him through the door and onto the sidewalk.

Peen grabbed Tora's hand and shouted, "We'll head across to the Seattle Center. I know where we can hide."

"Where's that?" she asked as they jaywalked, or rather ran, across First Avenue West after dodging two cars.

"Ever been underneath the Seattle Center?" yelled Peen.

"Underneath?" questioned Tora, "I never knew there was an *underneath*."

"How fast can you run? Do you think you can keep up with me?"

"I'll go through my credentials later. Anywhere you run, I'll be able to follow."

✳✳✳

"Get out of that fire escape and catch them," growled Damon into his headset. Once again, Peen had given him the slip. And now, some woman named Tora was helping him. Damon was furious that Erich and Peter hadn't known about the fire escape, but it was sure obvious Peen had known about it.

Standing next to the Escalade, he watched two runners sprint across First Avenue West, a man and a woman.

They were near enough to Damon for him to recognize the man as Peen Rogers. Based on the conversation he'd overheard in the apartment, he knew the woman was Tora. But where had he found her? And why was she with him?

Damon jumped into the SUV, shouting to his driver and pointing to the two runners, "There they are, go after them. Where the hell are Erich and Peter!"

For the second time that day, the driver of the Cadillac gave chase to Peen. Just as Damon's driver was about to pull out of the parking spot, the traffic light turned red and three cars lined up next to them, trapping the Escalade. Damon fumed. He glared at the Driver until he pulled out in front of a fourth car. The Driver rounded the corner at West Thomas Street. He accelerated to Queen Anne and turned right onto the one-way street.

Damon watched the pair of runners cross Queen Anne Avenue and enter a restaurant parking lot. As the Cadillac arrived at the place where the runners had been, Erich and Peter alerted Damon through their headsets that they were just behind the Cadillac.

Damon shouted back at them through his headset, "They have gone into the parking lot near the restaurant. We will circle around to the back side to catch them, while you two push them toward us."

Erich and Peter dashed across the street.

Damon's driver raced down the block, made a left, and turned left again, heading north on First Avenue North. Peen and Tora appeared on the sidewalk. One look at the Escalade racing toward them caused Peen and Tora to pause for a second, then Damon watched Peen grab her arm. The two sprinted across the street toward a three-story parking garage. A ticket machine with a single-armed horizontal yellow gate marked the entrance. A second gate marked the exit.

Damon saw Peen and Tora duck under the exit gate into the garage. He assumed they would run through the bottom level and out the back. Damon shouted, "Now, drive to the far side of this block, but go faster this time! We must cut them off at the next street."

The Driver drove as fast as he could, squealing hard right onto West Thomas Street and then right again onto Warren Street.

Damon watched Peen and Tora hurdle a short brick wall that marked the edge of the garage and land onto the sidewalk. The Cadillac was fifteen yards away.

Seeing the Escalade, Peen grabbed Tora and pulled her across Warren Street and up the stairs of a building.

His frustration overflowing, Damon ordered the Driver to stop. The Driver slammed on the brakes, bringing the Escalade to a halt. Damon jumped out of the car and aimed his gun at the two fleeing runners just as they bounded up a short flight of stairs onto the porch of a two-story brick house that had been converted into a business.

About to squeeze the trigger, Damon suddenly stopped. Over his gun sight, he'd spotted a large window with three tiny faces looking out. He watched the two runners as they disappeared through the front door. A banner over the front of the building read *Women @ the Center*. Damon wasn't sure what type of business that was, but he did know he was a poor shot. Even *he* didn't shoot at children. So, he holstered his gun.

Damon jumped back into the car and told his driver to look for an alley behind the house. Then he spoke through his headset, "Erich, Peter. Where are you?"

"We see you and we saw them enter the building."

"Good, flush them out. We will find out if there is a back alley."

✳✳✳

When Peen had emerged from the parking garage, he'd realized the women's shelter was just across the street. He hadn't initially planned to go there, but after seeing Damon so close, he panicked. The shelter seemed like a safe place, so he'd led Tora straight for it.

Peen knew the shelter. He'd even volunteered there for a short time two years earlier, because a woman Peen had dated had volunteered there. But, Peen had found the experience extremely frustrating. He'd befriended a woman resident who'd described the abuse she'd endured. Later, after thanking Peen for his kindness, the woman wanted to give her husband another chance. Over his advice, the woman returned to her abusive husband, who beat her into unconsciousness two weeks later. After that, Peen stopped volunteering.

Today, however, the building was something familiar, a place where he and Tora could catch their breath and wits. He also knew the building had an exit in the rear, so they could head there.

They were barely through the front door when he realized how stupid it was to use the shelter as an escape route. He could only hope his pursuers would never hurt women and children; they only wanted him. Well, maybe Tora now, too.

Tora had followed Peen's dash through the door unquestioningly. *He must have a plan*, she thought. Unaware it was a shelter, Tora surveyed the entry room, a long narrow rectangular area. Everything was beige: the vinyl floor, walls, and furniture. Florescent lights added to its institutional feel. A few women and several small children huddled near a television. Tora watched the women glare at Peen with suspicion. Tora wasn't sure if this was a daycare or something else, but she quickly sensed they should leave.

Tora looked ahead to where the room narrowed. At the far end of the hall, in the direction they were heading, was a set of doors.

Peen knew they were about to enter a dining and kitchen area. Past the kitchen, at the south end of the building, was a delivery entrance. His plan was to exit through the back doors, cross the alley and go around a church. From there they could reach Seattle Center's Pacific Science Center, another place Peen knew very well.

Peen glanced at Tora. She looked bewildered, as if she was trying to make sense of their surroundings.

"A shelter," muttered Peen, making momentary eye contact with Tora.

That brief interruption in Peen's concentration was poorly timed, because when Peen returned his focus to the doors his right foot landed squarely on a Tonka Jeep, which had rolled into the hall from an open door. As he planted his weight on the toy, his foot shot out from under him and he fell awkwardly to the floor onto his back. Though embarrassed, the fall wasn't too painful. Peen scrambled back to his feet. The sound of a crying little boy, distressed about his toy, bellowed through the hallway.

Peen and Tora entered the dining room through the double doors, then walked briskly into the kitchen where they skirted around two mobile warming ovens. After passing by the cooking area and then a short corridor with a counter along one side, they reached the back door. Tora grabbed the doorknob with both hands to open the door, but, before pulling on it, peered out a small window.

The sight of a black Cadillac Escalade pulling up to a stop in the alley made her freeze. Peen almost ran into her, catching himself with his arms against the door above her.

"Shit!" uttered Tora.

CHAPTER 12: CAROLYN HARPER

"Damon's here!" shouted Tora, pointing through the door window of the shelter's kitchen, "the Escalade just drove up!"

"Damn," said Peen panting, "we're trapped. Any ideas?"

"Nope. I was hoping you had one!"

Surprising both of them, a female voice barked angrily, "I'm Carolyn Harper, the Director, can I help you two?"

Peen and Tora pivoted to face a stocky woman. She stood with her hands on her hips, her jaw clenched and her eyes narrowed.

Peen had met her once before, briefly. He remembered tales of her fearlessness; Carolyn could back down the angriest of husbands.

Peen could see she didn't recognize him. He chose not remind her, to plead for assistance instead. "Yes you can help us. Is there any way out of here besides the front or back door? Some nasty guys are chasing us. We thought we could get through the building in time, but they are now in the back alley waiting for us."

"Listen, I don't know what you two are doing here, so LEAVE NOW!" commanded Carolyn.

Anytime there was an unusual threat, Carolyn called for a lockdown. Strategically placed alarm buttons allowed a resident or staff to electronically lock the front and back doors. Carolyn had seen many scared women over the years. She'd learned to read people quickly. Carolyn often had little time to decide between granting access to women who truly needed a safe haven and denying access to women who just wanted a place to stay. In Peen and Tora, she saw two people who looked like caged cats.

Peen responded, "Great. Call the police and lock the place down. We'd love to leave right now, but we can't go out either door because we're being chased by some thugs who are about to enter both doors."

Carolyn countered sarcastically, "Well, isn't that special. You led thugs to a place that's supposed to be a safe haven for abused women and kids! What were you thinking?"

"We didn't know what this place was!" argued Peen, lying to her. He knew she was right. He was furious at himself for making such a foolish decision. But then, he couldn't think of where else they could have gone.

Tora added, "We were running from them. We didn't know. We've done nothing wrong."

Carolyn's principle goal was to diffuse a situation and bring calm to the residents. Several residents had heard the commotion and were now watching the scene unfold. She could handle an angry husband, but multiple men would make the situation too complex. Yet, she also didn't want the residents to see her force the man and woman out the door, possibly to an ill fate. The residents needed to feel safe, even in an unusual situation like this.

"Alright, everyone back to their rooms, NOW! You two," ordered Carolyn pointing at Peen and Tora, "do as I say and follow me!"

Carolyn turned abruptly and escorted them back through the kitchen. After the last resident exited the kitchen she locked the entry doors. She coolly guided Tora and Peen around a corner to a door at the far end of the dining room that had several locks. Working quickly, Carolyn unlocked the door, pulled it open, and descended some stairs.

"Let's go. Careful of the steps! Shut the door behind you," ordered Carolyn.

Twenty steps descended to an underground tunnel and concrete walkway. The passageway was narrow, just wide enough to allow two people to walk tightly side-by-side. Carolyn led the way. Peen estimated they had gone about half a block, before arriving at another, taller staircase.

Carolyn instructed them, "At the top of these stairs you'll find a door. It's a one-way door that opens near the sidewalk. Once out, you can't re-enter." She stopped to take a breath, "But I warn you. Now that I have shown you the exit, I will return to the shelter and tell the people chasing you where to find you. I want all of you gone. And, please, do not tell anyone about this tunnel. The police are on their way. GO NOW!"

"We promise not to tell anyone. Thank you so much. You are literally saving our lives," said Peen.

"Good luck. Never come back," she warned as Tora and Peen ran up the stairs. Peen was sure she mumbled *idiots*.

The instant they reached the top of the stairs and examined their surroundings, discovering they'd emerged inside an exterior alcove of a church. Directly across the street from where they stood was the Seattle Center.

To their left was a children's theater. Looming above it was the familiar saucer of the Space Needle. To their right, fifty yards away, were the Pacific Science Center buildings.

Peen started to explain where they were headed, when a garbage truck heading south rumbled slowly by them, making it impossible for Tora to hear him. He pulled her and pointed to their destination, but the garbage truck was blocking his view. That gave him an idea. He motioned to Tora to follow him.

Leaping off the curb, Peen and Tora ran to the driver's side of the truck near the back wheels. The garbage truck moved slowly, so they caught up with it quickly. As they jogged along side it in the street, sirens sounded somewhere in the distance.

"Carolyn was serious about the police," yelled Tora.

Peen nodded in agreement, but didn't answer. He was focused on the intersection ahead of them, knowing one part of it ended at the Science Center's loading dock.

"Let's hope the truck keeps going straight," Peen shouted to Tora. Just then the truck began to turn right.

"I spoke too soon," he complained in frustration, "we need to make it to the Science Center's loading dock across the street. Let's cut in front of the white minivan parked across the street next to the sidewalk. Ready?"

"I'll follow your lead," yelled Tora, displaying no signs of fatigue.

Tora watched Peen veer away from the truck. Tora did the same.

Peen leaped to the sidewalk in front of the white minivan, ran past a small oak tree and onto a short pathway. Tora trailed just behind, but as she cleared the front of the minivan, she heard a loud voice quickly followed by the sound of shattered glass. Something hit her right arm, but she didn't dare stop. She focused on Peen, ran passed the oak tree and onto the concrete path. Again she heard yelling, but sirens drowned out the voices.

Peen and Tora sprinted across the small parking lot and bounded up a short flight of stairs to the loading dock. As they entered the loading dock's large open bay, both turned to see two men entering the parking lot area, running their direction. Knowing they were still being chased, they ran through the dock's staging area and through a door with a sign that read *Building Five - Pacific Science Center.*

In spite of everything, Tora continued to trust Peen. However, she thought it ironic that once again he'd taken them to a place, the Science Center, where there might be children. But then, she also understood these were places he knew. Besides, she had no better alternatives.

Peen led Tora into the building's gift shop. They wound through racks of books and toys for sale until they exited the doors of the gift shop and Building Five and entered Building Four, which opened into a cavernous space for large exhibits. Peen and Tora ran swiftly by some tourists marveling at a display of dinosaurs. Two angry volunteers warned them to slow down, but Peen and Tora ignored their pleas.

At the southwestern corner of Building Four, they exited the building and found themselves on the Science Center's central plaza. Peen quickly scanned around, looking up at the soaring white arches, then across the plaza's multiple levels and surrounding pools. Suddenly, he grabbed Tora's hand and said, "Let's go!"

They hurried along a service walkway that ran between the Laserdome building's aggregate concrete wall and one of the reflecting pools, then ducked around a corner toward Peen's objective: the underground exhibit space known as Building Three.

Having volunteered at the Science Center, Peen knew most visitors rarely explored Building Three. He directed Tora to a glass-enclosed staircase. They ran down the stairs and entered an exhibition hall. There was no one inside. The pair crossed the room and halted at a metal, unmarked door.

"Cross your fingers," said Peen.

He twisted the knob and gave the door a push. It opened. With a quick glance over his shoulder, he closed the door, and flicked the deadbolt shut. He was satisfied that Damon would never find them.

Whew, Peen sighed.

Tora looked around the brightly lit room. It appeared to be a makeshift employee break area with a refrigerator, microwave, table and chairs. No attempt had been made to hide the rough concrete walls and ceiling. Exposed plumbing and electrical conduit crossed overhead, leading to a dark passageway.

Peen turned from the door and began walking past Tora when he noticed blood on her right shoulder.

"Tora, were you hit?" asked Peen with concern.

She felt her right shoulder with her left hand, then looked at her hand. There was blood on it.

"My arm stings a little, but it doesn't hurt," she said. She spotted a short pile of napkins on the nearby table and wiped her shoulder. She spit onto a second napkin and wiped again. Sounding puzzled, she said, "This is weird. It stings, but I don't feel cut. What do you see Peen?"

Peen examined her shoulder, "I don't see any cuts either. If the blood isn't yours . . ," Peen stopped talking. He didn't want to know the answer. Both of them were a little shaken by the revelation.

After cleaning up her shoulder, Peen turned toward the utility tunnel.

"Where are we going now?" asked Tora.

"I want to go deeper. This room is one of the entry points for the maintenance halls under the Seattle Center. I know a quiet spot to hunker down where we can collect our thoughts."

"How long do you think we'll have to stay here?"

"What, bored already?"

"Hardly," was all that she could muster.

Peen led Tora through a maze of concrete hallways, a sharp contrast to the bright colors and open space of the gigantic buildings above. Eventually they arrived at a hallway that widened into a small alcove.

Some folding tables and chairs, along with chain link fencing, were stored in the alcove. A fluorescent shop light illuminated the area, however the dark concrete seemed to absorb it. Peen removed a chair from one stack and offered it to Tora. She plopped down onto its red fabric and found it uncomfortable.

"The Ritz it's not, but I'll take it right now," said Tora as she slumped forward with her elbows on her knees, "how'd you know about this place? I've been to the Science Center a dozen times, yet never knew anything like this existed."

"I've volunteered for computer and science camps here. Sometimes late at night, when our shifts were over, we'd roam around the Science Center. Occasionally, we'd end up down here."

"How'd you know that door would be unlocked?"

"You mean the door to this place? We always had a problem keeping it locked, due to the fact that just inside the door is a refrigerator where volunteers keep food. I just took a guess that it was unlocked."

"And if it had been locked?"

"We'd have gone out the emergency exit doors in Building Three, the ones with the big 'No Exit' signs on them. They open onto 1st Ave. But you'll see for yourself. We'll head out them when we are done here."

"Why's that?"

"Because the Science Center funnels visitors in and out of the plaza through a single point, all Damon has to do is wait there for us. However, each building has a set of emergency doors and I doubt they can cover all six. And, I'll bet they won't linger with the police around, especially since someone might have been shot. They probably took off as soon as we entered the building. Of course, we are better off assuming they're waiting for us, so I think we should still exit through the emergency doors."

Tora said, "And this feels like an emergency to me!"

"Once we leave the building we'll need to run again. Those doors will set off a general alarm."

Tora nodded her head in agreement, "Works for me." Then she suggested, "You know, we could just call the police and ask them to escort us out of here."

Peen stood up suddenly and patted his pockets. "Oh shit! I just remembered I put down Chase's phone at my uncle's apartment." He slumped back into the chair, Then he added, "Sure. Just tell the police I'm with you, Tora, and I guarantee they'll be here in no time."

"Oh really?" Tora raised her eyebrows and quizzed him, "is there something else you want to tell me?"

"Not that I *want* to tell you, but probably should. You see, this afternoon I was with the wrong guy at the wrong place at the wrong time," admitted Peen.

"What was the wrong place?"

"A hospital."

"And the wrong guy?"

"Well, he was the guy who chased me this afternoon. You know," he said, pointing to his face, "scratches and roses. Well, he died this afternoon from a bullet he received while I was at the hospital. And no, Tora, I did not fire the bullet. I don't even own a gun."

"Peen! They want you for murdering someone? But *of course* you didn't do it. Isn't that what they all say?" she replied sarcastically.

"I didn't do it," he defended, "one moment he was alive, albeit barely. I left the room and returned a minute later to find him dead. So, I ran."

"Do you think Damon had something to do with it?"

"I don't know, but he's my number one suspect."

"Why would Damon have his own man killed?" asked Tora, perplexed.

"He was of no use to them anymore."

"Oh, that's cold." A shiver went down her.

"That's why we don't want them to catch us or my uncle," responded Peen. He was grateful she was finally taking him seriously.

"Speaking of your uncle, what's next? Should we try to find him?"

"What do you mean *we*?"

"Well, it just seems to me you need some help. You're face is scratched, you've been shot at and chased twice, and you are wanted for murder. And that's just today. Besides, helping to solve one of the world's greatest art mysteries ever has its own appeal. Might even look nice on my vita."

"You academics, anything for your resume," teased Peen. Then he held up three fingers on his right hand, "By the way, three times."

"Huh?"

"I've been chased three times. Once at the park, once at the hospital, and once minutes ago."

"Hopefully, it's the last time today."

They fell silent for a moment.

"I would welcome your help," Peen acknowledged. What he didn't say was that he was beginning to find this athletic, smart and beautiful female appealing.

It had been a while since his last girlfriend dumped him: seven months and six days to be exact. And he knew it was his fault. While he threw a lot of energy into early relationships he usually had a problem later on, when he began focusing on his own interests, which usually meant working too much.

Lately, due to the economy, he'd scaled back his work, because there was little of it. However, the habit of staying busy remained, so he directed his energy into learning new things. For example, when his neighbor moved and couldn't take her piano, he adopted it. Never much of an audiophile, Peen had few songs on his phone and never learned to play an instrument. But, he was curious, so he downloaded some how-to instructions from the internet and began playing. He was surprised to discover he enjoyed playing.

But, it was a solitary event that took time away from Peen's most recent relationship and was another reason his girlfriend had dropped him. Fortunately for Peen, women found him attractive, so he had few problems obtaining dates. Lately, though, he just hadn't found anybody that triggered his interest.

Tora seemed different. Maybe it was the way they'd met or what they'd been through in just a couple hours. She could think on her feet and generate ideas, but didn't need to be the center of attention. Thus far she'd been very much a partner without complaint. Sure, it had only been two hours, but he liked what he'd seen.

Peen shifted in his chair, bored. His mind thrived on stimulation. He asked Tora, "You said you have your phone? Can you find out more about the panels?"

"Yep. Let me text Les to let her know we'll be much later than planned."

"Who is Les . . . oh Leslie your roommate. Yeah, good idea. I don't need her reporting me to the police."

Tora held up her phone, "Or, maybe not."

"No service?"

"Not a single bar."

"I can't say I'm all that surprised. The ceiling is constructed from thick concrete."

Tora slid her phone back into her pocket, "How long should we stay here?"

"I was wondering the same thing. The longer we stay, the more likely Damon and the police are likely to leave the area. On the other hand, something is bothering me."

"What's that?"

"I was just replaying my kidnapping. Damon never said he didn't know where my uncle was; instead, he implied that he couldn't get to him. My sense is that my uncle needs help sooner rather than later."

Tora added, "There's another issue. If the Professor really is trapped, he might not have access to his medication. I don't know what medication he started taking after his heart attack, but he could be on a blood thinner like Warfarin or an antiarrhythmic drug to combat irregular heartbeats. He might be taking other drugs, too. Do you know what the doctors prescribed?"

"I don't remember. But, depending on where he is, just obtaining water could be a big issue. On the plus side, he told me last week he was feeling better than ever."

"I was surprised the Professor returned to school at all," admitted Tora.

"Well let me tell you something. He had his heart surgery on December 5th," Peen told her. He held up two fingers for emphasis and said, "Two days later he complained about being bored. To keep him busy, I spent a great deal of time shuttling books and papers between his apartment and hospital room. But, I can't complain too much, because there was one blessing about his heart attack. It was the most time we'd spent together since I was in high school and Dad was around. I hadn't realized how far apart my uncle and I had drifted."

Tora liked Edmund Rogers and found him pleasant to be around. She also found Peen pleasant, so she couldn't understand why Peen and Professor Rogers weren't closer. She asked him, "Did you two have some type of disagreement?"

"Not at all. We get along just fine and always have. We just hadn't made time for one another. We are both workaholics; it's a family trait I guess," admitted Peen.

"Doesn't your family get together for holidays?"

"He and I would call each other on holidays, but there's only us two. It's not much fun with my parents and grandparents being gone."

Tora felt stupid for bringing up the subject of family. She knew how difficult losing a close family member could be. She also understood why finding his uncle was so important to Peen. They were all each other had left.

"I'm very sorry," she began quietly, "I didn't know they'd passed. My brother died three years ago and it seems like it happened just yesterday."

"Yeah, your roommate Leslie mentioned that. I'm truly sorry," he sympathized. He took a calming breath and said, "My mother died when I was twenty from thyroid cancer. It seemed to come out of nowhere. One day she was fine and a month later she was dead. And my father's death happened even more suddenly. He died five years ago from a heart attack, but really I think it was from a broken heart. He loved my mother and missed her desperately. Uncle Edmund is my father's brother. He never married and never had children. I was an only child. Dad and Uncle Edmund did a lot together with me when I was a kid. But, by the time Dad died, my uncle and I were too busy with our lives to interact. Maybe it was easier for us to avoid thinking about Mom and Dad by avoiding each other. It wasn't until my uncle's heart attack that we came together. There was no one else to take care of him. During his recovery I realized, as he got older, I'd likely be the one caring for him," Peen stared into the dark corridor, his chest felt heavy with emotion. He was saddened by the possibility he might not see his uncle again, "The time in the hospital together not only healed him, it also fixed us. We've made it a point to spend time more together. We try to share dinner at least once a week."

Peen admitted to himself that becoming closer with his uncle was more gratifying than he'd realized. It was the closest Peen had felt to anyone since his father's death. He needed his uncle, not as a father figure, but as a dependable person he could trust. Perhaps he wasn't the loner he'd thought he was.

Peen stared at the ground, "You know, at the start of spring semester, Uncle Edmund wanted to return to work, but the university told him he couldn't teach any more classes for the year. He joked with me that he was on injured reserve. He was good with that, because he didn't like teaching undergrad classes anyway."

Peen paused and looked directly at Tora, "My uncle preferred pursuing his research and working with grad students like you."

"Out of curiosity, did he ever mention me?" asked Tora.

"No. When we get together he never talks about work. Our discussions are pretty superficial, except when we talk about Mom and Dad. Otherwise, it is all sports or news. And, now I can see why. It seems much of his work was something he didn't want to discuss, so it was easier to avoid the topics altogether."

Tora smiled, "Well Peen, on the positive side, your next dinner conversation should be very interesting!"

"I think that's an understatement," Peen chuckled, then added, "I don't know about you, but I'm feeling useless sitting here. As much as I like the safety of this place, I don't like being out of touch with the internet. The last thing we need is Leslie calling the cops because she hasn't heard from you."

"I'm glad you said that. I feel the same way. We should head for Port Townsend," urged Tora, "that's the best lead we have."

"Yeah, but we have a problem. We can't reach your car without making a large circle around the women's shelter."

"We don't need it. We can leave it where it is," argued Tora, "instead, let's run down Broad Street to the waterfront. Then we can catch the trolley and ride from the waterfront to the ferry dock, where we can catch the ferry to Bainbridge Island."

"I thought they closed down the trolley system a few years ago?"

"They did, Peen. But I read last week that it's open for the summer to alleviate traffic problems caused by the waterfront construction. If it isn't working, we'll figure out something else."

"But, once we reach Bainbridge Island's ferry dock do you know of a way to reach Port Townsend? That's a long walk," noted Peen.

"Well, there is something you should know. I have a certain way with cars. They respond to me," bragged Tora with a hint of seductiveness.

"Is that your way of implying Grand Theft Auto?" asked Peen calmly. But, then he thought about all he'd been through today, "Jeez, why not. I'm already wanted for murder. Maybe we could get locked up together. What type of car do you prefer to steal?"

"Anything from the 70s and earlier. A Ford, if possible."

"Are you sure you can do this, Tora?"

"Yes, I'm very serious. I know how to start or hotwire older cars. The ferry's parking lot is pretty big. There ought to be an older car there somewhere."

"Good point, Tora."

"Have faith, Peen. Even better, on the ferry we'll have cell service."

"I like the way you think, Tora!"

"My only question is," wondered Tora, "can we can trust Stella? I mean, not that she would lie, but do you think she is correct about his place near Port Townsend?"

Peen grinned, "Yeah, remember one of her best skills is relaying information. Turns out her gossip is quite accurate. Trust me, if you want to know who is sleeping with whom, who is declaring bankruptcy, or whatever, she's the one to ask." Peen stood, offered his hand to Tora, and said, "Shall we go?"

She put her hand in his and rose to her feet, "Why Mr. Rogers, I thought you'd never ask."

Minutes later they were back in the employee break room. Peen quizzed her, "Do we need to let anyone else besides Leslie know where you are? Like a boyfriend or maybe your family?"

"No, no boyfriend. I'm quite single. As far as family goes, my parents are living in Europe for the next year. They operate an Italian Consulate."

"That's too bad, I mean you must miss them."

"It's all good. They love what they do and were just assigned to Italy last fall. When I complete my dissertation, I plan to visit for a month and unwind. I've never been there. How about you?"

"I've never been to Italy either, but have been to Eastern Europe. I spent a few weeks there."

"No Peen, I meant any girlfriend?"

"I too am very single."

"Good," she replied with a wink.

Peen walked to the door. He rotated the latch until he heard the deadbolt move. He cracked open the door and peered out. The view gave him a good slice of Building Three's floor. He saw no movement. Feeling confident, he opened the door wider.

Peen turned back to Tora, "It looks safe. Ready for a romantic ferry ride?"

"Is this really the time for romance?" she challenged.

"I suppose not. The exit doors are on the far wall over there," Peen said pointing across the room," as we open those doors, if everything is still the same, a loud buzzing sound will alert security the doors have been breeched. Ignore the noise and follow me."

"I'm ready when you are."

"You know what woman? I like your style."

Tora responded as they ran to the emergency exit, "You mean my haircut and clothes or are you referrin' to my dastardly, car thievin' ways?"

"Both," murmured Peen. *Definitely both*, he thought as he placed his hands on an exit door marked EMERGENCY ONLY - ALARM WILL SOUND.

"Ready Tora?"

"I was born ready!"

"Then let's go!"

With that he threw the emergency-exit door open and ran right into Bobby Moran's life.

CHAPTER 13: BOBBY MORAN

Seattle Center security guard Robert "Bobby" Moran felt his discomfort ease. He slumped into a deck chair and was now soothing his achy body with his favorite drink: a mocha double latte with extra foam. He leaned one elbow on a metal patio table at the south side of the Pacific Science Center. The tall white arches overhead cast lacey shadows across the plaza. The reflecting pools in front of him created the type of peaceful setting he needed, but also reflected the sun into his eyes, so he continued to wear his sunglasses. He'd position himself with a view to the Science Center's entrance; Bobby didn't want to get caught by his boss taking an unauthorized break.

Bobby set his coffee down next to his helmet and took a breath. A gentle breeze ruffled his thinning brunette hair, sweaty from running a slight fever. In the distance he could hear the sound of ball bearings clattering through an oversized pachinko machine. He was told the exhibit provided a visual example of how randomly falling balls created predictable patterns. The meaning was lost on Bobby, but he found the repetitive sounds comforting.

He reached for another sip of coffee. The coffee's heat and the caffeine combined to clear his sinuses, which helped his head feel better, but the rest of him suffered from the cold he'd caught. Bobby wanted to return to bed, bury himself in a comforter, and finish watching *Back to the Future III*. That's what he'd been doing earlier in the day. But, just as Marty McFly was driving Professor Brown's DeLorean through the red dirt of Monument Valley with braves on horseback chasing him, Bobby's phone had rung. He'd reluctantly answered it, because it had been his boss Duncan calling.

Duncan Schwartz was Chief of Security for the Seattle Center and had called to order Bobby to appear for work immediately. Bobby had tried to explain he was sick, but his boss was insistent; he needed Bobby's help. A popular local rock band, the De Haro Straits, had a concert scheduled at the arena and they expected big crowds.

So Bobby came to work knowing his day would really suck. His job required rolling his six-foot-four, two hundred and twenty pound body around the Seattle Center on in-line skates. He watched for problems, helped lost people, and enforced the Center's rules. Normally he didn't mind his job, but it was draining to do when sick. To complicate his day, Duncan had told him to train a new security officer, which meant he had to be on his best behavior. It also meant he couldn't easily sneak in breaks.

He'd been working with the trainee for four hours and was unimpressed. The trainee didn't have the expert control of skates necessary to do the job. The kid asked a lot of dumb questions and wouldn't shut up, which grated on Bobby's nerves. About the time Bobby didn't think the day could get any worse, an emergency erupted over his walkie-talkie. Reports of a shooting near the loading dock of the Pacific Science Center put the entire security staff on high alert.

Bobby and his new trainee received instructions from Duncan to coordinate with the Seattle Police Department and search the dock area, but they'd found nothing except a witness who'd heard the shots and watched two people run inside.

Bobby asked his boss what he'd seen on the security feeds. Duncan admitted to Bobby that he'd been in the bathroom when the police contacted him and hadn't been monitoring the cameras. He told Bobby he'd review the security video to see where the pair had gone. In the meantime, Duncan told Bobby to continue searching. Bobby rolled his eyes and asked his boss to hurry.

Bobby and his trainee searched Building Five, but found nothing suspicious. In Building Four they'd encountered two volunteers who'd spotted a man and woman running through the exhibition hall. Bobby had been sure that was the couple they sought.

Bobby and the trainee had exited Building Four to search Building Three. As they crossed the plaza, the trainee got distracted by someone shouting and skated directly into the reflecting pools next to the walkway. Bobby ordered the completely soaked trainee back to the office to find some dry clothes, telling him he'd wait at the plaza until they could explore Building Three together. Bobby had taken advantage of the situation and ordered a coffee from a nearby cart.

Bobby sipped his coffee, then reached up with his right hand and rubbed his bare head, hoping to invigorate himself. He lamented the fact that, at thirty-five years of age, he should suffer like this. He had twelve years of service under his belt and was the senior security officer, next to his boss. He'd even applied for the position of security chief two years earlier, but lost the job to Duncan, because the Seattle Center Director informed him, *he hadn't distinguished himself as a leader and he lacked initiative.*

Bobby had waited two years for a way to show he could lead and make difficult decisions, but the lack of opportunity frustrated him. It was difficult for Bobby to show initiative, due to the fact his day-to-day activities hardly varied. Disillusioned, he'd recently applied for jobs as a city police officer.

This shit isn't worth it, he thought. *If I were with the police force, I'd have more sick days. I'd be home right now. I've got to find something else to do.*

As Bobby sipped more coffee, static erupted from his radio. It was the same voice that had interrupted his movie earlier in the day.

"Hey Bobby, what's your 10-20?"

"Building Three of the PSC."

"Two people just set off the emergency exit on the Denny Way side of Building Three. The security cameras show a man and woman. Want to bet it's the pair we've been looking for?"

"Holey Donuts!" said Bobby, purposefully uttering a phrase he knew irritated Duncan. He liked to stick it to Duncan any chance he got. "I'll head down the stairs and check it out."

Bobby leapt from the chair and skated over to the glass-enclosed stairway. He kept his skates sideways as he descended the concrete steps, firmly gripping the handrail. Near the bottom he let go, but his blades rolled unexpectedly, causing him to crash onto the floor to the sound of breaking plastic. Lying on his back, stunned, he blamed being sick for the mistake. He hauled himself to his feet, looked at the floor, and realized his sunglasses had fallen off and been crunched during the fall. He grumbled at his misfortune as he skated across the floor to the emergency doors.

Bobby pushed the door open with his leg and held it open with the baton in his hand. Light flooded through the entrance, blinding him momentarily. Seeing no one, he raced to the sidewalk along Denny Way.

Bobby could see in three directions: east and west along Denny and south to Puget Sound. To the west, three elderly men were strolling away from him on the sidewalk. Bobby assumed none of the them had run anywhere recently and eliminated them as suspects. Looking east along Denny, the sidewalk was empty.

Bobby then looked across the four lanes of traffic toward Puget Sound. He spotted two silhouettes running at a fast pace. Bobby reached for his walkie-talkie to call his boss. It was then he discovered he'd broken his radio when he fell on the stairs.

Bobby shouted into his walkie-talkie, "Dammit! Duncan, Duncan? Can you hear me Boss?"

There was no answer. There was no static. There was nothing. The only thing he heard was the roar of traffic moving along Denny. He couldn't call Duncan using his cell phone. Duncan had banned them after a security guard ran into a tourist while texting and skating.

Watching the two runners vanish into over the hillside, Bobby wondered if he should chase them or not. He knew it would be a violation of the Center's security guidelines and knew that, away from Seattle Center property, he had no authority over them. Yet, he wasn't concerned about the rule. Bobby knew he wouldn't lose his job, because his overly protective mother, who was on the Board of Directors for the Center, would insure he kept it.

He realized this was an opportunity to show initiative. He thought the police departments he'd applied to would look favorably on such assertiveness. At the very least, by chasing the suspects he could watch their movements to determine if they were suspicious and then alert the police.

The situation invigorated him. Bobby felt better than he had all day. Certain this was the right move, he took advantage of a gap in traffic and quickly crossed all four lanes of Denny Way.

From there, Bobby rolled toward the intersection of Third Avenue and Broad Street. He now had a clear view down the Broad Street hill and waterfront piers sixty-nine and seventy that stretched into Puget Sound. While skating down the hill, Bobby observed the two runners crossing to the south side of Broad Street just beyond Second Ave, putting them on the opposite side of Broad Street from him.

Bobby could see the pair was moving fast. Creating a mental log he planned to share with police later, he noted she wore a t-shirt and jeans and the guy had on a gray hoodie and jeans. He was about six feet tall, she was maybe six inches shorter. Convinced they were guilty of something, he rolled expertly down Broad Street's steep sidewalk, slaloming on one foot while dragging the other to control his speed. As Bobby approached Second Avenue, he slid to a stop to wait for traffic.

Bobby checked and saw the two had already crossed First Avenue and were on the next block. Two blocks beyond that a waterfront trolley was waiting at its northernmost stop. He wondered if that's where the couple was heading.

After the last car passed, Bobby launched himself across Second Avenue. He raced down the hill until the First Avenue light turned red and forced him to stop. Bobby again waited for a break in traffic, saw a chance, and traversed the rough pavement, narrowly missing a speeding a small car.

When he caught sight of the two targets, he was surprised to see the female returning his gaze. She nudged her companion, who then looked toward Bobby, too. Their faces registered concern.

Bobby assumed he looked like a cop to them. His dark blue security uniform, designed to look similar to a police uniform, confused Seattle Center visitors, making them believe he was a police officer. Bobby hoped it would confuse the couple, too, and cause them to surrender. Instead, they sprinted across Western Ave down to Elliot Ave, looking back frequently.

With two green lights in a row, Bobby closed the distance between them. Now, only the red light at Elliot Avenue and a stream of traffic momentary separated Bobby from the couple. Stalled, he watched the suspects scurry across the railroad tracks, and hop aboard the waterfront trolley as it began its trek south.

"Shit," mumbled Bobby as they escaped.

The trolley, while not speedy, moved at a steady pace. Bobby surveyed the tracks and the terrain. He had to find a different way to chase them or abandon the chase and climb back up Broad Street, an option he didn't relish.

This is MY time. I will be a leader and show initiative!

Flooded with adrenaline, Bobby considered his options. Three vehicles waited at the light near him: two passenger cars and a large rental van. He thought the van gave him the best option, so Bobby skated to the rear of it.

Bobby hopped onto the diamond-plate bumper and grabbed hold of a handle to the right of the cargo door. The van lurched forward, bumped across a series of train and trolley tracks, and turned left onto Alaskan Way, the four-lane arterial that follows the waterfront.

Now this is the way to skate, he thought, re-energized by his ingenuity.

A half mile later, the van caught and then passed the trolley. Bobby felt elated at outsmarting the couple. But then, the van drove through three green lights in a row and passed the Aquarium. He noticed a dramatic increase in automobile and foot traffic along the central waterfront area with its shopping, restaurants and tourist activities. Not only was it jammed with tourists, but he was too far ahead of his prey. He was concerned they would jump off the trolley and escape.

To his relief, the van rolled to a stop at a red light. Bobby hopped off the truck, jumped onto the crowded waterfront promenade, and raced to the nearest crosswalk. When the Alaskan Way traffic stopped for the crosswalk lights, Bobby skated across the busy street and slid to a stop at a small concrete trolley platform. He looked north and spotted the trolley rolling his direction.

I got'em now, he thought, feeling victorious.

When the trolley slowed at the stop next to Bobby, two people leapt from the back, hurdled a low concrete barrier, and sprinted across Alaskan Way to the crowded sidewalk, just beating two lanes of fast cars bearing down on them. The couple darted south along the promenade, weaving around strolling tourists.

Bobby reacted too slowly. He couldn't beat the string of fast cars. By the time he skated across Alaskan Way and gave chase along the sidewalk, the runners were only a block ahead of him.

With his considerable crowd experience, Bobby skated around and through the tourists, closing ground on the couple. However, the heavy crowds were slowing him down. He considered skating in the street, a perilous option; the last thing he needed was to get hit by a vehicle.

After two minutes of chasing them, Bobby still lagged by a half a block, but he was convinced he'd catch them soon. He thought they'd be forced to duck into one of the shopping piers to hide. Then, rather than follow them, he'd locate a cell phone, call Duncan, and convince him to send the Seattle Police to arrest the couple. In the meantime, he would remain on the sidewalk in case they tried to escape.

At least, that was his plan.

Unfortunately for Bobby, the couple didn't enter a shop; they entered the Coleman dock, the Seattle terminus for the Washington State Ferry System. Bobby hadn't considered that option. Faced with the possibility they could escape aboard a ferry, he needed a new plan. Worse, there were two major ferry routes from the Coleman dock: Bremerton and Bainbridge Island. Since Bobby wasn't actually part of the police force, making his case to the hold the ferries would be difficult.

Taking the initiative once again, when he reached the terminal Bobby entered the two-story building, clumsily made his way up the stairs with his skates sideways, and stopped at the only ticket window. Looking at him through the glass was a young woman.

"Hey," said Bobby with authority, "I'm with security at the Seattle Center. Did a man and a woman just buy some tickets from you?"

Puzzled, the ticket booth operator responded, "That's not much of a description. Several couples have bought tickets. Is there a problem?"

"Yep, I, uhmm, the Seattle Police need to question them. Is there any way we can keep the boat from leaving?"

Rolling her eyes at the crazy request, she answered, "Sir, I don't have the authority to do that."

"Then whom should I talk to?" Bobby said, trying to sound important.

"I can call my manager."

"No, that will take too long," he growled.

"The police will be here shortly," fibbed Bobby, "locating this couple is very important. Can I enter and look for them?"

"Sir, I can't just let you board the ferries. You'll need to buy a ticket."

"I don't want to board the ferries. I just want to access your lobby so I can track them for the police."

The ticket taker glanced at the growing line of commuters, then looked back to Bobby. "Okay sir," she told him, "I'll let you through, but you need to take off your skates inside the waiting room."

Bobby pushed off from the ticket window and sped down the hall, ignoring her request to remove his skates. When he entered the passenger terminal's waiting room, Bobby slowed to a stop and searched the crowd. He saw couples, some with children, a glut of commuters in suits, and tourists in shorts carrying shopping bags. But, he didn't see any signs of the couple he sought.

He scanned the terminal's west wall. The right ramp indicated the Bainbridge ferry; the left ramp indicated the Bremerton ferry. Just then, Bobby glimpsed the couple entering the Bremerton ramp. They saw him looking their way, then bolted up the ramp and into the boarding tunnel, disappearing from view. Bobby gave chase again, weaving through waiting passengers with little caution. Just before entering the boarding tunnel, a large man in a blue Seahawks shirt stepped backward. Unable to dodge the man, Bobby smacked right into him, sending them both flying.

Bobby felt his elbow burn as he skidded across the industrial carpet. He jumped back to his feet, his apologies to the man echoing through the covered walkway as he raced onto the ferry.

He soon found himself on the third deck of the ferry. He slid to a stop on the vessel's slick tile floor and scanned the rear passenger area. Convinced they weren't there, he skated down a long corridor to the front passenger area. They weren't there either. He pondered his next course of action. Feeling over-confident, Bobby went straight to the captain and to warn him the suspects wanted in a shooting at the Seattle Center might be aboard his vessel.

Maybe I can convince the captain about the seriousness of the situation, he thought.

Emboldened, Bobby skated through deck three to a set of stairs. He ignored a *No Admittance* sign and climbed to deck four, but missed seeing two people climb up a different set of stairs and leave through the boarding

tunnel. He would never understand how they'd eva him and snuck off the ferry.

Just as he reached the bridge level, Bobby f sideways tug. The ferry had begun its trip to Bremert

***

Bobby would successfully convince the captain the Bremerton police about the couple by claimin a police officer trainee, temporarily interning at t Center. The Bremerton police would hold the hostage. Bobby would scrutinize everyone depa the ferry, but would see no one he recognized.

Following Bobby's folly, the Bremerton p would personally contact Duncan as Bobby v ferry. After speaking to Duncan, the captain Bobby the phone so Bobby could learn that Center grounds and for impersonating an fired. Even his mother wouldn't be able Bobby's effort to make a difference wo complete disaster.

Chapter 14: Potsdam Giants

"Tora, great plan! I hope that guy enjoys his trip to Bremerton," Peen said, congratulating Tora as they re-entered the ferry terminal's waiting area, then veered onto the Bainbridge Island ferry's boarding ramp. Peen imagined the security officer's face and chuckled, "The poor guy's going to be super mad when he realizes we aren't on that ferry."

"Thanks. I knew it would work," replied Tora.

She'd hatched the plan after jumping off the trolley and seeing the security officer still on the chase. She thought if the guy followed them into the ferry terminal, they could board the wrong ferry, leave that ferry, and then board the Bainbridge ferry. So, they'd waited at the boarding ramp until the guy appeared inside the terminal. Assured he'd seen them, they'd executed the plan.

"So, you knew that would work because you've used that strategy before?" asked Peen.

"Some guys just won't take no for an answer," she replied, "when someone asks me out, and I don't want to go out with them, I try to be polite. However, sometimes at a bar I'll get a guy who is too drunk to understand the word *no*. I've had to employ some misdirection strategies to disappear."

"Well, I'll be the first one to admit that some guys are jerks," Peen told her, "but I can see why they'd hit on you."

She looked at him and smiled, "And some aren't jerks."

"Well, don't make up your mind too quickly about me, Tora. We've only just met."

"Who said I was talking about you?" she replied flirtatiously without looking at him.

"Do you think the guy is still on the other ferry?" asked Peen as they walked onto the Bainbridge Island ferry.

"As long as he isn't on *this* ferry, I don't care!"

Peen and Tora were walking toward a long row of padded benches when movement caught Peen's eye through the portside windows. Peen said, "Well, there goes the ferry; hopefully that guy is on it!"

"Thankfully! Maybe we can relax for a short while."

"It's a good thing you're sneaky. I'll bet you were a handful as a kid," suggested Peen.

"Yeah, I'm sure my parents thought so. I wasn't super bad, but my parents were strict. As a teenager I'd sneak out my window after dark. I'd walk along the roof and shimmy down a tree next to our house. I was determined to have my fun even if I had to sneak out to do it."

"So what happened to you? What turned you to the dark side, the side of boredom and staidity, better known as academia?"

Tora laughed as they reached the benches, "Staidity? I am not familiar with that word."

Tora and Peen collapsed onto opposing padded benches that faced each other. "Okay, so I made it up. Now you understand why I never pursued a PhD. I tend to color outside the lines, not an endearing characteristic to grad schools."

"I disagree," countered Tora, "my experience is that there are a number of abnormal, dysfunctional people pursuing graduate degrees. They got in somehow. I suppose you could too."

"Wait a minute, Tora. I didn't say I was dysfunctional or abnormal. What I said was I don't play by the rules all the time. Or put differently, I play by my own rules. I figure that doesn't lend itself well to institutions which value and adhere to rules and bureaucracy."

"Oh, I know you didn't say you were abnormal. I'm just reading between the lines," teased Tora, "besides, I don't think I've ever met a normal person. Who is normal?"

"I once met some normal people from Normal, Illinois," said Peen.

"Ohhhh, that's so painful it's beautiful." Then she added, "I'm sure it's your *normal* Midwest town."

"What do you suppose happens if you are crazy in Normal?" wondered Peen aloud, "do they ostracize the crazy people, chase them out of town?"

"I have no idea," responded Tora. She was having fun bantering with Peen. He brought out a fun, egg-headed side of her. "Did you know there's some cool history behind the word *ostracize*?" she asked.

"Actually I don't, but why do I think you do?"

Tora continued, "You know how the participants on the television show *Survivor* vote people off their show? In the Fifth century, when Athens was a city-state, Athenians would gather to manage state business. During those meetings they could attempt to banish a citizen by calling for an election."

Peen liked how much Tora enjoyed sharing her trivia, "You mean someone could arbitrarily decide to vote a person out of Athens?"

"Sort of, Peen. It worked like this. Citizens scratched or carved the name of whomever they wanted to banish onto a broken piece of pottery, otherwise known as an *ostrakon*. Then they deposited the pieces into a giant urn, their version of a ballot box. So, we get the term *ostracism* from the Greek term for the piece of *sherd* used to vote a citizen out of Athens."

"That's a sweet factoid," exclaimed Peen, "history is just so interesting! I love stuff like that. Do you know if anyone was actually voted out of Athens?"

"Yeah, but to be kicked out, someone's name had to appear on at least six thousand pieces. If that happened, the unlucky person had two days to leave or they would be killed. If they tried to come back into the city, again, they faced the death penalty. The good news was they were allowed to return to the city after ten years."

Peen chuckled, "Like you'd want to return to a city that banished you?"

"I know, right?" laughed Tora, "after learning about it I can't ever read the word ostracism without thinking of pottery pieces."

Puzzled, the ticket booth operator responded, "That's not much of a description. Several couples have bought tickets. Is there a problem?"

"Yep, I, uhmm, the Seattle Police need to question them. Is there any way we can keep the boat from leaving?"

Rolling her eyes at the crazy request, she answered, "Sir, I don't have the authority to do that."

"Then whom should I talk to?" Bobby said, trying to sound important.

"I can call my manager."

"No, that will take too long," he growled.

"The police will be here shortly," fibbed Bobby, "locating this couple is very important. Can I enter and look for them?"

"Sir, I can't just let you board the ferries. You'll need to buy a ticket."

"I don't want to board the ferries. I just want to access your lobby so I can track them for the police."

The ticket taker glanced at the growing line of commuters, then looked back to Bobby. "Okay sir," she told him, "I'll let you through, but you need to take off your skates inside the waiting room."

Bobby pushed off from the ticket window and sped down the hall, ignoring her request to remove his skates. When he entered the passenger terminal's waiting room, Bobby slowed to a stop and searched the crowd. He saw couples, some with children, a glut of commuters in suits, and tourists in shorts carrying shopping bags. But, he didn't see any signs of the couple he sought.

He scanned the terminal's west wall. The right ramp indicated the Bainbridge ferry; the left ramp indicated the Bremerton ferry. Just then, Bobby glimpsed the couple entering the Bremerton ramp. They saw him looking their way, then bolted up the ramp and into the boarding tunnel, disappearing from view. Bobby gave chase again, weaving through waiting passengers with little caution. Just before entering the boarding tunnel, a large man in a blue Seahawks shirt stepped backward. Unable to dodge the man, Bobby smacked right into him, sending them both flying.

Bobby felt his elbow burn as he skidded across the industrial carpet. He jumped back to his feet, his apologies to the man echoing through the covered walkway as he raced onto the ferry.

He soon found himself on the third deck of the ferry. He slid to a stop on the vessel's slick tile floor and scanned the rear passenger area. Convinced they weren't there, he skated down a long corridor to the front passenger area. They weren't there either. He pondered his next course of action. Feeling over-confident, Bobby went straight to the captain and to warn him the suspects wanted in a shooting at the Seattle Center might be aboard his vessel.

Maybe I can convince the captain about the seriousness of the situation, he thought.

Emboldened, Bobby skated through deck three to a set of stairs. He ignored a *No Admittance* sign and climbed to deck four, but missed seeing two people climb up a different set of stairs and leave through the boarding tunnel. He would never understand how they'd evaded him and snuck off the ferry.

Just as he reached the bridge level, Bobby felt a sideways tug. The ferry had begun its trip to Bremerton.

✳✳✳

Bobby would successfully convince the captain to alert the Bremerton police about the couple by claiming he was a police officer trainee, temporarily interning at the Seattle Center. The Bremerton police would hold the passengers hostage. Bobby would scrutinize everyone departing from the ferry, but would see no one he recognized.

Following Bobby's folly, the Bremerton police captain would personally contact Duncan as Bobby waited on the ferry. After speaking to Duncan, the captain would hand Bobby the phone so Bobby could learn that for leaving the Center grounds and for impersonating an officer, he was fired. Even his mother wouldn't be able to save his job. Bobby's effort to make a difference would turn into a complete disaster.

"I can see why," said Peen, as he stretched out on the long padded bench and stared at the ceiling. Tora did the same on the other bench. They fell silent, grateful to relax for a little while as the rumble of the ferry's engines soothed their stressed bodies.

Without looking at Tora, Peen said, "Wow, does this bring back memories. When you're tired and need a rest, there's nothing better than napping on a ferry. If I wasn't so wired, I'd be asleep in seconds."

"You've ridden a lot of ferries? Been chased onto them often?" joked Tora.

"Nope. I saved this experience just for you Tora. My other ferry rides have been pretty tame, though one time I did have to push-start my car off a ferry. How about you?"

"This is definitely the first time I've been chased onto a ferry as well," chuckled Tora. She paused and then said, "Seriously though, I've never been chased like this. This is absolutely crazy!"

Peen tilted his head, "Tora, you need to get out more often. Hang around with me and I'll have you chased through places you never knew existed."

"Oh, you mean like dimly lit, subterranean utility tunnels? Secret passages? Fire escapes? Yeah, I'll bet you show all your dates a good time like this," she challenged.

"But, of course. So, what do you think those guys want with the panels anyway? Money? Political power?"

"Your guess is as good as mine," Tora answered, "certainly those are plausible reasons for hunting the panels and, by extension, us. Another question is, how did your uncle and Damon get connected?"

Tora paused for a moment, lost in thought. Before Peen could respond, Tora started talking again, "Maybe he got talking to the wrong people? Maybe he has a colleague that tipped them off? Or, maybe he said too much to the MFA&A group. Who knows?"

"Hold on," Peen said. "What's the MFA&A group?"

"That's the acronym, well initialism really, for Monuments, Fine Arts, and Archival. It was an American organization established to protect any art and artifacts recovered by Allied forces as they moved into the interior of Europe."

"Initialism?" asked Peen, "you are full of interesting words. I knew there was a reason I liked you. How does that differ from an acronym?"

"An acronym is pronounceable, while an initialism is a collection of letters that represent the longer words," she said before stopping to think, "for example, NASA is an acronym, while FBI is an initialism."

"Well, no shit. I didn't know that," said Peen sitting up. His mental wheels were spinning, "So, CIA is an initialism, while the term RADAR is an acronym. Do I have that right?"

"You've got the right idea. However, RADAR is a special kind of word. It's a backronym. I wasn't going to go there, but since you brought it up, a backronym is an acronym with specifically chosen words so the resulting acronym is pronounceable. In other words, the acronym was chosen and the full name of the organization was altered to back into the acronym. In fact, backronyms are often used to create brandable legislation. For example, the letters in the U.S. PATRIOT Act legislation stand for individual words," noted Tora.

"Hmmm. You are just full of information. I guess that makes sense. Now, back to the MMFAA."

"No no," corrected Tora, "just one *M*. The MFA&A. They were also known as the Monuments Men if that makes it easier."

"Yeah, let's go with that," said Peen with a smile.

"If you think that is hard to remember, try the Soviet version of the same group following World War II. Their Monuments Men counterpart was . . . let me think," said Tora as she tilted her head to jog her memory, "it was called the Extraordinary State Commission on the Registration and Investigation . . . ummmm . . . of the Crimes of the German-Facist Occupiers and Their Accomplices and the Damage Done by Them to the Citizens, Collective Farms, Public Organizations, State Enteres, and Institutions of the USSR."

Pumping her fist into the air, she yelled, "Sweeeet, I remembered it!" then added, turning toward Peen, "check it out. I didn't even need to google it!"

Peen stared at her in amazement, "Why in the world did you spend the time to memorize that name?"

"Just think of it as a gift for remembering the unusual," she boasted.

"I see, do you have a photographic memory?"

"I wish! But sadly, no, not photographic. I forget plenty of things," responded Tora. "Now, where did I leave off? Anyway, there were millions of artifacts stolen, misplaced, and destroyed during the war. Locating and preserving art was a priority, which led to art-recovery organizations on all sides. The Allies feared that the retreating German Army and the advancing Allies might destroy irreplaceable works of art. So, Monuments Men traveled with Allied armies to identify and secure any works they could locate. I read that after the war, they restituted over five million artifacts and documents. However, there've been reports that the United States still holds valuable treasures from World War II."

"I feel like a whole new world is opening up. What do they, or I guess we, have?" asked Peen. He couldn't understand why the United States would continue to hold onto European art.

"That's a pretty gray area. According to what I've read they've been declared a national security issue by the CIA and kept hidden," explained Tora.

"If they are a secret, how do we know there are any treasures here at all?"

"Well, for example, in 1978 President Carter issued an executive order to return the Hungarian crown jewels that had been found in a German salt mine during World War II. Supposedly, the jewels had been held at Fort Knox with other historic treasures until Hungary could verify the jewels would be returned to the people of Hungary rather than to the Communist Government of the time."

"So," said Peen suspiciously, "if the United States government could hold a country's crown jewels for so long, it begs the question about what else is buried in government vaults."

"Exactly, Peen. Not surprisingly, among the items the Monuments Men hoped to uncover were the Amber Panels, but no one ever found them. In 1952 the Monuments group was disbanded. However, some history professors still donate their time as members of an unofficial restitution group. They communicate over the Internet and hunt for missing artifacts. I know your uncle volunteered with the organization a little, but I don't know to what extent. It's entirely possible he uncovered something important about the panels. How anyone else would have found out about his involvement is anyone's guess. The panels have been so shrouded by confusion," explained Tora.

"I sure hope he's still around to explain all this to us," said Peen.

"Yeah, me too. He's a good guy," added Tora, "I've been doing graduate work for three years now. I've known your uncle the whole time. I'm always amazed at the breadth of his knowledge. Sometimes it makes me want to quit the whole process, because I can't imagine learning as much as he knows, even if I live to be one hundred."

Tora stopped talking and looked out the window at a tugboat pushing a gravel barge into Elliott Bay, "He told me he was lucky, that he had the ability to remember most everything he read and the good fortune to have an interest in wide-ranging subjects. But the most important thing he told me, and what inspires me to this day, is that it doesn't matter how much you know. What matters is that you take an informed, unique approach to looking at the world. And sometimes that fresh approach requires an absence of knowledge, or an absence of experience."

Peen nodded in agreement, "That sounds like my uncle. It's his work ethic translated for academia."

Two children ran noisily along the aisleway. Peen watched a couple walk hand-in-hand toward the aft deck. A child pleaded, "But Daddy, you said we could!"

The father picked up the crying child and walked away.

Tora shifted and pulled the phone from her pocket. She told Peen, "I almost forgot to text Leslie."

Tora tapped out a message that started a brief exchange of texts. She assured Leslie that her time with Peen had been an unexpected adventure. Leslie informed her that their guests were enjoying the food despite her absence.

After that, Tora launched the phone's web browser. She searched for a few minutes before finding a long article about the Amber Panels. She looked up at Peen. He seemed lost in thought, staring south at Vashon Island. She followed his gaze, then looked east toward Mt. Rainier. The sun lit the mountain brightly against a deep blue sky.

"Peen. Earth to Peen. Are you there?"

Peen blinked, then turned to look at her, "I was just thinking how surreal this all is. Getting chased, meeting you, learning things about my uncle I never knew. Crazy, isn't it?"

"Hello, that's what I said earlier! I haven't felt this alive in months. I've been buried in my little box researching and writing for way too long."

"In your box?"

"Yes, my special place I go in my head where I can think. It disconnects me from the planet."

"Makes sense," observed Peen, "speaking of boxes, please share with me what your little cellular box knows about the Amber Panels."

"Yes sir," answered Tora. She looked down at her screen, "It says here the idea for the panels was hatched by King Friedrich Wilhelm of Prussia, who controlled most of the southern coast of the Baltic Sea." She paused, "You do know where the Baltic Sea is, right?"

"Generally, yes. It's north of Germany, south of Sweden. I'm sketchy on the rest."

"Not *too* bad, but you really need to spend more time in Europe," suggested Tora.

"I hate getting geography questions wrong. Book my tickets and I'm there, especially if you go with me."

"Sounds doable. As for the Baltic Sea, it's bordered at twelve o'clock by Sweden and Finland, and at three o'clock by Estonia, Latvia, and Lithuania. Kaliningrad is about 4:30. Poland and Germany are at six o'clock. At eight o'clock is Denmark. At the very edge of the Baltic Sea, just above Estonia, a small tip of Russia touches the Baltic, allowing St. Petersburg to have a port," explained Tora as she returned to reading. "In the early 1700s, while Peter the Great was consolidating his power, he chose to make St. Petersburg the capital of Russia due to its location on the Baltic Sea. He was determined to see St. Petersburg and Russia become the equals of the great cities and countries in Europe."

Tora stopped. She asked Peen, "Can you find me a bottle of water. I just realized how thirsty I am. Here's some cash left over from our tickets."

Peen took the money and returned two minutes later with peanuts and water. Tora sipped some water, then continued, "The beaches on the Baltic Sea in the southeast corner are natural amber depositories. The theory is that a petrified pine forest exists under the Baltic. Major storms release amber from the sea floor. The amber floats to the surface and the currents carry it to the southeastern shores. You can still walk along the beaches near Kaliningrad, the new Königsberg, and collect amber."

Peen chimed in, "Sounds romantic."

Tora looked up at him and smiled. He winked at her. She suddenly felt uncharacteristically shy and returned to her phone.

"With that geopolitical background in mind, in 1701 Prussia was officially recognized as a Kingdom and Frederick I of Prussia became the first King. Importantly, he was King *in* Prussia and not King *of* Prussia. The distinction honored the true King of Austria and the Holy Roman Empire, Leopold I, whose blessing was required to allow Frederick to become King. Around the same time, Frederick's wife Sophie-Charlotte argued that a uniquely spectacular work of art would attract leaders to Prussia, because, like Russia, Prussia sought legitimacy in Europe. Her efforts paid off when the King commissioned Andreas Schlüter to design and build the Amber Panels. Schlüter remained in charge of the panels until 1707, when he was replaced by another artist."

"Does it say why he was replaced?" asked Peen.

"Nope it doesn't. Instead, it skips ahead to 1713 with the death of the King in Prussia Frederick I. At that time the panels were incomplete. When his son Frederick Wilhelm I King in Prussia assumed the throne in 1713, he halted work on them. He felt the panels were a waste of money, so he had them boxed and stored in Berlin. The new Prussian King was interested in the military, not art. Specifically, he gathered the tallest men he could locate for a special regimental unit nicknamed the Potsdam Giants. According to a French Ambassador at the time, the King told him he was indifferent to beautiful women, but *had a weakness for tall soldiers . . .* "

Peen interrupted Tora, "Not to sound judgmental, but I have to admit that sets off my gaydar."

Tora looked at Peen. She thought he was a little rough around the edges at times, "Maybe he was gay or maybe he wasn't. It's easy to misinterpret what that statement meant centuries earlier. Even ideas of personal space and privacy were different back then. For example, it was common for more than two men to share a bed. Travelers, even as late as the 1850s, often rented a space in a bed rather than rent an entire room."

Peen realized he'd touched a nerve, "I understand that. But, I'm a product of our current culture and, good or bad, it's just what flashed through my imperfect brain."

"Fair enough," she responded, "I wouldn't be honest with myself if I didn't admit that it occurred to me, too. Anyway, in 1716, Frederick Wilhelm agreed to an alliance with Peter the Great. As part of their agreement, Frederick

Wilhelm asked for fifty-five very tall soldiers in exchange for the unfinished Amber Panels."

"Hmmm. That's not weird at all," cracked Peen.

Tora smirked, but ignored him, "This was a win for the Prussian King, because not only did he get more soldiers, he also rid himself of an art project he never wanted. For Peter the agreement was likewise a big win: he'd desired the uncompleted Amber Panels for years. This was likely the result of Andreas Schlüter, who, after leaving the Amber Room project in 1707, was invited to work in St. Petersburg by Peter. Some historians speculate Schlüter brought the original plans for the amber panels with him to Russia."

"You just can't make this stuff up," joked Peen. He was enjoying this history lesson. Then it occurred to him just how little reading he'd been doing on his own. He told her, "I need to get back to reading. I've been to busy to read many books."

Tora looked up from her phone, "Well, I have the opposite problem. I've been reading so much I haven't had the time to enjoy present day life. It feels really good to be away from my desk, though ironically, what am I doing? Reading about history!"

Peen looked out the window. "Hey," he said having lost track of time, "we're almost to the Bainbridge dock. Put your phone away, it's time to return to reality and find some transportation."

Chapter 15: Katya Ballheim

Damon's assistant, Arista, was clearly agitated as she spoke into her cell phone, "What happened? The police scanners are buzzing from a Seattle Center shooting!"

"We missed them again. Peen Rogers has proven resourceful," explained Damon calmly from the front seat of the Cadillac Escalade. The car was idling in a parking spot next to a tiny well-worn building that housed the Shanty Cafe, "Arista, we need to get to Port Townsend, wherever that is. What is the fastest route?"

"Wait a minute," she responded typing madly on her keyboard. Arista was in a downtown Seattle hotel room she'd rented, where she monitored breaking news and coordinated the men. While talking with Damon, she was simultaneously intercepting chatter from the Seattle Police department's radio communications.

Arista spoke, "Damon, you are a couple of hours away from Port Townsend. It is located northwest of Seattle on the tip of the Olympic Peninsula. But, there are islands between here and there with no direct route over them."

Damon considered what she'd said, then replied, "Why not rent a helicopter and fly there?"

"Renting a helicopter requires identification," she cautioned, "and *you* can not risk being identified. Your best option is to take the downtown ferry to Bainbridge. You will likely miss the 6:00pm boat, but according to my information, there is another one at 7:05pm."

"You mean driving will not get us there faster?" asked Damon impatiently.

"Even with the one ferry delay you will still reach Port Townsend faster than driving south to Tacoma and then heading north."

"We will take the ferry," Damon declared as he ordered his driver to head for the ferry dock. While his driver inputted directions into the GPS, Damon changed subjects, "Arista, have we breached the door of the silo, *ach*, I mean the *Ant Farm* yet?" inquired Damon, momentarily forgetting to use the silo's code word.

"No, Damon. The men were forced to locate more equipment . . ."

Damon interrupted her and vented his frustration, "Arista, I do not need the details. Just breach the door of the silo. Whose stupid idea was it to turn off the electricity in the first place."

Arista answered, "That was your idea, boss. You blew the power circuits."

Damon closed his eyes and exhaled. Getting angry would only add to his stress. He waited several seconds before talking again, "Arista, the question was rhetorical. Remember, we could not risk having them broadcast a message for help." Changing the subject again he asked, "Have you heard anything from Kaliningrad's city council about moving forward with phase two of the Königsberg Castle restoration project?"

She gave Damon the same answer she'd given him the day before. She knew Damon could be impatient, but there was little she could do to speed up the slow pace of the city's political machine, "I am still waiting for a response from council member Peter Chiacov."

"He is stalling. The council continues to get opposition from Moscow. If I hadn't pushed, this would be going nowhere," argued Damon. Privately, Damon relished that without him nothing would be happening. He wanted as much credit as possible for restoring the city, "We must schedule a meeting with our social media crew next week. We have to create more noise on blogs and build controversy regarding the delay in renaming the city. It will take time to build a groundswell of popular opinion, so we have much work left to do."

"I will add that to the schedule, Damon. And, I will inform you when Peter calls."

"Is the meeting with the Russians finalized for the *Ant Farm* yet?" he asked.

"Yes," she replied, "You'll be meeting Andrei at 7am at the *Ant Farm*. The Russians said he is a special envoy."

"Good," said Damon, close to completing a decade long dream, "I have heard of him, but never met him. I just want a witness present when we open the doors and find the art."

Arista brought up a touchy subject, "What about the old men in the vault?"

Damon replied with confidence, "Andrei will see the bigger picture once we show him the panels. The old men will fade into history. But, I would still like to find Peen and the woman named Tora. Based on the conversations I overheard in the professor's apartment, they can identify me and connect me to the panels, so I need to deal with them one way or another."

Arista knew what that meant, "That is all I have. I will call when we make more progress."

"Goodbye," was all Damon said as he abruptly ended the conversation. He relaxed, leaning his head against the dark tinted window of the Escalade for a short nap. He expected it would be a long night. But, his mind was racing, juggling countless issues. Most importantly, he was close to the panels. He knew it. All he needed was to get inside the missile vault. He had to admire the clever hiding spot for the treasure.

As his driver maneuvered through Elliot Avenue's traffic, Damon thought of the girl, Katya Haider, whose diary had yielded the answers he'd long sought. When he first heard about the diary, Damon assumed it was another false rumor from someone hoping to be rewarded for panel information. Offers of cash to researchers he knew in Poland, Germany, and Kaliningrad had proven effective for generating leads. Most rumors were useless and he dismissed those without payment, but when Petra Bork appeared before Damon three weeks ago, she provided more than a rumor.

Petra handed him actual copies of a teenage German girl's diary. Damon browsed through some of the entries Petra had highlighted. The words' tall, lean script was difficult to parse, but Damon was experienced enough to recognize the value of the diary. He rewarded Petra for it, reminding her that if it was a fake, she'd be sorry. The woman assured him it was genuine.

As he read through it, Katya Haider's diary proved compelling. In short entries, she wrote how her life in Königsberg had collapsed like the city around her. She yearned for a life of routine, to revisit her days of walking to school or meeting her father at the university, where she'd sometimes sit in on his English classes. Or, she'd dream of leaving the city altogether for Sunday visits to her grandmother in the East Prussian countryside.

Other entries described the disappearance of people she'd met, mostly older men. One by one, her family and friends disappeared. She complained of loneliness. She desperately longed for the return of her father. Her diary became a time machine, portraying the good, the bad, and the death all around her. She explained how her classmates, the older boys, were increasingly absorbed by the Volkssturm. Sometimes she wrote about the food she'd eaten or the places she'd explored, as the city had a wholly revised landscape due to the bombings in 1944. One day she described sneaking into a movie theater whose roof had collapsed. The movie still played, but only at night.

She wrote how some men tried to trade food for intimate relations. One woman told her that she could charge two cans of condensed milk for each encounter. Katya told the woman that she'd rather die than trade her body. The woman responded that Katya would probably get her wish. However, Katya couldn't bear the thought of her father returning and discovering she was unclean.

As the months passed, the diary entries indicated hunger and fear had taken their tolls on Katya. Damon thought about the entry from December 2, 1944: *Three men were hanging near Duchstrasse today. They weren't there yesterday. On one was a sign that read, 'These soldiers were cowards'. Dressed in their soldier uniforms, the bodies were stiff from the cold. They swung silently to gusts of wind. I was so relieved to see you weren't there, but where are you father? Why don't you come home? I'm so tired and cold and need you more than ever.*

This had been the tone of many entries during the cold winter of 1944-1945. But, on January 20th, 1945, her life changed dramatically. The entry for the day was long. She described her day in short sentences. *Went to castle to find food. Overheard men talking end of war. Many soldiers dead. Russians are coming. They will defeat us. Dr. Rhode has plans for famous Amber Panels. They were so beautiful. Do you remember Papa? Have plan.*

And then in a different style of pencil, as if the second part was added later, she'd written. *Located Oskar outside castle. I asked him to join me and leave Germany. He agreed. We parted and resolved to meet at the abandoned Begelhaus one hour later. I was so relieved and thankful when he arrived! Together we climbed to the third story of Begelhaus, which no longer has a roof. There, while holding his Bible, we exchanged vows and married ourselves under the eyes of God. I am no longer Katya Haider; We are now Oskar and Katya Ballheim. He says I am now a Saint. I told him I didn't feel a saint for what we had to do. He said we can spend our lives redeeming ourselves, by giving ourselves over to God. We prayed for forgiveness, because we had to kill to survive.*

Damon had read those pages several times. Sure, he'd killed people, but most either deserved or expected it, though when pressed he'd admit a few were collateral damage. But, he'd never killed a teenage girl on purpose.

He realized Katya had grown up that day. She understood the overall picture and that being a survivor was paramount. Like Katya, Damon would have to seek forgiveness some day, too, for all that he'd done. But not yet; his quest was incomplete.

Damon's driver turned right into the ferry terminal and stopped behind a silver Honda at the ticket booth. It was 6:10pm. They had about an hour to wait before they could drive onto the ferry, so Damon closed his eyes and drifted off to sleep.

CHAPTER 16: THE FORD FALCON

Tora and Peen walked quickly through the long covered elevated ramp that connects the ferry with Bainbridge Island's ferry terminal. Soon they were standing at the edge of a large parking lot scanning the cars. Some ferry commuters drove new BMWs, while others used "island cars", older ones with little theft value.

Tora spoke, "It looks like we have some options. If we can find a 1960s Ford, I might even have a key."

"Huh?" said Peen, "how do you have a key to a vehicle we haven't found yet?"

"You'll seeeee," she replied confidently.

"Unless it's a Mustang I'm not sure I can easily spot a different make of . . . "

Before Peen could finish his sentence Tora grabbed his arm and said, "Follow me! I see exactly what we need."

Peen trailed Tora as she marched behind a row of cars, turned, then walked to the far side of the lot toward an older white vehicle. Peen spotted two round taillights, but couldn't determine the model. As they neared the car, a chrome trim piece stretching between the taillights identified it as a *Falcon*.

As if reading his mind Tora explained, "It's a two-door Ford Falcon Futura. It could use some bodywork, but hopefully the drive train is okay. Let's start it up and see how she sounds."

Peen was puzzled, "And you have the key to this?"

"Patience," she advised.

Tora stepped to the driver's side and pulled out a ring of keys from her pocket. She picked through the keys and selected one. He watched her look around as she fiddled with the lock, which suddenly popped up. Then, she opened the door and climbed inside. She reached across to the passenger side, unlocked the door, and said, "Welcome to our new, old car!"

Amazed, Peen slid onto a dark blue bench-seat surrounded by coordinating blue doors and headliner. The dash was chrome with a classic horizontal speedometer, an AM radio, and a glove box.

"Here we go," announced Tora as she slid her key into the ignition switch. It didn't turn at first, so she wiggled and twisted it. The engine turned over, but didn't fire. On the third try, the engine started.

"Impressive!" exclaimed Peen, "but how?"

"It's a long story, but here's the short version. Years ago Grandma took Grandpa's truck to the store using the wrong key. After some experimentation, Grandpa discovered that 1970s General Motor keys could be used to start 1960s Fords. He always told my brother and me to carry an extra GM key, because you'll just never know if you'll need one."

"And what if the key hadn't worked?"

Tora backed the car out of the parking spot while responding, "Grandpa taught my brother and me how to hot wire a car, too. Old cars are pretty simple. There are two basic steps. One, the coil needs to power the distributor, so a power wire must be attached to the ignition wire. Two, the starter must engage so the motor turns over. To do that, just cross the starter wire onto a power wire."

Peen nodded, "I suppose that's a good skill to have. My grandparents never taught me cool stuff like that."

Tora pulled out of the lot and stopped for a light, "Looks like we have nearly a full tank. That ought to get us to Port Townsend. Who shall we thank for this loaner?"

"Let me check the registration," said Peen. He opened the glove box and explored some of the documents, "The Washington State Department of Motor Vehicles believes the vehicle is owned and registered to a kind and generous gentleman named Keith E. Borchard, Jr. You know, I've always thought highly of him and shall have to thank him if I ever meet him, which I hope never happens."

"Don't worry, he won't be too unhappy with us. We'll make sure his car gets back in one piece. Besides, Keith Borchard is the least of our worries," noted Tora.

"On the bright side Tora, at least we have a cool stolen car to drive to Port Townsend thanks to you!"

"Hey, if that's the bright side, I don't want to think about the dark side."

"Well my young Jedi," said Peen, trying to lighten the mood with a terrible Yoda-like impression. "Be wary of the dark side. Clear your head of evil thoughts. Open yourself to the force. Let me be your guide. I can show you wonderful things."

"Master PeenYoda, if you get fresh with me I'll demonstrate the use of my knee-force right between your scrawny Jedi legs."

"Hmmm . . . you'd be wise not to threaten Master PeenYoda, for I am experienced in the use of the force and I shall use your force against you. You shall know what it means to be bested by a temperamental muppet," chuckled Peen. "In the meantime my young Padawan, take a lesson from Harrison Ford and pilot this car like you want to make the Kessel Run in less than twelve parsecs."

"As long as you lay off the terrible Yoda impressions, I will do my best Han Solo impression. Deal?" giggled Tora.

"Agreed!" He promised, "let me check your phone and see how far we have to drive."

The light turned green. Soon, Tora and Peen were heading northbound on State Highway 305 toward Port Townsend. The highway passed through rural surroundings with mailboxes marking driveways that disappeared into leafy underbrush.

Looking down at the phone, Peen pressed the *home* button. The iPhone requested a key code, "What's the code to access your phone?"

"1899," she responded, "the year my grandmother Elsie was born. She was one of my favorite people growing up."

"Well, that just begs me to ask why?"

"Grandpa always said Grandma Elsie had *sand*. If she wanted to do something, she did it. When Grandma was sixteen, she went to a circus show and saw a woman ride a horse while standing. When she returned home, Grandma took her horse Buster into the pasture and started practicing. She claimed she fell off twenty-three times before she could completely ride around the pasture standing up."

"I'm amazed she didn't break any bones," said Peen, "did she ever join the circus?"

"Noooo," laughed Tora, "Grandma Elsie said that completing the challenge was the objective; she had no interest in entertaining people."

"Did she try any other tricks with Buster?"

"She never mentioned any horse tricks. Her next big challenge was a road trip when she was twenty-two years old. She came into some money and decided she wanted to see the world, so she bought a 1919 Winton Six. Grandma told me those were expensive cars back then. There weren't many roads to choose from back then, so she drove from Seattle down the Pacific Highway to San Francisco. There she turned east and planned to take the Lincoln Highway all the way to Chicago. However, she broke down in Salt Lake City. The trip had been more expensive than she'd planned, so she sold the car, purchased a train ticket, and made her way back to Seattle."

"I'll bet that was an amazing trip back then. Did she ever buy another car and try again?" asked Peen.

"She lost interest in solo exploring after her car broke down in Utah, because on her train ride back to Seattle she met my grandfather, the same man who taught my brother and me how to hotwire vehicles. He'd been on his way back to the Seattle area after serving in the army. That trip was a highlight of her life and she shared many stories with me. Grandma said at the time she didn't realize it, but later she'd learned it was her Hero's Journey. She said someday I needed to take mine. But, I've been in school too much to travel for long periods."

"A *Hero's Journey*? Isn't that from Joseph Campbell, the same writer who coined the phrase *follow your bliss*?"

"One and the same," answered Tora. "Peen you are full of surprises. I would never have guessed you'd have known that phrase."

"Never judge a book," he countered.

"So true. You know, people interpreted Campbell's *following your bliss* mantra to mean a person should pursue instant self-gratification. But, Campbell never intended that. Instead, he wanted to suggest the value of pursuing one's own journey and gaining insight by leaving behind the familiar, if only temporarily. Eventually, he coined an alternative phrase: *follow your blisters*."

"Interesting," said Peen, "that was something I didn't know. Have you taken Campbell's and your grandmother's advice? Have you followed your blisters on your own hero's journey?"

"Nope. But, I've read a few books about other women's journeys, like *Eat, Pray, Love* and *Where did you Go Bernadette?* Does that count?" asked Tora wincing slightly.

"I think they might be inspiring for your own journey, and you can learn a lot from reading, but in my experience you can't get blisters without putting your feet to the ground," responded Peen.

"Maybe this is my journey? I'm certainly well beyond my comfort zone, driving a stranger's car to a strange place with a strange stranger next to me! And, how much more heroic can we be if we save the Professor and the Panels?"

"I don't think you're on a Hero's Journey; I think you're just plain nuts," chuckled Peen, "but then again, I'm here too. I don't know what that says about me."

Tora glanced at him and smiled.

She doesn't look a bit crazy, he thought, *in fact, she seems very happy.*

Peen looked down at Tora's phone to see how much farther they had to drive, "The almighty Googler says we have about an hour and twenty minutes before we reach Port Townsend."

"Since we have time to kill, let's find out more about the panels. Would you please?" requested Tora.

Peen switched pages on the web browser and found the page she'd been skimming, "Hmmm. Where were we? Ah yes, the Prussian King gave the panels to Peter. In return,

Peter gave the Prussian King fifty-five very tall, perhaps very sexy, soldiers."

"You sure seem fixated on those soldiers," she teased.

"No no, just makes me laugh," chuckled Peen. "In 1716 Peter the Great had the panels packed into eighteen crates and carted to St. Petersburg. Despite Peter's intention to have them completed, he was forced to put the panels into storage. The panels remained in storage until Elizabeta Petrovna, also known as Empress Elizabeth, Peter the Great's daughter, assumed the thrown in 1725, following Peter's death. The Empress was an art lover who spoke French, German, Italian and Russian fluently. In order to honor her father, she had the Amber Panels moved to the Winter Palace in Saint Petersburg and asked Italian artist Francisco Bartolomeo Rastrelli to finish them."

Tora interrupted him, "Have you ever seen the movie *The Russian Ark*?"

"I've heard of it," said Peen. "Now that I think about it, wasn't that filmed at the Winter Palace?"

"Correct. The movie shares the history of the Russian Empire from the era of Peter the Great until the start of World War I. The most amazing part of the movie was that they shot it in one continuous eighty-six minute take. The camera had to move constantly from room to room and film thousands of actors as the story revealed Russia's effort to be recognized by Europe. The creators of the movie only had one day to film the entire thing. The first two takes failed. Finally, on the third take they nailed it."

"That's cool," replied Peen, "I'll have to see if I can find that on Netflix." Looking back at the phone, he continued,

"It says here that when the Italian artist opened the Amber Panel boxes for the Empress they discovered interlocked amber pieces: some ornately carved and some flat. The amber shapes had been wax-bonded onto a thin sheet of gilded brass, which was attached to massive oak panels. The technique produced a bright, illuminating effect as light penetrated the amber, reflected off the brass, and returned through the amber, resulting in a golden, glittering effect."

"That sounds beautiful," injected Tora. "I wonder if the reconstructed panels equal the originals? Much of that type of artisan knowledge has been lost."

"It doesn't mention that here," said Peen. "After unpacking the panels Rastrelli discovered they weren't large enough to completely fill all the wall space. So, more design and construction was necessary. The added complexity delayed the completion of the Amber Room until 1746, more than four decades after work had started. But, when it was completed, the room was instantly considered a World Wonder. The Russian Empress held social events and meetings within the amber space, making it a popular destination trip for foreign dignitaries. So, you'd think the Empress would have been happy with them, but she wasn't. In 1755, she decided to move the Amber Panels to a larger room at her Summer Palace in a town called . . . "

Peen paused for a moment wondering how to pronounce the name Tsarskoe Selo. Turning to look at Tora, he asked, "Is the town called Zarsco Say Lo?"

"Close. It's more like Sars-Kay See-Low. I believe the town is located just south of St. Petersburg. However, the new name for the town is Pushkin, honoring the famous Russian poet and writer. Pushkin and St. Petersburg are two places I plan to visit someday."

"Strangely, I have a sudden interest in both, too," said Peen nonchalantly as he pursed his lips and raised his eyebrows. Tora smiled, but didn't respond.

He read on, "In 1755 the Empress moved the newly expanded panels to Sars-Kay See-Low. To increase their size, architects added mirrored pilasters with gilt bronze candelabras between the panels. Above them were Florentine mosaics made of multicolored jasper framed in amber. In addition, artists added a carved and gilded wood frieze that ran around the upper portion of the room. Finally, they lit the entire chamber with over five hundred candles," explained Peen before he stopped reading. "I just described a room that I can't picture. Can you?"

"I can see it; let me help you out," she said. "To fill the extra space on the walls that lacked amber, the workers added mirrors, mosaics of reddish-rust-colored stones, and carved borders. How's that for a rough translation?"

"That I understood," responded Peen. "Until her death in 1762, Empress Elizabeth was a patron of the arts who embraced extravagance. She literally never wore a dress twice and was said to have 15,000 dresses at the time of her death. She went so far as to ask her guards to stamp the gowns of women attending balls, so that they could only wear their dresses to her balls once."

"Wow, no control issues there," interjected Tora.

Peen nodded and clicked on a link. He skimmed through an article about Elizabeth, "Oh, it get's better! She passed laws insuring that all French fabric salesmen had to sell to her first. Also, Russian women could not wear her hairstyle. Given her vanity, it is easy for me to see why she would embrace an expensive and unusual art project like the panels."

Tora laughed, "It's funny how some of the oddest people with the worst intentions can create some of the most amazing things."

"You know," said Peen, flexing his intellectual muscles, "De Tocqueville, in his 1800's book, *Democracy in America*, marveled at how some of the kindest rulers in Europe made some of the worst policy decisions with the best of intentions. He compared that to the self-interested decisions made by our Congress. He believed that, despite the self-interest, or because of it, their overall policy enactments did more good than bad. De Tocqueville marveled at that conundrum."

"Well," responded Tora, "I'm marveling at you. I didn't expect that you'd have read De Tocqueville."

"Haven't you learned yet Tora? I'm not all good looks and charm," teased Peen, "but seriously, I believe the old adage that those who don't know their history are doomed to repeat it."

"And I'm a believer that history repeats itself whether we know it or not. It's our failings as human beings that doom us. It's more of a Jeffersonian *Past is Prologue* philosophy," argued Tora.

"You know that's not a Jeffersonian quote, but one that Shakespeare penned," countered Peen casually. "He wasn't claiming that history repeats itself. He used that dialogue to assure the audience that the early acts of *The Tempest* were only precursors to the really good stuff."

Surprised once again by him, Tora asked, "Where did you come up with that?"

Peen replied, "It started with a framed poster of Thomas Jefferson my parents hung on a wall that included the phrase *The Past is Prologue*. When I asked her, my mom explained it meant the best was yet to come. Then she pulled out the play and read it. I'll never forget that."

"Can I rephrase my position on history?" said Tora without sounding upset that Peen had challenged her regarding the root of the phrase.

"Please do," replied Peen glancing at her with a smirk.

Tora thought for a second. Then she said, "I believe in a bastardized Shakespearean philosophy whereby the past, in terms of people fighting each other for land, of boom and busts, of love and heartbreak, and the life and death of civilizations will continually repeat itself in familiar forms."

"Okay, I can agree with that, too," responded Peen, impressed that Tora took no personal offense to his comments. He'd met plenty of people who didn't like their ideas challenged. But Tora, rather than being insulted, appeared to have the self-confidence and humility to re-examine her positions. He liked that about her.

Peen looked back at his screen, "Now, where was I . . . Empress Elizabeth died in 1762. From that time until World War II the panels hung at her palace. Because of the extreme hot and cold temperatures at the Summer Palace, due to limited heat and no air conditioning, the wax adhesive would expand and contract, causing some pieces to detach. So, during the 1800s some of the panels underwent restoration. Over the years the room was used less and less. The original amber encrusted furniture, built specifically for the room, fell apart. After the 1917 Bolshevik Revolution, the Communist Party assumed control of Russia and changed the country's capital of St. Petersburg to Leningrad; during this time the Amber Panels were neglected even more."

Peen looked from the phone to Tora, "That's why I find Russian history so confusing. They keep changing the city names, so how's a person supposed to remember which city is which?"

"It does complicate history, Peen, but history is messy. That's part of the attraction for me. I like the challenge of uncovering the stories that underpin history and properly contextualizing them."

"I get what you are saying," replied Peen, "but you managed to make it sound so academic just now that I want to yawn."

"It's a gift," said Tora laughing, "go on."

"So, the panels hung for almost two hundred years on the summer palace walls in the town of Pushkin until the Nazis stormed into Russia in 1941 as part of Operation Barbarossa, the surprise German attack on Russia during World War II. When word reached Leningrad that the Germans were on their way, an order was given to remove anything of value from the palaces surrounding Leningrad.

This herculean task entailed moving three million items to safe locations using only horse drawn carts in a few months time. Impossible under the best of conditions, the Germans aggravated the situation by bombing Leningrad and the surrounding areas. Palace and museum windows had to be boarded, forcing curators to pack art by candlelight. In some cases heavy objects, such as statues, were buried rather than moved."

Peen stopped reading to take a sip of water and chew a few peanuts left over from their ferry ride. He wasn't used to reading aloud and was surprised at how quickly his throat dried up. He chewed on a few more peanuts, offered some to Tora, and continued reading, "When the Russians turned their attention to the Amber Panels, an attempt was made to remove them, causing some damage. With so many more objects to move and uncertainty surrounding the practicality of removing the panels, the decision was made to cover the panels with fabric in the hope the Nazis would be deceived. But, the ruse failed. One reason it didn't work was that prior to the onset of World War II, the Nazi Party had sent art students throughout Europe to locate major works of art and record information about them. The Amber Panels were not only included in that lengthy list of items, they were at the top. Three months into the war with the Russians, the Germans arrived at the Summer Palace and Baron von Kunsberg arrived with them. He was leading his Second Battalion of Sonderkommando Ribbentrop, who were attached to the German Army at the Eastern Front to identify, protect and appropriate items of cultural interest."

Tora speculated aloud, "Had the Russians known how sophisticated the German art plunder was, I wonder if they would have expended more effort to remove the panels."

"I doubt it. I bet they suspected the worst already," responded Peen. He continued, "It says here the German team removed all the panels in less than a day and a half, leaving only a few pieces of amber behind." Peen turned to Tora, "I would have thought the Russians could have done the same. I'd have to guess the Russians didn't have the right people available to remove the panels."

"Yeah, I agree, that's strange," she said.

Peen went back to reading, "Some experts argue had the Germans not removed the Amber Panels from the Summer Palace walls, they would have been destroyed by the German Army during their retreat following the Siege of Leningrad in 1944. During their forced withdrawal, the Germans plundered and scorched the inside of the Summer Palace, leaving only the walls in place." He stopped reading and said, "I don't know anything about the Siege of Leningrad. What do you know?"

"I know that the Germans surrounded Leningrad at the end of 1941," explained Tora. "Hitler wanted to destroy the city through starvation. Over a period of nine hundred days more than one million soldiers and citizens died by starvation, making it the most costly siege on a city in modern history. The Germans devastated a city that was once the heart of Russia, which was Hitler's plan. He wanted to destroy the hearts of the Russian people."

"So give me some perspective, Tora. If more than a million were killed in Leningrad, how does that compare with, say, the atomic bombings in Japan?" asked Peen.

"I don't know the answer," she replied, "you'll have to look that one up."

Peen took a minute to search Google, "Roughly 300,000 people died between the two bombings in Japan."

Tora noted, "Numbers like that just underscore how immense and unprecedented the scale of death was during World War II."

"I'm just beginning to understand that myself," agreed Peen, now searching for more information on the Siege, "it says here the German blockade successfully halted the flow of food and services into Leningrad. It also stopped people from leaving the city. So many people died that the living couldn't accurately count the dead. As bodies piled higher and the starvation situation worsened, cannibalism became a problem. A lack of heat and electricity compounded their misery. Millions more citizens would have died had the Russian Army been unable to force the Germans to retreat in 1944, which saved the city. There's a Russian saying: *Troy fell, Rome fell, Leningrad did not fall.*"

Eyeing Tora, Peen said, "If I ever learned this in high school, I forgot it."

Tora nodded her head in agreement, "Me too."

Peen switched back to the Amber Panel website, "After removing the Amber Room in 1941 the German Army sent it, along with other valuable artifacts, to Dr. Alfred Rhode, the curator for the Prussian Fine Arts Museum at the Königsberg Castle. Apparently, Rhode was more than just a museum curator; he was the world's expert on amber, having authored several books on the topic during the 1930s. One of his books was titled *Amber — the German Material*, which hints at his perception that amber was somehow uniquely German. It says here that Rhode felt an immense sense of pride, because he was curating the world's best example of amber art: The Amber Panels. After receiving the panels, Rhode installed them onto the walls of the Lovis Corinth Gallery in the Königsberg Castle. Then, the museum printed postcards and distributed them around the country. German newspapers carried front-page articles about them. One paper claimed German soldiers saved the panels from being destroyed within the wrecked castle of Catherine the Great."

Tora guffawed, "That's like a bank robber entering a bank, stealing money, torching the building and then releasing a statement claiming he saved the money from the fire!"

Peen added, "Thank goodness for the German Army! Can you imagine how many items would have been damaged if they hadn't been there to save the artifacts? Nothing like a little disinformation."

"Right?" exclaimed Tora.

Peen looked back at the phone, "Under Rhode's care, the panels were repaired to a reasonable degree. At some point during Rhode's tenure, Hitler contacted Rhode and requested the panels be delivered to Berlin. Despite having sent other artifacts to the Führer, Rhode, in a show of defiance, declined the request. How Rhode defied Hitler on this matter and survived isn't clear, but apparently Dr.

Alfred Rhode's passion for the panels and his motivations for saving them weren't in lockstep with the Nazis."

"He defied Hitler?" said Tora, surprised, "pretty ballsy. I sure wish I could have listened in on *that* conversation!"

Peen took another swig of water and resumed reading, "During 1944, German losses accumulated rapidly, while the Allies grew stronger. The D-Day landing on June 6th, 1944, along with the Allies' southern advance from Italy, added to Germany's growing challenges. In Russia, the Eastern Front had grown to nearly 3,000 miles. The changes forced Germany to fight a two-front war and losses became more frequent. For most of the war, Königsberg had escaped damage, but on August 26 and 27, 1944, the British finally launched a major attack on the city, killing many people and destroying several areas of the city; however, the bombing left Königsberg Castle and Altstadt, the old city center, nearly intact. Because of the bombing, Rhode ordered most of the castle's art packed and taken down into the subterranean parts of the castle. High on his list were the Amber Panels. Since the panels hung in the castle, rather than being a permanent fixture like they had been in Russia, packing them took less time. In only one day, thirty-one crates of panels were safely stored below ground."

Peen stopped reading. They'd arrived at the Hood Canal floating bridge. On either side of the bridge, calm gray water shimmered in the summer sun. Looking west, the Olympic Mountain's snow-capped peaks stood high above the surrounding dark green forests. After they crossed the bridge, the forest encroached on the highway once more.

Tora said, "Hey mister manservant, no lollygagging. Keep reading!"

"Leslie warned me you were demanding," teased Peen.

"She said what?" responded Tora, before realizing he'd made that up.

Peen continued, "Dr. Rhode's foresight saved the panels. Two days after the first bombing, a second series of bombings by 179 British planes loaded with highly incendiary bombs destroyed most of the city center, the old Cathedral on Kneiphof Island, and much of outlying Königsberg. The destruction and winds were so fierce people were sucked into flames or had their clothes ripped from their bodies. Over 200,000 people lost their homes that night and for weeks life came to a halt in the eight-hundred-year-old city. The Gautleiter of East Prussia, Erich Koch, who served directly under Hitler, ordered people to stay and rebuild the city. Koch and Hitler expected Königsberg to be defended at all costs."

"What's a Gautleiter?" asked Tora.

"Just a sec while I look that up," said Peen as he tapped on the phone's screen. He read, "Originally, the position of Gautleiter coordinated regional Nazi Party events. However, the position evolved into one of immense power. In Koch's case he was, for all practical purposes, King of East Prussia, a kingdom of his own under the blessing of the Führer."

"You know, that sounds exactly like King Frederick and his son under the Holy Roman Empire three centuries earlier!" said Tora. "See, history does repeat itself, whether you know the history or not, and I'm sure many people in Königsberg knew their Prussian history."

Peen nodded and returned to reading about the panels, "In late January of 1945, the Russians stormed through East Prussia and surrounded Königsberg. But, the Germans in the city refused to surrender, in part because the SS would have shot them if they had. It wasn't until May 8, 1945, with Gautleiter Koch missing and ninety percent of the city destroyed, that German General Lasch relinquished the city. Upon hearing the news Königsberg had surrendered, Hitler ordered Lasch executed and his family arrested and killed."

"Was Lasch's family really killed?" asked Tora.

"It doesn't say here, but I can looked it up."

"Naw. Don't worry about it."

Peen returned to the text, "Once the Russian Army took the city, Rhode was summoned to appear before a Russian team seeking the panels. Rhode recounted how the panels were lost in a fire and guided them to the cellar where he showed them burned fragments of gilded wood and hinges. Based on this evidence, the Russians informed Moscow that the panels were destroyed, so they ended the search for them. The following day, Rhode failed to appear for a second round of questioning. The Russians searched the city, but couldn't find him. That same day a prominent local Nazi Party member signed Dr. and Mrs. Rhode's death certificates, claiming they died of dysentery. The Nazi Party member who signed their certificates was killed the same day. Soviet intelligence looked for the Rhodes' graves, but didn't find them until 1946. When the Russians opened their caskets, they were empty."

"Jeez, how much crazier could this story possibly get?" Tora wondered.

"Bizarre is what I'd call it. However, after our day today, it seems the final chapter of the panels probably hasn't been written yet," said Peen.

Tora asked him, "Does the article indicate what happened to Gautleiter Koch?"

Peen scanned through the text, "He escaped East Prussia, leaving Pillau in May 1945. He managed to make it to Hamburg where he lived under the assumed alias of Rolf Berger until 1949. Captured in Hamburg, he was sent to Poland where he was sentenced to death. However, the sentence was never carried out. His execution was continually postponed at the request of the Soviet government, because he claimed he knew the Amber Panels' location. He died in 1986 still imprisoned in Poland, proclaiming: *Where lies my treasure, there also lies the Amber Room.* Just before he died, he indicated the panels were in a brewery in Königsberg, or Kaliningrad as the city is now called, but they were never found. Paradoxically, his life depended on him not revealing the location of the hidden panels. Had he given up the panels, he would . . . "

Peen paused as a text alert interrupted his reading, "Ummm . . . you've got a text from Leslie asking if you are still having fun with that sexy man."

Peen looked up at her, "I assume she means me? Well, are you still having fun?"

Tora's face turned red. "Yeah, just ignore that text," giggled Tora trying to laugh off the awkward moment.

Peen laughed, but didn't comment, "It says here that most think Koch was lying to the very end. Several witnesses report that some time in late January of 1945, Rhode, under the supervision of Gautleiter Koch, ordered the crating and loading of the panels onto a convoy of trucks. Yet, other reports indicate that they were put on a ship that was torpedoed and sunk in the Baltic Sea. Still other rumors claim the panels were stored in a beer cellar under the city or buried in mine shafts. All these competing theories have kept treasure hunters, intelligence officers, and reporters busy for decades."

"And," added Peen, "I'm sure this is no surprise to you by now, Tora, several people have died investigating the panels' disappearance. One famous European reporter named George Stein earned his fame during the 1980s uncovering plundered loot. In 1987, he was found dead next to a scalpel and two pairs of scissors, with several slices to his abdomen. It was rumored he'd been spreading secrets about the panels, so he was executed . . . uh oh, there's another alert. Your battery is down to five percent."

"Oh crap. And I don't have my charger with me either. Better shut it down for now. The battery doesn't last much longer once it hits that level."

Clicking the top button, the screen went black. He looked over at Tora as she concentrated on the road. His body was tired, but his mind was spinning. Peen turned his gaze back to the road and its undulating, hypnotic terrain carved by glaciers long ago. He leaned against the passenger door and closed his eyes.

He began thinking about his life. This crazy quest with Tora to find his uncle was just another odd experience after several years of unexpected life changes. When his business crashed during the downturn, he'd had to downsize his entire life. He sold his Indian Motorcycle, his power tools, and the runabout boat he'd used for fishing. His father had bequeathed him an entire household of stuff, which he'd kept in a storage locker. Sadly, that went too. He'd thrown sentimentality out the window and forced himself to be practical. In fact, he had little desire for stuff any more. He found the so-called American Dream too stressful, a burden. After spending time away from the work world and traveling around the country, he didn't want to work hard just to own stuff any more.

"What are you thinking about so deeply, partner?"

"Oh, are we partners now, Tora?"

"I'd say we are partners in crime at the very least."

"Well then, partner, I was just thinking about my crazy life," Peen responded. Then he quickly changed the subject, "But I really need to focus on our situation. Where could my uncle be if he's not in Port Townsend? What did happen to the panels?"

"Let's hope he's learned a lesson from Gautleiter Koch," said Tora. "If Koch told the Soviets where the panels were hidden, they would have had no reason to keep delaying his execution. Likewise, if someone has your uncle, he'd better not reveal the location of the panels or what he knows. His knowledge of the panels is his ace-in-the-hole, just like it was for Koch. Maybe that's where you come in. They need you to make him reveal the panels' location."

"Could be," acknowledged Peen.

"As for Koch," continued Tora, "if the panels really were in a brewery, it is doubtful he could have found them again. The Soviets razed most of the city after the war. So, even if Koch knew where the panels might have been, the city he'd known no longer existed."

"Why put them in a brewery at all, Tora?"

"Breweries used to have underground curing rooms that had cool and stable environments. They made excellent places to store and preserve art. In fact, the Germans hid art in underground areas all over Germany: in salt mines, gold and silver mines, basements, and caves, any safe place they could find."

"So, what do you think happened to the Amber Panels?" asked Peen.

"I think there are at least three possibilities. One, the panels were moved by convoy a short distance and then buried. Two, the panels were convoyed to a train where they were railed to a special location, probably a mine. Three, the panels were convoyed to a waiting ship. Germany's infrastructure was imploding near the end of the war, so moving the artifacts a long distance by truck was impractical. Though the panels were an important artifact, I doubt the Germans could afford to send a convoy of trucks on a long drive. So, I think there's a high probability that Koch was correct in his statement that the panels were hidden in the cellar of a Königsberg brewery."

"Sounds reasonable to me," agreed Peen.

"Yep," replied Tora, "and maybe your uncle stumbled onto an old map that shows the distinct locations of businesses within the city, or perhaps a list of all the breweries up to 1945 that he can globally position using today's maps."

"Okay, if that's true Tora, then how did those assholes chasing us get involved?"

"That I don't know. Your guess is as good as mine, Peen," said Tora.

"And I don't have any good guesses," he responded, "but, let me ask you this, are you sorry that you missed your party."

"No way," countered Tora. "I would have paid good money to go on this adventure."

"Really? Does that mean I can charge you next time?" he joked.

"Next time? Let's see how this turns out first."

"Well, only twenty minutes to Port Townsend," said Peen, "I guess we'll find out how it ends pretty soon."

CHAPTER 17: DANA WILFERT

Agent Michael Jorden drove his white Jeep Grand Cherokee down Seattle's Capitol Hill on Denny Way toward Professor Rogers' apartment. Evening commuters clogged every arterial. While stopped at a red light, his phone beeped. He glanced at the screen and learned there'd been a shooting near the Pacific Science Center. It immediately caught Jorden's attention because he knew that was only a few blocks from Peen's uncle's place. He decided to head there in case it involved Peen.

As traffic moved forward, he reviewed all that had happened so far. Following the call from Officer Jacobs about Gristo's death, Jorden had gone to the hospital and investigated the scene. He'd discovered Gristo had been shot once in the head and found the bullet lodged in the mattress. Unfortunately, the staff had contaminated the rest of the physical evidence while attempting to save the man's life.

A security camera focused on the third floor nurses' station recorded Peen walking by, but it didn't cover enough of the hallway to show him entering or leaving Gristo's hospital room. When Jorden requested footage from other cameras, the head of security had explained that two other cameras with better angles were tampered with shortly before the killing.

Jorden recalled the head of security explaining, "all we can see is a hand reaching to the camera and a finger smearing grease onto the lenses."

"Someone took the time to mess with the cameras and no one noticed?" Jorden had replied.

Security explained that two nurses had identified the man as a six-foot tall Caucasian man with a beard. At the time, nothing about him stood out, because he was the wearing the proper uniform.

"And nobody noticed the cameras go blurry?"

Security responded by telling him that they'd had a higher priority: the hospital's central oxygen system had stopped working. They figured the cameras could wait until later."

Jorden remembered the frustration he'd felt. He suspected the mystery maintenance man had created the oxygen problem as a diversion.

After he'd finished with security, Jorden had left the hospital wondering if Peen was capable of killing Gristo. If that were the case, where did he get the gun?

Jorden was also suspicious of Damon Kant, but was Damon really cold-blooded enough to kill his own man? Jorden was left with more questions than answers.

***

When Agent Jorden arrived at the scene of the Seattle Center shooting, police were still actively investigating the area. Jorden explained his purpose and requested a quick briefing with the lead officer. A few minutes later an officer named Jan Camplette shared what she knew.

"At approximately 5:15pm witnesses say that as a man and woman ran by the front of the minivan, shots were fired into it. Inside the minivan were forty-year old Dana Wilfert and her daughter Brianna. Brianna was the driver and Dana was sitting behind her in the middle seat of the van. Brianna was not wounded, but Dana was pronounced dead at the scene. Based on the evidence, we estimate at least three shots were fired. Unfortunately, witnesses can't agree on how many shots they heard or where they originated. When the gunfire started, most witnesses fell to the ground. Only a few could provide anything helpful. One witness saw people running in all directions. Another witness heard people yell, doors slam, and a car roar away."

"Where's the minivan?" asked Jorden.

Ms. Camplette pointed and said, "It's still parallel-parked along the sidewalk over there."

Jorden squinted at the vehicle parked by itself against the curb. From where he was standing across the street he could only see the driver's side. Beyond the minivan a secondary entrance led into the heart of the Seattle Center. To the right of that was the Science Center's loading dock. To the left was the Seattle Children's Theatre.

"Where's the daughter, Brianna?" Jorden asked.

"She's in the ambulance getting checked for wounds and being treated for shock," responded the officer.

"Who's your best witness?"

"Agent Jorden, that would be the deceased's son Garrison. He's right over there," said Camplette motioning at a fourteen year-old boy sitting nearby. "He says he saw the glass on the minivan explode. His father, Ken, should be here soon."

Jorden thanked the officer and approached the boy. He was slumped on the curb, arms wrapped around his legs pulling them close to his chest. His hair was cut short, probably for summer. He wore a gray t-shirt and red shorts. Jorden introduced himself and asked the young man what he'd seen.

"It was horrible," Garrison began, sniffling. "We'd stopped here so I could run in and buy tickets for the Imax movie. I was like running back with the tickets in my hand. I was so happy. I'd spent the last month mowing the old woman's lawn across the street so I could pay for the tickets myself. I was running fast because Mom said we were late for dinner with Dad. I wasn't far from the van when I heard sirens. They got louder and louder."

"That's good Garrison. Do you mean you were running back from the Science Center ticket booth along that walkway?" asked Jorden as he pointed to the pathway between the Children's Theatre and the Science Center.

"Yes sir. And with all the sirens, I was paying extra close attention. It seemed like the police were coming in our direction. Then I noticed a man followed by a woman run across the street and pass in front of our van. Then they ran down the sidewalk past our van. After that they ran that way," explained Garrison, pointing at the Science Center's loading dock, "they looked like they were running as fast as they could."

"Did the man look like this?" asked Jorden, showing him a picture of Peen.

"Yes, that could have been him."

"What happened next, Garrison?"

"Just as the lady was passing by the van, I heard loud noises like gun shots. The window on the sliding door blew out at the same time. It like all happened at once."

"Garrison, what did the man and woman do when they heard the gun shots?"

"They kept running."

"Garrison, was the man or woman hit by any bullets?"

"I don't know," the young boy replied.

"Did you see who fired the gun?"

"No sir. After the glass exploded out of the minivan, I quit running. Then I saw the glass on the ground and the blood and could hear Brianna screaming and saw Mom leaning over and I just couldn't imagine it was all real. It makes no sense. Why would someone shoot my mom?"

Garrison looked at Jorden, but Jorden shook his head, "I don't know. It doesn't make sense to me either."

The young man nearly cried, then took a breath and composed himself, "And then I looked through the broken window into the minivan. Mom's head was resting against the door. I saw blood, but, it didn't seem real. She was alive only minutes ago. The next thing I remember is my sister Brianna crying."

Tears began steaming down Garrison's face. The young man soon became inconsolable and was unable to give any more information.

After a medic came to examine Garrison, Jorden approached Officer Camplette again and asked if the police had arrived *prior to the shooting.* She confirmed that and explained the police had been responding to a trespassing call at a nearby shelter. Then she directed Jorden to Carolyn Harper who was standing a few feet away.

Harper identified Peen and described Tora, at the same time explaining all that had happened earlier. From Ms. Harper's interview, Jorden concluded that Damon must have chased Peen and Tora into the shelter. After the two of them left the shelter, Damon or his men shot at them as they passed by the minivan. Since it appeared they were running away from where Edmund Rogers' apartment was located, Jorden concluded they must have been there as well. It was time to pay the building's manager a visit.

***

Jorden pushed the buzzer next to a first-floor apartment door with a plaque on the door that read *manager.* A feminine voice answered from the other side of the door, sounding happy someone was there, "Just a minute please. I'll be right there."

Moments later an older woman in a Seattle Sounders bikini opened the door.

"Oh, I'm sorry," said a flustered Jorden. Unsure what to say, he gulped and presented his badge for her, "I'm Agent Michael Jorden of the FBI. Did I interrupt something?"

"No, No. I was just getting dressed before I came to the door. Oh, okay, the FBI? How wonderful! I'm Stella Campinelli and I'm the manager here. Is your name like Michael Jordan the basketball player?" she inquired.

Her stance reminded Jorden of a teakettle. One hand gripped the edge of the open door near her head while the other hand rested on her popped hip as if to say, *here I am boys, what do you think?*

"Yes, well no, my name is spelled with an *e*. It's Jorden with an *e*."

"Oh yes, of course. What can I do for you Mr. Jorden with an *e*?"

"I'm looking for the apartment of Professor Edmund Rogers. I know he lives here. Can you take me there?"

"Why I'd love to! Anything to help out the FBI. I'm sure he isn't there right now, but we can check anyway. We are close friends you know. Let me grab my keys, Mr. Jorden," she said emphasizing the *e*. After getting her keys, she walked him to the elevator.

He asked her, "Has anyone else been here to see the Professor today?"

"Why yes, as a matter of fact, his nephew Peen dropped by earlier. I ran into him and that lovely friend of his in the hallway maybe an hour ago. He's such a good boy. Well, I guess he's a man, but I will always think of him as a good boy. Did you know his face is all scratched up? The poor boy," she remarked as she walked into the elevator and pressed the third floor button.

Jorden followed her inside, "As a matter of fact I also spoke with Peen today. I know all about his face. Do you know the woman's name?"

"Okay, I was just trying to think of what that was. My memory has always been so bad. Oh, I wish there was a memory pill. Someone really needs to invent one, don't you think?"

"Ma'am, in my line of work, that would by very handy."

"Oh, Mr. Jorden, don't called me ma'am. It makes me feel old. Call me Stella, please," she said sweetly.

"Stella it is. Think of her name yet, Stella?"

"Her last name was Armstrong. That part is easy. As soon as I heard her name it made me think of that bicycle fellow. It's her first name I was trying to remember. I think it was Oria, like Victoria? No, okay, wait, it sounded short for Victoria. Yes, her name was Tora. Tora Armstrong. Such an unusual name, don't you think? Tora. She was nice. She reminded me of my niece, Becky."

"Tora Armstrong," said Jorden, typing the information into his phone as they exited the elevator on the third floor, "are you sure?"

"Well, as sure as I can be. That's how I remember Peen introducing her, but as I said, my memory it terrible. It could use a boost."

"What did Tora Armstrong look like?"

As Stella escorted Jorden down the hallway to Professor Rogers' apartment, she described Tora, "Peen's lady friend had fair skin. She was medium height, maybe five-foot six, blond pony tail, and cute as a button. She had a medium build and wore a t-shirt and jeans. She seemed a little conservative in her pants, but then I prefer shorts myself."

"Very good," said Jorden. The description matched the one given by Carolyn Harper, more or less.

"What's all this about anyway?" asked Stella.

"Stella, I really can't comment on it. However, I can say that either the Professor or Peen or both might be in trouble. Do you know where Peen went after he left here?"

"As far as I know, Peen and Tora are still in the apartment. I never saw them leave."

"Anything else memorable about your conversation?"

"Okay, well," said Stella, wondering if she should say anything more. She didn't want to violate Peen's trust. Choosing to keep some details to herself she added, "After introducing his friend, Peen said he wanted to know if Edmund was home. Peen drops by occasionally, so it didn't seem that unusual."

"Anything else? Any other place he might be heading?"

"No no, not that I remember," answered Stella.

As they approached the apartment they saw the damaged entry door. She commented, "Well isn't that unusual? I wonder what happened?"

"Stay back, Stella," ordered Jorden, as he drew his gun.

Stella backed away from the door until she felt her body press against the corridor's far wall.

"This is the FBI. If there is anyone inside, please respond," shouted Jorden.

Hearing nothing, he stepped cautiously through the debris and explored each room until he was satisfied the apartment was empty.

"Stella, can you come in here? Do you know the apartment well? Is there anything out of place? Please don't touch anything!"

From the hall she yelled, "As a matter of fact, I know Edmund's place very well." She stepped inside and examined the living area. "This is certainly odd. It's clean! He's usually so messy. I can't tell if anything is missing because it looks so different."

Stella walked into the bedroom, noticing the window to the fire escape was ajar, "Well, okay, that's not right! Maybe Peen and Tora left using the fire escape, though I can't imagine why." She walked over to the window, "Mr. Jorden, can I shut this window?"

"No, please don't. This is very possibly a crime scene. We need to examine it more closely."

Walking back into the living area, Stella surveyed the walls, "You know, that painting on the wall right there is askew. That's not like Edmund to leave a painting that way. He told me it's very old and had something to do with some amber panels."

"Hmmm, the Amber Panels again," mumbled Jorden.

"What did you say Mr. Jorden?"

"Nothing, Stella. Just thinking. When I spoke with Peen earlier today he mentioned the Amber Panels. Do you know anything about them?"

"Not really. All I know is that the Professor was curious about them. He told me the story of them, but that was all. To be honest, it was all pillow talk. I just enjoyed hearing him talk, no matter what the subject. I never paid that close of attention."

"Very good. I think that's all for now. I will send over a team to sweep the room for evidence right away. They'll be here soon."

As they stepped back into the hallway, Stella said, "I'd better call the handyman and get this door fixed. When can I do that, Agent Jorden?"

"I couldn't say for sure, Stella."

Turning to him, more serious this time, she asked, "Do you think they are okay? What's happening here?"

"I can't say, because I don't know. Can I have your phone number? I will have my team call you when they arrive or if I have any more questions."

"Sure thing, Mr. Jorden. I will help any way I can."

"Thanks. Here is my business card in case you think of anything else. If you hear from Peen or Edmund, please call me immediately. Their lives may be in danger."

After adding Stella's phone number to his contact list, she walked him to the elevator. Jorden plotted his next move. He hoped Tora Armstrong's name would prove useful. He needed to determine the connection between her and Peen.

Chapter 18: Ian Cadmeyer

"Welcome to Port Townsend, Washington's Victorian Seaport and Arts Community," Peen read aloud to Tora. After they passed the city's entry sign, the evergreen trees lining State Highway 20 slowly yielded to homes and businesses. The road meandered down a bluff revealing a scenic view of the bay and the open water of Admiralty Inlet beyond. Soon the highway transitioned to Water Street as they entered the historic city's downtown area. To his right Peen looked at the ferry dock for the Whidbey Island ferry.

"Pull over here for a second," said Peen pointing to an empty parking spot along the road. "Cadmeyer's place has to be somewhere near here."

Tora came to a stop while Peen tapped on her phone. To conserve power, they hadn't been using the GPS. Peen checked a map for the exact location, while Tora looked out her window. The mid-June sun wouldn't set for another hour and downtown Port Townsend was humming with evening activity. Tora watched a group of teenage girls with ice cream cones giggle their way down the sidewalk. Behind the girls, a well-dressed elderly couple walked briskly as if late for some event. Along the opposite side of the street, a young man with long hair that dropped below his shoulders softly peddled a pink beach cruiser, oblivious to the cars. He appeared to be in no great hurry.

"It feels earlier than quarter to eight," noted Tora.

Peen didn't hear her, instead he responded, "1008 Water Street is two blocks north of us on the left hand side. Let's go!"

Pulling back into the street Tora asked, "Where's the battery at on the phone?"

"I believe," responded Peen, "the battery is on the back of the phone." Peen dramatically held up the phone and flipped it to show her the back. He added, "Well, I can't really see it, but I suspect it's in there somewhere."

"You knooowwww what I mean, mister!"

Peen laughed in response, "Yeah, I know. The battery is at three percent. It'll be dead soon."

They passed through an intersection. Peen looked across the street and spied a three-story brick building that filled half of the block. They continued along Water Street until Peen shouted, "Look, there it is, Bernstein Fine Arts. It's between the Palace Hotel and the Wine Seller. It's got an OPEN sign, too."

Tora made a left onto Tyler Street, a block-long side street that dead-ended at the foot of the bluff. She pulled the Falcon into an angled parking space. As they started walking, Tora said, "This town is certainly narrow. Look, this street is even shorter on the other side."

And indeed it was shorter, ending after a half-block at the water's edge. Tora and Peen walked passed the Palace Hotel, a Victorian three-story red brick building on the corner wrapped by carefully pruned street trees.

The hotel's entrance was marked by a red and white striped awning and flanked by American and Canadian flags. Pots of colorful flowers bordered the sidewalk. Charmed, Tora remarked, "Oh, that's pretty!"

Just past the hotel was a white storefront door with a painted sign above it that read *Bernstein Fine Arts*. The tinkle of a small bell announced their entry. Inside, instead of the amber-related items he expected to see, he saw walls filled with paintings that satisfied a wide variety of tastes. Some were abstract, just swirls of color, and others were classic still-lifes, portraits or landscapes. In the rest of the store, beautiful cabinetry, sculptures, chairs, and tables crowded the space. It seemed part museum, part antique store. The smell of dust and old furniture polish lingered in the air.

A man emerged from the back and approached them. A little taller than himself, Peen estimated he was six foot one or two. He stood straight, but moved carefully among the items. His bushy gray mustache widened as he smiled, apparently happy to see customers. Despite an air of vitality, he appeared tired, ready to be finished for the day. His hair was full, a blend of blond and gray that gave him a youthful appearance from a distance. He wore a light gray V-neck sweater over a white shirt and dark Levis, a casual contrast to the formality of the surrounding items.

"I'm sorry, but it's almost eight o'clock. I'll be closing soon unless there's something you're particularly interested in viewing?"

Tora stepped toward him extending her hand, "Hi Professor Cadmeyer, it's me, Tora Armstrong. We've met a few times at the University of Washington Humanities academic functions."

Peen watched Cadmeyer study Tora. A look of uncertainty appeared on his face. It was quickly replaced by a warm look of recognition.

"Of course, Tora. Call me Ian. Professor is a little too stuffy for me these days. Yes, I remember you. I must say seeing you outside the hallowed halls of academia threw my abacus off a bit," said Cadmeyer, pointing to his head. "I'd call it a computer, but my poor brain isn't nearly that responsive. My goodness, when did we last meet?"

"Last autumn at the faculty get-together. I was too deep in the throes of my classwork to attend the spring party."

"Oh, good. Are you ready to tackle your dissertation?"

"As a matter of fact, I am. Everyone on my dissertation committee is ready to sign off on it, except for Professor

Rogers, which brings us to the reason for our visit." She turned to Peen, "this is Professor Rogers' nephew, Peen."

"Of course, of course," interrupted Ian, grabbing Peen's hand and shaking it, "but I know you as Ulysses. Do you still go by Peen? Forgive me. It's been quite a while since we've seen each other. Did you know your uncle still refers to you by your given name? "

Peen gave a sigh, then a wry smile as Tora turned to look at him, her eyebrows raised. With Tora's look, Ian guessed Peen had kept his given name a secret from her.

"It's okay, Ian," said Peen, "I tried to explain to Uncle Edmund that I'd legally changed my name, but he likes the connection the name has with Mom and Dad, which is why I kept Ulysses as my middle name."

"Peen Ulysses Rogers?" exclaimed Tora.

"Guilty as charged."

"I'm afraid I'm guilty as well. My apologies, Peen."

"Really, it's okay. Ms. Armstrong and I have become good friends over the past three hours."

"Has it only been three hours Peen? I feel like I've known you at least six."

"Being chased and breaking laws will do that," said Peen, "but all joking aside, we need to have a serious conversation. Have you seen my uncle?"

"Hold on. I'm going to close up for the night." Ian walked over to lock the door. He flipped the sign from OPEN to CLOSED and turned down the lights. Pointing to a doorway at the rear of the store he said, "Why don't you two head upstairs to my loft and make yourselves at home while I set the alarm down here."

Peen followed Tora up a long slender staircase that ended at a second floor landing and a door. Peen opened the door and the pair stepped into the loft. Scuffed softwood floors were partly covered by a long oriental rug that led them to the loft's center. On their near left was a butter-colored interior wall, probably the bedroom, where three landscape paintings hung in lavish gilded frames. Against the far right wall, beyond what was most likely the bathroom, was a galley-style kitchen. To this side of the kitchen stood an old library table with claw-foot legs surrounded by not-quite-matching chairs.

"Elegantly shabby," offered Tora.

Peen surveyed the loft's original red brick walls half-covered by bookcases and artwork. The paintings were colorful, mostly modern. Peen stared at a large painting of an underwater diver suspended beneath a rippled surface.

"Well, not *that* shabby," countered Peen.

Just then Ian Cadmeyer stepped through the door and turned on some lights.

Peen and Tora immediately looked up, their eyes drawn to three huge chandeliers that hung nearest the loft's window-wall above the living and study areas. It was then they realized the ceiling soared higher in that part of the loft, maybe sixteen feet

"It's a beautiful effect, isn't it? Those chandeliers have inlaid amber pieces that reflect the light and cast a warm glow. I love this space," said Ian proudly, "can I get you something to drink? Water, wine, soda?"

"Water would be great, thanks!" responded Tora.

"Me too," seconded Peen.

Peen and Tora sat in upholstered chairs opposite a dark leather couch with a worn depression at one end surrounded by books, tablets, pencils and reading glasses. Beneath their feet was a large rectangular oriental rug, blue and gray.

Ian delivered their water, took a seat in his usual chair, a glass of wine in hand, and asked, "Alrighty then. Did you two really just meet or are you pulling an old man's leg?"

"Nope, we weren't joking," replied Tora, "and we really do need to find Professor Rogers. He may be in danger."

With that, she and Peen told him about the Amber Panels, Damon, and all that had transpired. As they talked, the sun dropped lower in the western sky, washing the buildings of Port Townsend in a glow that matched the amber ambience of Ian's loft.

✳✳✳

At the conclusion of their story, Ian walked to a phone and dialed a number. The call went to voicemail, "If you get this message, Edmund, please call me back," said Ian.

He returned to the sitting area and perched himself on the arm of a couch.

"So do you know were Professor Rogers is?" asked Tora.

"No, I don't. But he could still be at his house. He's been known to shut off all communication when he's in the middle of a project. He can disappear for days."

"So you aren't surprised he didn't answer the phone?"

"Not at all. I suggest you run over there. He bought the house with twenty acres of land several years ago. It's on Marrowstone Island near Fort Flagler, about thirty minutes from here by car," explained Ian.

"Do you know the address?" requested Peen, "I can't believe he didn't tell me about the house."

"Well, he needed a safe house," replied Ian. He formed his thoughts then spoke deliberately, "I am quite familiar with the Amber Panels . . . chased them for years myself. Truth be told, I was the one who got Edmund interested in them in the first place. But while I became convinced they would never be found, your uncle embraced the search with increasing zeal. If he's in trouble, I'm afraid I bear some responsibility for that."

"Do you know if he found a clue to their location? Why do you think Damon would attempt to kidnap me?"

"I don't know if he found the panels. I do know his search for them yielded other pieces of missing art," admitted Ian. He drew a big breath and began," I know this because he saved my livelihood when the recession hit in 2007. You see, I retired in 2002 and moved up here to start this antique and fine art shop, putting most of my retirement money into it. Despite giving up my search for the panels, I still have a fondness for them. The German word for amber is bernstein, which I thought was perfect for a fine art shop."

Ian took a sip of wine, then continued, "At first, my decision to open this place was validated by a brisk business. But in 2007 everything changed. That summer customers stopped walking through my door. Sales plummeted, forcing me to dismiss all three of my sales people. No one was spending money. I used my savings to keep the doors open. In 2009, during a third miserable summer, Edmund visited, as he did most every year. When he asked how the antique store was doing, I admitted to him that if I didn't get some business I'd be forced to close my doors. Edmund told me he could help. He revealed he'd discovered a number of looted artifacts from World War II and suggested I use my shop as a middleman between restorers and himself. His only request was that we keep the transactions quiet. He assured me at the proper time these would be sold or returned to the rightful owners. *Most importantly*, he told me, *we are saving and restoring these old pieces.*"

"Where did he find the art?" asked Tora.

"I never asked. One look at the pieces and I knew they were European and very nice, but none were obvious masterpieces. However, as you know Tora, millions of pieces disappeared during World War II and are still floating between private collectors. I suspected these were pieces brought back by Americans. The truth is, if they were looted, the original owners are likely long dead. Peen, I have always known your uncle as an honorable man, so I trusted him. I still trust him."

"And he never said anything more about the panels?" asked Peen.

"If he found the panels, he would have kept them secret until he and the panels were safe. Too many people connected to them have disappeared or died. We agreed early on that the less the other knew, the safer we would be. After all, there are many serious researchers looking for the panels, along with treasure hunters, reporters, the Germans, former East German Stasi officials, the KGB and former members of the Soviet System's MVD. Those latter groups don't screw around. In fact, they're a huge problem, because they spread a great deal of disinformation."

"What kind of disinformation were the different groups promoting?" asked Tora.

"The answer is complicated. Let me step back for a moment and provide a wider context. For me this didn't begin as a search for the panels, but as research into the city of Königsberg, a city that was the heart of my PhD dissertation. Königsberg began life as a military city built by the Teutonic knights in the thirteenth century. Soon the city overtook both sides of the Pregel, or Pregolya River as it is called now, and Kant Island, where the Königsberger Cathedral and Immanuel Kant's tomb are located. In fact, foot traffic across the Pregel uses Kant Island as a stepping stone, a central connection point. It had been that way for hundreds of years, because seven different bridges used to connect two islands in the Pregel River with the mainland. The bridges themselves became a favorite debate topic among the citizens of Königsberg. The big challenge was, could a person walk along a single trajectory and cross each of the seven bridges once without doubling back over a bridge?"

"I'm having a problem picturing that," admitted Peen.

Ian walked over to his bookcase and retrieved two books. One, a photographic retrospective on Königsberg, he handed to Tora. The other book he opened and handed to Peen. He pointed to a diagram of the seven bridges problem. "Peen, start at point A. See how the path can't cross *all seven bridges* and *end at point B* without crossing a bridge twice?"

"And there's no solution?" asked Peen as he futilely tried different paths with his finger.

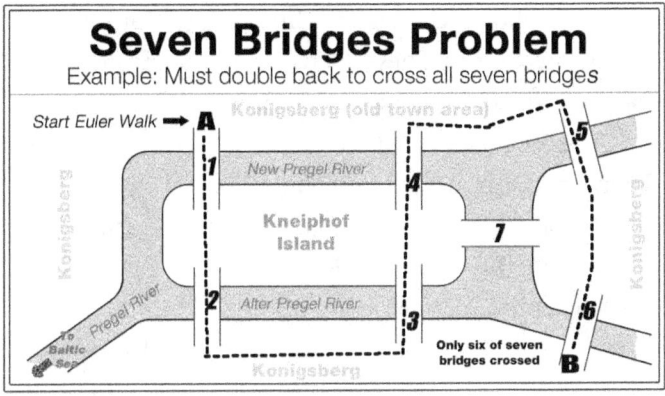

Ian explained, "There was much debate about the issue until Leonhard Euler answered the problem mathematically in the 1700s, by demonstrating that it was impossible. It is called the *Seven Bridges Problem*. Over time the term *seven bridges* or *sieben brucken auf Deutsch* came to represent an impossible situation. Sort of like our saying, *we are between a rock and a hard spot*. In fact, by solving the bridge problem, Euler went on to create an entire field of mathematics known as graph theory. But, of course, the Seven Bridges problem is only a footnote in the long history of the city, because for centuries the cosmopolitan city sat at the nexus of Russia and Northern Europe and was a center for cultural interchange. It was flush with unique amber resources and became popular among artists, especially amber craftsman. With a large population, active trading community, one of the largest libraries in Europe and one of the earliest tram systems, it stood as a great modern European city even though it had only one tenth of the population of Berlin."

Tora, who'd been leafing through the Königsberg book interrupted him, "These pictures are beautiful. The castle has a fascinating mix of architectural styles."

"Yes. You can see why I fell in love with the former city. Königsberg translates as the King City and Hitler understood the symbolism of it. The day before the Nazi Party won the German election, Hitler gave a dramatic speech from Königsberg, the first live speech to be broadcast throughout Germany. He rallied there, because he knew it was an ancient coronation city and I believe he wanted to be viewed as a King. Unfortunately, the bombings in the summer of 1944 damaged most of Königsberg. After difficult fighting and more destruction, the Soviets captured the city and forced the remaining citizens, perhaps 100,000 people, to leave. Later, the USSR flattened the city, replacing the historic buildings, streets, and culture with Soviet versions. You can hardly blame the Russians for burying a symbol of German strength, since the Russians endured way more death and destruction at the hands of the Germans than any other country during World War II. After all, when you add together the deaths of French, British and the U.S. troops, the total reaches just over one million. Don't get me wrong, that's a significant number, but contrast that with an estimated *ten million* Russian soldiers who died. Estimates vary, but an additional *ten to seventeen million* Russian *citizens* died as well, resulting in a total of twenty to twenty-seven million Russian deaths during World War II."

"Wow!" exclaimed Peen, "I knew Russia had suffered. We even talked about that in the car on the way up here, but I had no idea it was anywhere near *that bad.*"

"The Germans expected the Russians would fight hard. When Hitler attacked Russia, and I say Hitler, because many of his staff did not approve of the idea, he sent three million troops, many tons of equipment, and more than a half million horses. The scope of operations was mind-boggling. For example, the Germans had almost two hundred and fifty companies of veterinarians and at the height of the war the veterinarian hospitals serviced around 100,000 horses a day. To give you another example, in June 1944 at the start of D-Day, Allies in the west were fighting fifty-nine divisions, while the Russians were fighting one-hundred and fifty-six divisions, or *three times* what the invading Allies faced. The immensity of the Eastern Front in terms of scope, death, and destruction is unequaled in the history of warfare and, I hope, will never be equaled again. That is why the Russians refer to their fight against Germany and the other Axis powers as *The Great Patriotic War.*"

Ian took another sip of wine. Although Peen was anxious leave and find his uncle, he was gripped by Ian's story.

Ian continued, "By the time the Russians reached East Prussia, they were out for revenge. Horrific acts were committed by both sides, which led to more horrific acts being committed. There was a saying among Russian soldiers, *the first wave gets the watches, the second wave gets the women, and the third wave gets what's left.*"

"And, yes," nodded Ian, reinforcing the story as true, "some Russian soldiers wore watches up and down both arms. When the Soviets surrounded Königsberg in early 1945, citizens of the city were forced by the SS to defend it to their deaths. The Russians obliged by bombing, destroying and killing people in the city until the Germans yielded. So, while I loathe the destruction of Königsberg, I understand why it happened. If the Japanese awakened a sleeping giant in the West, the Germans attacked a Russian bear in the East until the bear returned the favor, giving as good as it had gotten. Königsberg's death and the disappearance of the panels were nearly simultaneous, both beauties forever lost. In my youthful exuberance, I was certain that if I could find the panels, I could save the city, too."

"How could you save the city by finding the panels?" asked Tora.

"Oh, there was nothing rational in my thinking. I was young and naive. I felt that if I found this singular treasure, the city would embrace it, which would lead to a rebuilding of the castle and city traditions. That was in the mid-1980s and hope was blossoming. During my research, the Arm's Reduction Treaty talks began between the U.S. and Russia. Then, Gorbachev rose to General Secretary and hastened a Cold War thaw. As the geo-political borders melted, so did the informational ones. New documents about the panels emerged. Unfortunately, as we approached the 1990s, Kaliningrad, the name the Soviets gave Königsberg, got worse."

Tora interjected, "Was part of the reason for Kaliningrad's troubles related to its physical distance from the main part of Russia?"

Ian replied, "That likely had something to do with it. Just like East Prussia was a political island, separated from Germany following World War I, Kaliningrad Oblast is a satellite, disconnected from Russia. Kaliningrad Oblast is the name of the region, with Kaliningrad its largest city, and it is separated from Mother Russia by Lithuania and Poland. The only reason it is Russian at all is because the Soviets wanted a warmer Baltic naval port. It became a forgotten stepchild as Russia struggled through the 1980s, a tiny satellite whose significance diminished even more with the ending of the Cold War. By 1990, the citizens of Kaliningrad were worse off than many other Russian regions. The economy was poor, joblessness was high, and organized crime feasted off the hopelessness."

Ian paused, appearing to ponder something before continuing with the discussion.

Tora spoke up, "But, how does that fit in with the post World War II disinformation campaigns of the Russians and East Germans?"

"Oh my dear, you did ask that. Here I am off on a tangent. That's a good question. I promise I'll get to that in a moment," he replied. "By April of 1945 the Russians were inside Königsberg searching for the Amber Panels. From the day the Russian soldiers first entered Königsberg, they heard multiple stories about the panels' fate. Some claimed they were carted away after the 1944 bombings. Others said they were buried under the rubble of the castle. Still others claimed they had burned in a fire caused by the bombings of Königsberg. And therein lies the confusion for me. After a great deal of research I arrived at a crossroad. Had the mystery surrounding the panels been fueled by innocent rumors? Or had they actually been part of a web of deceit, a complex disinformation campaign directed by Dr. Alfred Rhode to throw everyone off the trail? I concluded it was the latter, yet, I also know Rhode didn't act alone in spreading disinformation. Even Dr. Rhode's death is part of the mystery."

"How so? Wasn't it obvious when he died?" asked Peen.

"You'd think so, wouldn't you? During my initial research, I learned that Dr. Rhode and his wife died in April of 1945. Later, when the Russians opened their graves, there were no bodies in them. That story was published in respected magazines and repeated elsewhere."

Tora added, "That's what we read on the way up here."

"Except, that's not what happened. Dr. Rhode lurked around the castle in April and May of 1945 before the Russian investigator Brusov identified him as the lead curator. Then, Dr. Rhode was given special access privileges, only to abuse them by burning important documents. In late June, when confronted by Brusov with a letter Dr. Rhode had written in 1944 claiming the panels were in a specially built bunker, Dr. Rhode agreed to reveal the bunker to Brusov. He took Brusov and witnesses to a building, leading them down to an underground shelter more than four stories below street level. When they arrived at the shelter, Brusov was shown several valuable artifacts, but he found no indication the panels were there.

That convinced Brusov that Dr. Rhode was purposely misleading him. When Brusov aggressively interrogated Dr. Rhode, Dr. Rhode claimed that he'd planned to move the panels in January of 1945, but couldn't find any way to transport them. So, he claimed to have stored them in the Knights Hall area of the Königsberg Castle, where they'd burned. Unbeknownst to Dr. Rhode, this is what Brusov had concluded after seeing amber remains in the heavily damaged Knights Hall. Satisfied with the explanation, and fitting Brusov's theory, Dr. Rhode's deception dovetailed with the facts to confirm the panels' fate, a fate he officially reported to Moscow. However, the Soviets kept Dr. Rhode under surveillance in Königsberg until December 1945, when he mysteriously died. So, even the time frame of Dr. Rhode's death, the central figure in the disappearance of the panels, has been reported differently by a variety of sources. And, there are no reports on what actually happened to his wife. It begs the question, how could the date of Dr. Rhode's death be such a mystery? And if that's a mystery, what else do we really know?"

Tora noted, "I explained to Peen that history is often messy. But I've never run into anything quite so messy as this story."

"Neither had I, Tora," responded Ian. "To complicate the tale further, over the years different maps surfaced indicating where the panels had been taken, all resulting in dead ends. People would claim they knew the location of the panels, then they'd deny it later. As the Cold War thawed in the 1990s, documents and sources surfaced with increasing frequency. It became a disorienting landscape of lies, half-truths and truths. The more I looked into it, the less I could tell the truth from the lies. I ultimately decided that one or all the groups were purposely disseminating misinformation to confound searchers of the panels. Frankly, it's a brilliant strategy. I became discouraged and then disenchanted, so I turned over my research to Edmund in the summer of 1995. I wished him good luck and said I would never ask him about them again. In fact, this is the first conversation I've had about the panels in many years."

Peen couldn't help himself, "This is just crazy. It's a funhouse with no exit, a puzzle with no answer."

Ian nodded and then spoke, "I'd forgotten about a quote by Winston Churchill in 1939 until you mentioned the word puzzle. Churchill once said, *I cannot forecast to you the action of Russia. It is a riddle wrapped in a mystery inside an enigma, but perhaps there is a key. That key is Russian national interest.* In this case, I suspect the Russians don't know the truth, so they've flooded the landscape with false information to insure that everyone remains confused."

Ian fell silent. Tora and Peen exchanged glances.

"Thanks for the information Ian. That was fascinating, but we really need to get going," Tora explained.

"I understand. I'm sure you are both itching to find Edmund. Hopefully he's at his house asleep or writing. His disappearance may be easily explained."

"Let's hope so. Thanks again," acknowledged Peen.

"Don't make yourself a stranger Peen, nor you Tora," replied Ian with a friendly tone. Then, more seriously, he added, "Also, I have no idea who this Damon character you told me about is, but I think you can assume the worst. Be very, very careful. And, please let me know when you find Edmund!"

"Yes sir, we will," Peen promised.

Ian quickly wrote down the directions to the Professor's house on Marrowstone Island, telling them a rusted jeep marked the entrance. With directions in hand, they exited out the back of his loft to the carport and the alley.

CHAPTER 19: SAVIOR OF KÖNIGSBERG

Ian's mind was spinning as he pulled the iron skillet from the cabinet and placed it on the stove. It had been years since he'd thought seriously about the Amber Panels, but tonight they gnawed at him anew.

He placed two sliced brats onto the heated skillet. They sizzled for a minute. Then he added fresh sauerkraut and beef broth. He covered the pan and turned the knob to simmer. He started the spaetzle noodles following his grandmother's recipe: flour, water, eggs and salt blended into a gooey batter. He wasn't one to cook often, but good spaetzle noodles were impossible to find in grocery stores, so any time he wanted them he had to make them himself.

Just as he set aside the batter to rest, the doorbell rang. He half hoped it was Tora and Peen, returning to ask more questions. He turned off the stove and moved to the door.

What did those kids forget? Maybe they need me to go with them. There. I finally admitted it. I miss the chase. I want to help. What can I do?

Thinking it was Tora and Peen, he flung the door open without checking the peephole. Three men he didn't recognize filled the doorway. All three were dressed in black windbreakers and jeans. One had a trimmed beard and the other two were clean-shaven. All three were shorter than him.

The bearded man spoke, "Excuse me sir, you wouldn't happen to be Professor Ian Cadmeyer?"

Ian answered, "Yes I am, but who are you?"

He'd said the words automatically, but already Ian wished he could take them back. How did these guys know his name or that he'd been a professor?

Damon flashed a badge, then lied, "We are with the FBI. I'm Agent Kline, this is Agent Jones, and this is Agent York. We have reason to believe that Peen Rogers came to see you. Is that true?"

Ian hesitated, wondering whether to tell the truth or lie. Ian's hesitation was all Damon needed to see.

"I'm sorry Agent Kline," answered Ian, "I've met a lot of people, but I don't recognize you and I'm very busy . . . "

A handgun interrupted Ian's answer. Damon pushed his way passed Ian. One of Damon's men, Johann, followed Damon inside and shut the door. The other stayed outside as a guard.

"Let's not waste time," said Damon firmly, "we know who you are and that you met with Peen and Tora. Do you deny this Professor Cadmeyer?"

"No," replied Ian flatly, "are you here to eliminate me like you want to eliminate Peen, Agent Kline, if that's even your real name?"

"So my reputation precedes me. True, I am not Agent Kline, but there is no need to tell you who I am," stated Damon. "I realize our tactics are crude. If you cooperate, we will leave and you will still be breathing. I am not an assassin. I experience no pleasure in torture or death, however sometimes it is useful for getting information. Besides, I want Peen alive, not dead. Our only goal is to obtain the panels and Professor Rogers has them."

"What in the world makes you think Edmund has the Amber Panels?"

"Ahhhh," said Damon. He was quite satisfied at tricking the professor, "I never said which panels. But you already know about the panels, don't you?"

Damon watched Ian hesitate. He could see him searching for the right words.

"Yes, I know about the Amber Panels. I searched for them, but gave up. There is too much disinformation to unravel. The rumors about the panels are like the spaetzle noodles over there on the stove. They interweave and stick together; the true story of the panels is an impossible mess to detangle."

Damon's satisfaction was obvious as he smiled, "Professor Cadmeyer, for the last twelve years I have hunted them also, never uncovering their true location.

However, they say that *luck is when opportunity meets preparation*. It seems my hard work finally paid off and opportunity has come my way, for I have proof the panels came to the United States."

"What?" blurted Ian, jolted by the news, "I've never heard *that* rumor!"

"Nobody had. But think, what a great hiding place! No one ever imagined the panels left the continent. However, I don't believe Dr. Rhode intended for them to come here. He was sending them to an unknown Icelandic location so that even he couldn't reveal it."

"How do you know all this?" asked Ian.

"Indirectly, Edmund Rogers helped me discover their trail. However, I believe only he knows the full secret. You must be curious about the truth?"

"I am. I'm even more curious about what you plan to do with them."

"I believe the panels are more valuable as a sign of hope than as a monetary treasure. Years ago I realized if the panels returned to Kaliningrad they might create a powerful symbol for restoring the city to its former glory. You might know that Immanuel Kant is called the Sage of Königsberg; I aspire to be the Savior of Königsberg," announced Damon arrogantly.

Admittedly, Ian felt some sympathy for Damon's cause, "I too wanted to see that happen. My dissertation was about Königsberg. I also once dreamed of seeing it restored to its former glory. But, do you believe that the end justifies the means? Wasn't Immanuel Kant more interested in the means than the end?"

"Kant wanted to follow the highest moral path for the greatest good," replied Damon, a little irritated by Ian's interpretation of Kant. "Only the greatest good is the highest moral path."

"I don't agree with your interpretation of Kant," countered Ian.

"Yes, but after studying Kant, I learned that despite his call for experience in the real world, he himself never worked to accomplish anything substantive with ordinary people whose values and interests diverge. He might not have admitted it, but his philosophical world was wholly intellectual. I deal in the real world. I pursue high moral goals that benefit many, including myself, sometimes at the expense of others. Kant understood that people need a leader, a moral guide. I am no more of a perfect moral guide than Kant was, but I try. Which is why, though I'd prefer not to hurt you, I will if I think it's necessary. In your case, it's nothing personal, really. In fact, I skimmed your dissertation on the Internet during my trip here. I appreciate your passion for the city, so I will make you a deal. Let us trade information. Professor Cadmeyer, how about a trade? I will tell you about the panels if you give me Peen and Tora's location."

Ian considered Damon's offer. He really didn't think he had a choice, "So all I have to do is tell you Peen and Tora's location? That's it?"

"That is it. Of course, you are going to lie and tell us the wrong location. I know that. I understand you don't want them hurt. We don't want to hurt them either. Our sole interest is finding the panels. But, I don't like it when people lie to me. If I find out you lied, I will come back and you'll regret it. Nothing personal."

"You've said several times now that you don't want to kill them, yet you've shot at both of them. I'm confused on that point," said Ian.

"Excellent point. But, if I wanted to kill Peen, I could have shot him at the intersection where we first met. After he started to run, I only wanted to injure him. But now, I no longer have time to waste. If he cooperates, I will not shoot him. It is that simple," countered Damon.

Ian froze his gaze. He was sure Damon was lying, but thought it useless to argue with the man. Then, an idea struck. He could tell Damon where they'd gone, yet still make it to Edmund's before Damon arrived.

"Okay, you have a deal. I will tell you exactly where I sent them. But you must promise not to hurt them. Are those conditions agreeable?"

"Yes," lied Damon, tired of this game and ready to go.

"They've gone to Edmund's house on Marrowstone Island. It's the last house on the right before Fort Flagler. There's a rusty jeep on the road next to the driveway. You can't miss it. They left shortly before you arrived."

"Thank you, Mr. Cadmeyer. And as I said, I'll tell you how the panels left Königsberg. They left by truck heading west to the Baltic. From there, they went by sea. From there, well, you'll have to wait on that. For now, of course, you won't mind if we tie you up? Johann, use the plastic ties and bind him to that pole."

"Hey, that wasn't part of the deal," argued Ian.

"True, but it was not *not* part of the deal. Besides, you are a smart man. You will escape in time and, when you do, we will be gone. Also, I'd advise you not to contact the police, because I just confirmed the police are looking for Peen," said Damon. Arista had called before their arrival to share the news that the police had issued a warrant for Peen, "Did Peen mention he shot and killed one of my men at a hospital? He was involved in another shooting of a woman as well. Did you know that there's an arrest warrant out for Peen?"

The surprise on Ian's face told Damon all he needed to know. Damon spoke, "No? He didn't tell you, did he Professor? I can assure you it is true. Therefore, if you care about Peen, do not call the police."

As Johann tied him up, Ian stared at Damon and said, "It seems you leave me with no option."

"As I promised, no harm has come to you," stated Damon. Then he asked Johann, "Done?"

"Ya. He von't be going anyvhere soon."

"Good. Let's go find those two."

Ian heard the door shut. He was alone. A short time ago his greatest concern was what to have for dinner; now he had to save the lives of Tora and Peen. While he believed Damon wasn't interested in killing Peen or Tora, he also felt Damon wouldn't hesitate to do so if necessary.

Ian knew what he had to do. First, he employed a trick he'd learned as a kid, something a doctor had warned him to stop doing or he'd ruin his joints. He held his breath and snapped his thumb out of position.

"Ouch! Boy, that hurt a lot more than it used to," Ian said as he slid his hand from the bindings. He quickly released his other hand and was free. His doctor would be relieved to know that his joint was painfully tight still.

Ian stood, grabbed his jacket, and headed for the door. He estimated it would take him fifteen minutes to reach Tora and Peen, which was approximately fifteen minutes faster than it would take Damon to get there by car.

CHAPTER 20: WILLIAM STEPHENS

Ten miles south of Port Townsend Tora steered the Ford Falcon east onto a secondary road. Though the setting sun still lit a narrow band of sky above them, the meandering country road was a dark canyon of tall evergreens and thick underbrush. The road lightened briefly as they traveled over the Marrowstone Island bridge, but the darkness quickly returned as they plunged into another stand of trees, forcing Tora to turn on the car's headlights.

"The good news is that we've just crossed onto Flagler Road," said Peen. "We should be there soon. According to your phone's map, the bridge back there is the only entrance to the island. We're at the south end of the island

and the road travels five miles due north to Fort Flagler State Park. So, unless swimming in very cold salt water is your thing, we'll be coming back this way."

"What's the bad news, Peen?"

"The bad news is your phone just shut down. The battery is dead."

"Great," sighed Tora. "So, do you know what the rusty jeep will look like?"

"Not really. All I know is Uncle Edmund used to have an old flat fender jeep like they used in the army. He named it *Not Safe*."

"I'd guess his jeep wasn't safe to drive?" asked Tora.

"Nope, just the opposite. He used to joke that my aunt, who left him years ago and didn't care for jeeping, thought there were places he *ought not to go*, as she put it, when driving; he countered that his jeep was perfectly safe for going places others *ought not to go*. So, he told me he named it *Not Safe* because he was able to go places *not safe* for others. I went jeeping with him a few times when I was a kid. I'd forgotten about that jeep."

"Sounds like you know more about jeeps than I do," said Tora. "Based on what Ian told us, the rusty jeep should be on your side of the car anyway."

"I know a little, but not much," replied Peen as he cranked his window down for a better look. A cool wind rushed inside. The grassy ditches alongside the road appeared and disappeared as the Falcon's headlights passed over driveways.

A few miles later they came to a country store where a bay, a silvery mirror, opened up to the west. The flash of water reflected blue sky with pink wisps, and then vanished as the road plunged back among the dense trees with long evening shadows.

"What a peaceful looking stretch of water that was," remarked Tora.

"Didn't you see the sign? It said that was Mystery Bay," responded Peen. "Kind of adds to the mood, doesn't it?"

Tora nodded in agreement.

Two miles later, they passed by a thick stand of trees that reached the edge of the ditch. Peen looked into them, but only saw darkness. The stand ended, followed by dense underbrush. Just then Peen shouted, "Stop. I think I just saw a reflection."

Tora stopped the car and shifted into reverse. She backed up slowly.

"There it is," said Peen. Like a prisoner held hostage in a thicket, the nose of a rusted jeep was barely visible. Near the jeep was a driveway, two dirt paths separated by a strip of grass that disappeared together into the dark.

"Is that a jeep?" asked Tora.

"That's what's left of one. There's a pretty creepy driveway next to it. I guess we ought to give it a try," suggested Peen with a shrug.

Tora shrugged back, "I guess."

She swung the Falcon into the driveway. Tora drove slowly between the trees, whose branches formed a canopy above them. They intersected a minor cross trail and continued past it. A quarter mile in, Peen spotted dim lights through the trees. A fork in the drive forced them to turn right or left.

"Let's turn to the left," suggested Peen.

Tora took the left fork, then followed it a short distance before the drive wound to the right around some trees. A two-story cedar-shingled home appeared before them. It looked more like a software executive's getaway than a professor's writing cabin. Attached to the far side of the house was a large garage of some kind.

The dirt driveway transitioned to gravel as the circle widened in front of the house, then continued on to the right. That's when Tora realized the drive was circular: either fork would have brought them here.

Tora rolled to a stop twenty feet from the front door, where she shut off the car. Three porch lights cast a soft glow over the area.

Unlike the unkempt driveway, even in the dwindling light Peen could see the landscaping and yard were trimmed and tidy, a strange contrast to the country feel of the island. All the lights were off upstairs. Downstairs, light filtered through frosted glass on both sides of the front door.

"Normally I'm not a paranoid guy, however after today I can't help but wonder if this is a trap," admitted Peen.

"I agree."

"Tora, why don't you stay with the car while I ring the doorbell. If anything bad happens, you get the hell out of here and find some help."

"Okay, but be careful!"

Peen quietly exited the car and climbed two stairs to the doorstep. He put his ear to the door and listened, but heard nothing except his pounding heart. He looked back at Tora, shrugged, and, unable to find a doorbell, rapped on the door with his knuckles. There was no answer.

He tried a second time, only louder. To his surprise, he heard the faint sound of footsteps.

"WHO'S THERE?" came a deep and forceful voice through the door, a voice Peen didn't recognize.

"My name is Peen Rogers. I know this sounds strange, but I think this is my uncle's house. However, you don't sound like my uncle. His name is Edmund Rogers, Professor Edmund Rogers."

***

William Stephens froze. Two days ago he wouldn't have feared a knock at the door, however in the last twenty-four hours his world had turned upside down. His grandfather Chester Stephens wasn't who he claimed he was. The life William knew, his tribe and his traditions had come completely undone.

Worse, the man who'd played a central role in his life, but about whom he now questioned everything, was in trouble. William didn't even know if his grandfather was still alive.

The second knock at the door was more insistent. Could it be a neighbor or friend of Edmund Rogers? He couldn't be sure of anything. Yet the person was knocking, so maybe it wasn't one of the men he feared. Trusting his instinct, he shouted, "Who's there?"

The person on the other side said it was Edmund Rogers' nephew Peen Rogers.

William responded, "Just a minute!"

Without opening the door, William snuck over to a window in an adjacent room so he could see the porch and driveway. He saw a slim, tall man in a gray hoodie and jeans standing in front of the door. An older white car sat in the driveway, but he couldn't determine the make. He saw no guns or evidence that this was anything other than what the man claimed. William decided to give the nephew a chance.

In his right hand he held the 10mm Sig he'd found in the house when searching a little earlier and walked to the door. He figured he couldn't be too careful. William tested the visitor, "If you are Edmund's nephew, then you will know his wife's name."

Peen answered without hesitation, "I think you mean the wife who divorced him. It was my aunt Emma. She left years ago."

Satisfied with the answer, William unlocked the door, then backed down the hall a ways. "The door's open," he yelled, "come in, slowly. I have a gun."

✱✱✱

Peen turned the doorknob and pushed on the door. As it swung open he saw a man with a gun about ten feet away. The man was of average height, with black hair, a dark complexion, and an intense gaze. He held the small gun firmly with his right hand. Peen noticed an unusual square-shaped scar below the man's left eye that gave him a menacing look. Peen stood still, unsure whether to step forward. Peen thought it best to start talking, "Now that you know who I am, who are you?"

"My name's William."

"Normally at this point, I'd say it's good to meet you, William, but I'm feeling a bit nervous with a gun pointed in my direction."

"Well, *normally* I'd say I'm sorry, but I've had a bad couple of days."

"I can relate to that," said Peen, "I've been shot at, nearly jailed, accused of murder, and chased for reasons I don't quite understand. My life has been anything but normal."

"Well, it seems like we have something in common."

William lowered the gun. His eyes softened as relief replaced the concern he'd felt just a minute ago, "Are you really Edmunds' nephew?"

"Yes. Do, you know who my uncle is?"

"I do. He's the one that told me where to find his gun. What I . . . "

Peen interrupted him, "My uncle owned a gun? Why don't I know any of this?"

"I know why you aren't supposed to know," responded William, "what I don't know is whether Edmund and Grandpa are alive or dead."

CHAPTER 21: CONTACT LOST

The Mariners were ahead four to nothing at the top of the sixth when Jorden's cell phone vibrated in his pocket. He retrieved his phone with a feeling of guilt as he glanced at his little brother Isaac, a twelve year-old he'd met through the Big Brother program. While Isaac munched peanuts and sipped water — no soda allowed on Jorden's watch — he read the text: *Contact Lost.*

Jorden slipped his phone back into his inside jacket pocket and returned his attention to the game from their seats behind first base. The Mariners were tossing the ball between bases while waiting for an Atlanta Brave to take the batter's box. Meanwhile, Jorden surveyed the stands. Most of the seats were empty. He glanced at the Safeco Field sign above left field and then beyond it to the

Columbia Center, Seattle's tallest building. The setting sun shone onto the western side of the skyscraper, turning it a brilliant orange.

Despite the baseball game, he couldn't stop thinking about the day's events. He was especially confused about Peen's movements. He knew Peen had been chased in the morning and later taken to the North Precinct. After that he'd gone to the hospital to see Gristo. After tracking down Tora's condominium in the University District and speaking with Tora's roommate, Leslie, Jorden learned that Peen had gone to the University of Washington to look for his uncle. There he'd met Leslie, who eventually introduced him to Tora. Leslie reported that Tora and Peen had left her condo to visit Edmund Rogers' apartment. There, the apartment manager, Stella, talked with both of them. He couldn't verify it yet, but it seemed Peen and Tora were then chased from the apartment to the women's shelter and from there to the Pacific Science Center where Dana Wilfert was killed in the minivan.

After his interview with Leslie at Tora's condo, Jorden drove directly to Safeco Field to meet Isaac, whose mother had dropped him off at the ballpark before the 7:30pm game. Jorden never cancelled on Isaac, because the kid had endured too many disappointments in his young life. So, while Jorden watched the game, his people tracked Tora's phone and then texted him updates.

He'd received his initial update at the bottom of the first inning. His phone had buzzed with a text message: *heading north toward Port Townsend/Port Angeles. Signal intermittent.*

That's strange, he thought at the time. Maybe the two were driving for Port Angeles where a ferry could take them to Canada. Or, perhaps they planned to disappear into the Olympic National Forest, making them hard to track. Jorden didn't know.

At the top of third inning, his phone had buzzed again: *Arrived in downtown Port Townsend. Stationary.* That made no sense to Jordan. Nothing he'd learned about Peen indicated any connection with Port Townsend.

During the bottom of the fifth inning, with the Mariners at bat, he'd received another message: *heading south from Port Townsend.* Jorden wondered if they were heading back to Seattle.

During the sixth inning he'd received the last text: *Contact Lost.*

Jorden puzzled over what Peen and Tora's movements meant. He began to second-guess his decision not to take a helicopter to Port Townsend, yet he didn't want to waste resources by making a useless trip, especially since they kept losing Tora's GPS signal.

He thought about the likely reasons the signal had terminated: one, the phone had no service; two, the phone was out of battery; or three, the phone was destroyed. But, it didn't really matter. The signal was lost and he had to deal with that fact. But, again, why had they gone there in the first place? And why were they heading south again? He'd issued an alert for Tora's Volkswagen, but the Port Townsend police hadn't seen it. So, how were they traveling? Maybe someone else was involved.

Jorden had too many questions and too few answers. He decided that after the game he'd take Isaac home and return to the office. That wouldn't make his wife happy, but somehow he had to find a way to locate the two fugitives.

CHAPTER 22: CHESTER STEPHENS

"Hold on a sec. I'll have Tora come in so we can compare stories," Peen said to William as he waved her inside. A moment later, Tora was walking inside the house, immensely curious. She shut the front door.

Peen introduced them, "Tora Armstrong meet William Stephens, grandson of a friend of Edmund's."

William eyes surveyed her *Artist's Do It Colorfully* t-shirt as they shook hands.

"Nice to meet you, William."

"Good to meet you, too, Tora. Let's go to the kitchen where there's more room," he suggested.

Next to the oval-shaped kitchen table Tora saw a set of sliding glass doors. Outside the glass doors a deck with plastic chairs was barely visible. To the right of table was a kitchen. The cabinets had glass fronts with light wood frames, displaying a few plates and cups, but not much else. Obviously the Professor did little entertaining. To the left was a family room with two leather reclining chairs, a fireplace and a television. On a wall near the fireplace Tora noticed a framed photograph of Professor Rogers and Peen, the two men perched on a rock, grinning, with Mount Rainier in the background.

Tora spoke, "I'd say the picture on the wall establishes the house as the professor's. I can't imagine who else would have a picture of you two."

Peen turned to look at it, "Wow! That was outside Ohanapecosh at Mount Rainier National Park. We spent a couple days camping and hiking there. Sure is strange to see the picture. I didn't know he had it . . . let me amend that comment. On any normal day this would seem strange, but since I dumped reality out the window a few hours ago, encountering the unexpected seems the norm."

William consoled Peen, "If it makes you feel any better, I've never been here either. I only arrived about twenty minutes ago."

"Where's your car?" asked Tora.

"I rode my Harley and, after checking out the place, I parked it at the state park just up the road. This long driveway looked like a trap. If I need to make a quick getaway, I figure I can escape out the back, run along the beach, and hide at the state park until things cooled down."

"So, William, why are you here?" probed Peen.

"I'm here because your uncle and my grandfather, Chester Stephens, are in trouble. They sent me to this house to get my tribe's bomb shelter plans . . . well, it turns out that it wasn't a bomb shelter, but a missile silo of some kind. Jesus, I learned my tribe isn't even real. Talk about bizarre, try growing up a proud member of the Tamanachee Indian Tribe, having your own reservation, your own culture, only to find out that none of it is real. It's nuts."

Puzzled, Tora spoke, "Hold on. I'm confused. Just how does this relate to Professor Rogers?"

William responded, "The professor and the reservation and my dad and the trouble are all linked . . . "

Tora interrupted him, "And the Amber Panels, too?"

"Huh? What you mean. What are Amber Panels?"

"Clearly, we need to exchange information. We are all part of a bigger puzzle that none of us understands," said Tora. She explained her frustration at not finding the Professor when she needed him for her dissertation, how she and Peen met, their escape in Seattle from Damon, and their need to safely return the car they'd *borrowed*.

Peen went next, describing how an attempted kidnapping interrupted his bike ride, his leap onto a boat mast, the police interrogation, and Gristo's death.

William spoke next, "I'm an electrician. I work for the Tamanachee Utility Company, which contracts with public utilities. Most of the time I'm on the road, but when I have a long break, I stay with my grandfather on our reservation near Yakima, where he's head of the tribal council. Like me, he's an electrician. He manages both the reservation's hydroelectric plant and our tribe's bunker, which it turns out is a missile silo, but more on that later. Yesterday morning Grandpa asked me to accompany him to the bunker, because he wanted to share something important with me. We weren't out of the driveway before he began telling his story. He stumbled at first, dancing around the truth. I think he'd kept it bottled for so long that sharing it was difficult, but once he started, it poured out. It was pride mixed with pain, the pain of deceiving our tribe."

William hesitated. Should he be saying anything? How much should he tell them? He looked at Peen, at the fresh cuts crisscrossing his face. *These two are fighters,* he thought, *and already they feel like friends. Right now, I need friends with fight in them.*

Feeling confident he was doing the right thing, William shared with them the story his grandfather Chester had told him on their drive to the Tamanachee Missile Silo:

William. There's the life you are born into and the life you make. The life you are born into is your childhood. The path you take in adulthood is the one you make. My life story is a little different. What I'm about to tell you will shake your view of me as well as the world you have known. You are twenty-five years old, so you know a little about making your own way in the world. I probably don't tell you often enough how proud I am of you.

I know I've told you I left the military in 1947, but that wasn't true. I've lived a secret life for decades, however now I feel I have to tell you the truth. As I've told you, I entered the United States Army Air Corps in December of 1942. By the time I entered, the Air Corps had become so desperate for recruits that they'd dropped the college diploma requirement. That meant kids like me who'd placed near the top of their high school classes could join. Though I'd done well in high school, there was no way an orphan like me could have gone to college. The Air Corps opportunity changed my life forever and has shaped yours in ways you are about to understand. You know I've shared a couple stories about bombing runs into Germany and returning in planes that were flying on fumes. Those were terrifying flights, but my most important mission was top-secret.

On January 3, 1945, our crew completed a mission over Berlin. On our way back, flak damaged two of our engines, destroyed our communications and killed four people, including one of my closest friends Spence Davis. With only two engines, we slowed and lost some altitude. Pretty soon, we found ourselves flying alone, unable to keep up with the other planes. We left the German mainland and saw the Baltic below us when an enemy fighter spotted our plane and began firing. Our pilot was hit, but could still fly. I thought that was the end of us. Miraculously, a P-38 appeared and shot down the German plane. We considered abandoning the plane and jumping, however the cold water would have killed us.

When we neared the southern tip of Sweden, we discovered the hydraulics had been leaking, making it impossible to turn. We resolved to crash-land in Sweden. Our pilot, despite bleeding badly, still held the plane steady. Thankfully the weather was good. The pilot was able to maneuver to a farm on a hill with a downward slope. Unfortunately, the pilot misjudged the landing and we came down hard, rolled a couple times, and the plane's fuselage split into two parts. Only the pilot and I survived, pure luck on my part, though I had cuts and bruises. It was late when we crashed and the pilot didn't want to move, so I stayed with him. I fell asleep during the night and when I woke up, I discovered he'd passed. Then I was alone. I hiked to the nearest road, which led to a small Swedish town called Tomelilla. I remained there for a month. The people of Tomelilla were helpful and kind. In fact, I bet you recognize the town's name; it is how I came up with your mother's name, Melilla.

Eventually, I found a way to notify the Air Corps I was alive and the only survivor. On January 27, 1945, I received new orders. I arrived at a Swedish airbase and boarded a C-54 before I learned we were flying a top-secret cargo of passengers and boxes to an Airbase in the U.S. A day later we landed in Blackstone, Virginia. When the plane landed, we were immediately routed to an empty hanger. The crew was quickly ushered off the plane. I was directed to a room by myself and never saw anyone from the flight again.

I remained alone in the room for an hour until a four star general entered followed by another man he called Joe. After introducing us, the general left the room. Joe told me he needed a volunteer for a special mission and that I was an ideal candidate.

How so, I asked? What had I done? Joe said a combination of my military service coupled with the fact that I was an orphan was critical, because I'd have to die, at least on paper. Then Joe told me something I'll never forget. He said that occasionally in life a person confronts a choice that changes his life forever. This was one of those times.

After some back and forth questioning, I learned that by agreeing to the life-long mission I'd be given property, a home, and the education to live and work well. I'd also receive a new identity. So, my life would be forever altered.

To be honest the decision wasn't that difficult. My experience in the military had been positive, so I'd planned to remain in the service anyway. The other men respected me and I was a top-notch navigator. I readily volunteered for the mission.

That's when Joe laid out the entirety of what had happened. He explained to me that a German ship had beached in Sweden a week earlier. He told me that everyone on the ship had died. It appeared there had been a mutiny, but nobody knew for sure. Most importantly, the cargo consisted of Russian art treasure that needed to be hidden and guarded. The Swedes got word to an Office of Strategic Services agent stationed in Stockholm about the art and shared the news that an American salvage ship in a nearby harbor, whose crew was hiding from the Nazis, could be utilized to retrieve the art. That way, the Swedes could maintain plausible neutrality. The reason I was recruited to join the rescue effort was because the navigator had became extremely ill on the flight to Sweden, so I was needed to navigate the plane and the cargo back to America.

With the art in the United States, Joe told me the next step was to hide it indefinitely in a remote location. He hoped the panels would be returned to Russia some day. Until then, he didn't want to create an international incident by revealing their existence. Joe told him that relations between the U.S. and the Soviets were fragile and that the war with their common German enemy was the single bond that united them. He also ordered me to avoid any contact with the Monuments Men or any other restitution group. He said they were great people doing important work, but they would argue the art should be returned to Russia right away and didn't have a full understanding of the Soviet-American political tensions. For those reasons, said Joe, my job for the next few years was to keep them safe and hidden. I did not realize my decision would last a lifetime.

Joe didn't do anything half-assed. Given the significance and size of the art, he said he wanted to assign a steward to manage it and give the steward tools to be self-sustaining, rather than become a line item expense of the defense department. He felt this helped create a long-term security plan safe from the whims of government.

What Joe told me next led me to believe that he was a high level agent in the OSS, before he moved on to the CIA. To fulfill his vision, he altered history by creating a fake tribe he called the Tamanachees. The backstory he created was that the federal government had unfairly lumped the Tamanachee in with other tribes of Eastern Washington. Through fake court documents and some revisionist history, he created the foundation for the tribe's existence. He even had a fake treaty from 1890 magically unearthed by a well-known scholar that proved the tribe had been given sovereignty. To complete the ruse, I would become one of four returning Indian war heroes who were given new backgrounds. We supposedly sued and won the right to be recognized as a forgotten tribe.

Then, Joe managed to convince the Federal Government to recognize the fake old treaty. Furthermore, he claimed that former Tamanachee lands northwest of Yakima, Washington, and claimed by Bureau of Land Management and the Forest Service, should be returned to the tribe as part of the agreement. The whole thing was a farce, but somehow Joe pulled it together.

To lend legitimacy to our story, the Tamanachee claimed to be an offshoot of the Yakima Tribe. Joe made an agreement with the Yakima Tribal Council to overlook the sudden appearance of the new tribe, but I never knew the details. In addition, there was already a program in place called the Indian Reorganization Act of 1934. Through that act, even after World War II ended, the U.S. government continued to recognize and un-recognize tribes and tribal lands. In fact, several tribes, like the Klamath had their tribal sovereignty terminated as late as 1954, though they later won back their recognition. So for our tribe to suddenly appear, or reappear, was perceived, and articulated, as just another government injustice. At that time, people were so relieved to have World War II over that the emergence of a new tribe was never scrutinized.

When the original four of us met for the first time in 1945, we realized we came from different tribes in different locations. None of us looked much like the other, so we figured no one would believe we came from the same tribe. But the one thing we did have in common was that we were soldiers and we'd fought proudly for our country. Our country was calling again and we'd do our best to honor that commitment.

Joe explained to us that the land we'd been given had a storage facility and barracks used during the war by the government. That's when he revealed that the Japanese floated bombs over the Pacific to the U.S. during World War II. The bombs would detonate in remote forest locations, so the Forest Service had to train fire fighters to parachute into the woods to fight them. Though the war was over, the Forest Service still wanted to train forest fighters to parachute into difficult areas, so Joe saw to it that the Tamanachee got the contract to provide the land and facilities for training them. That generated our first tribal revenue. I bet if you search that old warehouse with the winter plow trucks you might still find some of the old fire fighting equipment. I haven't thought about that in years.

Of course, four people weren't enough to make a tribe, but Joe had an answer for that, too. The four of us, as tribal council, could select military veterans to move to the reservation through a homestead act-like legal device. We chose twenty-three men we felt would fit into the tribe. We began as a mish mash of ethnicities, a melting pot of an Indian kind, a micro-American experiment.

We also welcomed military female veterans. Few people know that Indian women served in World War II. Your grandmother served in the Army Nurse Corps in Belgium and France. She said that after seeing the world, she could never return to her previous life. Marrying a woman veteran was a way I could find someone who understood the mission I'd undertaken. Your grandmother was a great woman, William, and I miss her every day.

Through Joe, as our small tribe grew, I secured small contracts to build facilities under the auspices of fire training, but were really for the storage of the art. During those early years Joe made sure I received the training and experience necessary to build a secure underground complex. But, Joe ran into several funding delays.

Eventually, Joe spurred the DOD to build an F-type Titan missile complex on the reservation. It was never intended to be used as a missile silo. It was built as a prototype to train our construction company to build an actual silo in Royal City, Washington. Not only would construction of the prototype provide an opportunity to test and work out problems in the design, it also allowed the creation of an underground storage facility without red tape or questions.

As the years passed and our tribe grew, I felt a tremendous amount of guilt for lying to tribe members about our history, even if it was for the best of reasons. And, when I speak of our tribe, I do mean our family and our extended family of brothers and sisters of different names and backgrounds who have come together to build and support this tribe. If I have learned one lesson from this experience, it's that my definition of a tribe altered from bloodlines to community. I feel closer to these folks, our tribal lands, and our customs, than I do to my birth tribe. I am and will always be both a proud Tamanachee and an American. I've spent a lifetime serving both.

***

What had taken William's grandfather an hour to tell, William had retold in a quick ten minutes. "I couldn't believe what my grandfather told me. I was in shock.

Numb. I couldn't even look at him, so I stared at the sagebrush and dust as he drove his truck along the reservation road. I thought I knew the man. As we approached the entrance to the bomb shelter, I mean missile silo, I finally decided to ask him a question. I asked what his birth tribe was, but he refused to tell me. Instead, he repeated that he *was and will always be a Tamanachee*."

William fell silent, looking slightly lost.

"That's quite a story," acknowledged Peen, "I don't know about Tora, but I've got all kinds of questions. The one I want to ask most is, where is my uncle?"

"He's trapped at the silo with my grandfather. That's why I'm here. He and . . . "

Tora interrupted William, unable to contain herself, "Wow, the implications are amazing! The U.S. Government has been hiding Russian property all this time? What are they waiting for? If they truly are the Amber Panels, then why not turn them over to the Russians following the collapse of the Soviet Union . . . wait . . . they couldn't. They'd have destroyed the little trust they'd established as we emerged from the Cold War."

A rap on the sliding glass door jolted all three.

When they turned to look, it was Ian Cadmeyer standing outside the window. He knocked again.

"Who the hell is that," yelled William, pointing his gun at the stranger.

Ian thrust his hands up and yelled something they couldn't decipher.

"Put the gun down, William," ordered Peen, "he's a friend. He's one of us."

"Did he come with you guys? Why didn't you mention him?" yelled William aggressively, agitated at the unexpected event.

"The short answer is he didn't come here with us," explained Tora, "why he is back there and how he got there we won't know until we talk to him."

William lowered the gun as Peen unlocked and opened the door.

Peen introduced them, "Professor Ian Cadmeyer, meet William Stephens. William's grandfather, Chester, is a friend of Uncle Edmund. William, Ian is also a long time friend of Uncle Edmund."

Ian stepped into the house and grasped William's hand. Both men considered the other carefully.

"What are you doing here?" gasped Tora.

"I had to warn you. That Damon fellow you mentioned is on his way here. We might have ten minutes."

"How'd he find out we were here?" exclaimed Peen.

"It's a long story," replied Ian, "the short version is he arrived at my place shortly after you left. He made some threats and then tied me up, but my hands are double jointed. I slipped out of my bindings in only a few seconds. I figured it would take Damon about a half hour to get here, because the route is so much longer than the fifteen minutes it takes to cross the water and round the point at Fort Flagler. Since my friend keeps his boat moored near my place and I know where he keeps the spare key, I stole it and raced over here as quickly as I could. It's tied up at Edmund's dock below the house. "

"Damn," responded William, "I wonder if that's the same guy who broke into the silo?"

"Someone broke into the silo on your reservation?" asked Peen. "It wouldn't surprise me if it was Damon!"

William announced, "It's urgent that I get the silo plans and get out of here. That's why I came here. The plans are key to helping the Professor and Grandpa."

"What are the plans for William?" probed Tora.

"We need them to reroute the power into the vault. The guys who attacked the silo blew the power right away, probably so Grandpa couldn't contact anyone for help."

"How were you attacked in the silo?" Tora asked.

"Listen, there's no time to explain. Let's focus on getting the plans and I'll explain more later."

"Okay. Where are the plans William?" Peen asked.

"In a safe behind the refrigerator."

"Edmund's in a silo? There's a safe behind the refrigerator?" asked Ian, raising his eyebrows in surprise. "I think I've missed some important information."

"We'll fill you in, Ian," assured Tora. Yet, she was still puzzled about one thing, "I'm confused. Why were the plans kept here?"

"Grandpa told me there were two sets of plans. One set is kept on the reservation and the other set is buried in some government archive, probably impossible to find. After my grandfather's company bought this property and remodeled the house, he put the plans here. However, they never got around to making a second copy of the plans to keep on the reservation."

"So, it isn't really my uncle's place?" asked Peen. "That explains why I didn't know about it."

"I'm not sure who legally owns the place. I'm just repeating what I was told before sneaking out of the silo through an emergency escape vent. I was looking for the safe when you knocked on the door. As I said, the safe is supposed to be in the kitchen behind the refrigerator."

"I've never heard of putting one there," observed Tora.

The four of them inspected the kitchen's refrigerator, a stainless model with an icemaker and water dispenser. To its right was a wall and to the left was a kitchen counter with top and bottom cabinets that stretched the length of the kitchen.

"Let's see what's here," said Peen. He placed his hands on either side of the refrigerator and pulled it forward. The appliance rolled smoothly toward him. Peen moved aside and rolled it until the front touched the kitchen's island.

William slipped between the counter and back of the refrigerator. The refrigerator's outlet was installed near the bottom of the wall and a long fresh water tube disappeared into the wall.

"It looks like a normal wall back here," said William.

"Are you sure he said it was behind the refrigerator?" asked Tora.

"Yes, they said behind the refrigerator . . . ahhh, I see. What looks like trim at the top edge actually slides," noted William. He bent down, "Same thing down at the bottom. I've slid them both."

Peen and Tora peered into the space as William stood up and moved backward a little, gently tugging on the electrical cord. The back wall rotated toward the side of the wall on door hinges. William stepped under the electrical cord and over the water tube.

"Pretty clever, but not very convenient," commented William looking at the way the electrical wire and the water tube ran out the back of the door and up to the ceiling with enough slack to allow the hidden door to open, "I never would have thought something was back here. But then, I guess that was the point."

"Ian?" said Peen, turning to look at him, "given we're about to enter the rabbit hole, would you mind keeping a watch at the front door for our visitors? I'd suggest the room off to the left, since that room is harder to see into from outside."

"How do you know that Peen?" asked Tora.

"Because, I couldn't see into it when I walked up to the door. The room on the other side of the door had some back lighting and I could make out furniture in there."

"Hmm . . . can't say I noticed that," responded Tora.

Ian piped up, "Good idea. We can always head out the back door and take the boat if necessary." Ian walked down the hall to position himself near the front door.

Tora and Peen slipped behind the refrigerator. Peen remarked, "Not the quickest method for accessing a safe, but as a hidden entrance it satisfies the goal."

Tora, William and Peen stood at a large vault door with a combination knob and lever. The steel door ran from floor to ceiling.

"All this for some plans?" asked Tora.

Peen added, "William, did they tell you what was inside of here?"

"Nope, they just said in the left hand corner were some tubes of plans. I was to get three tubes marked Tamanachee F Missile Silo."

"Do you have the combination? If you don't, I think I do," said Peen.

"Do you? Let's see," replied William.

Peen took the paper from his pocket that had the four numbers he'd written down from the text Chase had helped him with earlier in the day, "I wondered what these numbers meant. Now I'm pretty sure I know. I hope I don't have to pass any of the numbers as I spin the dial."

Looking over his shoulder, Tora saw the numbers for the first time, "You know, those could be dates relating to the panels. The first two numbers are the year the work began. The second two are when the panels disappeared."

"That would make the combination easy to remember. Another clue my uncle was neck deep in them."

Peen spun the dial. He clicked back and forth from 17 to 00 to 19 to 45. Grabbing the horizontal bar, he pulled up with no effect. So, he pushed down. The bar rotated clockwise until it gave way accompanied by the sound of the door unlocking. He pulled the door toward him. It was heavy and gave way slowly.

CHAPTER 23: EDMUND ROGERS

The two old friends sat together in the dark underground vault room, each minute dragging slower than the last.

"How long do you think it's been since William left?" Chester Stephens asked once again.

"Oh," Edmund Rogers groaned, "maybe ten hours, but I can't be sure anymore." Edmund's chair squeaked as he shifted his position.

"You doin' okay there professor?"

"Yeah, I guess so," Edmund lied. His head and body ached from stress. He was tired, hungry and thirsty, the trifecta of misery.

Despite his friend's stoic response, Chester wasn't fooled. Edmund's fragile health concerned him. Chester had already given Edmund the rest of his water. He wished there was more he could do for Edmund, but for now all Chester could do was distract him with conversation.

Edmund sighed, "Are you sure we can't turn on one flashlight for a few minutes? The darkness is depressing."

"We'd best save them for when we really need them,"

311

Chester advised, "why don't you picture this room in your mind so you can find your way around in the dark. It might come in handy. I know this room like the back of my hand, but you need to memorize it for yourself."

The incessant banging caused by the men trying to access the vault made it difficult for Professor Edmund Rogers to focus. He took a few breaths hoping to relax and block out the sounds. Then he began to visualize the square room, forty feet each side, white-painted concrete all around. Centered on one wall was a high-security blast door that was theoretically unbreachable. Centered on an adjacent wall was the two-foot diameter emergency vent that William had ascended so many hours ago, a simple round opening in the wall located three feet above the floor that led into a horizontal shaft ten feet in length. At that point the shaft turned ninety degrees to vertical and shot up fifty feet to the desert surface above them. William had climbed the ladder attached to one side of the vertical shaft and made his escape, but Edmund was too weak and Chester too old to make such a climb.

Edmund imagined looking up at the fourteen-foot concrete ceiling with the exposed electrical conduit. To one side of the room were forty wooden crates. Most held the panels, a few held other artifacts. Several boxes were empty, because Edmund had given the art to his friend Ian Cadmeyer for restoration. On the other side of the room, where he and Chester waited, Edmund knew there was furniture, three desks, a few large tables, and some metal chairs. So here they sat, in blackness, dependent on William to rescue them.

Edmund's thoughts were disrupted by another round of banging and clanging, just like the intruders had been doing for hours.

Chester remarked, "I figured everyone had forgotten about the Amber Panels after all these years. If I weren't afraid of revealing the secrets of the Tamanachee Tribe's beginnings, I'd have gotten rid of these damned things years ago."

Edmund knew that wasn't true. He recognized that Chester was proud he'd dutifully protected them. But, Chester was getting too old to guard them anymore. He needed to hand them off to someone else and, until his heart attack, Edmund had been that someone. They'd planned to move the panels this year to the new location near Fort Flagler, but now those plans were on hold. *That crusty eighty-nine year old man is in better shape than I am*, lamented Edmund. As much as he tried, Edmund couldn't shake his feelings of disappointment and despair. The darkness was an ally of both.

"No offense to you, Chester, because you know I enjoy your company," said Edmund, "but this just might be the worst birthday party anyone has ever thrown for me."

"It's your birthday?" replied Chester in surprise, "I'm sorry I didn't know that. How old are ya?"

"Sixty," responded Edmund somberly.

"If it makes you feel any better," confessed Chester, "my wife always said I was horrible at birthdays. She told me I was too practical."

"Practical is what I need. This thirst is unbearable. I took my last drink of water about five minutes ago."

"Sorry birthday boy, I don't have any water left either," replied Chester. "When we get out of here I promise you a nice tall bottle of the coolest, freshest water I can find. I'll hike up Mt. Rainier and carve off a chunk of glacier myself if I have to. I'll even wrap the bottle with a ribbon for ya. But, I'll only do that if you promise to relax."

"You old man. You'll never make it up there. What are you, a hundred and ten years old now?" teased Edmund. He still had a little sense of humor left.

Chester chuckled as the distant sounds stopped and quiet enveloped them again. He took Edmund's teasing as a good sign. He commented, "I sure feel like a hundred and ten sometimes. I never thought I'd live to be eighty-nine. I used to think by the age of seventy I'd be sittin' on a porch relaxin' on a rockin' chair preparing myself for the man with the scythe. But, for some reason, I just keep ticking along. You just hang in there, because I know you'll be fine, too."

"That may be, Chester, but I doubt my ticker will go as long as yours. My heart attack knocked the wind out of me. I never saw it coming," acknowledged Edmund.

The far off clatter began anew, signaling the team of unknown men was still trying to breach the first of two doors that separated the vault from what would ordinarily have been a control room in a working missile silo, but now was an empty space, a bomb shelter, of the Tamanachee silo. Chester remembered joking with Joe the first time Joe proposed they build a missile silo on the reservation property. *Are you sure this isn't some plan to paint a bulls-eye on the chest of the Tamanachee and other*

Indian tribes and let the Soviets finish the job the Federal Government started?

Joe had laughed in response. However, by the time Joe had finished explaining why the missile silo was a perfect solution to their storage problem, Chester was on board.

The plan had been simple. Build a freight elevator and stairs down to a control and utility room to demonstrate the design for the F-type Titan Missile Silo. During the construction they'd covertly added a hidden sliding door from the control room that would lead to a short corridor, ending at a blast door. Beyond the blast door would be the vault. As was standard in the F-type Silo, an emergency vent was added, but in this case it was connected to the vault room. Chester informed Joe he didn't want to get stuck inside the room in case the electricity went out and the doors back into the control room wouldn't open. His foresight proved important, because Chester and Edmund found themselves in that exact situation now. The flaw in his plan was that Chester never imagined he'd get too old to climb up the escape vent ladder.

As if reading his mind, Edmund asked Chester, "Do you think it was a good idea to tell William not to contact the police after he escaped through the vent?"

"Yes," argued Chester, "I'm certain if the police hear about this it will make the news. I haven't spent my life guarding this secret to reveal it now. I'm confident William will return with the plans. I'd rather get the CIA or DOD involved, but I'm not sure how to contact them other than to use the equipment we have in here. We just need a few tools to rewire the overhead wiring and we should be good to go. Have faith in my grandson."

Chester went on to explain to Edmund that the sliding door could be opened without electricity, but someone would have to know how to do that from the utility room. And, the blast door lock was made to withstand a blast, not necessarily to withstand an attack. The blast door in particular could be disassembled, but that would take patience and know-how. However, the intruders were proving to be relentless. Chester feared it would only be a matter of time before they accessed the vault.

A new noise, a series of dull thuds, echoed through the walls. Chester found them discomforting, like warnings of an approaching storm. His concern about Edmund grew, so he thought he'd better get him talking again. Chester decided to resume their earlier conversation they'd had.

"Edmund, you still believe this is all the result of the notebook scans you were sent?"

"I do," responded Edmund, "you and I have been working together for twelve years and never had an inkling of a problem until Godfred sent me that diary."

Two weeks ago Edmund's close friend Godfred Berg, a professor of North American History at the University of Sweden, had contacted Edmund about a diary he'd received. A doctor friend of Godfred's had witnessed a deathbed confession by a woman named Katya Ballheim. She'd shared a guilt-ridden tale of her escape from Germany in World War II. She told the doctor that she'd recorded journal entries into a notebook and wanted him to retrieve the notebook and see that it reached someone who could use it. She wanted something good to come of the information and hoped it might unravel the mystery of the Amber Panels.

The doctor found the diary, handed it to his neighbor, Godfred, and relayed Katya's request. Godfred realized the implications of the diary and called Edmund, thinking Edmund might be the best person to review the information. Edmund agreed to look at it and asked Godfred to send him digital scans of it. Edmund wondered if the diary might hold the key for how the panels got from Königsberg to Sweden, something he and Chester had always wondered.

When Edmund received the scans, the diary's old formal German script was too difficult for him to decipher. So, Edmund forwarded the scans to Kjell Hansen, another professor from the University of Sweden who was on sabbatical in Poland. Edmund trusted Kjell and thought Kjell would have the time to quickly complete a rough translation of it.

Last week, Kjell emailed Edmund a translation and also included an important note. He wrote about a history professor at Gdansk University who'd seen a printout of the notebook on Kjell's desk. The professor had taken a keen interest in its contents.

Shortly after Kjell finished interpreting important aspects of the notebook, someone had burgled his office and stolen a printed copy along with his laptop computer. Fortunately, he'd kept all the scans and his translations on the University of Sweden's network, where he kept all his important files.

As a result of the theft, Kjell spoke with other professors at Gdansk and learned that a man named Damon Kant had offered a reward for information about the panels. He'd also learned Damon was dangerous.

Kjell wrote in his email that he understood the importance of the notebook and the danger that knowledge might present. He destroyed his digital copies and decided to return to Sweden. He expressed to Edmund how sorry he was for accidently sharing the scans.

A muffled sawing sound interrupted Chester's concentration. He asked Edmund, "How come you didn't tell me about the email when you received it from Kjell?"

"As I told you before," explained Edmund, "I didn't want to put you or the panels at risk. I felt it was best to meet in person and discuss it. I had a few things to finish this week and then I planned to surprise you. I figured we could go have some dinner in Yakima, enjoy some wine, and discuss what we should do. But, three days ago I thought for sure I was being followed. I saw the same black Cadillac five times. That's why I texted you *Aetheria*, to warn you there was a problem. After that, I shut down my phone and raced here."

Chester apologized, "I'm sorry I didn't have my phone with me. I'd left it in the truck. It wasn't until I went to buy some gas that I saw your text. I was so worried about why you sent the message that I thought I'd better bring William along with me. I know we talked about including him sooner, but I've had a hard time telling him about the tribe's true past."

"I understand. I was happy to see you enter the room together. I could tell his mind was swirling. I thought he'd tip over he looked so disoriented," said Edmund.

"Yep," agreed Chester, "I'm disappointed we didn't get a chance to show William one of the panels. Heck, I never even got a chance to describe the type of treasures we've been guarding. I wanted to surprise him. However, barely had a chance to say *hello* to you before those thugs blew the top door and entered the silo. I never in a million years thought they'd cut the electricity."

"Chester, I can't help but wonder if someone was monitoring my phone. Do you think my text allowed them to track us here? I pulled the battery from my phone as soon as I sent the text."

"We'll probably never know how they found us," lamented Chester, "let's just hope William returns before they breach the vault's door."

"Amen," seconded Edmund.

The sound of the sawing stopped and silence returned. Chester could hear Edmund breathing. Then he heard Edmund make a sound he hadn't heard before.

"What are you doing Edmund?"

"I'm lying on the floor, Chester. I didn't make any sounds. I thought that was you."

"Ssshhh," whispered Chester. He listened carefully. Then he heard a *clink, clink, clink*, followed by a quiet grunt of frustration.

"Chester, you know what that sounds like to me?" uttered Edmund quietly, "it's similar to the sound William made when escaping. I think those are the sounds of shoes on the ladder rungs."

"That's what I think too, Edmund. But, is it William or someone else?"

"Good question."

Chester quickly devised a plan with the resources they had: two flashlights and two shotguns. They'd been conserving the battery power in the flashlights for emergencies. He whispered to Edmund to take both flashlights and circle around to a position behind a crate twenty feet in front of the emergency vent entrance. Meanwhile, Chester positioned himself to one side of the opening. He'd wanted to crouch behind a desk, but his knees couldn't handle that position any more.

Despite the person's attempts to remain quiet, the intruder made noise as he worked his way down the escape vent's ladder.

Edmund waited in position, his heart beating quickly and sweat dripping down his forehead. He waited for something, anything to happen.

Eventually, the intruder emerged from the emergency vent and stepped onto the floor. Edmund switched on the flashlights and yelled, "Who's there?"

The answer was flashes of light, as repetitive gunshots filled the dark void.

Chapter 24: Jolo

The safe's interior lights blinked on when Peen opened the vault's door, revealing a large walk-in space lined with shelves. Tora gasped in amazement. Old paintings, sculptures, small boxes, and other artifacts filled the room, leaving only a narrow pathway. A small tapestry hung on the far wall.

"Wow!" gasped Tora. "Why are these things here?"

"Grandpa told me it was a storage facility for the items from the silo. This safe is just the beginning. They built additional storage underneath this house for more items."

"Why build here?"

"Edmund and Grandpa told me that security was a primary concern. Did you see the naval station as you passed by Indian Island to get to Marrowstone?"

"Yes," replied Tora.

"That's protection right there. Second, this place has a nice dock, so they could move boxes by truck or boat.

Also, Port Townsend is an artist community with the art supplies they could get for restoration without attracting attention. Finally, the natural isolation would allow them to come and go unnoticed."

"Did they plan to move all the art here?"

"That was the plan Tora, until Edmund fell ill last December. Grandpa said he wanted everything removed from the silo so the tribe could end all responsibilities for the art."

"I'll bet Ian will recognize some of these items. He probably helped restore them," said Peen.

William stepped inside to a shelf with cardboard tubes. After shuffling through them, he found three brown tubes marked *YAKIMA F MISSILE SILO*. He removed the tubes and all three of them slipped back into the kitchen. William closed the safe and secret door, then pushed the refrigerator back the way they'd found it.

Tora walked toward the front door calling quietly, "Ian, where are you?"

No one responded.

"Ian, are you there?"

Tora was concerned. She nervously whispered to Peen and William, "Guys, Ian isn't answering me. Where could he have gone?"

Peen put his finger to his mouth signaling them to be quiet. The three of them crept to the front door. Peen and Tora moved left toward the study, while William moved right into the living room.

Peen continued through the dark hall, while Tora entered the study and examined a small desk. A white wire snaked across the top.

"An iPhone cord," she whispered. She pulled out her phone and connected it. The battery was completely depleted, so the phone refused to turn on. The display indicated it was beginning to charge.

Suddenly a toilet flushed, a door opened, and Ian's voice called out, "Who's there?"

They all shuddered. Peen said, "Jesus Ian. It's us. We didn't know what happened to you."

Approaching from a side hall, Ian issued an apology, "Sorry, but I had to go to the bathroom. I didn't realize how badly until I was standing guard."

From the other room William sounded a warning, "Everybody shut up!" He crossed the foyer pointing to the door and whispered loudly, "Our visitors are here!"

The three men joined Tora in the study. Outside they saw a dark SUV with two men standing next to it. A third man was walking toward the side of the house.

"Maybe these guys just want to borrow a cup of sugar?" quipped Peen, sarcastically.

Tora announced quietly, "Noooo, they don't look like bakers to me. I think they want a cup of our hides."

"Should we run for the boat?" suggested Ian.

"Not with the guy circling around the side of the house. It's too dark to run fast. We'd be sitting ducks," responded Peen with concern.

William whispered, "Look, one of them is heading around the other side of the house. And one looks like he's coming straight for the front door."

"Wait here," said Peen. "I'm going to buy us time."

He returned to the kitchen and turned off the lights at the rear of the house. Suddenly they heard shouting and saw flashes of light from the living room. Tora realized Peen had turned on the television, apparently to a noisy action movie.

They looked at him, confused, "They won't be able to hear us over the noise from the television, which should give us a little more freedom. However, just before I turned on the television, I heard the sound of footsteps on the back deck. So, that exit is no good. Any other ideas?"

No one responded. From the family room the noise level increased as the voice of a used car salesman argued his dealership offered the best used-car pricing in Seattle. Peen pointed to the man approaching the house, "He's still coming our direction."

"Why don't we return to the hidden room behind the refrigerator? They'd never look there," suggested Tora.

"I don't think we'd make it past the guy on the deck. There aren't any blinds on the windows to keep him from seeing into the kitchen," argued Peen.

Ian spoke, "May I suggest we head to the garage? We have more options in there and could use tools as weapons if necessary. Edmund once told me it had a fire door, so it might be hard to break down. Or maybe we can use one of his vehicles to escape?"

No one answered Ian. They were focused on the man outside, who'd stopped at the porch steps. He looked cautiously across the front of the house.

"That's him. That's Damon," whispered Peen. "Ian, show us the way to the garage."

Damon knocked on the door as Ian led the way to the garage, using the wall as a guide in the dark. Tora grabbed her iPhone and followed Peen down the hall. William stayed behind.

Ian opened the garage door and flicked on the lights. As Tora and Peen's eye's adjusted to the brightness, a single gunshot rang loudly from inside the house. Tora, Peen and Ian froze. A second later, William bolted into the garage, "Sorry about the gun shot. I hope it didn't startle you too much, but I wanted to spook those guys, maybe slow them down a little."

As his heart raced, Peen surveyed the garage, amazed at the sight before him. The space was three cars deep and eight cars wide with four extra large double doors, the ones he'd seen from the exterior. It looked far bigger from the inside. Toolboxes, equipment and a long workbench were against the back wall. There were no windows in the concrete walls, only the four doors. The ceiling was high, maybe fifteen feet.

Four-wheel-drive vehicles packed the garage, most of them green military jeeps without tops. There were also glossy CJ-5s, including a white one with red, white and blue stripes running along the hood and down the sides. Over in the corner was an aqua green jeep with a matching striped top bordered with fringe. They were tightly packed together, some facing forward, some facing backward and a few sideways.

"What the hell? My uncle has a car collection? He works on vehicles?" gasped Peen.

Ian answered, "It always seemed like a large collection on a professor's salary, so I'm not sure whose it is."

"It might be my grandfather and your uncle's combined. Don't feel bad, I just learned about it yesterday along with everything else," lamented William. "Now, follow me around this Willys M-38. We need to push it against the door."

Peen and Tora moved around to the driver's side of an old flat fender military jeep painted army green. They followed William's lead as he put his hands on the driver's side and pushed. That's when Peen noticed each wheel of the jeep had its own small dolly with four casters, making the jeep easy to maneuver in the tight space. Together, they pushed the jeep sideways until it was hard against the interior door they'd just come through. With the jeep in place, William showed them how to release the dolly's ratchet lever and drop each tire to the floor. The door was now blocked and impossible to open.

"Ian was right. The door is a heavy fire door," said William. "With the jeep in front of it, it will be difficult for them to break through. That buys us some time. Meanwhile, as you can see, we have quite a few transportation options."

"Why are these old jeeps here?" asked Tora.

"Look at all the vehicles you could hotwire, Tora," teased Peen.

"I'm going to hotwire you to a battery and see how you spark if you aren't careful mister," she responded.

"My grandfather loves old jeeps. All I know is that they said I *had* to check out the garage before I left the house. From what I can see, about half of these are restored MB and GPW jeeps from World War II. Over there is a really rare Bantam BRC-60, the second type of jeep ever produced," explained William. He caught himself and said, "Sorry, this isn't the time for a history lesson.

"Perhaps we can use one of these as a getaway vehicle?" asked Ian.

"Do they run?" asked William.

"Most do. Edmund's taken me for rides in several of them," said Ian.

"Which one can outrun an SUV?" asked Tora.

"I doubt any of them could," cautioned William.

"But we out-float them," Ian said. "That front one floats like a boat. Edmund called it a seep, a sea-worthy jeep."

Tora responded, "So It floats? Like those duckmobiles in Seattle that carry tourists into Lake Union?"

"Yes, it's a floating jeep from World War II. It's similar to a DUKW, only smaller," explained William as he walked past several jeeps before stopping at a boat-shaped jeep painted the same olive drab green as the other military vehicles. Gesturing toward the seep, he continued, "More importantly, for our protection, the hull of this jeep, or seep I mean, can resist bullets better than anything else in the garage. Safety, rather than speed, seems a priority at this point."

Ian added, "And, if we can get into the water, they can't follow us."

"Did you ever ride in it? Or, float in it?" asked William.

"Yes. It was a kick, but it's not very fast," warned Ian.

"How do we get to the water from here?" asked Peen.

"We can't get down the bluff behind Edmund's house, but we can access the water from Fort Flagler State Park just north of here. A fire road intersects the driveway that leads directly to the park. From that beach we can enter Puget Sound. Edmund and I went in from the other side of Marrowstone Island. But, that would take too long. We don't want to give those guys more opportunities to catch us."

"I agree," said Peen nodding. "And, if we can reach the water we can cross Admiralty Inlet to Whidbey Island. There'd be no way for them to follow us by ferry tonight."

"Theoretically, yes," responded Ian, "but Admiralty Inlet often has strong currents and heavy ship traffic. We'll have to be lucky and cautious, but my boat trip over here this evening was calm, so I expect the ride to Whidbey could be fairly smooth as well."

"I think that's our best option. I'd rather take my chances with the tides than Damon," said Peen.

As he climbed into the driver's side William said, "If I can get this seep started I can drive it, but the water portion will have to be learned on the fly."

Peen noticed the word JOLO painted in white on the seep's hull. "Is the seep named Jolo?"

Ian replied, "Yes, Edmund mentioned he named it Jolo, because the guy he bought it from said it was used in the Philippines during an attack on Jolo Island . . . "

With an escape plan in mind, William interrupted Ian, "Tora and Ian, hop in. Peen, you stand by the door opener that's against the wall." William pointed to a space between two of the garage doors, "Peen, when I tell you, hit the button and hop into the passenger side."

"Ian, why don't you sit up front, since you're the tallest. You'll fit better there," suggested Tora.

"Thank you my dear," replied Ian. "But William, I'm afraid I don't *hop* too well anymore. Instead, I shall climb in with haste."

With no doors, Tora put her hands on the side of the hull and vaulted into the rear seating area. After landing hard, she painfully learned the back seat wasn't a seat at all, but a flat piece of sheet metal covered by thin olive drab pads. The front seats were similarly cushioned. Between them were two gearshifts. In front of those shifters were three additional shifters, two short ones and one tall one. Tora figured the tall one was the transmission shifter, but had no idea what the others did.

A large three-spoke steering wheel topped a narrow steering column that angled to the floor. Several brass plates were attached to the dashboard with diagrams and d instructions for operating the vehicle.

"Ok, how do we start this Jolo?" wondered William aloud as he puzzled through the brass plates.

"Don't we need a key?" asked Tora.

"No, the Army didn't want keys. Generally, there is an ignition switch to power up the electrical system and a button to start the motor."

"Are you sure you know how to drive it?" quizzed Peen.

"Oh sure, driving a jeep is pretty easy. But, I've never driven one as a boat. Let's see what the instructions tell me," said William looking at the plates on the dash.

Ian added, "I'm afraid I wasn't paying attention to Edmund while he drove, so I'm no help. I was enjoying the scenery too much."

Just then, a thud followed by frustrated shouts echoed through the garage. The men were trying to open the garage's interior door, but the M-38 blocked it. Thinking they could overcome whatever was blocking the door, the men slammed against the door several times.

"Uh oh. That's gonna leave a dent in the jeep," deadpanned Peen.

"I think I have this figured out. If I twist the ignition like this," William said while turning a knob on the dash and pressing a button. The seep vibrated as the engine turned over.

"It might take a couple times to get the gas to the carburetor," continued William.

Two more attempts failed, but, to everyone's relief, on the fourth try the engine ignited. It wasn't the rip-roaring sound Tora had expected, but rather a quiet chugging.

"This sounds like a real-life Chitty Chitty Bang Bang. Go Jolo!" yelled Tora.

"Hit the button, Pete!" shouted William.

"Peen," corrected Ian.

"Yeah, that's what I meant. Let's go, Peen!"

Peen pressed the garage door button, then jumped into the back of the seep next to Tora. As the door slowly lifted, William browsed the directions. He reached down and shifted the farthest lever to the right forward.

"Low range," he shouted to no one in particular. Then he reached for the middle lever and pulled that backward saying, "Four wheel drive. That ought to help us start a little faster."

After examining one particular data plate, he glanced down at the shifters between the driver and passenger seats. He nodded to himself, comprehending how the different levers worked.

Additional banging came from the fire door. The large garage door continued its slow upward grind. William turned and motioned to Peen with his gun, "Know how to shoot this?"

"Aim and pull the trigger, right?" shouted Peen.

"That'll work," said William as he handed Peen the gun. Figuring he didn't know much about guns, William advised Peen, "Keep hidden until I tell you when to shoot. Hold the gun tight and fire at the SUV. It's a big target that will make noise when you hit it. That should scare them and buy us a little more time."

"Don't hit the Ford Falcon, though. I already feel bad enough about stealing it," warned Tora.

"No guarantees," replied Peen.

A shout came from outside as the garage door reached a high enough point where William could engage the clutch and roll out of the garage. With only seventy horsepower, the vehicle wasn't designed for speed. However, with four-wheel drive and the low range, Jolo's ability to move quickly at low speeds was improved.

Peen, Tora and Ian squished down into the seep as far as possible. They heard angry shouts from the house. As the seep accelerated, William steered it to the left side of the driveway. He angled it onto the upper circle of the drive, leaving the Cadillac, the Falcon, and the men on the lower part of the drive.

"Now Peen!" yelled William.

Peen peeked over the side of the seep, pointed the gun at the Escalade, and fired. His first two shots went wide. They were answered by a series of rapid shots. He fired two more rounds, one of which hit glass, causing more shouts.

"Wow, I had no idea guns had so much kickback!" shouted Peen, "it looks so easy in the movies. It's freaking loud, too!"

William coaxed Jolo around the backside of the circle drive before turning onto the long drive. He heard yelling behind him and then the roar of the Cadillac's engine.

Part way down the driveway, Ian pointed out the fire road. William slowed, then turned north onto a straight trail, so narrow the underbrush scraped both sides of the vehicle. Twigs snapped under the tires and the uneven ground caused Jolo to pitch and sway. The trail was dimly lit by the old headlights, poor at best, but the straight dirt road reduced the need for them. William threw caution aside and shifted into third gear. Jolo's four-wheel drive helped him maintain control over the rough road.

Bright lights pierced the darkness behind them as the Cadillac turned onto the fire road. Despite a more powerful engine, the SUV's wider body had to push aside the underbrush, keeping it from gaining any ground. A minute later, Jolo emerged from the bushes onto a grassy, wide-open space, part of Fort Flagler State Park.

The seep bounced over a curb and onto a park road. As Ian gave him directions, William turned to the left and then immediately to the right.

Jolo's headlights barely illuminated the blacktop of the state park's main road. The tiny engine powered the bulky steel hull down a hill, allowing them to pick up speed. Dashing through a deserted intersection, William steered the seep up a slight hill. The lights from the Cadillac appeared from behind, causing the seep's own shadow to stretch grotesquely before them.

"Damon's catching us," yelled Tora.

They crested a hill and swung left, temporarily disappearing from Damon's line of sight. The park's headquarters building, museum, and the former military barracks appeared before them.

"I know where we can hide," announced Ian. Pointing, he said, "Take this immediate right, shut off your lights, and then turn again. We can hide behind that building."

William followed the instructions and stopped next to a windowless one-story building. They were parked only a few seconds when the Cadillac crested the short hill, rounded the corner, and raced past them. The SUV sped northward, beyond the museum shop and several other

333

buildings, before entering the old parade grounds. Now in a wide-open space, the Cadillac slowed to a stop.

Ian directed William, "We need to get to the road that follows the bluff on the east side of the park's parade grounds. We'll take it northward until it forks down to the spit where the lighthouse is located. We'll start with the lights off. Just slowly drive across the grass behind these old buildings. They can't see us as long as we are sneaking behind them, but when we emerge into the parade grounds, I'm sure Damon will come after us. If we can get to the lighthouse quickly enough, we ought to make it into the water."

William let off the clutch and rolled the seep forward. When they reached the road at the edge of the bluff, William turned onto it, still hidden behind the buildings. He paused for a moment, just behind the last building, as a cool breeze swept up the bluff from the saltwater. Peering onto the parade grounds, he could see the Cadillac sitting motionless, its headlights aimed northward, like a cat waiting to pounce. The road was only the width of a single lane, so William knew he'd have to steer Jolo carefully.

William shifted one of the levers.

"What are you doing?" asked Peen.

"I shifted into high range."

"How come? I thought low range made us go faster."

"High range allows us to reach higher speeds, but driving fifty miles per hour in a seep is not a good idea. We could break the front driveline if the thing isn't properly balanced."

"That would be bad," agreed Peen.

"And we need to keep it in four-wheel-drive so that we can cross the beach and reach the water," added Ian.

"Can't we just shift Jolo to four-wheel-drive when we get there?" wondered Tora, already developing an affinity for the seep.

"This isn't like a modern four-wheel-drive jeep. There's no shift-on-the-fly option. To shift we have to stop completely. Even then, it doesn't always work smoothly."

"I guess we'll just take our chances," said Peen. "Go for it, William."

The trees looked black against a purplish sky that cast just enough ambient light for the road to be visible. William saw it stretch slightly up hill for half a mile or so before it reached the fork where a branch dropped down the bluff.

William motioned to Ian, "Here, take my flashlight. I might need you to light up the dashboard once we hit the water. That's in case I forget which way to move the power-take-off levers for the propeller and bilge pump."

"Aye-aye captain," said Ian, grabbing the flashlight.

His nerves belying his cool exterior, William let the clutch out a little too fast, causing Jolo to lurch forward. He quickly depressed the clutch pedal to stop the lurching before releasing it again. As they slowly picked up speed, William shifted into second, his foot pressing the gas pedal to the floor. The slow acceleration was agonizing.

"I think they've spotted us," hollered Peen over the sound of the struggling engine, "the Cadillac's lights just shifted this direction."

"Are you sure? I'll turn on the headlights if that's the case. This road is damned hard to see," yelled William while keeping his gaze focused on the road.

"Just keep driving straight," shouted Ian, "it looks like they're trying and head us off. They're driving straight over the parade grounds."

William reached down and pulled the light switch. A rush of relief accompanied the glow of lights that made the single-lane road slightly more visible.

The Cadillac approached fast. Tora was concerned. "It looks like they'll cut us off before we reach the branch road down to the spit. I got a bad feeling they're going to beat us. Come on Jolo!" she urged.

"Try shooting at them, Peen. Maybe you can distract them," yelled William.

Peen had forgotten he was holding the gun, but didn't think he had a good angle with Tora in his way. He tapped her on the shoulder and motioned for her to shoot the gun. She took it and pointed it at the Cadillac as it bounced over the uneven parade grounds.

Using the side of the seep as a brace, she aimed. With nothing else to draw upon, she copied what she'd seen in movies. She exhaled, took careful aim, and fired four quick shots at the SUV. Three missed completely, but one pierced the glass on the passenger side. The driver of the Cadillac veered to the left, which sent the Escalade in the direction of a small utility building. They watched the Cadillac brake and turn to evade the building, altering the vehicle's intended trajectory.

"I think it worked! I think it worked!" exclaimed Tora.

"Great shot!" Ian shouted, "it looks like we'll make it over the bluff first, but they'll still be right on our tail."

As Jolo reached the top of the bluff, the lights of the amphibious jeep faded into the darkness. William instinctively hit the brakes, unsure which direction the road would take them. The seep plunged downward until, to William's relief, the lights revealed a narrow paved road carved into the hillside. In the distance, Peen spotted a lighthouse surrounded by one-story buildings and realized the road they were on led straight to it, dead-ending at it. Peen looked back. The lights of the Cadillac blazed brightly as it crested the bluff.

"They're right behind us. We have no margin for error," announced Peen.

Looking ahead, William asked, "I didn't expect to see so much driftwood on the beach. Is there a way through it?"

"Yes," said Ian confidently, "you'll have to steer to the far end of the parking lot. It's actually a walking path, but it should be wide enough to allow us through . . . I think."

"You think?" questioned William.

"Well, I'm pretty sure."

"I guess that'll have to do," responded William.

Peen looked toward the beach. The lights of the seep and the SUV illuminated piled driftwood that had accumulated along the high-tide line. It formed a natural barrier between the parking areas and the beach.

The hill gave way to the flat spit where the road widened. William pushed the gas pedal to the floor. The seep's tires picked up gravel on the road and shot it against the wheel wells, causing a loud racket.

337

Ian shouted, "Head for the sign at the far end of the gravel parking lot. That's where the walking path snakes through the driftwood. It's narrow, but I'm sure Jolo can make it."

The Cadillac was closing the distance between them.

Jolo entered the flat gravel parking lot. William steered toward a wooden sign anchored by two posts at the far end of the lot. While the sign was obvious, the existence of a path through the driftwood was not.

William downshifted into second and shouted, "Anyone see the path? I can't see anything between the seep's weak lights and the Cadillac's bright lights."

"Patience William," responded Ian, "it's there."

"I see it!" yelled Peen, "it's just past the sign."

William stared intently, then felt a rush of excitement as he spotted the trail. "Got it. I see what you mean."

William slowed the seep, but kept it in second gear. He wanted to maintain momentum, because they were about to leave the firm gravel parking lot and enter the soft sand of the beach. William swung Jolo left for a straighter line, "Hold on to anything you can."

The trail wasn't a path so much as a spot where driftwood had been removed. Hanging tight to the steering wheel, William sped up at the end of the parking lot to take advantage of the hard gravel.

The opening was too narrow. William was forced to steer the right wheels over a piece of half-buried driftwood. The impact launched Jolo's right side into the air. The seep came down hard, but kept moving. The four wheels propelled the clumsy amphibious vehicle in and out of dips and over rocks, knocking the occupants back and forth. In no time, they'd cleared the driftwood barrier and were racing across the soft sandy beach toward the water. Near the water's edge, the sand got harder and the traction improved, allowing William to shift back into third.

"Shouldn't you slow down?" yelled Peen as he clung to the back of Ian's seat.

William shouted back, "The directions on the dash plate say to hit the water at full speed. So prepare for impact everyone!"

Jolo plunged into the cold salt water with a hard jolt. The force of the impact splashed water over the top of the seep. The impact also caused Jolo to slow dramatically. Despite the sudden deceleration, the four riders held tight and no one was injured. Jolo settled into a gentle rocking motion as ripples echoed away from the tiny boat.

William pushed in the clutch and hit the brakes to halt the transmission's turning. He pulled the four-wheel-drive lever into neutral, then reached for the lever on his immediate right between the seats and pulled it backward, engaging the power-take-off propeller. William shifted Jolo into first gear. Holding his breath, he released the clutch and pushed on the gas pedal sending power from the drivetrain to the propeller, forcing it to spin. They were no longer adrift as Jolo motored into deeper water.

Figuring there were a few bullets left, Tora turned around and pointed the gun aft. It was then she realized the Cadillac had failed to drive through the gap in the driftwood. "We did it, we're safe!" she exclaimed.

William shifted the seep into second gear and Jolo moved faster through the water. A moment later he shifted into third.

"Jolo might not be a jet boat, but anything that takes us away from those guys is fast enough for me," said Tora.

Ian spoke up, "Ernie Pyle once wrote the jeep *was as faithful as a dog, as strong as a mule, and as agile as a goat.* And, in the case of Jolo, he should have added, *it floats like a boat.*"

Peen remarked, "Ernie Pyle? The name seems familiar."

"He was a famous World War II correspondent that died at the end of the war. He was shot by the Japanese after jumping out of a jeep."

"Oh no, I was thinking of Denver Pyle," Peen said shaking his head at his mistake.

William chimed in, "You mean the actor from Gilligan's Island?"

Tora corrected him, "No, that's Bob Denver. Denver Pyle was Uncle Jesse in the Dukes of Hazzard show."

"What about Gomer Pyle?" remarked Ian, "or is Jim Nabors before everyone's time?"

"Well that's *pyling* it on don't you think Ian?" joked William, feeling giddy with relief.

"Ouch, that was bad!" laughed Tora, energized by their lucky escape.

"How fast do you think we are going?" Peen asked no one in particular.

Ian responded, "Oh, I'd say about five knots. Jolo can't go much faster than six knots, at least that's what Edmund told me."

"How did the Professor say Jolo got his name again?" inquired Tora, remembering they hadn't gotten the full explanation in the garage.

"Edmund told me that in 1945 Native Moslem islanders combined forces with American GIs to remove the Japanese soldiers from the island of Jolo. At the beginning of the assault a small group of GIs and Islanders barely survived a counter-attack by using this very seep to escape into the Sulu Sea. Edmund wanted to name it Sulu, but that name was already taken by Gene Rodenberry's character. So, he named it Jolo instead."

"That's where the name Sulu came from? The Sulu Sea in the Philippines?" asked Peen.

"That's what Edmund said," responded Ian.

"I'll have to fact-check when I get power to my phone. I didn't know that either," remarked Tora.

Though the water around them was calm, they'd taken on water upon entry. William reached for a lever between the seats and shifted it forward saying, "That sound is the bilge pump. At least, that's what the data plate says it is."

Tora turned to Peen, "This is so cool! You really know how to throw a girl a first date!"

"A date? Who said this was a date?" replied Peen with a smile. He turned to look behind them. The lights of the SUV were heading back up the bluff to the parade grounds, "And, I think we've finally shaken them."

"That's a win for the good guys," announced William, turning to Peen and Tora for a couple of high fives. Ian turned and raised his hand to join them.

"How far do you think we have to go?" asked Tora.

Ian looked across Admiralty Inlet toward Whidbey Island where he could see a few house lights twinkling in the dark. "It's about two miles straight across, but we'll be going down there." he said, pointing south.

When Tora looked south, she saw Mount Rainier in the distance shrouded in silvery shades of blue. Then she noticed a large vessel with white lights blazing. "Is that ship headed our way?" she asked.

"No," said Ian, "it's going away from us. We'd see a red port light if it was coming this way. But we do have to worry about the large vessels that use this channel. Every cargo ship and ocean liner that enters Puget Sound has to go through Admiralty Inlet. They are guided by mid-channel buoys that mark the center of the shipping lanes, like highway centerlines."

As he listened to Ian, Peen settled into the seat. He was comfortable wearing the hoodie, but he wondered if Tora was warm enough. Concerned she might be cold, he slid his arm around her. She didn't object. He couldn't have imagined that his crazy day would have transformed into an even crazier evening.

"I'm just happy we are heading away from Damon," William noted.

"I'm happy it's a calm night," commented Ian. "There's often a swift current through here because it's as much a highway for the tides rushing in and out of Puget Sound as it is for the ships that travel through here. These waters can be treacherous during extreme tides and high winds.

William noticed a different set of lights to the south. "Is that another ship?" William asked.

"Yes," Ian answered, "and this one appears to be coming our way."

Wanting to ignore more talk of danger, Tora changed the subject, "How'd they find us at Ian's? No one knew where we were going."

"I don't know," answered Peen. "We had your cell phone, but I highly doubt they tracked it."

"Maybe the apartment was bugged," suggested Tora, reaching for her pocket. She pulled out her iPhone. She fiddled with it for a moment and then said solemnly, "It didn't get charged enough; it's dead."

"Yeah, I wished we'd been more careful when we were there," remarked Peen. "Anyway, the dead phone is all for the best. That way no one can track us."

William added, "Peen's correct about that. For at least ten years the FBI has had the technology to geo-locate modern cell phones and auto-launch the microphone, even when the phone is off. It's called a roving bug. They can also use car systems like OnStar as a roving bug. That's why I only own old vehicles. Call me paranoid, but I like simplicity and privacy."

Tora responded, "Normally my life is so boring that no one would want to listen to anything I have to say."

Ian added, "Life was so much simpler when I was younger. Given my recent art restorations, I suppose watching what I say and do is important as well."

Silence fell over them as they decompressed from the chase. A buoy in the distance beeped a warning sound, reminding boaters of the underwater dangers.

Ian took a deep breath. He loved being on the water at night, but on this evening he felt extra fortunate. Looking into the sky he saw red and white lights from several airplanes twinkling against a deep royal blue sky. He could see faint stars appearing in the east. The water was black and seductively calm, lapping gently against the hull as they motored toward Whidbey Island.

Peen broke the silence, "I don't understand how a silo disappeared from the government's radar."

"I was curious about that as well," answered William. "Grandpa explained that this project was Joe's baby. Since the relationship between the U.S. and the Soviets devolved into the Cold War, Joe felt revealing that the U.S. held important Russian treasures would degrade things even more. Joe kept the project so secret that by the time the Berlin Wall fell, Joe and Grandpa were the only two left that knew the whereabouts of the panels. Apparently, Joe passed away twelve years ago, but before he did, Joe approved the idea of recruiting an expert to evaluate and restore the artifacts since there'd been some deterioration. Fortunately, the reservation company Grandpa started grew large enough that an expert could be well paid and the cost absorbed without notice. So, Grandpa hunted for an art expert he could trust."

Listening intently, Ian finally put the pieces together. It wasn't private collectors that owned the art Edmund had been funneling to him for restoration. These were treasures from the Tamanachee vault.

"Oh my goodness!" uttered Ian.

"What's the matter?" asked Tora.

"Twelve years ago I was contacted by an anonymous group asking if I could help restore sensitive artifacts. I never knew how they found me, but they were interested in me due to my Eastern European expertise. And, somehow they knew I had been researching the Amber Panels. I always wondered why they chose to contact me, but now it makes sense. The U.S. Government must have tracked my trips to Eastern Europe. I must have raised a few eyebrows within the State Department and maybe wasn't as anonymous as I'd imagined. When they first contacted me, I said I wasn't interested and recommended they contact Edmund Rogers. I'm sure that's how the Tamanachee tribe learned of him."

"Grandpa never said how they'd met," explained William, "but then, as you have learned, he didn't share much with me. However they met, they became good friends over the last twelve years. He joined us for dinner several times a year. I just knew him as Grandpa's friend."

William proceeded to describe arriving at the Tamanachee Reservation's desert bunker near Yakima with his grandfather and seeing the professor's Subaru wagon sitting next to the bunker's entrance, "We drove up the access road, which ended at the top of a large knoll, and saw Edmund's car. Since there's nothing else around there but a concrete pad, a large gravel parking lot, and sagebrush, the only place he could have been was inside. So, we walked to the center of the concrete pad where some stairs descended into the ground. We stepped down the metal staircase until we encountered a heavy door. Grandpa typed a code into a panel that opened the door.

We entered and took an elevator at the far side of the landing to the main floor. I'd always been told the main floor was a bunker or bomb shelter. But this time, Grandpa revealed the space would have been the control room for a missile silo. He also explained that was why the utility room was built underneath the control room, so that the wiring and systems could be easily maintained. Then, Grandpa crossed the control room and showed me a small box I'd never noticed. He produced a key from his pocket that turned a switch, which caused a large door, or more like a portion of the wall, to slide open. It was so well hidden I never knew it was a door. Behind the sliding door was a twenty-foot corridor. We entered it and Grandpa used the key again to shut the sliding door."

Tora interrupted him, "I don't understand. Why'd the tribe think they'd need a bomb shelter?"

"I don't know," replied William, "people never talked much about it. We all just assumed it was there because of the Hanford Nuclear site."

"So, where was my uncle?" asked Peen impatiently.

"I'm getting there," responded William, "Grandpa led me from the sliding door in the control room through the corridor to a second door, which he said was another blast door like the one at the bunker's surface. He repeated the process with another key and switch. This time a door with enormous hinges swung open toward us. That's when we entered a room with maybe fifty old-looking, large wooden crates of different sizes. Nearby were some desks, chairs, and an electrical console with a few display screens and switches. When he heard the door swing open, Edmund welcomed us. A short while later, Grandpa and Edmund explained that they needed my help. But before they could say any more, a high-pitched alarm interrupted our conversation. Grandpa went to the security console and discovered three men had somehow accessed the blast door at the top of the silo and were standing at the doors to the elevators. We caught a quick glimpse of them on a security camera before the screen turned to snow. One minute later we watched the men enter the main floor. They looked around, unsure where to go next."

Ian interrupted, "We might have a problem. That cargo ship William spotted earlier is going faster than I thought. I doubt we can get across the shipping lane before it reaches us. I think we'll need to turn south, wait for it to pass, and go behind it."

"It still looks pretty far off, Ian," observed Peen. "Are you sure it's coming too fast to cross in front of it?"

Ian cautioned, "Better to be safe than sorry. Even if their radar picks us up, there's no way they can maneuver around us. If we let it pass by and go behind the ship, we'll have to deal with its rolling wake. So, pick your poison."

"As captain it is time for me to make an executive decision. We'll head south," announced William.

"No end of challenges tonight," sighed Tora, then asked, "William, tell us what happened after you saw the bad guys in the control room."

William continued his story, "Grandpa pushed an intercom button and told them they were trespassing. He ordered them to leave and claimed the police would arrive shortly. The men laughed. One shouted that he didn't believe him. He said he knew Grandpa and Edmund were inside somewhere, then threatened to shut down the electricity if they didn't appear immediately. My grandfather's kind of stubborn and answered the man with a single word, *no*. A few moments later the power went off and everything turned black. I thought we were in a world of hurt until Grandpa told me about the escape vent. When I suggested they come with me, Grandpa told me they'd never make it up the long ladder. The next thing I knew, they were sending me up an old ventilation shaft to retrieve the design drawings so Grandpa could re-establish power and communications to the vault. So, despite my concerns, I climbed up the shaft, unlocked a metal hatch, and carefully peered out. Seeing no one, I shook loose the rocks and debris from on top of the hatch. After I closed the hatch, I kicked some dirt back on top of it and ran down the hill. I walked, then hitched a ride back to town to get my motorcycle and raced here."

"So you just left them there?" complained Peen.

"They said they were safe!" countered William, "they said no one could reach them without electricity."

"Why don't you contact the CIA?" inquired Tora.

"Grandpa said no one would believe my story. I had to go along with their plan."

"Why not alert the police or the FBI?" asked Peen.

"Hey, no need to attack me. I suggested they do that, but their primary concern was to maintain secrecy. Again, Grandpa was very worried about the effects of the news on the tribe. Even telling you guys was a risk, but I needed help. I can't take on that crew by myself. From what I glimpsed on the monitor, they entered the silo with semi-automatic rifles."

"Well, I'll tell you one thing, I'm going back with you. You won't be alone," announced Peen.

"Works for me. I'm there too," said Tora.

"I'm on board," added Ian.

"Okay then, we're all in agreement. But, first things first. We need to get to Whidbey Island and then to the mainland," argued Peen.

Tora spoke up, smiling, "That's when I find us a ride."

"I've got a better idea," suggested Peen, "we'll visit my friend Corvair in Everett. He can store Jolo and provide us with a vehicle we don't have to steal."

"Can we trust him?" asked William.

"Yes, we've been friends a long time. Last time I saw him was during a hike in North Cascades National Park where we were stranded for two days due to a freak snow storm, but that's a long story."

"What kind of name is Corvair?" wondered Tora.

"Yeah, Corvair Smith. His dad owned a 1963 Corvair that he loved. Corvair explained that with a last name like Smith, his dad thought he needed a first name that would stand out."

"Wasn't the Corvair the vehicle that Ralph Nader said was unsafe at any speed?" probed Ian.

"Yeah, the Corvair people point to a 1972 National Transportation Study that proved Nader wrong, or so claims my friend. I only know that because every time we'd go out to play pool someone would make fun of his name and he'd have to defend it. And, since he's a total geek and a car nut, he did the research. He said one secret to keeping the car stable was to maintain the correct tire pressure. He's fanatical about details like that. I always felt that begged the question, that if you have to monitor the tire pressure so closely, maybe it really isn't so safe. Eventually, I learned to avoid the entire subject, unless I wanted to get under his skin."

"Will we be borrowing a Corvair?" asked Tora with a dash of sarcasm.

"We'll take whatever he has available."

Tora draped her arm over the side of the seep and dipped her fingers into the cold water. "The water comes up pretty high on Jolo," she commented.

"Yes it does," said William. "These were made to float low. Unfortunately, they float so low they sink easily, too. They weren't too popular in the war for that reason. They also couldn't carry much in the way of cargo, so they were abandoned for the larger six-wheeled DUKWs."

"Can we avoid the factoid about the potential for Jolo to sink? I am blissful in ignorance," noted Ian.

"Agreed," seconded Peen.

"When was Jolo built?" asked Tora, ignoring the comments about sinking.

"Around 1942. Some people call this a seep. Others call it an amphibious jeep. Ford designated it a GPA."

"Hmmm.... GPA makes me think of school."

"The *G* stands for government vehicle. The *P* stands for an eighty-inch wheelbase or a quarter-ton vehicle. I'm guessing the *A* stands for Amphibious vehicle. I'm only guessing that, because Ford built jeeps during World War

II that were designated GPWs with the *W* standing for Willys style or a jeep with a Willys motor, depending on the source. It gets confusing kind of quickly in the jeep world. Only people who truly suffer from the dreaded Willys disease know those kinds of details."

Tora tilted her head, "Willys disease?"

William responded, "Yes, a disease that makes you obsessive over learning the history of the jeep."

"What's the cure for this disease?"

"You'd think the cure would be to own a Willys Jeep. But, few people can own just one. No matter how nice your jeep is, there are so many different models and varieties, people can't help but want another one. In the end, there is no known cure. We just suffer through it."

"Have you considered a psychiatrist? I'd suggest you seek mental help after we save your grandfather."

"Strangely, that's not the first time I've heard that."

"Is there anything about jeeps you don't know?" asked Peen with a yawn. He could feel the day's events catching up with him.

"Probably, but I never know what I don't know until I learn that I didn't know it. For such a simple vehicle, their history is complicated."

Peen paused, "Speaking of jeeps, what was up with all those jeeps in the garage? How long has my uncle been collecting them?"

William shrugged, "Well, you'll need to ask him yourself. I knew my grandfather liked old vehicles, but I didn't know about the collection either. I grew up exploring the trails and logging roads around the foothills of Eastern Washington in an old Willys Wagon. Every time I went exploring, I'd never know if I'd be walking or driving back, as the wagon didn't always work right."

"Do you still have your jeep?" asked Tora.

"I have a wagon, but not the original one. I've owned a few other jeeps over the years. Now all I own is the wagon and a 1949 CJ-3A."

Peen surprised Tora when he closed his eyes and dropped his head onto her shoulder. He was exhausted after his long day and the gentle motion of the water only made it worse.

William listened to the sounds of water slapping against the hull. He looked at Ian, who sat in the passenger seat at an angle watching the water in front of them. Ian's right shoulder leaned against the seep's side wall. His long legs bent awkwardly beneath the dash. William looked back at Tora and Peen, who were squished together in the back seat, but didn't seem to mind.

Tora spoke, "William, if you don't mind me asking, how'd you get that interesting scar on your face?"

"It's not a pretty story. Still want to hear it, Tora?"

"Now I'm even more curious William."

"Okay, but I warned you. There were some bullies at school who called my friend Ray a square because he wore glasses. One afternoon while walking home, I saw five of them had cornered Ray and were pulling him into the woods. I ran over and told them to stop. They got mad at me, so they let go of him, pinned me down, and used a knife to carve a one-inch square outline shape into my cheek. It hurt like hell, but I was still glad Ray got away.

They laughed and said that from now on everyone would know I was a square like Ray."

Tora gasped, "That's horrible! What happened to them when you told your parents?"

"I never told anyone what happened, even when my parents demanded. But, over the years the strangest thing happened. One by one all five of those guys disappeared," explained William coldly. "That's all I'm going to say."

Tora was uncertain whether to believe him or not, but his cold voice suggested he was *dead* serious.

Ian hadn't been listening too closely. He'd been studying their heading. He remarked, "That slow blinking light on Whidbey is Bush Point. We'll be landing south of that somewhere, probably at either Mutiny Bay or Useless Bay, depending on the wind and current. It will take us about an hour or so."

Ian shined his flashlight on the dash, "Three-quarters of a tank. We sure got lucky on the gas. I'd hate to be adrift out here with an empty tank."

William added, as he pondered the vessel passing by, "Ian, you were right about the size of that ship. It's huge! It couldn't have avoided us at all. Do you think the wake will really be that large?"

"Oh, yes. We're in for a bit of a roller coaster."

"Hmmm," said Tora, "Mutiny Bay or Useless Bays. Both sound ominous."

CHAPTER 25: ARISTA KHARKOV

"Yes, a drivable boat or floating jeep. We chased them onto a spit. We had them trapped on a beach, but they drove the jeep-boat into the water and floated away. That Peen is too damn lucky. He can't be lucky forever and then I will get him. I *will* get him," growled Damon into the phone. He'd been ranting for several minutes about losing Peen again. Getting him had become a matter of pride.

Arista didn't say anything, but cringed when Damon used Peen's name. She preferred using code names, however she chose not to correct Damon. She knew he needed to vent, that he was used to getting his way. Damon was a man who rarely lost at anything. His relentless drive for success and confidence was unmatched by anyone else she knew. Damon wouldn't give up on Peen any more than he'd give up on returning the Amber Panels to Königsberg, which was the principal reason she worked as his assistant—to return the panels and restore the City of Kings to its former glory.

As Damon ranted on, she idly twisted a lock of her black hair around her finger. Her hair was like her grandmother Henrietta's, who'd been one of the few Germans to remain in Königsberg after the war. Arista was young when her grandmother died, but she could remember stories her grandmother had told about surviving World War II.

Henrietta explained how demoralizing it had been when Russian soldiers entered Königsberg in April of 1945. Henrietta was eighteen. She described how the dead were everywhere, rotting. She'd seen naked women nailed to walls, ones she'd prayed were dead and at peace. One deceased man had a sign tacked to his body that read, *Fritz, you did this to yourself.* Babies lay dead on the sidewalk, some with smashed heads. Russian soldiers, fueled by vodka, fought German soldiers and citizens who refused to honor Königsberg's surrender. Women hid in fear, but they were found and raped. Some screamed, *Schiess doch! — Shoot me now!*

Arista's grandmother and great grandmother Anke had been forced to live through the agony of the Russian's capture of Königsberg, because Henrietta was too sick to travel that winter. By the time she was healthy, the Russians had surrounded the city. So, Anke and Henrietta hid in the Königsberg flat that had been their home for fifteen years.

One day a Russian soldier burst through their front door. He stomped through the apartment overturning tables and searching cabinets and drawers. Finally, he entered their bedroom and found them. The two women were certain they'd be raped and killed.

The soldier who stood before them was unshaven. He stank and had a beastly look in his eyes. He wore four wristwatches on one arm and two on the other. He grunted like an animal when he saw them. They watched as the man lifted his gun and viewed them over the top of the barrel. Holding each other close, they cowered against the wall expecting the worst.

The eyes of the animal stared at them, cold and unblinking. Henrietta had explained to Arista how, like the man, time stood still. The two women waited silently for their executioner to pull the trigger.

Then something unexpected happened. The man lowered his gun, slumped to the floor, and began to weep. The animal had transformed into a pitiable human being. Henrietta and her mother, not knowing how to react, remained against the wall, waiting.

Eventually, the soldier started speaking in broken German. He said his name was Lev and that he was twenty-six years old. The Germans had raped and killed Lev's pregnant wife at the start of the war while he was at a nearby town gathering supplies. He felt immense guilt that he hadn't been there to protect her.

Later, he'd joined the army to seek retribution. Since 1942, Lev had seen nothing but inhumanity, first from the Germans, and then by his own people. He too had done terrible things. Like the others, he'd become a monster, a crazed warrior, always looking for his next victim.

He admitted to Anke and Henrietta that when he burst into the bedroom and saw Henrietta, it brought back powerful feelings, because she looked like his dead wife. Lev felt he was standing before his wife, having to answer for all his sins.

That night he slept on the floor of the living room. During the following weeks he protected and fed them. He taught them a little Russian to survive. Eventually Henrietta and Lev fell in love, married, and moved to a house outside of the city. *Lev and I saved each other* is what Henrietta told her granddaughter Arista.

When Arista was a little girl, Henrietta and Arista would wander Kaliningrad and imagine the old Königsberg. It was this love of the city, imparted to Arista by her grandmother, which prompted her to join a political group called the Königers. They hoped to transform the city into one that would embrace its Teutonic and Prussian history.

Her involvement in that group led to a chance meeting with Damon. They were lovers at first, but it cooled into a friendship. When Damon asked her to be his assistant eight years ago, she eagerly accepted the challenge. Since then she'd traveled and experienced the world in ways she never could have imagined. She didn't always like Damon, but respected his desire to save art and to resurrect her native city. She tolerated Damon's lesser qualities.

Damon's voice interrupted her train of thought, "Arista, are you there?" he asked more calmly.

"I am here. Are you done venting?"

"Yes," he responded curtly.

"Great, because I have some good news. We've broke nthrough a door at the *Ant Farm*."

"Excellent! Does that mean we are inside the vault?"

"No, that is the bad news. There is a second door."

"Can we blow the second door?"

"No. It will likely do more damage to the structure than to the door," explained Arista.

"Do you have a plan for accessing the second door?" asked Damon.

"Yes. I am told the second door is a blast door rather than a security door. The door has a massive lock that can be dismantled, but it will take time, possibly most of the night."

"Push them to work quickly. We are on our way there from Port Townsend. It is 10pm right now. We will arrive at six a.m. Tell them I don't want anyone entering the room without me there."

"I understand."

"Tell everyone else to head there too. We must focus our resources," ordered Damon.

"We will have nine people on site including you."

"Why not all ten?"

"We have one man unaccounted for at the *Ant Farm*. We are still waiting to hear from him."

"Where was he last seen?"

"He was acting as a sentry," she said, "and reported finding a possible access shaft. No one has heard from him since. The team at the *Ant Farm* plans to check the perimeter at first light."

Damon informed her, "I will be there by morning. I will direct that myself."

"Should I remain in this room?" asked Arista.

"Yes. You stay there. In case something happens, we will need you to coordinate."

"Yes sir."

"I want to nap. You do the same. Nothing will happen for a few hours."

"Thanks. I will check in at 5am," said Arista.

Damon turned off his phone and pulled the battery. Arista was a good woman. If he had time for a relationship, he thought he could woo her back. But he was much too busy for a relationship.

He knew Arista's family history and wondered if her grandmother had known the fifteen-year-old Katya in 1945, unlikely because Königsberg was a big city, but not impossible. Henrietta had been luckier than Katya. She'd endured fewer hardships. One lucky and one not. How different their fates had been.

Outside the window, the tall evergreens alongside the highway formed a dense, dark blur. Damon felt claustrophobic in this place of towering trees and jagged mountains. He longed for the gently rolling hills and flat plains of his native Gdansk. He was ready to go home, but he was too close to his goal to leave just yet. He must secure the panels.

Damon closed his eyes. His mind fell back to Katya, how she and Oskar had married themselves in an impromptu ceremony at the Begelhaus.

Damon pondered her husband Oskar's bravery: to run from his duty was a death sentence, yet, in hindsight, staying in Königsberg to fight the Soviets was a death sentence, too. *Would I have run away with Katya? No, I would have stayed and fought. I likely would have died, but it would have been tough to kill me.*

After writing about her marriage to Oskar, Katya had described her plan for leaving Germany. She believed if she could take the place of the nanny, she could gain entrance to the boat captained by Fritz that was leaving from Pillau. She told Oskar he could join her aboard.

Katya wrote that Oskar balked at the idea. Katya wrote, *I argued that war is ugly and if we are to survive, we too must be ugly. I asked him if Heavenly Father would forgive us? Doesn't he evaluate all sins equally? Oskar was unsure and confused. He told me he felt trapped, should he kill for his new wife or kill at the command of the Volkssturm? He sat quietly, reflecting. Finally, I told him I would do it alone, but he told me no, that he would help me. He said he had been considering a lesson from the Book of Mormon, how Nephi's murder of Laban was sanctioned by the Spirit of the Lord. God kills people, too, the Spirit had reminded him. Oskar said his options were clear, he could take one life now or wait for the Russians to arrive and kill them, until they killed him and, probably, me. Oskar announced that if Nephi could kill on behalf of God, he could kill on behalf of his wife. So, he agreed to do what I asked. Before we*

embarked on our mission, we prayed to Heavenly Father for
his strength and his forgiveness.

In her diary Katya explained how they located Dr.
Alfred Rhode's flat. When they knocked on the door, a
woman they presumed to be the nanny answered. Katya
and Oskar entered with a load of laundry, claiming they'd
been told to deliver it to Dr. Alfred Rhode's residence.
While the confused nanny questioned the laundry
delivery, Oskar stepped past her, turned around, and ran a
knife through the front of her neck as he'd been taught in
the Volkssturm. Katya described how they coldly moved
the young woman's lifeless body to the couch and covered
it with a blanket.

That's when they heard Mrs. Rhode calling to the
nanny, asking who was at the door. Katya and Oskar
remained silent and waited for the woman to appear. Mrs.
Rhode approached them from a side room. As Katya said
hello, Oskar attacked again. However, Mrs. Rhode pivoted
to fight off her attacker. Katya swung her foot at the back
of the woman's knees, causing them to buckle. The woman
collapsed. Oskar fell on top of her, plunging the knife into
her abdomen. Mrs. Rhode was wounded, but not dead. She
pleaded for mercy. *We ended her life quick*, wrote Katya.
The black of death has turned my hands red.

After moving Mrs. Rhode's body to the couch and
covering her too, Katya called for Weinhold, the Rhode's
child. She convinced the young boy she was his new nanny
and lied to him about Mrs. Rhode's whereabouts. Katya
said Mrs. Rhode was at the candy shop with uncle Fritz

waiting for them. The child seemed excited about seeing Uncle Fritz and ran off to get a toy.

Before they left the residence, Katya and Oskar removed their clothes, quickly cleaned themselves and selected outfits from the Rhode's closet. Oskar traded the Volkssturm uniform for a formal suit with pants, shirt, vest, and jacket, while Katya traded her shabby clothes for a plain gray wool dress. They also took jewelry, a watch, money and several family photos. The jewelry would secure their journey by boat to Pillau, with the least number of questions. The photos identified Weinhold as the Rhodes' child. When all was ready, they exited through the building's back door.

Weinhold behaved well, convinced he was on way to see his mother and uncle Fritz. We could not have made it to Pillau without his cooperation, wrote Katya. *We felt ruthless, scared, cold-blooded and frightened. Who could be so horrible? The world made no sense. My new husband is a killer and I stand by his side in support.*

In Pillau, Katya and Oskar found the shipyard, then the docked vessel. After the cargo was loaded onto the vessel and the trucks drove away, Katya and Oskar approached the ship's gangway with Weinhold in tow. They steeled their nerves and asked for the captain. When Fritz appeared and introduced himself, Katya explained she was the new nanny and that Dr. Rhode had asked her to accompany the boy and keep him safe.

Then Katya explained Oskar's presence to Fritz, telling him he was her brother and that Dr. Rhode had agreed to let Oskar aide them. Finally, she supplied a password. She said *panels*. She knew that would get his attention and it did. He welcomed them aboard and directed them to their quarters on a lower deck. Soon the small freighter was at sea.

Katya described winter weather that quickly turned the ship adventure into a brutal trip. For two days the rough Baltic Seas tossed the ship about. She summed up those days briefly: *Sick. Tired. I hate ships.*

At the end of the second day, Katya wrote. *FOUND OUT! Fritz confronted Oskar. Oskar pulled his gun and killed the captain in front of Weinhold. Locked Weinhold in a closet and tried to pull the captain's body into the captain's quarters next to ours. The sound of a gun brought the crew to investigate. They attacked Oskar. He shot three sailors before running out of bullets. He was bravely fighting with a fourth sailor on the top deck, when the ship lurched. Both went over the side. My poor Oskar, GONE! I ran back to Weinhold and hid with him in the closet. A sailor broke down the door and found us in the closet. He pulled me from the boy and threw me to the floor. He was going to punish me for what happened. But, he didn't know I had Oskar's knife. Weinhold screamed as the man held me down and pulled up my dress. But I showed him. I shoved the knife into his side. When he pulled away, I yanked out the knife and stuck it into his neck like Oskar had demonstrated. I pushed upwards as hard as I could. It made a sickening sound. I recoiled as the man fell to the floor still thrashing about. Finally the man stopped moving and making any sounds. He was dead.*

She described waiting several hours in the room with the knife in her hand. After no one came, she ventured onto the top deck and then up to the bridge. Next to the radio she found a sheet of paper with handwritten notes: *my son. yes. my nanny. dead. wife. dead. Imposter!* She realized Dr. Rhode had discovered the grisly scene at his home and had contacted the ship.

She didn't know how many people were left on the vessel. She searched, but found no one else. She assumed the crew had been kept small to keep the secret safe. With no one to operate the ship, it was up to Katya to steer it, but she had no idea which direction to go. To make matters worse, several hours after the shooting, fog engulfed the boat. Katya stayed on the bridge with Weinhold. As the boy slept, she wrote to her father again, describing her sadness at losing Oskar and everyone else around her.

And, most importantly for me, thought Damon, *she described Dr. Rhode's plan, the plan she'd overheard. It was a misinformation campaign to the fullest.* According to Katya, Dr. Rhode said he would send boxes on trains and on trucks, some filled with items from the museum, others filled with stones from surrounding buildings. He sent false telegrams and spread lies whenever possible. He knew people would hunt the treasure and would follow leads no matter how crazy. He even burned amber artifacts of lesser value in Knights Hall to confuse investigators.

The true path of the panels, Katya wrote, *was by ship with Fritz to Sweden and then to Iceland. No one would ever suspect Iceland, Dr. Rhode had told Fritz. When I heard their plan, I knew I had to find a way onto that ship. The only way I could think of was to replace the nanny.*

The last entry in the diary read, *Survived the shipwreck in Sweden. Americans took me and Weinhold to a safe place. I hid this notebook under my clothes. Should my father ever appear, I will share it with him. He must know what it took for me to survive. When the Americans came, I denied knowing Weinhold. I couldn't bear to look at his face, knowing what I'd done. I denied knowing about the cargo and denied knowing what happened to the crew. I am denying everything I knew. I have a chance at being reborn. I want a new life. I am no longer a killer. God willing I will live as a saint, helping rather than killing people.*

Yes, thought Damon, as the Cadillac wove southward on the Olympic Peninsula highway, she preserved the diary in the hope her father would return, an unlikely outcome. At any rate, with her recent death, her nightmare had finally ended.

And now, Damon was growing sleepy.

Chapter 26: Corvair Smith

The cargo ship's wake was a series of huge swells that first lifted the seep and its four member crew to the wave's crest, then sent them surfing in a downward rush into its trough where Jolo's front edge smacked the water with a hard splash.

"The seep doesn't have a normal hull, so it has to take the waves straight on," Ian had advised.

"What's happening?" Peen shouted, suddenly awake. After a few more large swells, the water calmed and everyone relaxed again. William followed Ian's directions to Whidbey Island, while Peen feel back asleep.

William estimated it was around 11pm when he finally spied the sandy boat ramp near some houses at Mutiny Bay. Jolo's headlamps provided little visibility, so it had taken twenty minutes along the sleepy island's shore to find the location. The lights from beach homes were welcoming beacons as they approached the boat ramp. William disengaged the bilge pump by shifting the lever next to the passenger seat backward. Then, he engaged the clutch and pulled the four-wheel-drive lever backward

367

from neutral into four-wheel drive. He felt the lurch of the seep as the front wheels contacted the bottom and churned against the sand. The front lifted out of the water as Jolo triumphantly pulled them from Puget Sound.

"Ahoy mates," barked a relieved William as he slowed the vehicle to a halt at a stop sign. He pushed in the clutch and shifted the propeller out of gear, "Welcome to Mutiny Bay Beach. Your captain has retired for the evening and your chauffer will now take over. Thank you for boating with us and please come again!"

"Not so fast," replied Ian, "don't forget, we have one more crossing."

"A trivial detail," said Tora, "we are old deck hands now, right Peen?"

Peen responded with a sleepy *yep* and looked around.

"Where do we go from here?" asked William looking forward at one road that disappeared into the darkness of the island's underbrush and another to his right that headed south paralleling the beach.

Peen spoke, "Uhhmm . . . we're at Mutiny Bay, right?"

"That's right," replied Ian.

"William," said Peen, "go straight up the road in front of us. Since there is no direct way to reach the east side of the island, without taking the main highway, we'll have to follow a few back roads."

"Aye aye navigator," responded William shifting into first gear. He released the clutch and the four of them began a trek across the southern part of Whidbey Island.

"Why can't we use the main highway? Isn't this seep fast enough?" shouted Tora as they picked up speed.

"It's not licensed and the lights are crap. There's not even a place to put a license plate," responded William.

"Yeah, and the last thing we need is to get stopped by the police," added Peen.

***

Twenty minutes later and several miles of unlit country roads behind them, Peen instructed William to make a sharp right off Whidbey Island's Soundview Drive. William slowed the seep down as the paved country road transitioned to gravel with holes and ruts. On the left were two cottages with their porch lights on.

"This is where it gets interesting," remarked Peen. "I walked this path a long time ago. I hope it's still open."

"You hope?" asked William, turning to look at Peen.

Peen shrugged, "Yep. We can always make a U-turn."

The gravel road narrowed to a rough dirt road. The springs squeaked as Jolo bounced and groaned.

"It looks like the road is ending," said William spotting a gate and a no trespassing sign, "do we need to go through the gate?"

"Yeah, that's new. Stop here and I'll deal with the gate," responded Peen.

Peen hopped over the side of the seep, opened the gate, and waved them through. William drove far enough ahead for Peen to shut the gate behind them.

The dirt road was now an overgrown tangle. Though it might have once been a road, the underbrush had narrowed it to a path.

"Are you sure the trail is wide enough for the seep?" asked William.

Peen slipped in front of Jolo, looking for the trail he'd walked as a teenager.

"Yep, it's still here, just narrower than I remember."

"Really? All I can see is a black hole."

William watched Peen disappear into the dark trail and then heard him call, "Come on!"

Despite reservations, William engaged low range, released the clutch and began slowly grinding forward. He focused on keeping the seep centered on the single-track trail. Ian and Tora leaned towards the middle, ducking branches and bushes that scraped along Jolo's hull.

The motor chugged dependably, powering them to their uncertain destination, the wheels occasionally dropping into ruts. Jolo's hull scraped the ground several times, but it always kept going. The headlight beams bounced this way and that, causing the trail to appear and disappear. The crackle and snap of twigs and brush accompanied their progress. Soon the smell of saltwater and seaweed permeated the trail, but it was impossible to see how close the water was.

As she bounced around in the back seat, Tora thought there was nothing comfortable or nice about Jolo, yet she was thoroughly grateful for its dependability and utility. It had transported them away from their enemy and carried them across the water just like it had probably done decades ago. For the first time, she could feel and appreciate why soldiers had become so attached to their vehicles. She'd read fond accounts about them jeep over the years as part of other research, but now she understood—when they'd needed this jeep to work, it had come through.

After fifteen minutes of following Peen through the uncertain terrain, the underbrush thinned and opened to a wider trail. Then the bushes disappeared altogether and William could make out a large open space that he assumed was some kind of field. Peen stopped and looked down at something. William brought Jolo to a halt and all three jumped out to see what had caught Peen's attention.

"I don't remember this canal being here," said Peen with his hands on his hips. As the four of them surveyed it, he added, "But, it doesn't look very deep."

"Famous last words," William laughed. "It never looks deep until you get stuck in it."

"I guess there's one way to find out," said Peen as he pulled off his shoes and socks. Then off came his pants. He teased Tora, "I really didn't expect this is how you'd first see me without my pants."

Tora fired back, "A typical man. Any excuse to take them off."

Ian added, "William, I sure hope there's a room on the other side of this canal where we can leave these two."

"Amen!" agreed William.

Just in case there were sharp rocks or glass, Peen put his shoes back on and made his way down the bank of the canal, descending about four feet. A second later he was standing mid-canal in a foot of water.

"Good news, the bottom feels solid. It's definitely a saltwater inlet. It must flood during high tides," explained Peen. He took a step, then another. Ten feet later he confirmed the entire bottom was firm with the deepest point being one and a half feet. He walked to the other bank, estimating it rose five feet, which would make Jolo's exit a challenge.

"What do you think?" shouted Peen to William, "can we get through?"

"Oh yeah, we can get through the water, but whether we can make it up the bank or not I won't know until we try. But, if necessary, we have four people to push, so I'm sure we can do it."

"Four people?" asked Ian puzzled. He turned to look at William, "Who'd be driving?"

"Nobody has to drive. We just keep it in low range, let out the clutch, and steer. The seep will crawl slowly on its own just fine, especially if we give it some help by pushing it up the far bank."

"But that means we'll all get wet," said Tora.

"If you're afraid of getting wet, you can just take your pants off, too," teased Peen.

Ignoring Peen, Tora argued, "But why get wet if we don't have to. I suggest we try making it over with everybody in it first. If we can't get up the other side, then we can back down and push."

Everyone agreed that made sense. So, they piled back into the seep. William let out the clutch and slowly inched Jolo to the edge of the bank. The angle of the drop-off was so steep that the seep high centered momentarily before the weight and momentum forced the steel hull into the water with a splash. The seep's weight allowed the wheels to dig into the canal's bottom and propel them forward.

As Jolo approached the far side, William gave it some gas. The front of the seep caught the canal bank, its nose rising higher and higher as it climbed. But instead of cresting the hill, the engine sputtered and coughed. With no power to the wheels, Jolo rolled backward. William held tight to the steering wheel as the seep re-entered the water with a splash, and wound up straddling the inlet.

"I didn't see *that* coming," said William in frustration. They sat quietly in the dark, with Jolo's engine no longer puttering, its illusion of dependability was shattered.

"What happened?" asked Tora.

No one answered. William tried restart the engine. It turned over several times, fired, and then died. He repeated this several times until the engine stopped firing at all. Then he spoke, "Guys, I have a bad feeling we are out of gas."

Ian checked the gauge with a flashlight and groaned, "The gas gauge reads three-quarters of a tank, which is exactly where it was when I checked last time."

"I guess the gauge doesn't work," sighed Peen.

William agreed, "It wouldn't surprise me at all if it didn't. The gas gauge relies on a simple resistance circuit to calculate the fuel level and that isn't a dependable system."

Tora offered, "I can steal a different car."

"Yeah, that's an option, but I hate the idea of leaving the seep here. It's just a thing, yet if there's any way to find some gas, I'd like to get it out of here. Besides, the ferry to the mainland won't run again until morning, so we need this seep to get across," cautioned Peen.

"No, that's too late. We've got to return as soon as possible," urged William.

Silence returned to the seep's occupants. An owl hooted in the distance.

"I may be able to help," said a deep, loud voice from somewhere in the field.

Startled, they all looked up. So absorbed in their plight, they hadn't noticed a dark figure observing their predicament. The man stepped their direction, flashlight in hand, and stopped at the edge of the bank. He spoke again, "Couldn't any of you see the no trespassing signs?"

Peen took the lead, "This was my idea. We're taking a short cut to reach the east side of the island. I'm sorry if we trespassed, but our decision was made with the best of intentions. Can you really help?"

The man's flashlight beam slowly crossed over the seep and its occupants.

"I'll be damned! Is that really a Ford GPA?" he asked, his stern demeanor disappeared, replaced by curiosity.

"Yes sir," answered William, surprised.

"That's what I thought. Your vehicle triggered an infrared sensor my son installed at that gate you opened. It sets off a buzzer in the house and a camera to photograph intruders. I couldn't sleep tonight and my wife is visiting her friend Judy, so I was playing solitaire when I heard the alarm. When I checked the computer, I couldn't believe my eyes. To be honest, I had to reference my jeep book to remember the name. I figured it would take you a while to get through the trail with your rig."

"Are you a World War II buff?" asked Tora. She could see he was an older man, tall like Ian. He looked about fifty-five years old. He had little hair on his head and wore a large smile that pulled higher up on the left side of his face. He was dressed in a long-sleeved plaid shirt and jeans. Appearing affable and grandfatherly, he seemed curious about their plight.

"Though I don't have any experience with seeps, I do own a CJ-5. I also used to work on transmissions and transfer cases for extra income. I helped my son build a jeep, too. My wife and I belonged to a jeep club for years."

"I guess we've found the right man," noted Ian. "Can you help us? I know our explanations sound weak, but we really do have an important mission."

"I can only imagine you are doing something important if you are negotiating my property in the dead of night with a seventy year old seep."

Peen climbed the bank, still without pants. Meanwhile, one at a time, Jolo's occupants climbed onto the cowl of the seep, each jumping to the embankment.

Peen stepped forward and shook the stranger's hand, "My name's Peen, this is Tora, next to her is William and over there is Ian. Sorry about my lack of pants!"

"No problem. Nice to meet you. My name is Karl, Karl with a *K*. Let's see if we can fix this thing."

"Do you think it's out of gas, too?" asked Tora.

"Probably. I heard the sputtering. Most likely either you've lost your fuel pump or your tank is empty. We can easily test both."

"Thanks Karl, we really appreciate it."

***

An hour later, they were waving goodbye to Karl and heading to the east side of the island along a few more remote country roads.

Ian spoke, "Good thing Karl keeps a couple full containers of gas for mowing and chainsaws at his shop. I'd say he saved the day! "

"Yes he did," agreed Peen, "did you know he's in his seventies? He told me stories of being in the Navy, working for Boeing and how his wife judged gymnastics before they retired to the island. He said he lifts weights every day."

"Maybe that's why he looks fifty-five? He made me guess his age, then he pulled out his driver's license to prove he was seventy-nine," said Tora.

"He sure was thrilled with the ride in Jolo to his driveway," noted Peen.

William was less enthusiastic, "Yeah, but he also had plenty of advice about driving the seep. He said the axle bearings don't last long and the bearing retainers expand at speeds over thirty miles an hour. He warned me not to drive any faster than that or the bearings would fail prematurely. In fact, he *insisted* I didn't."

Tora laughed, "Didn't you remind him we're kind of in a hurry?"

"No, I didn't want to argue. I just thanked him for the information and gas. He's probably right, but we have bigger issues than bearing wear," said William.

"Well, we can always replace the bearings, but we can't replace our family," added Peen.

It took another fifteen minutes to cross the remainder of Whidbey Island and find the small boat ramp near the Clinton Ferry Dock. William navigated Jolo through the calm waters toward the mainland. Twilight had passed and twinkling stars filled the sky. It was a quiet scene, interrupted only by the noise of a southbound freight train on the opposite shore.

Ian bent his head slightly backward over the seat. "Isn't it beautiful! So many stars, but not as many as there are out on the ocean," commented Ian. He was silent for a few seconds, then added, "Anyone familiar with the Greek Mythological character Phaethon?"

No one answered.

"Phaethon was the son of Helios, the Sun-God," explained Ian. "Phaethon begged his father to let him pilot the Sun chariot. Reluctantly, Helios agreed. In no time, Phaethon lost control of it. The Sun chariot plunged toward Mother Earth, scorching her in places and threatening to set her completely afire. Mother Earth pleaded with Zeus to save her, so he hurled a thunderbolt at Phaethon, killing him and sending him into the river Eridanos. Phaethon's three sisters — Aetheria, Aegle, Aegiale — mourned him for months, before they were transformed into poplar trees. As trees they continued weeping, but instead of tears they wept amber."

"That's a beautiful, albeit tragic story," remarked Tora. "What made you think of that?"

"The river, Eridanos, into which Phaethon plunged is a constellation. The stars in the sky and all the talk of amber reminded me of it."

"Where's the constellation?" asked Peen looking up.

"Oh, you can't see it from here, Peen," responded Ian. "Like the more well-known Southern Cross, it's only visible in the southern hemisphere."

Quiet enveloped Jolo. Soon, they returned to land using the public boat launch at Mukilteo and headed north to Everett. Using back streets the tired crew soon arrived at Corvair's house, the romance of the seep having been replaced by the reality of its bone-jarring ride and unforgiving seats.

***

Peen rang the doorbell of the modest one-story house. Behind him, Tora, William and Ian stood waiting for Peen's friend, to respond. Despite repetitive ringing, no one answered the door. Peen yelled, "Corvair, it's Peen. I've got something to show you."

Tora clutched the drawing tubes while looking at the gray wood-shingled house with white trim. She thought the cookie-cutter house was unremarkable in a forgettable 1970s suburban housing development. Next to a small patch of grass that made up the front yard was a driveway the width of three cars. Two-thirds served the garage, the remainder vanished into the sideyard behind a gate.

"By Grabthar's Hammer Peen! It's 1:30am!" shouted a voice from inside the house.

"Huh?" Tora uttered, turning to William, "what's a grabbers hammer?"

William shrugged.

Peen yelled back at Corvair, "We don't have time for Galaxy Quest! Let *us* in dammit. We're in the middle of a shit storm."

"When you say us, who do you mean?"

"I'm here with Tora, Ian, William, and Jolo, but you don't know any of them. We've just driven Jolo across the sound from Port Townsend."

A groggy Corvair opened the door a crack. "What's a Jolo?"

"We drove an amphibious jeep named Jolo across Puget Sound."

Corvair snapped awake, "Really? That sounds cool. But, you should try doing that in the middle of the day when the *rest* of us are *awake*!"

"Sorry about the timing, Corvair, but get over it and let us inside. You'd probably be working in the middle of the day anyway."

"True,"

"Corvair, do you want to hear the best part of this whole gig?"

"Sure, why not Peen. I'm up anyway."

"We need to leave Jolo with you. You get to drive it."

Corvair thought for a moment, then slowly said, "Ohhh, I get it. You need something from me. That's why you're here."

"C'mon, what are friends for, Corvair? Just let us in so we can talk. This is important."

"You can come in, but I'm naked."

"I really didn't need to know that. Go get some clothes on or I'll open the door myself."

379

"Okay, okay. Give me a few seconds, then come on in and grab whatever you want. I'll be right out."

William was surprised by the home's interior. While the outside was forgettable, the inside was precise, balanced, clean and organized. The colors were muted, mostly grays and off-white with black accents, masculine, yet peaceful. Three different puzzle cubes were arranged on a black side table.

Peen led them into the dining room, which opened into a small kitchen with light gray walls and natural wood cabinets. They each took a chair at the dining table, relieved to be sitting on something soft and comfortable.

Corvair re-appeared sporting a vintage Sounders t-shirt and blue jeans, his dark hair pulled into a ponytail. Even with an olive complexion his eyes looked red around the edges, probably from the rude awakening. He had a slim physique and an athletic stride.

"Give me just a second," he said as he retrieved a large glass pitcher from the refrigerator. He poured a dark liquid into a coffee cup and took a sip, then took a gulp.

"That's Corvair's go-juice," explained Peen.

"Yep, and proud of it," responded Corvair. "Black fermented Pu-erh tea with a dose of lemon for flavor. Lots of caffeine without the sugar. Now, for introductions."

He walked over to the dining table and extended his hand to greet Tora, "Hi, my name is Corvair."

"I'm Tora," she responded.

Corvair gave Tora an up and down assessment in a way that slightly unnerved her. Then he shook William's hand and repeated the process. Finally, he greeted Ian.

"Would anyone like something to drink? Tora, Ian, William? Peen, you can get your own."

"I would like something. What do you have?" asked Ian.

Before Corvair could respond Peen interjected, "You'll only find tea, water or raw milk. And maybe some fresh seafood of some sort; he loves to dive."

"Yes. My soon-to-be-ex-friend is correct," said Corvair giving Peen a dirty look, "you can't get any better food than a freshly harvested dinner of shrimp, sea cucumbers or scallops. And if Peen knew anything about body chemistry and hormones, he too would eat like I do and stop consuming drinks and food laced with sugar and fake vitamins. The producers of the film *Idiocracy* nailed the future; we'll become a population evolving to embrace our most basic and banal desires. It's a crime really . . ."

Peen interrupted him, "Oh, knock it off professor. We don't have time for that. Just get them something to drink. We need to tell you what we've been through."

"A professor?" asked Ian in surprise.

"Yes, Corvair doesn't look much like a former professor, does he? It's been a long fall from the hallowed mountain top of academia."

"True Peen, but a giant leap in salary!" Corvair noted. He looked at Tora, "What can I get you to drink?"

"I'll have water," said Tora.

"Me too," said William.

"Me three," said Ian.

"I'll take the tea," added Peen.

"Yeah, he makes fun of my tea, but he likes it just the same," replied Corvair, eyeing his friend.

Peen chuckled. They'd been torturing each other since their first meeting at Camp Orkila on Orcas Island during the summer after seventh grade. They fought each other twice during their two-week stay, with Peen giving Corvair a black eye and teasing him about his name and Corvair giving Peen a bloody nose and teasing Peen that his name—Ulysses—was a 'sissy' name.

Their mutual disgust with each other altered dramatically after they were placed on the same capture-the-flag team. Winning several days in a row formed a bond that has lasted two-plus decades.

Corvair was quiet as Peen summarized their long day, though he never mentioned the panels specifically nor Königsberg. When Peen finished the story, he added, "We need to trade in our trusty seep for a vehicle that will take us to the Tamanachee Reservation near Yakima."

Corvair walked over to the kitchen, tapped his phone's screen, then smiled, "I know what you're not telling me, but you found them. You or your uncle or someone found the Amber Panels!"

All four were dumbfounded.

Pleased by their reactions he said, "You're wondering how I figured it out?"

"Yes," said Tora as the others nodded.

"You mentioned Bernstein Fine Arts. I thought bernstein was the German word for amber, but had to look it up just to be sure. The term Amber Panels also appeared in the search. Then I figured, what piece of amber art has disappeared and is worth all this effort, both yours and your nemeses? The answer was logical: the Amber Panels."

There was silence all around.

"Peen, I'm familiar with Graph Theory, the Seven Bridges Problem, Kant, Königsberg and I've read about the disappearance of the panels. I just did the math. Remember, I'm a professor of mathematics."

"Was," interjected Peen.

"Ok, was! But, it *was* Immanuel Kant — who lived and died in Königsberg — that claimed Euclidian Geometry to be, and I paraphrase here, *the one true geometry*! Even the famous Seven Bridges Problem of Königsberg is based on flat geometry, as is Euhler's graph theory, which evolved out of his attempts to prove that traversing the bridges without doubling back is impossible. However, if you start bending space, or bending geometry, then you enter non-Euclidean geometry, which alters the answers to both. One additional reason I know about Euhler is because Google uses his node theories to better organize networks of Internet information."

"Umm, I totally disagree with your interpretation," countered Tora. "Kant never meant Euclidian Geometry was the one true geometry; what he meant was that Euclidian Geometry was a creation of man, a synthetic way to explain the flat world around us. Non-Euclidian geometry is, again, just another synthetic creation by man to describe a world beyond Euclid's flat one. Therefore, Kant is in fact consistent."

"Interesting. I'll have to mull that one over," responded Corvair. People didn't challenge him often, so her response surprised him, "Peen, where did you find this woman? I like her!"

"I found her in a kitchen, actually. She can cook circles around you," bragged Peen.

"At this point, that wouldn't surprise me, given she's survived your antics," countered Corvair.

"Hold on," said Tora, "did you say the Seven Bridges Problem is unsolvable in flat geometry, but under non-Euclidian Geometry it is solvable?"

"Exactly. Start with a circle. The longest distance between two points is represented by the diameter," explained Corvair.

"That makes sense," Tora quickly agreed, enjoying the intellectual turn the conversation had taken.

"Now, bend your circle into a Pringle's potato-chip shape, which is roughly a hyperbolic paraboloid. As you bend the potato chip, the points along the bending edge of the circle move closer to each other, becoming closer together in terms of three dimensional space. Non-Euclidean geometry describes mathematical objects and systems that shift from two dimensions into three dimensions."

Corvair stopped to let them ponder what he said. Then he continued, "Here's a simpler example. Most maps make it appear that San Diego is much closer to Hawaii than Portland is to Hawaii. The truth is Portland is only about sixty miles farther than San Diego. If Portland was on the coast of Oregon, it would be closer than San Diego. The important takeaway is that flat geometry doesn't always tell the whole story. We live in a three dimensional world and often have to express the three-dimensional space accurately. If we don't, our conclusions can be false."

"But how does that solve the Seven Bridges Problem?" asked Peen.

"Go back to our potato-chip-shaped circle. You just have to bend the circle until the island meets with the mainland in a way that allows you to walk off the island without crossing a bridge."

"Wait, that's cheating," replied Tora.

"No it isn't Tora," explained Corvair. "It just seems like cheating because you've been taught to adhere to Euclidian Geometry. You have to think outside the box, pun intended, on this one."

"I don't quite follow it," said Ian, "but, I can see why Google hired you."

"Thanks Ian. I can always put in a good word for you at the company. The historical implications of organizing and presenting massive amounts of history will need smart people like you who know history."

"Maybe so Corvair, but I'm not sure this old dog is ready to pursue new computer tricks."

"If you people are through, I'd sure like to get a vehicle and get out of here," announced William impatiently.

"Right, right," said Corvair, "you can take my new Lincoln. I think I'll play with Jolo today."

Everyone began to rise when Tora dropped one of the tubes she was holding onto the floor. It rolled over toward Corvair, who bent down and picked it up.

"Are these the plans to the silo you mentioned?" asked, Corvair as he removed the end cap.

William responded, "Yes, we still haven't decided how to breach it. The biggest question is, do we go through the silo's top-side door or attempt to slide down the air vent?"

"It depends on how many are guarding the entrances I suppose," remarked Tora.

"Let's roll them out and examine the options," suggested Corvair.

As each sheet was unrolled, William filled in details not explained by the drawings. When they were done, "Back in Euhler's day, the only way to complete the seven bridges challenge was to cheat by crossing the water at least once. Water is your answer. That's how you get in. You cheat."

"You mean like we used to do with the snorkel in capture-the-flag?" asked Peen, smiling.

"Exactly. Now, here's what I suggest."

CHAPTER 27: THE FBI STRIKES

FBI Agent Michael Jorden forced his eyes open and reached for the phone. It read 3:00am. *It must be important*, he sighed.

"Hello," answered Jorden quietly, trying not to wake his wife.

"We have another hit. Tora's phone is on and stationary. It's in Everett."

Jorden remembered the short conversation they'd had before he'd gone to sleep. Tora Armstrong's phone had mysteriously re-appeared on the GPS tracking system at a location just south of Fort Flagler. From there it had moved northward through Fort Flagler, then, strangely, into the middle of Admiralty Inlet before it disappeared. Jorden hadn't known what to make of it. He'd told Agent Eric McIlvaine to watch for the signal and call him if it reappeared. Meanwhile, he'd gone home to get some sleep.

"When is the last time it moved?" asked Jorden.

"It hasn't moved since it turned on five minutes ago," responded McIlvaine.

"Get some folks from the Everett office there immediately. I want Tora and Peen apprehended."

***

Twenty minutes later, Jorden arrived at the FBI building in Seattle, rumpled and unshaven. Jorden walked into McIlvaine's office.

"The team is waiting for your order to enter the house," announced McIlvaine.

"Whose home is it again?"

"Corvair Smith. He's worked at Google for three years and before that was a mathematics professor. There's no evidence of gun ownership and no record of arrests or tickets. No kids and no wife."

Jorden took a chair next to Eric so he could view a large flat-screen monitor. The image showed the dark outline of a one-story house.

Jorden picked up an earpiece from the table and put the microphone and receptor onto his ear. He cleared his voice, then said, "Okay Folks, let's see who's at home. Approach the door and knock on it."

Jorden watched an agent with an FBI jacket approach the door with gun drawn. He thumped on the door loudly and shouted, "Corvair Smith, this is the FBI. "

A loud reply quickly followed, "Don't shoot, it's me, Corvair Smith. I'm unarmed and alone. I want no trouble."

The agent backed away from the door, "Come out slowly with your hands on the back of your head."

"Yes sir," responded the voice from inside.

Jorden watched the man exit the house. He expected to see the man dressed in pajamas or sleepwear. Instead, he was fully dressed for the cool night as if he expected this might happen.

"Lie down on the sidewalk face first," ordered the agent.

Corvair did as he was told.

"Ask him if he knows Peen Rogers or Tora Armstrong," requested Jorden into the microphone.

The officer repeated the question.

"Yes sir. Sir, am I being charged with something?" asked Corvair loudly.

"No, we are just asking questions."

"Am I under arrest?"

"No."

"May I get up?"

"No."

"Sir if I'm not under arrest or being charged, then I want to stand up. May I stand up?"

"No."

"Sir, if I'm not under arrest then by what authority are you holding me here?"

"We are holding you here while we search the house."

"Do you have a warrant?"

"Yes."

"May I read the warrant?"

"No, you may not. Just stay right there."

"Sir, am I under arrest?"

"No."

"Then I'm free to go?"

"No."

"Then I want to stand up. And, by the way, this is being recorded by my security camera and is being forwarded to my attorney."

Jorden slammed his hands on the desk and, without irony, shouted, "Shit. I hate these freaking surveillance cameras! We can't do anything without being recorded!" he paused, then said, resigned, "tell him he can stand up. Ask him where Tora and Peen are."

The agent helped Corvair to his feet, handed him the warrant, and repeated Jorden's question.

"I don't exactly know where Tora is," responded Corvair as he attempted to read the warrant in the dark.

"Well, we know Tora is here," argued the agent.

"How would you know that? Because I'm pretty sure she's gone. Oh wait, you must have tracked the phone she accidently left here."

Jorden realized he was being played, "Tell him we are going to charge him with obstruction of justice."

The agent relayed the threat.

"How was I interfering? I didn't know there was an investigation until two minutes ago. All I'm doing is innocently charging Tora's phone. How was I to know you were tracking it? In addition, I'm answering your questions with accurate and timely responses. You are the ones asking poor questions."

The agent speaking with Corvair was becoming impatient, "I'll ask you one more time, what do you know about Tora and Peen?"

Corvair pondered this question. He realized the police knew about Tora and Peen, but not about William or Ian,

"That's different from your initial question. I can tell you that I heard they have been falsely accused of crimes they did not commit."

"Again, are you trying to hamper this investigation? Because, if you are, you are committing a crime."

Knowing he full well meant to delay the FBI, he remained quiet. It had been his idea to distract the FBI just in case they were monitoring her phone, "Not in the slightest sir, but I'd also hate to accidently incriminate myself should I say something either untrue or inaccurate. Therefore, I'd like to speak to my attorney."

"Damn police shows," muttered Jorden to himself. "Okay, let him call his attorney. This is going to take longer than I thought."

Chapter 28: Ian-Tovs

It was Tora's turn to take the wheel. They were switching drivers so everyone could get some rest during their drive to Yakima. Ian rode in the passenger seat of Corvair's Lincoln, while William and Peen slumped into the back seat. Tora pulled away from the Factoria Mall near Bellevue.

Ian opened a discussion about the task he and Tora had been assigned: to come up with a distraction at the top of the silo while Peen and William entered it.

"Tora, I think Molotov Cocktails are the solution. They're easy and quick to make with readily available supplies," suggested Ian. He gulped down more of the lukewarm coffee he was drinking to stay awake.

"Well, that seems like a good solution," responded Tora. "But, are you sure they are powerful enough?"

"Despite their simple ingredients, they have been surprisingly effective weapons. In the 1930s they were made from gasoline, kerosene, and tar in a bottle with a rag at the top, used first by the Spanish against Russian tanks in the 1930s. They didn't earn their Molotov title until the Winter War of 1939 between Russia and Finland," explained Ian. "At that time a Soviet Foreign Minister named Molotov claimed over the radio that the Soviets were dropping baskets of food to aid the starving Finnish people. The problem was the Finn's weren't starving. Instead of food, the Soviets were dropping bombs, which the Finns branded Molotov Bread Baskets. In retaliation, the Finns successfully employed the Spanish bottle weapons against Soviet tanks; however, the Finns called their improvised bombs Molotov Cocktails, claiming they were *drinks to go with the Molotov Breadbaskets*. Despite their simplicity, Molotov Cocktails proved very effective against the tanks."

Tora asked Ian, "Have you ever made one?"

"Nope! But, I'm sure some enterprising nutcase on the Internet has done all the work for us. Where'd we put Corvair's phone?"

"It's right here," said Tora.

As the Lincoln dropped down the long slope toward Issaquah, Ian launched the phone's web browser. Its light washed his determined face, but he grumbled about the small print and his poor eyesight. By the time they were approaching North Bend, he'd found all the information they needed to construct a modern version of the Molotov Cocktail from ingredients available at any super store.

Ian explained how it worked, "Salad oil, melted wax, and cotton balls are combined to create a sticky, yet stable mixture that compels the gasoline to burn more evenly and thoroughly. We pour the mixture into a bottle until half full, then cork it. Next we tape some strings tied to rocks to the side of the bottle. Finally, for our igniter, we adhere a women's panty liner to the bottom of the bottle. This replaces the old-fashioned and more dangerous dangling-rag-igniter that you always see in the movies. With the panty liner on the bottom of the bottle the thrower can hold the bottle by the neck, dip the liner into a container of gas to wet it, and light the panty liner with a portable cook stove. Then it is aim and throw. I call it the Ian-tov!"

"Professor, I think you missed your calling as a weapon's specialist," she teased. "What are the strings and rocks for?"

"The hope is that one or both of the rocks will hit the bottles during impact, improving the chance the bottles will break."

"I guess if they are powerful enough to stop a Russian tank, they are good enough to cause distractions. So all we need is some way to transport them to the silo entrance and make it safe for us to throw them," said Tora.

William, offered a sleepy suggestion from the backseat, "You know, you could use our reservation's snowplow truck. It's big and would protect the thrower if they hid in the dump bed and it would be a hard vehicle for them to damage. I can show you what I mean when we get there."

"William, good idea," said Ian, "now get some sleep."

"Yes sir," William mumbled.

"I sure hope the Molotovs will work. We need a pretty big distraction," said Tora.

"Agreed. Let's hope Corvair's plan works."

Ian's plan seemed a good one, thought Tora as she sped up Snoqualmie Pass. *But, Peen and William will need to complete their tasks, too.*

CHAPTER 29: ANDREI NIKOLAEVICH

"Andrei Nikolaevich, welcome. I am pleased to meet you and gratified you could make it," said Damon, using Andrei's full name in a formal greeting. Damon smiled broadly and thrust his open hand toward Andrei as the Russian stepped from of his car, "This is a historic day. I wanted you to see this for yourself, to assure the Russian government I am working with your interests in mind. This is not my treasure, it is yours."

Not warming to Damon's charm, Andrei stepped away from the black Audi and firmly shook his hand. His stern manner and grimace conveyed his unhappiness at this clandestine 6am meeting with an underworld character wanted by Interpol.

Caring little about formalities Andrei responded curtly to Damon, "Good morning Damon Severloh."

Andrei purposely addressed Damon by his given name, rather than his current alias, Damon Kant. He wanted to send a clear message: *We know your real identity, so do not screw with us.*

A desert breeze slightly ruffled Andrei's blond hair as he analyzed his immediate surroundings. Andrei heard his two trusted security men close their car doors. He didn't care what Moscow had told him; he wasn't meeting Damon alone.

Looking beyond Damon, Andrei noted that, in addition to his Audi, there were five vehicles parked on the gravel lot. Next to them was a concrete pad with a set of stairs that disappeared into the ground. There was no security fence, only a rocky landscape dotted with clumps of sagebrush. A portable generator by the stairs suddenly kicked on, noisily breaking the silence. A fat orange power cord slipped down the stairway.

Seven men dressed in jeans and jackets stood at attention, armed with semi-automatic weapons. Damon started talking, but Andrei wasn't listening. So extraordinary was the mission that the Consulate General had banned the use of the normal consulate car. Instead, Andrei had switched between several vehicles at safe-car locations to insure no one had followed him. His boss, the Russian Consulate General in Seattle, had made it clear he didn't trust Damon. But, it was imperative that Andrei make the trip, because a directive had come from a higher authority than his boss. That directive instructed Andrei to meet with Damon at an undeclared missile silo on an indian reservation near Yakima.

Andrei's reputation for cleaning up sticky situations had made him a valuable man. With a military and intelligence background, forty-year-old Andrei had taken a position in the Seattle Consulate to align himself with the head of the consulate, an old friend, who everyone expected would become Russia's Ambassador to the U.S. Until then, he was a fixture in Seattle.

Andrei was given a specific goal. He had to determine if the Amber Panels were real, and if so, whether Damon was serious about handing them over to the Russians. He was informed that Damon appeared to be a friend of the Russians, with his work in Kaliningrad being evidence of that. Just the same, they reminded him to remain vigilant for Damon's motives were not entirely clear.

"Is not this surreal?" asked Damon, attempting small talk, "a Polish entrepreneur and a Russian Diplomat standing on an American Indian reservation at a decommissioned U.S. missile base hunting for a lost Prussian artifact."

"Russian," responded Andrei, coolly.

"Pardon me," asked Damon.

"The artifact is *Russian*. It is Russia's property. Let us be clear about that. It was stolen from Russia by the Nazis. It is not Prussian."

"Right, correct. I just meant its origin was Prussian."

"Its origin does not concern me. Ownership concerns me. I want *no confusion* on this."

"And I make no ownership claims," Damon continued, "I hunted this for the benefit of the Russian people, in the hope that it will find a proper home in a rebuilt castle in Kaliningrad, celebrating all that is Russian and Prussian."

"Mr. Severloh. Enough talk. I make no promises. My singular purpose is to view what you have to show me, to verify that something worthy of the Russian government's involvement exists."

"Fair enough, Andrei. Let me call down to my team to make sure they are ready."

Damon pulled a black rotary dial phone from a metal box that appeared to have been hastily installed near the stairs. A hard line ran from the phone, crossed ten feet of the concrete pad, and disappeared down the stairs.

Damon spoke into the receiver, "Our Russian friends are here. Have you heard anything from our two guests? No? Okay. Do not go in until we get down there . . . huh? Well, clean it up. See you in two minutes." After putting the phone away Damon turned to Andrei, "I have two men cleaning up and re-lighting the area to make it safer. It should only be a few minutes."

"Are there no building lights inside the silo?"

"There are lights, but the power is not working. The power system was accidently damaged," lied Damon, "and we have no instructions for returning power to the facility. So, we have had to cut through the doors. There are two men trapped inside the vault and we hope to get them out before they die. We just disassembled the vault's locking mechanism a few minutes ago. You and I will pull the vault door open together; I dared not do it without your participation."

Damon was lying again. In actuality, he hoped the two men inside were dead. And if they weren't, he'd make sure they were.

"I was not made aware there were men trapped inside the vault. Who are they?"

"We believe they are the men who have guarded this secret for decades. Unfortunately, we have had no way to communicate with them. We tried tapping, but we heard nothing in response."

That, too, was a lie. Damon wasn't worried about tapping. In fact, when daylight had broken an hour earlier, they'd been more concerned about searching the area for a missing comrade. That's when they discovered an access hatch, a hundred yards away from the silo's entrance, a vertical shaft with a ladder that descended to an unknown location. Damon had ordered a man to go down it. He and three others watched as the man descended into the dark. After a minute, they lost radio contact. After several more minutes passed they heard gunfire echo from the vent hole. They'd heard nothing more after that.

If he could, Damon would have delayed the meeting with Andrei. But, the situation was a delicate one. The meeting had been very difficult to arrange. Damon concluded he had no choice but to open the vault door, face Edmund and Chester in the silo, convince them he meant no harm, and then kill them. Damon assumed that Andrei would find such actions unsettling, yet Damon was convinced that Andrei would see the bigger picture.

Finding the panels would be an incredible coup and the two men guarding them would be quickly forgotten.

The vintage phone at the silo's surface rang. Damon opened the box and lifted the handset to his ear. Damon responded to the caller saying they'd be right down. But, as soon as he'd spoken, the sound of a diesel truck rumbling up the silo's access road distracted him. It appeared to be, yes, it was, a snowplow truck, a strange sight to see on a summer morning. Damon figured it was a maintenance crew arriving to do work. He'd order his men to detain the workers until their all-important meeting was over. Once the Russians saw the panels, no maintenance trucks, tribes, or governments would prevent them from immediately taking possession of the them.

"Who is that?" asked Andrei, uncomfortable with this unexpected intrusion.

Damon leaned toward his men and told them to put their guns in their jackets until he and the Russians entered the silo. Then, they were to detain the truck until they received additional instructions.

"Just a maintenance truck," responded Damon, "I am told they check the facility every few days. My men will ask them to leave. There is not a problem. It is time for us to head down the stairs."

Andrei and the two other Russians followed Damon and two of his men into the stairwell. They passed through the silo's blast door and continued down four flights of stairs to the control room. Two more of Damon's men trailed them, but stopped and closed the blast door until it nearly pinched the phone cable and electrical wire powering the lights below. The two remained at the door to guard it.

Up on the surface, two of Damon's men eyed the approaching truck. A third man crouched a hundred yards away monitoring the entrance to the vent. They all watched as the snowplow truck came to a stop, black bursts of diesel smoke tumbling from its exhaust pipes. It was idling only a few feet away from the Russian's Audi.

The blinding morning sun was behind the truck, forcing the guards to squint. They could just make out that the driver was a young woman with blond hair. Surprised by her presence, they started walking toward the truck when the blade suddenly slammed to the ground. They stopped, staring at the woman. Just then the blade lifted, partially blocking their view of her, and the truck's horn sounded, adding to the strange scene.

The loud noise threw them off guard, so they were astonished to see a flaming bottle rise into the sky and tumble in their direction. It was strange looking, with strings and small rocks attached to it. Before the first bottle hit, two more bottles arced toward them. Damon's men drew their guns and fired off several rounds at the driver, but the snowplow blade blocked all but two of the bullets, which hit the windshield.

✳✳✳

Welcome to the siege on silo-grad boys, thought Tora. She watched the men scramble to avoid the first bottle as it crashed onto Edmund's Subaru, lighting its hood on fire. A black cloud flashed upward. It was followed by two other bottles that landed twenty feet to either side of the first.

403

Ian's plan to force them into the silo was working. Tora watched them scramble into the stairway, then watched three more bottles fly into the air and land near the silo's entrance.

More bottles spun through the air. This time there was no escape; the bottles crashed directly onto Damon's men in the stairwell.

Chilling screams and cries for help accompanied the flames and smoke. The horrific scene shook Tora; she couldn't take any more of it. She pressed the horn for a second time, alerting Ian they were leaving, just as two more bottles arched overhead. One landed on the Audi and another landed on a Ford Taurus, setting them ablaze.

Tora hoped Ian had flattened himself on the dump bed. She shoved the gearshift into reverse and backed up. She took aim at the biggest vehicle, the Cadillac that had chased them so relentlessly, shifted into first gear, and rammed it with the snowplow blade. She expected she'd feel triumphant, but the sounds of the burning men horrified her. So distracted by the men's screams, she didn't notice that the man guarding the escape vent had crumpled to the ground.

She backed away from overturned SUV, swung the truck around, and headed back down the access road as fast as she dared. Stealing glances from the mirrors, she could see black smoke billowing from the burning vehicles. Half way down the silo's access road she felt a large whoomp rattle the truck, which she attributed to a gas tank explosion. At the bottom of the road, Tora turned off the truck, hopped out, and ran back to help the professor down from the back of the dump bed.

Ian yelled with pride, "Wow, did you hear that? The Finn's Molotov Cocktail has nothing on the Ian-tov Cocktail, a dish best served flaming!"

Tora nodded in agreement. Her heart was pounding with adrenaline, but it was also heavy with the knowledge they'd just burned two men to death. As Ian lowered himself to the ground, they heard another explosion.

"Two cars down," said Tora flatly.

"Did we get them?" Ian asked.

She waited a second before replying. Maybe it was best Ian didn't know exactly how the men had died, "We created a distraction that will keep them busy for a while."

"Good," replied Ian, "it's up to Peen and William now."

CHAPTER 30: THE TAMANACHEE SILO

William crept on his elbows between clumps of sagebrush, hugging the hard desert floor to avoid detection as he moved toward the silo's escape vent. So far, the early morning temperatures had kept the surface cool, but it would soon be hot. Sand clung to the front of his clothes and filtered into his socks and shoes. Tucked inside a belt loop against his back was a handgun. Next to the gun was a sheathed knife. A small backpack held food bars, rope, duct tape and water. In his right hand he dragged a four-foot long steel pipe, one and a half inches in diameter.

William crawled to a point where he could see a man with a semi-automatic rifle crouching over the silo's vent hole. He wasn't surprised to see the guard, which was why William had approached his target with the morning sun behind him.

His caution had paid off, because William was within thirty feet of the guard when Ian and Tora began their assault on the silo.

William checked his watch as the sound of a diesel motor broke the desert's silence. It was 7:00am. Their timing was perfect.

He watched the vent guard's head wheel around toward the sound of the crashing metal. The man raised his gun, but remained at his post. The noise from an explosion reverberated across the desert followed by black smoke billowing into the air. Gunfire and more explosions erupted. The guard ran his hand nervously over his shaved head. Fixated on Tora and Ian's attack, the man didn't notice William rise onto one knee, aim, and fire two bullets. The man fell instantly.

William glanced around to see if anyone else was near, but saw no one. As Tora drove the truck down the access road, William ran to the fallen man and checked for a pulse. It was slight. He unsheathed his knife and coldly ended the man's life.

William slid the dead man's walkie-talkie into his backpack and secured the rifle. After he dragged the body into the sagebrush, he again checked his watch. It was 7:07am. Peen was scheduled to open the sliding door at 7:15am. William needed to hurry.

He grabbed the metal pipe and positioned it over the vent. He tied one end of a 100ft nylon rope to a heavy belt around his waist, then coiled the rope twice around the bar to act as a pulley. He planned to slide the other end of the rope through gloved hands and descend down the vent quickly and quietly. He didn't dare step on the rungs, because the noise might reveal him to anyone in the vault.

Ready to go, he flicked off the safety of his grandfather's Walther P99 and secured the handgun to the front of his shirt with two pieces of duct tape. He wanted to keep the gun close, since there was little room to maneuver.

He put on the heavy gloves, slipped into the vent headfirst, and grabbed the rope tightly. Slowly, he released the rope and began his descent. After a few seconds, what had seemed like a good idea had become uncomfortable. Blood rushed to his head, making it throb. Tom Cruise's movie character had made it look way easier.

An agonizing minute later he reached the bottom of the shaft where it turned ninety degrees to horizontal. He untied the rope from his belt and crawled quietly on his elbows toward the vault. He halted at the sound of a deep clunking noise. Sensing no immediate danger, he moved to the edge of the vent and peered into the vault. It was pitch black.

He was about to crawl out of the vent and ease himself down to the floor when a single loud *clunk* rang out, followed by beams of light sweeping the room. William held fast, realizing that, somehow, Damon's men had breached the vault. He watched the light beams dart back and forth, but detected no movement inside the room. Even with the light beams, the room was still very dark.

A voice William didn't recognize called out, "Hello, anyone there?"

No one answered. If his grandfather and the Professor were alive, it seemed they needed his help more than ever.

William couldn't see the men controlling the light beams from the corridor, but assumed they were armed. Lying on his stomach in the vent, he felt vulnerable. He needed to get to the floor without Damon's crew seeing him. After considering his options, he devised a test to see if they had itchy trigger fingers. William removed his gloves and quietly peeled the gun from his chest. He grasped the P99 with both hands and fired one shot at the floor. It was deafening, far louder than he'd expected.

The single bullet ricocheting off the ground was answered by a torrent of gunfire. Flashlight beams added to the chaos as they swept through the darkness in search of the shooter.

The firing stopped. The light beams were extinguished as well, because the shooters were rotating the door closed to shield themselves. Everything returned to black except for thin shafts of light slipping around the nearly closed vault door. Though the firing had stopped, the smell of gunpowder and the loud ringing in William's ears continued, disorienting him. He waited, and as the ringing subsided, he heard the muffled sounds of people arguing, partly in English and partly in Slavic or Russian. It seemed a jumble of languages.

In the confusion, William exited the vent, slid to the floor, and rolled to his side. He pulled off the backpack. His heart beat steady, but fast. He wondered if he should call out to his grandfather. Around him the smell of sulphur combined with the smell of urine. Of course, his grandfather and Edmund had no other option, but to pee against a wall or into a cup.

Just then the vault door moved. Light poured inside the room from the corridor, but the door wasn't opened enough for William to see who was there.

"Hello," announced a voice, "We mean you no harm. Please let us in."

"I don't believe you," barked William. He wanted his grandfather to hear him, to know that he'd returned. He lied, "Everyone else in here is dead and I'm badly injured. But, I'm not going to surrender without a fight."

More arguing ensued from the other side of the door. Eventually the door swung open revealing four men at the front with three others behind them. One of the men in the front row stepped into the room and announced, "Please don't shoot. We mean you no harm. Drop your weapons and we'll get everyone out of here safely."

"Bullshit," whispered William under his breath. To test them, he unzipped his backpack and grabbed the walkie-talkie. He tossed it to the far side of the room where it hit the wall. One man stepped forward and shot in the direction of the walkie-talkie.

As the men were focused on the far wall, William peered over the top of a desk, aimed his pistol, and fired two rounds into the group. One bullet missed, but the other hit a man in the back row, dropping him instantly.

***

Andrei was shocked to see his bodyguard drop to the floor, blood flowing from the side of his head. Highly suspicious of Damon, Andrei concluded they weren't there to rescue anyone, but to take the panels by force, assuming there really were any panels. Whatever the truth was, he wanted no part of this or the potential diplomatic results. He hadn't started this, but he would damn well finish it. To take control of the situation, Andrei ordered his remaining bodyguard to fire on Damon's men.

As soon as he gave the order, Damon bolted into the vault's blackness. Andrei's bodyguard opened fire, killing two of Damon's men. Damon's third man took several bullets in the back, yet continued to shoot as he spun and fell. Bullets ricocheted off the concrete walls, two of which hit Andrei's bodyguard. The bodyguard roared in pain, yet continued to fire more bullets into Damon's man until he stopped shooting.

Andrei turned to look at his bodyguard when something pierced his right thigh. He instinctively reached down with both hands to his leg, accidently dropping his gun. When the gun landed on the concrete floor, it fired, hitting his already injured man in the left foot. The guard yelled out again, cursing loudly in Russian. The kick from Andrei's gun sent it flying into the vault.

Andrei held his pulsing right thigh as he ordered his man to back down the corridor into the control room. Andrei's bodyguard did as he was ordered, stumbling awkwardly away from the vault. Andrei limped backward away from the vault, watching for Damon.

Strangely, Andrei heard a *thump* behind him as the bodyguard's cursing suddenly turned to wet gurgling noises. Andrei pivoted to see his man on the ground, a diving spear lodged in his chest, his shirt discolored with blood. The man writhed and kicked as he desperately grabbed at the spear, but his movements slowed, then stopped altogether.

A spear? Andrei thought. *What the hell is going on?*

Standing in the corridor at the control room's open door, Andrei surveyed the control room, hoping to identify the person who'd fired the spear, but couldn't see anyone from his vantage point. Damon's two men stationed at the top of the stairs hadn't come down, so Andrei couldn't figure out who'd shot the spear.

He weighed his options. He could stand where he was and possibly be shot in the back by Damon or he could surrender to whomever it was who was in the control room and possibly be shot with a spear himself. He chose to put his fate into the devil he didn't know.

He put his hands on his head and stepped forward into the control room. Pain seared through his right leg as he walked. Once he'd cleared the corridor, he shifted to one side and planted his back against the wall. He felt safer now that he was no longer exposed. He rotated his gaze around the room until he saw the source of the spear.

A man stood off to his left in a doorway. Behind the man a set of stairs appeared to lead to a floor below. The man wore shorts and a t-shirt. Water dripped from his hair and clothes as if he'd just been swimming. The man was studying Andrei with a piercing gaze. The grimace on his face, along with a handgun in one hand and a speargun in the other, told Andrei what he needed to know, that he shouldn't move.

Loud stomping and clattering disrupted the standoff. Two of Damon's men appeared in the control room across from Andrei. They had just come down the stairs from the silo's entrance. Andrei stared at them and they stared back at him. Everyone was confused. Andrei was unsure whom to trust more, Damon's men or the unknown man in the doorway, a person Damon's men had not yet seen.

CHAPTER 31: INTO THE PIPE

Peen tugged on the sleeve of the wetsuit, which was tighter and more uncomfortable than he remembered. He peeled back the left sleeve to read the time on Corvair's watch. It was 6:50am, time to enter the water. He smeared spit on the inside of his dive mask to keep it from fogging, then grabbed Corvair's speargun and strapped it to the wetsuit. Despite borrowing his dive equipment from Corvair, his friend hadn't complained, because the entire attack on the silo had been Corvair's idea.

While scanning the silo's plans, he'd pointed out a drainpipe running from the silo's utility room to the nearby river. As soon as Corvair mentioned it, William realized he was right. One reason Chester had built the silo near the river to test the silo's ability to repel or counter underground water. William explained that Chester finally had to install a sump pump to expel water that kept accumulating in the utility room due to the area's hydrodynamics. No matter how much they'd tried to seal the utility room, the water seeped in. Chester had installed the pump and drainage system to solve the problem.

William went on to explain that with the silo's electricity shut down, the sump pump couldn't work. Water would have immediately started to collect in the utility room, which was just under the control room. So, even if they could re-establish power to the entire facility, they shouldn't, because it might cause a massive short in the entire system.

Once William confirmed that the drainage system existed, Corvair suggested someone could start at the river, swim through the pipe, and climb into the utility room. William agreed it was feasible, and that once a person was inside the utility room, the sliding door from the control room to the vault corridor could be manually opened. Peen volunteered to swim up the pipe and William agreed to return to the vault via the vent pipe. If William could open the vault's blast door, Peen could access the corridor. With both doors open, William could shepherd the two old men from the vault, through the corridor to the control room, and down into the utility room.

To confuse Damon's men inside the silo, Ian and Tora planned to create a major distraction at the silo's surface, which they hoped would cause Damon's men inside the silo to be called to the surface.

Peen still had one concern. The distance between the river and the utility room was seventy feet. He didn't think he could swim that far holding his breath and it sounded like the pipe was too small to accommodate wearing a scuba tank on his back.

Corvair said he owned a Third Lung, an air pump that floated on the surface of the water with a one hundred foot long breathing line that allowed a diver to explore under water unencumbered by scuba tanks. Since the drawings indicated the pipe was only seventy feet long, Peen would have more than enough line to reach the utility room.

Peen was still concerned about running a noisy pump that might draw attention. He suggested connecting the breathing line to a tank of compressed air. Corvair agreed that could work.

The plan had sounded great in the warmth and comfort of Corvair's kitchen. But, as Peen stepped into the river near the silo, he found the entire idea nuts. Even so, he had no choice. Everyone depended on him to execute his part of the plan.

"Okay, let's do this," he said out loud. He placed the breathing regulator into his mouth and double-checked that the tank was secure on the bank. Peen pulled the mask over his face and slipped below the crystal river water fed by the melting snow from the Cascade Mountains. Shivers rippled down his spine as the chilly water filled the areas inside the wetsuit. His one comforting thought was that his body would warm the water inside the suit, eventually.

He groped around until he found the entrance to the drainpipe and swam inside. It immediately felt like an elongated casket, dark and claustrophobic. Peen shook that image from his mind and focused on what was in front of him. In his right hand he held a small diver's flashlight, but it failed to illuminate much beyond the green moss that waved eerily all around him. He was sure the Creature from the Black Lagoon feel right at home inside this hell.

Peen wasn't wearing flippers, so he got little push with his feet. Instead, he used his left hand to pull himself along the corrugated pipe. To his surprise, instead of angling upward at all, it continued horizontally. He wasn't going fast, but he was making progress. The breathing tube flopped against him as he moved forward, even thought he'd strapped it to one leg so that he could pull it along without using his hands.

He'd been swimming for several minutes and felt he was nearing the end when he was jerked to an abrupt stop. He realized the breathing tube had no more slack left, which meant either the breathing tube was shorter than Corvair claimed or the silo's drainpipe was longer than they'd anticipated. Rather than tug on the tube and risk pulling the tank on the riverbank into the water, Peen had another plan.

After he untied the tube from his leg, he located the rope he'd brought with him and tied one end to the breathing tube. The other end he held in his hand. He took three deep breaths, stuck the flashlight into his mouth, and used both hands to move quickly forward. Ten feet later the pipe turned upward. He shifted the flashlight to see how much further the pipe went. The pipe ended only five feet above him, but a metal grate the size of a manhole cover blocked his exit. Still holding his breath, he maneuvered around, stood up, and pushed on the grate with his back, but it didn't give.

William had told him there was a grate and assured him it wasn't locked, but he had said there might be a latch he'd have to release.

Peen stuck his fingers through holes in the grate and felt with his fingertips, trying to ignore his aching lungs. He touched a piece of loose metal and wiggled it with two fingers. Something seemed to release, so he pushed up on the grate. Part of it gave way, allowing him to lift it to a slight angle, but it still didn't open all the way. He thought, *Damn, there must be a second latch.*

By now, Peen's lungs were burning for oxygen. He needed to turn back and find the regulator, quickly. He slid feet-first down and around the pipe's bend and followed the rope back to the regulator, churning his arms to speed his descent. His entire body ached for air and fought the urge to gulp water. When he finally reached the regulator, he quickly shoved it in his mouth and took in one long breath, then another. Peen took a minute to calm himself.

He checked his watch. It was 7:10am. He was running late. Peen wondered if he could make it past the grate, then wondered what would happen to Chester and his uncle if he failed.

No, he didn't need to wonder about that. They'd probably die and Peen would lose his last remaining relative, but there was no way that was going to happen without a fight. He'd rather die trying to help than live with the guilt of giving up.

Peen cleared his head except for an image of his uncle Edmund and the task before him. He took a few deep breaths, stuffed the flashlight into his mouth, and hurried back up the pipe. Peen turned the corner and launched himself upward to the side of the grate opposite the one he'd unlatched. His fingers probed the grate as he mentally visualized the latch, but he couldn't locate anything.

Peen planted his feet and pushed hard with his shoulder against the grate. It gave way some. He repeated the same move, this time employing the anger he felt toward Damon for screwing with his life. The grate lifted a bit more. His lungs began to burn again, but he didn't want to give up. The anger of losing his business, his mother and his father surged through him. He must save Uncle Edmund! With revenge fueling his legs, he roared upward against the grate, the pressure causing air to escape through his mouth and roil past the flashlight.

Suddenly, the gate gave way and he was standing. He forced the grate and swam upward until his face broke the water's surface. He pulled the flashlight from his mouth and inhaled the stale, dank air of the utility room.

Peen climbed from the basin, stepped to the floor of the utility room and tied off the rope, so he could use it as a guide to find the regulator. Then, he surveyed the room with the flashlight. On one wall were vintage electrical panels with dials and switches. The ceiling was full of conduit. On another wall hung equipment, but nothing he understood. On the floor, the water that had seeped inside the room reached halfway up his shins.

Peen checked his watch. 7:17am. *He was late*!

Just then he heard gunshots coming from the stairway. Startled, Peen stripped off his wetsuit, assembled Corvair's speargun, and removed a handgun from an airtight plastic bag William had given him. He waded through the water, silently ascended a short fight of stairs, then turned and peered up at a second flight. He saw that it opened to the control room. That's when he heard a conversation, but was unable to make out the words. Peen assumed it was Damon's men talking.

He crept up the stairs. As he approached the top he could see the sliding door to the corridor was already open. Confused, he tried to make sense of it, water dripping into a small puddle around him. Peen was cold and exhausted. He didn't feel very ready for a fight, despite the adrenaline now pumping through him.

A voice startled him, "We mean you no harm."

It was Damon, but Peen couldn't tell to whom he was speaking. Gripping the handgun in his right hand and the speargun in the left, Peen decided to step into the control room when another round of gunfire erupted. Bullets ricocheted through the corridor into the control room and several voices screamed in agony. Peen retreated into the stairway. A moment later, a man, obviously in pain, stumbled from the corridor into the control room.

The sight of the man was so unexpected Peen accidently squeezed the speargun's trigger. Though he'd never admit it to anyone, hitting the man in the heart had been a complete accident. Peen watched the man collapse, kick violently, and then cease all movement. Next, a man with his hands on his head limped from the corridor and flattened himself against a wall inside the control room. He was clearly injured.

As Peen pondered what to do he heard footsteps trample down the long stairway. Two men entered the control room. The injured man, continuing to lean against the wall, turned to look at them. The two men came into Peen's view as they approached the man against the wall, their guns trained on him. Peen wondered why two of Damon's men had their guns trained on another of Damon's men.

Peen spotted a large birthmark on the side of one man's cheek. He realized that it was the Driver, Damon's chauffer from the day before. Peen concluded that the two men were definitely Damon's men, but then who was the man against the wall with his hands on his head?

Peen watched the man's expression. He appeared worried. No, worried wasn't it; he was challenging these two men. He was insuring they'd keep their gaze on him, and furthermore, he wasn't giving Peen away. With one look in Peen's direction, he was sure the two would turn and fire. Of that, Peen was certain. But the man held their gaze as they approached. It seemed Damon's men were having trouble making sense of the man's position against the wall.

Peen gambled. He lifted the gun and fired five shots at Damon's men. Two bullets hit Damon's driver in the kidney, knocking him to the floor. The other man turned toward Peen and fired just as Peen thrust his legs out behind him, his knees crashing hard onto the staircase. It hurt, but the move was a smart one because Peen had dropped just below the man's bullets.

Of course, the man wasn't done. He aimed his gun lower to fire again. Before he could, Andrei swung his right forearm at a specific spot on the man's neck. The man yelped, stumbled, and collapsed to the floor.

The room was silent. There was no movement. Andrei looked at Peen, who was now pointing a handgun in Andrei's direction. Not wanting to rattle Peen, Andrei slowly shook his head back and forth and pointed at himself trying to communicate, *not me.* Then he pointed down the corridor toward the vault. Finally, he held up a single finger.

Feeling unclear about what the man's gestures meant, Peen whispered, "What are you trying to tell me?"

"Only Damon remains in there," responded Andrei with a Russian accent.

"No one else?"

"Another man, a shooter, is in their, too. Is the shooter with you?"

"I believe so," Peen nodded.

Peen pulled himself to his feet, his knees still throbbing. He edged toward the vault's corridor and planted his back against the wall opposite where Andrei stood.

"My name is Peen. Who are you?"

"I am Andrei. I am with the Russian Consulate. Damon misled us. He must pay for killing my men. He must die for that."

"I'm okay with that."

✳✳✳

William was crouched behind a desk in the vault. A moment earlier a man had dashed into the vault just as the shooting broke out from the direction of the control room. William had wondered if it was Peen or someone else. Then he heard Peen's voice and someone named Andrei. Andrei confirmed that it was Damon wbo had dashed into the vault.

"Damon, if you don't give up, you'll surely die," said William, the sound of his voice echoing through the room.

Damon didn't respond, but Peen did, "Hey bud, you still alive? So am I. Me and my new friend Andrei are ready to rid the world of Damon. Can you flush him out?"

"Give me some time and I can."

"We'll slide a couple portable lights into the corridor so you can spot him. When you do, shoot him," said Peen coldly.

Out of the darkness of the vault came Damon's voice, "Wait. You need me alive."

"No, we do not," answered Andrei.

"Yes, you do," countered Damon.

"Why do you think we need you?" asked Andrei.

"Because I know where the missing Russian Crown Jewels are located, the missing jewels of the Romanov family," responded Damon.

"The same as you knew where the panels were hidden?" asked Andrei.

"They are here!" shouted Damon, "I am sure of it now!"

Andrei and Peen exchanged glances. Peen nodded, "He's right, the panels are in there."

Andrei's eye's widened. He returned Peen's nod and shouted down the corridor, "Where are the jewels?"

"In Poland, near my place in Gdansk. That is all I will say until I am safe. I will trade my life for them. Now you have the panels, too. You will be famous, a hero in your country. I have kept my word. I said I would get you the panels for the country of Russia and I did!"

"Hold on, the panels aren't yours," said William, "They're staying here . . ."

A voice interrupted William, "No, William. It's time for them to go home. This old soldier has done his duty."

"Grandpa!" cried William, from behind a desk, unable to see where Chester was. William's eyes welled up, because he'd fully expected to find his grandfather's lifeless body on the floor.

"Yes, my boy, nothing seems to be able to kill me. Don't ask me why, but accept Damon's offer. I don't want any more blood shed today."

"Is it a deal, Andrei?" asked Damon.

"Yes, it is a deal. Kick your gun toward me and lay on the floor. We are coming in slowly."

Peen added, "William, turn your flashlight on him. I want to make sure he's doing as he's told."

William flicked on his flashlight and edged out from behind the desk. It took a little searching, but he finally found Damon, "Yes, there he is. You can come on in."

They entered the room. Andrei approached Damon, pointed a gun he'd retrieved off his bodyguard, and fired directly into Damon's leg as he laid on the ground, shocking everyone.

Damon clutched his torn thigh and rolled back and forth on the floor, howling in pain.

Andrei responded calmly to their shock, "Now he can no longer run, but he can supply information to us. It will heal, just like my injury will. Do not be a baby Damon."

While Andrei kept watch over Damon, Peen and William searched for Edmund. They found him near a desk lying flat and looking peaceful. Peen knelt and felt for a pulse.

Chester approached him and said, "Edmund was terribly thirsty and anxious when a second intruder tried to enter the vault from the escape vent about an hour ago. We killed that guy like we did the first. It must have been too much for Edmund, because he laid down here, complaining about feeling dizzy. He didn't say another word. One moment he was here, the next he was gone. When I checked for a pulse, well, there just wasn't one. I think he probably had a second heart attack. Your uncle Edmund was a good man, Peen, and a good friend."

"Yes he was," said Peen barely audible, "he was all I had. I wish we'd had more time together."

CHAPTER 32: THE SIEGE ENDS

The stairway proved a long climb. Damon went first, limping up the stairs as the blood seeped through a makeshift bandage. Any balking and Andrei hit his leg. Peen helped Andrei, acting as his crutch. William, in turn, aided his grandfather, who was weak and shaky from dehydration. So, they ascended slowly.

While Chester felt relief at being freed from the vault, the fact that Damon had discovered the silo bruised his pride. Chester and William had barely started toward the surface when Chester snarled weakly, "So Damon, how in the hell did you know where we were?"

Damon didn't answer at first, but Andrei's kick prompted him to speak, "I found a set of diaries written by Katya Ballheim in Poland."

Chester responded angrily, "You didn't *find* them, you son of a bitch. You *stole* them! Edmund told me."

"No, Chester," countered Damon, weakly. The painful climb was sapping his energy, "If they were stolen, someone else did it. I merely acquired them."

Taken aback, Chester blurted out, "How'd you know my name?"

"Easy," explained Damon as he stopped to take a breath, "I tracked the text message Professor Rogers sent you, the *Aetheria* message. It took nothing to track you down."

Peen thought he'd heard that name before, *but where*?

Sweat dripped from Chester's forehead onto his grandson. He was tired, each step draining him a little more, yet he still didn't have all the answers he wanted. He shouted up to Damon, "How'd you know the diaries weren't faked? Edmund said there were many rumors. Why trust the diaries?"

"There are two reasons," replied Damon. He grunted from the pain in his leg as he took another step, "One, Katya described a chain of events I had never heard rumored. That was a lead worth investigating. And, two, I managed to track down information on a Katya Ballheim who died in Sweden. Her age and date of death suggested the notebook was real. I also researched her life story. She never married. Her friends explained Katya devoted her entire life to nursing and to the church, but she never seemed truly happy. Like many people who survived the war, she was strong when it counted, yet the woman fought demons for the rest of her life. She fit the profile."

Peen felt sadness for Katya. There seemed to be no happy endings for people connected to the panels.

When they reached the landing at the blast door, Peen let go of Andrei and pulled open the heavy door. Not knowing if all of Damon's men had been captured or not, he drew his gun and peered around the door. The hideous smell of burned flesh blew past them. Peen knew he'd be looking into a stairwell that led to the surface, but what he couldn't have foreseen were the two half-burned bodies lying on the steps.

He slipped past two bodies and peered over the top step. Peen sighed in relief as a familiar authoritative voice ordered him to put down his gun and exit the stairwell with his hands on his head.

***

Standing near FBI Agent Michael Jorden, Tora watched as the top of Peen's head rose out of the stairwell. Immediately, Agent Jorden shouted at him to drop his weapon. He repeated his request, adding, "We have the silo surrounded. Come out with your hands on top of your head."

As Peen complied he yelled, "We need medical help. Andrei is a member of the Russian Consulate and has been shot."

FBI agents ran toward Peen, guns drawn. They guided Peen to one side. Next came Damon, then Andrei, and finally William and Chester. It was then Tora realized someone was missing: Professor Edmund Rogers. His absence told her what she feared. Tora's eyes watered as she hurried toward Peen.

Peen was escorted toward a police car accompanied by an FBI Agent. He noted the burned cars, little more than blackened metal carcasses. He heard footsteps on the gravel and turned to see Tora running at him. She threw her arms around him as the FBI agent backed away to give them room.

He hugged her back and whispered into her ear, "I take it Ian's cocktails were a big hit? Looks like you two had yourself quite a party up here. Why wasn't I invited?"

Tora deflected his attempt at humor as tears dripped down her face, "You were invited. And so was your uncle. Did you leave him down there to guard the panels?"

Peen fought back tears, "Yes we did, but it will have to be his ghost working overtime to keep those panels safe."

"I'm afraid he might have died for nothing," whispered Tora. "They won't tell me what will happen to the panels, though Agent Jorden did promise to drop the charges against you if we sign a non-disclosure."

"In other words, we can't talk about what happened here," sighed Peen. "Does that mean the panels will disappear again?"

"I don't know," answered Tora.

"I think we'll have to forget about them. Too many forces beyond our control are at work here. But no matter, because I think we can focus elsewhere."

"What do you mean, Peen?"

"Chester said there was a code, *Aetheria*, that somehow referenced this silo. After all we've learned, do you think they would have hidden everything in one location? Do you remember the story Ian told? Phaethon had three Greek sisters, I just can't remember the other two sister's names."

Tora's wet eyes brightened. "Aegle and Aegiale, if I remember correctly," Tora mumbled, fighting her tears. "So, it's possible there are other hiding places?"

Peen nodded. His voice trembled as he added, "For Uncle Edmund, his past is no longer a prologue to a better time. But for us, maybe, our future has brighter days in store?"

She smiled a little, then began to weep. An exhausted Peen Rogers grabbed this amazing woman tightly as his own tears fell onto her shoulder.

THE HISTORY BEHIND THE BOOK

The first edition of this book was published as a limited pre-release version (thirty copies) so that eWillys website readers could submit errors and feedback. The comments readers provided, from questions about the narrative to specific errors (in an early draft somehow I added a car door to the normally door-less SEEP — thanks Keith), proved invaluable. Apart from their submissions, many readers asked about the accuracy of the history. So, I decided to include a section that I hope answers at least some of the questions.

First off, I tried to make events prior to the loss of the panels in 1945 as accurate as I could. For example, the history of the Amber Panels creation, from their commission by the Prussian King, to the trade with Peter The Great, to their installation in the Königsberg Castle during World War II is factually accurate.

Dr. Alfred Rhode was the person directing the castle's museum in Königsberg during the war. The history surrounding his life and death was mostly true (though I can't verify he was ever a Boy Scout — I added that part). However, the history about the Boy Scout's founder was factual. Dr. Rhode had two children, not one, and was married. I don't know what happened to his wife. I did read an account of him refusing to deliver the panels to Hitler. Dr. Rhode was a world expert in amber, so it is easy to believe he had a special affinity for the panels.

The accounts of Dr. Rhode misleading the Russians following the capture of Königsberg were true. Dr. Brusov was the early lead Soviet investigator and concluded the panels had been destroyed by fire.

For me, an interesting part of writing this book was that the information I unearthed in 1994 (when I first started writing and researching the book) about Dr. Rhode and his death contrasted sharply with the information I read when I renewed my research for the book in 2012. Like Tora and Peen, I first learned that Dr. Rhode died in May of 1945, but then later learned he died in December of 1945; this reflects both my personal learning curve about the panels and what I perceive was the very real disinformation campaign surrounding them. There are so many rumors, more than I included in the book, about the possible location of the panels, that I truly believe Dr. Rhode led a disinformation campaign of some type. How much disinformation was disseminated by other groups — such as the MVD, KGB, Kremlin, Stasi — since 1945 is unclear. One book that valiantly tackles this issue is the *Amber Room* by Catherine Scott-Clark & Adrian Levy (2004). It's a must read for anyone interested in the panels.

Gautleiter Koch really did control Eastern Prussia and, based on all the accounts I've read, had a notorious reputation. He successfully escaped Pillau at the end of the war, hid in Germany until after the war, and died in prison decades later, unwilling or unable to give up the secret of the panels.

Katya is a completely fictional character. I created her to describe pre-war Königsberg and set the stage for the rest of the book. I drew on actual reports about the condition of the city to frame her experience.

The Seven Bridges problem was a real puzzle debated by the citizens of Königsberg; however, I fictionalized its similarity to the *between a rock and a hard place* expression common in the United States.

Pictures and descriptions of Königsberg suggest it was a beautiful, clean, modern city prior to its total destruction. To defend the city near the end of the war, old men and teen boys, like Katya's Oskar, were drafted. The SS were killing those who refused to fight.

The bitter hate between the German and Russian soldiers was real. The cruelty and torture I relayed were just a few of the many examples I encountered during my research. I completed this book with a far better understanding of the sacrifices made by the Russians during World War II. Additionally, I believe the task of the Allies in Western Europe would have been far more difficult and the loss of life far greater had the Soviets not fought as hard as they did.

Peen's travels in the book reflect actual locations in the Pacific Northwest. My wife and I drove the entire path. Unfortunately, we didn't get to drive a seep across Admiralty Inlet. Given the strong currents and busy channel, I would not advise it. However, I can relate, with certainty, that if someone had traveled across Admiralty Inlet on June 15th, 2012, it would have been possible, due to the light amount of tidal variance that day (I changed

2012 to 2013 for the purpose of the story after my aunt completed that research.).

I made up the Tamanachee Indian Tribe and its history. The name came from a lonely sign off a spur road along the Chinook Highway just west of the Little Naches Campground. However, it is true that Native American women served in Europe during WWII.

There is no missile silo northwest of Yakima (at least I am unaware of one). However, there is a decommissioned ICBM silo in Royal City. When it was mothballed and the pumps were turned off, water seeped inside of it. Now partially flooded, guided dive tours are provided by a private company.

When my mom, a draftsperson prior to my birth, read an early draft of this book, she explained, to my surprise, that she'd drafted illustrations of silos for the Air Force in the 1960s as part of her work at Boeing, something she'd never before shared with me. It was a funny coincidence.

The panels' fate remains a mystery. In my opinion, Dr. Rhode determined their outcome. Until they are found, the 'replacement' panels, built by a joint Russian-German team and now on exhibit at the Catherine Palace in St. Petersburg, Russia, are the next best thing. I hope to see them some day.

ACKNOWLEDGEMENTS

A book is rarely the sole creation of one person and this one is no exception. Without these folks, the book would not be what it is.

First of all, I'd like to acknowledge my pre-release readers, twenty people crazy enough to purchase an error-filled, early form of the book so they could read and report on it. I owe them a debt of gratitude for their insights!

Guy Kathe

Keith Buckley

Matt Levelle

Buz Bowling

Roy Genger

Karen Johnson Cohoe

David Urbanek

Joe Snodgrass

David Fortenberry

John Scott

Robin Smith

Craig Brockhouse

Bill Deaton

Kyle Buchter

Sebastian Lobo-Guerrero

Paul Dunn

Rich Herron

Gerald Oswald

Dave Antram

Jan Schurink

I want to thank Dana Wilfert. She read my first book (*Finding Virginia*) and, when she heard I was writing a second one, asked to be included. She and her family are great neighbors and were (thankfully) humored by the final outcome of their characters.

I have to thank all my family members who read the book. In particular, I owe a debt of gratitude to my mother, Marjorie, who read and re-read each draft. She and my father, Karl, have fostered my writing efforts, as well as other endeavors, in selfless ways.

I must also mention my Aunt Marilyn. She read every sentence in the book aloud (over the phone usually) to me and made herculean efforts to reformat my obtuse descriptions and assemble my awkward narrative flows into something everyone could understand.

Finally, I have to thank my wife, Ann, whose patient support of my writing passion and jeep obsession will likely earn her sainthood one day.

About The Author

A writer, blogger, and entrepreneur, author David Eilers grew up in Renton, Washington. He earned a Bachelor's Degree from the University of Puget Sound in Tacoma, Washington, and an MBA Degree from the University of Utah in Salt Lake City, Utah. Naturally, he became a writer. He's long had an interest in history, especially family history. Challenging people's understanding of history in an accurate, compelling manner, is a common thread among all his books.

Finding Virginia was his first book, a memoir that highlights four tumultuous weeks in 2011. His second was The Amber Panels of Konigsberg, a historical fiction thriller. He recently finished his third book, SLAG & The Golden Age of Lead-Silver Smelting.

At his website, ewillys.com, David has authored more than 35,000 posts about vintage jeeps and served more than 20 million pages to jeep lovers world-wide. He lives in Pasco, Washington.

www.ingramcontent.com/pod-product-compliance
Lightning Source LLC
Chambersburg PA
CBHW070307040726
47501CB00018B/233